I
FELT HIM
DIE

David J Bailey

ArrowGate

Published by Arrow Gate Publishing Ltd 2019

15 14 13 12 11 10 9 8 7 6

A CIP catalogue record for this book is available from the British Library.
ISBN 978-1-913142-08-7

Arrow Gate Publishing 85, Great Portland Street, London W1W 7LT

Visit www.arrowgatepublishing.com to read more about our books and to buy them. You will also find articles, author inter-views, writing tips and news of any author events, and you sign up for our e-newsletters so that you're always first to read about our new releases.

This book is dedicated to my loving and patient wife Gillian, who has put up with me sitting at my computer for hours on end instead of affording her the time and attention she deserved.

"He who finds a wife finds what is good and receives favour from the Lord."

–THE HOLY BIBLE – NEW INTERNATIONAL VERSION

Contents

CHAPTER 1

MRS SHACKLETON

SERGEANT PAUL SHERIDAN BARELY looked up as the woman approached the desk. He was engrossed in completing a form from a previous incident.

"Good morning, Madam," he greeted absent-mindedly, "what can I do for you?"

At the front desk at Barber Street Police Station, a sixty-something year-old woman, well dressed and still attractive, stood before him. She had looked after herself over the years and maintained an air of respectability, even affluence. Paul Sheridan was an old-fashioned copper, and he prided himself that he could sum up a person with just a glance.

The woman knew she didn't have his fullest attention, so she coughed before answering.

"I've come to report a murder," she stated confidently and serenely.

"Right," he muttered, still not affording her his full attention. Then suddenly it registered somewhere deep in his subconscious mind exactly what she'd said, and he snapped himself upright with mouth slightly agape.

"A murder madam? Did you say a murder?"

She looked him straight in the eyes.

"Yes, a murder," she answered, speaking still in that same calm, matter-of-fact manner.

"I think you'd better give me some details," he responded, searching for a new report form as he did so. Having found one, he looked up at the woman's very composed, but serious-looking face.

"Firstly, your full name and address."

"It is Dorothy Helen Shackleton, and I live at 53 Palmer Mews, Kerington, KE44 2RT."

"Palmer Mews, we don't get many callers from there. So, is it Miss or Mrs?"

"Mrs Shackleton, the estate agent from Kerington, is my husband."

"Ah, yes," the sergeant nodded, "way outside my price bracket, so I'll not be putting business his way. So, this murder – who died, where did it happen, and who committed the crime?"

"My husband, Sergeant, he's been murdered, but as for where and by whom I just don't know."

"Excuse me, Mrs Shackleton, I don't quite understand what you're saying. Are you telling me someone killed your husband? But you don't know where, nor by whom. How do you know he's dead – where's his body?"

"I thought you might have problems understanding it all, but I know someone killed him, but where it took place and who carried it out, I don't know. I wish I could help you further, but that's all I know."

"Look, I'm sorry to push you on this, but how do you know he's dead if you don't know where his body is? Maybe he's just gone away somewhere."

"No, he hasn't just gone away, but I can see your problem Sergeant, it's not a lot to go on as far as investigating it is concerned, but I know he's no longer alive because I felt his presence depart."

Sergeant Sheridan looked at her in disbelief. In all his years as a police officer, he'd never encountered a case like this. It was beyond his comprehension. He didn't work on feelings, and he needed solid facts – a body, a weapon, a time or a place. He was at a loss as to how to proceed.

After a few moments of silently looking into her unruffled face, a question arose.

"How was he murdered and when? Please tell me you can help me there."

A worried look spread across Mrs Shackleton's face and then a faint glimmer of hope appeared.

"Ah, yes, I can partly help you there. It was at 4.10 pm yesterday. Yes, I distinctly remember glancing at the clock on the mantelpiece when I felt it happen. However, how my husband lost his life I don't know, the how doesn't come into it for me, I only know that he is no longer alive – I'm now a widow."

For the first time, a show of emotion appeared, as a tear formed in the corner of her eye and trickled down her cheek.

She quickly opened her handbag, took out a lace-trimmed handkerchief and dabbed the tears out of existence.

"Sorry to be so emotional, I thought I had my feelings under control, but that one escaped," she remarked with a trace of a smile.

"Er...no, no, don't apologise, it's er...sort of reasonable to feel as you do if your husband is dead. However, sorry to say this in the circumstances, but you haven't given me anything concrete to prove that he is dead. You said yourself. It's just what you 'feel'. Mrs Shackleton, please will you take a seat for a few moments? I need to talk to one of my colleagues."

She slowly walked across the room and sat down on a chair against the opposite wall. For a few moments, Paul Sheridan watched her. She had dignity, and that air of composure was self-evident as she sat there upright and in full control once more. She looked every inch the 'lady' with her matching handbag resting on her knees. Eventually, he called one of his constables to 'man' the desk while he, report in hand, left the office.

He mounted the stairs to the CID department, hoping that his colleague, Detective Inspector James Cartwright, would take over this strange, unlikely, case. In the event, DI Cartwright was out on a case, so Paul knocked on the door of Detective Chief

Inspector Johnstone's office. Paul swallowed hard as he came face to face with this senior officer because he knew from experience that he had no time whatsoever for time wasters. DCI Bill Johnstone was a brilliant detective and promotion could have been his many times in the past, but he didn't want a desk job, he preferred to be active, hands-on. Paul had hardly begun to explain the situation before DCI Johnstone began to shake his head in disbelief.

"Paul," he eventually exploded, "send her away, we can't waste our time and resources on time wasters. She offers no real evidence and yet insists her husband is dead – all based on a feeling. You must be joking. The powers that be would be down on us like a ton of bricks if we were to take her seriously."

"I fully understand your reaction, but there's something about her that seems...different, genuine, convincing even. I don't know what it is. I just can't put my finger on it. Can I ask you to see her Guv? Just for a few minutes, and if you still feel the same afterwards, then I'll go along with you – we'll send her packing."

"Paul, if it were anyone else, I wouldn't give it a second thought, but you're generally reliable, although this has all the hallmarks of being nothing more than a domestic. I hope you're not losing the plot, Paul. We could all finish up with egg on our faces. Show her up to the interview room – you can sit in with me and take notes, providing she has something more positive to offer that is."

"Thank you, Guv. We'll be there in a couple of minutes."

It took DCI Johnstone entirely by surprise when he saw Mrs Shackleton. She was not in the least what he'd expected – he could usually spot time wasters, but she didn't fit the profile.

"Mrs Shackleton, this is Detective Chief Inspector Johnstone," Paul introduced his superior, "please will you answer his questions as fully as you can, we need as much information as possible if we are to follow up your claim."

"Mrs Shackleton, may we begin with what you have already told Sergeant Sheridan. You said you 'felt' your husband died at 4.10 pm yesterday. What exactly did you mean by 'felt'?"

She didn't answer immediately but was carefully considering how to respond. "Can I ask you both whether you're married and if so, for how long?"

Both the officers immediately acknowledged that they were married, DCI Johnstone for eleven years and Sergeant Sheridan for eight.

"My husband and I got married forty-five years ago, and over this period, we have come to know each other extremely well – we know how each other thinks and understand how each other ticks. Most of all, we had become emotionally linked, so when I said I felt he'd died it was because I felt the emotional link was missing, broken."

"Hmm, I hear what you're saying, but it's not sufficient for us to pursue it as murder – feelings are not enough; we have to work on solid evidence. However, let's look at things from a different viewpoint. Your husband is an estate agent, how long has he been involved in that line of work?"

"All his life. His father started the business, and my husband went to work for him after leaving university. When his father died in 1984, Leslie took over and had been running things ever since. He has a total of eight offices now and employs forty members of staff across those offices."

"Have you checked with his staff as to when they saw him last?"

"Yes, that was the first thing I did. Only two shops said they'd seen my husband recently, one four days ago and the local one two days ago. No one saw him yesterday."

"Did you see him yesterday?" the DCI asked.

"No, but that's not unusual, he was often away for days on end. Sometimes he stayed in his studio flat above the shop and at other times he would stay with friends or in a hotel."

"Sorry, I don't quite understand, you mean he stayed away without telling you he was not coming home?"

"Yes, that's correct. If Leslie were coming home, he would call me, and I would have a meal ready for him. Otherwise, I ate alone."

"The friends that he stayed with have you contacted them? Is he perhaps staying with them at this present time?"

"Oh no, I haven't contacted them, that just wouldn't be right; they were his private friends, so I don't know them, or where they live – I don't have contact numbers either."

"Mrs Shackleton, these friends, are they men or women?"

"Oh, younger women, Chief Inspector, he had no gay tendencies. He enjoyed their company, but he always came back to me – we were inseparable."

DCI Johnstone shook his head at this incredible account, "Mrs Shackleton, let's be clear, are you saying that your husband had sexual liaisons with several women, and he stayed with them regularly; that you knew about his tendencies and you didn't mind?"

This time she did smile.

"You're shocked at our arrangement. You look at me, and you think I'm an old-fashioned fuddy-duddy and therefore ought to be outraged at his behaviour. Well, that's because you don't know anything about me nor why I didn't mind. Let me explain. Very soon after our marriage, we were involved in a serious road traffic accident. We were travelling behind a builder's lorry when suddenly a scaffolding pole slid off the lorry and travelled towards us like a spear. That pole went right though the radiator, through the engine compartment and then the dashboard, finally thrusting with force into my groin region. Months of surgery followed as they attempted to rebuild my shattered body and pelvis. You know how large a scaffolding pole is, so imagine if you will, the damage it was capable of inflicting. To cut a long story short, I could no longer have sexual relations with my husband, so having a family was impossible. My husband escaped without injury, and after a while, being a red-blooded male, he needed to find satisfaction. I suggested the arrangement with other women, and although he protested vehemently, he later agreed. I had no objections as long as he returned to me each time."

For quite some time, neither officer could respond but sat quietly looking at their notes, unsure of where to go next.

"Have I shocked you, officers, do you think the arrangement was wrong?" she asked casually. "Would you have done that for your wives if the situation were reversed?"

"Well, er...who can tell," stuttered the sergeant. "I'm certainly sorry to hear about your terrible accident, and I can understand the predicament you both faced. Where did the accident happen?"

"It was on the A38 near Taunton; in fact, paramedics took me to Musgrove Park Hospital – it was 1972 if you want to check my story."

"Well Mrs Shackleton, you have given us a starting point for an investigation," responded DCI Johnstone, "but in the absence of anything concrete, we can now only treat your husband as a missing person, though we will start making some enquiries. However, we need some help from you. Does your husband have a mobile phone, and have you tried calling him? Also, does he have a middle name?"

"Yes, he does have a phone, and of course I've tried it, repeatedly, but it simply goes to voicemail. I have one of his calling cards in my purse that will give you all his contact details. His middle name is Archibald."

"Thank you," the DCI responded, "that's very helpful. Does he have a computer at home?"

"Yes, one at home and another at the office, you're welcome to come and check it and indeed the one at the office too. I doubt if either will provide you with much information, he never seemed to spend much time on the one at home, but I suppose he could have spent more time on the one at the office."

"We must find out his list of lady friends; one of them might be able to shed some light on his whereabouts. We have to consider that he may have gone off with one of his 'ladies' – maybe he decided it would be easier to make one of his liaisons permanent. We will need to send a search team to your home, his place of work and all the other offices he owned. In the meantime, we need an up-to-date photo, which we can circulate. Are you able to supply such a picture and are you happy for us to proceed with all I've out-lined?"

"Yes, most certainly Chief Inspector, I'm ex-tremely grateful that you are willing to take me seriously. My husband always joked that I was Dotty by name and dotty by nature. I did know that he loved me, and whenever he was at home, he was always very tender towards me, Leslie never got angry with me, and he showered me with kisses. I couldn't have wished for a better husband."

"Well Mrs Shackleton, we can't do anything until we get that photo, neither can we do anything until twenty-four hours have elapsed. We'll get things moving tomorrow, but can one of our officer's give you a lift home and at the same time pick up the photo?"

"Oh, Chief Inspector, that would be most kind, and yes, I will give him a recent photo. I know I won't, but if I should hear anything from my husband, I will immediately let you know. He's dead I'm sure, I feel his loss very deeply; our special bond is no more. I now feel there's a void, a nothingness. Please find out what happened to him. I don't know how I'll cope without him."

A forlorn look spread across her face and once again, a solitary tear formed and trickled down her face. She wiped it with her handkerchief, and then they all shook hands as she left the interview room. Sergeant Sheridan led her back to the front office and there instructed a constable to transport her home and collect the photo.

CHAPTER 2

HOME GROUND

NEITHER OFFICER HAD encountered such a case as this. Mrs Shackleton was undoubtedly not their usual standard of customer. She was not under suspicion, but the reality was, they didn't know how to read her, and there was, even after interviewing her, no obvious clue as to whether her claim was a true reflection of fact. Feelings – there was no space on the interview sheet for recording feelings, such did not figure in a copper's way of thinking. Oh yes, some referred to a copper's nose, but Mrs Shackleton didn't make their noses twitch in the slightest.

On the one hand, they were inclined to conclude it was merely a domestic, but on the other hand, there was something about Mrs Shackleton's beliefs that was convincing. It was nonsense, of course, but the kind of joke that demanded a response, some action – yes, an investigation even.

"Well, what's your conclusion Guv now that you've met her?" Paul asked.

"I've said it before Paul, and I'll repeat it, logic says we should kick it out as a waste of time, but I can't do that. That woman has got under my skin, she's touched a nerve and stirred up my 'feelings' – but don't you dare quote me on that. So, what next, where do we go from here? Hmm, as I said to her, with all intents and purposes, we treat it as a missing person until something more concrete surfaces. We do nothing until the twenty-four hours have elapsed, and then we'll circulate his description. Car, what about his car, where is it? Get the details Paul and when we find it, search it. Oh yes and check her story regarding the accident. Anything else from your perspective?"

"Well, at some point, I think we should pursue his finances and his clients. We need more information from his wife about his clothing, jewellery, distinguishing marks, hobbies and the like. We'll need to search his office and studio flat too."

"Yes, good. Remind everyone. Leslie Shackleton is a missing person, no mention of murder at this stage; otherwise, the press will have a field day. Don't ask me why, but I want to preserve that woman's dignity for as long as possible, though one day it will have to go into the public domain if we get anything concrete. Incidentally, who's running his businesses in his absence, did you ask?"

"Ah, yes," Paul replied, "I did ask her if she had any hand in the estate agent businesses, but Dorothy Shackleton is not involved at all – Leslie had appointed managers to handle the day-to-day activities in all their outlets. They have a regular accountant and a solicitor on board too. I guess we'll need to talk to them at some point."

A short while later, Paul returned to his desk, picked up the phone and called the Shackleton home.

"Ah, Mrs Shackleton, we're beginning the process of trying to trace your husband's movements and whereabouts, so may we collect his computers, diaries, etcetera, anything that will provide us with information about your husband's activities or appointments. Then we need to know what he might have been wearing, what jewellery he wore – did he have any distinguishing marks anywhere. Did he have a regular doctor and dentist? If you could furnish me with as much information as possible, that would help us enormously. Perhaps someone could call in to see you tomorrow morning, say about 10 o'clock."

"That will be fine, Chief Inspector."

"Great, many thanks."

Next morning DCI Johnstone shouted across the office to DS Dani Taylor.

"Dani, grab your jacket, you're with me."

"Where are we going, Sir?" she asked as they exited the building into the carpark.

"We're going to collect computers, one from Mrs Shackleton and then perhaps another from the office belonging to her husband. Be very alert Dani; I would value a woman's perspective on Mrs Shackleton herself and the overall setup. If Leslie Shackleton has gone missing, we must determine why, where to, and who he's with and see if you can get a feel for the relationship the couple had – you may sense things I miss."

Thirty-year-old Dani had only been in the force for six years, having come via university and basic training at Hendon. She had displayed a real aptitude for the job – she was bright, observant and reliable. Dani had great potential, and that's why she fast-tracked to CID and the rank of sergeant. DCI Johnstone was keen to encourage her to advance – she was too good to stay in the lower ranks all her life. Throughout the journey, they chatted amiably. She could talk, but she could also listen. Something though was stirring in her mind and eventually she plucked up the courage to speak out.

"Sir," she began tentatively, "is there more to this case than is generally known? We've had missing persons before, but I get the impression there's something below the surface, something no one's telling. Ignore me if I'm out of order for asking or treading on thin ice."

The DCI couldn't help but laugh, "Dani, one of the things I like about you is that you miss nothing – and that's a good trait for a copper to have. I certainly don't mind you asking, but I'm not at liberty to say anything more at present. Say nothing to anyone about your impression, and I promise you that if or when something concrete emerges, you will be first to know. It is for your keen observation that I asked you to come with me today. I need someone who is on the ball and whose mind is not elsewhere. Let me know what you see, what you hear, or don't hear, what impression you get. There is something more to this case, and I want to know what it is."

"Thanks, Sir," she responded, "I appreciate your honesty and trust – I'll do my best."

Mrs Shackleton opened the door at the first ring of the bell and invited them in. The DCI introduced her to Dani and then she showed them through to her husband's office.

"I need to take a quick look at the computer and then search through the desk drawers. There may be nothing, but sometimes the tiniest detail can be an enormous help."

"That's no problem Chief Inspector, can I get coffee or tea for you both while you're doing that?"

"That's very kind of you Mrs Shackleton, yes I'd love a coffee – white, no sugar please."

"Same for me please," Dani responded with a smile, "but may I come with you, we can chat while you're making the drinks."

"Of course, I'd value your company. By the way, call me Dorothy, we don't have to be formal all the time, do we?"

Dani took the older woman's arm, "No, we don't Dorothy, and please call me Dani."

The two wandered off together, chatting as they went, and DCI Johnstone set to work. He switched the computer on, and once it had booted, he quickly realised that it was password protected. What could it possibly be? He tried different words engendered by the name 'Shackleton' - Ernest, explorer, Antarctic, aircraft, bomber and then turned to his wife's name, Dorothy, Dotty and various other combinations including upper- and lower-case letters, but nothing worked. He turned his attention to the desk drawers and shelves, but there was no sign of any diary, address book or any other papers that could be of help. Any records must be elsewhere, perhaps on his phone. Just then, Mrs Shackleton and Dani entered the room.

"Ah, Mrs Shackleton, do you by any chance know the password for your husband's computer?"

"No, sorry I don't know anything at all about computers, I've never used one in my life."

"Not to worry, our tech guys will gain access for us. Incidentally, do you have a safe anywhere in the house?"

"Now that I do know, yes, it's right there behind you. Press the spine of the book 'The Hanging', and you'll see it."

The DCI pressed the book as instructed and part of the bookshelf swung open, revealing the safe door behind.

"Ah, there we have it, but do you know the combination?"

"Not for certain, but I suggest you try Leslie's birth date, or possibly the date in reverse. So, that's 16-08-48 or 48-08-16. I've never touched it myself, but I think I remember him saying something about it – unless he's changed it of course."

On the second attempt, as the DCI turned the dial, he heard the mechanism click as he logged the last number. Now the door swung open, revealing quite a full interior. The most noticeable item was a pile of banknotes; he estimated it to be many thousands of pounds. There were numerous accounts books, house and business premises deeds, various other files and papers, but no sign of a diary or address book. It was not the end of the world, but it would have been good to have some records to set the ball rolling.

"When you're done here, would you like to come through to the lounge? It will be more comfortable there."

The DCI closed the safe and turned the dial to lock it and then they walked through to the lounge and sat down.

"Mrs Shackleton, do you know why your husband kept so much money in the safe – did you know it was there?"

"I don't know Chief Inspector. As I said, I've never touched the safe, nor seen inside. That was Leslie's domain. I'd seen him open it, but I never enquired about the contents. No, as regards money, Leslie always gave me whatever I needed whenever I needed it. I never questioned his business acumen, and we never talked about such things. His accountant might be able to throw light on such matters; I suggest you talk to him. I've nothing to hide, so feel free to make any enquiries necessary to resolve the matter. Also, would it be for me to instruct him to bank all that cash? I don't like it to be in the house."

"I need to get my team to go through everything and to catalogue the contents, but then you may certainly ask him to bank it on your behalf. You will need capital to draw upon for living purposes, so you need to be able to access the account accordingly. Did you by any chance have a joint bank account?"

"Oh, my goodness no, I've never had a bank account in my life – I wouldn't know where to begin. I always relied on Leslie, and he was generosity itself."

"Did your husband make a will, Dorothy, and if so, do you know where it is?" Dani asked.

The DCI looked at her quizzically, did she know more than he thought?

"Oh yes," Dorothy answered unhesitatingly, "we both did, and they were prepared in the presence of his solicitor, Andrew Hastings of Hastings, Arnott and Gerard – he holds the copies in his strong room."

"So, you know what's in his will do you and to whom his estate is bequeathed?" Dani asked.

"Most certainly. We have no children, so we both bequeathed everything to each other – oh, there were a few small gifts for long established friends."

The DCI stepped into the conversation.

"At some point, we will require you to arrange for us to see the will, would you be happy about that?"

"As I previously indicated," Dorothy replied, "I will entirely co-operate with you in any way necessary to hasten a resolution. No doubt you want to resolve things as soon as possible, so do I. I need closure so that I can plan where I go from here, how I am going to cope without Leslie? It won't be easy – I relied on him completely. After the accident I was a broken woman, I lost all self-confidence, self-worth and almost the will to live, but my husband refused to let me give up. He nursed me, encouraged me, rebuilt my life and gave me a reason to live – even dignity. What you see today is what he encouraged, so how do I pick up the pieces, how do I go forward, and how do I survive without him?"

For the third time tears formed although this time not just a solitary tear, but a stream of tears that again trickled down her face, and as before, she retrieved her handkerchief and tried to dab them away. This time it was in vain, they continued to flow, so Dani moved alongside her, wrapped her arm around the older woman's shoulder and drew her close. Mrs Shackleton, in turn, reached out a hand and took hold of one of Dani's.

"Thank you," she whispered, "you are very kind, but I will be alright, I will get through it."

"Do you have friends or family you can call upon?" Dani enquired, "Is there a neighbour who would be available if you need company?"

"I do have a sister, as did my husband, but I haven't seen them or even been in touch with them for years. As for neighbours and friends, I speak to people as I pass, but there is no real connection between us. After the accident, I felt a deep sense of shame, and I felt I was no longer a woman, so I became a recluse. I didn't want to see anyone. I couldn't cope with people asking me how I was. Looking back, I know I was wrong for thinking and behaving as I did, but at the time, it was my way of coping. Ever since that awful day, I have only ever wanted Leslie. He understood, and he just let me be; he never pushed me into anything. Maybe he should have done so, but I don't think I would have let him. Oh, how I miss him, please find out the truth, even if it's an awful truth. Truth is better than speculation. Help me, please."

"Rest assured, Mrs Shackleton; we will solve the case. It might take time, but we will get there eventually," DCI Johnstone assured her.

CHAPTER 3

JUST A GLIMMER

BACK IN THE CAR, THE DCI turned towards Dani.

"Hmm, Sergeant, you seem to be more in the know than I realised. How did you come to know about the possibility of Leslie Shackleton's demise?"

"Ah, yes, Dorothy volunteered the information while we were in the kitchen. Dorothy said she 'felt' his passing at a specific moment – 4.10 pm yesterday, Wednesday. I didn't question her about it. I didn't think it was my place to do so without your presence. Was that okay?"

"Perfectly. Incidentally, you handled things well today, well done. However, please don't pass on to anyone that this might be a murder – that's for me, you, Paul and Superintendent Mann alone to know. For the present, he is a missing person, and it will remain that way until we get some positive evidence of foul play. Dorothy Shackleton seems genuine. But we can't launch a murder enquiry just on her feelings."

"I agree with you, Sir, but she believes her husband is dead. So, what's next?"

"The only hope we have is that either a body turns up, or we find a diary with records of his contacts. There needs to be a thorough search of his home and his business premises. I hope that his work computer will turn up something if the one from his home proves fruitless."

Back at the station, DCI Johnstone passed Leslie Shackleton's computer to the technical department to gain access.

"As quick as you can please," he instructed.

DCI Johnstone hoped Leslie Shackleton's computer would bring something by way of revelation to the case. He felt they were playing something of a waiting game, tiptoeing around, unable to share openly or investigate thoroughly. They desperately needed a firm lead and people to pursue. If it later transpired that Leslie Shackleton was a victim of murder, there was the danger that the trail could go cold while they were pussyfooting around. It was a fact, that in murder enquiries, the first twenty-four hours are crucial, leave it longer, and the villains could cover their tracks, rig alibis and dispose of weapons. However, all they could do under the guise of it being a missing person case was to search – his home, his businesses, places he frequented, people he knew. It was time to step up the action.

He called his team together, circulated Leslie's photograph and description, and sent some officers to the Shackleton home to do a thorough search. He instructed Paul Sheridan to send a team to do door to door, asking if anyone had seen Leslie during the last twenty-four hours. The media already had details of Shackleton as a missing person, so he was optimistic that someone somewhere would be in touch to inform them if they saw him around.

"Paul," the DCI continued, CCTV; get tapes from street cameras, shop cameras and any other cameras in and around his home, his local workplace and any others in premises that he owns. Check with his phone provider. Check activity at his bank. Ask everyone when they last see him; do they know any of his contacts? Has he told any of them his intentions? We're clutching at straws at present, so leave no stone unturned – we need a decisive lead. We're looking for his car, and that could be crucial to locating him, so circulate a full description. Someone somewhere knows something. It may be small, seemingly insignificant, but whatever it is we need it."

"Right away, Guv," Paul responded, "leave it with me, and I'll get all hands on deck."

"Oh, and Paul, we debrief tomorrow morning at 0900. Get me something – anything."

Later that afternoon, DCI Johnstone and Dani set off for Shackleton's Estate Agency.

"When we get there Dani, they will no doubt insist we have a search warrant, but we have permission from Mrs Shackleton, so don't let anyone intimidate you or prevent you from searching the premises. Tell them straight, in a missing person case we need their full co-operation and any opposition may be viewed as suspicious, indicating they have something to hide."

"Right Sir, but I doubt they'd have the nerve to try to obstruct you, so that gives me confidence."

The estate agency was on the main road with double yellow lines on both sides, but fortunately for clients, it had a small carpark at the rear. The DCI pulled in and parked. As they walked into the premises, a young sales woman greeted them, obviously hoping to gain business. They produced their warrant cards and asked to see the manager. She picked up the phone.

"Mr Roberts, two officers, want to see you." She listened briefly on the phone.

"Please will you go into his office through the door in the corner," she instructed calmly.

A bespectacled, smartly dressed man in a suit and tie was seated behind a mahogany desk, and as they entered, he rose to greet them.

"Good afternoon to you both, my name is Giles Roberts. How can I help you?" He addressed them with a rather pompous air. "I assume it's to do with the disappearance of Mr Shackleton, am I correct?"

"It is, indeed, Sir. I'm Detective Chief Inspector Johnstone, and this is Detective Sergeant Taylor. We are here in the hope that we might be able to get some idea of Leslie Shackleton's movements – his appointments, both private and business. We will need to examine his computer and probably take it away, but also we need to go through his desk and any other records that might throw some light on his activities."

"I'm sorry Chief Inspector, but unless you have a search warrant, I don't think I can allow you to pursue such a course of action. Mr Shackleton's computer is private, and only he can touch it, and as for our records, our clients' records are for our eyes only."

"Mr Roberts, I admire your loyalty, but may I remind you that your employer is missing, and we have been asked to trace him. It is imperative, therefore that we glean as much information about him as possible – even the tiniest detail may point us in the right direction. Mrs Shackleton has already given her blessing to our pursuing every avenue unhindered, so please ring her if you wish to confirm that, but I tell you here, and now, we are going to carry out a thorough search. We may view any further obstruction as an indication that you have something to hide, so unless you'd like us to arrest you, might I suggest you change your tone and co-operate with us."

By now, the manager's face had turned a bright crimson, and he was finding it difficult to contain his anger.

"Chief Inspector Johnstone, there is no need for you to adopt that officious tone, I'm only doing my job and seeking to protect both my employer and our clients."

"I understand, but in the circumstances, I believe our investigation eclipses your loyalty. Mr Roberts, you may baulk at this request, but I need a full and detailed list of your current clients and please mark any that Mr Shackleton alone handles. Does Mr Shackleton have his own office here? I need to see his computer and desk."

"He shares this office when he's here, and the other desk is his. You may find it locked and I'm sorry, but we don't have a key. He also has accommodation above this office, accessed via the door next to the shop door. Again, it is locked, and we don't have a key."

"Dani, go through the shelves and the papers on the desk, you know the sort of thing we're looking for."

The DCI opened Leslie Shackleton's computer and turned it on. Once again, he couldn't access it because of the password. He tried all the various combinations again, but all to no avail.

"Mr Roberts, do you know the password for this computer?"

"I have no idea; I have never touched it."

It was frustrating; every avenue seemed blocked.

"Dani, any suggestions as to a possible password?"

She hesitated for a moment and then suggested.

"Try Leslie followed by his birthdate, or perhaps his birthdate in reverse."

The DCI typed in her suggestion, and immediately, the computer opened. "You are a genius, Dani. What would I do without you? You'll probably go on to solve the whole case without me."

Dani smiled and continued her search, while the DCI began to search through the various files. He came across one file marked 'Personal' – he clicked on it, but again it was password protected. This time it was not the same password, so again, he tried all the former possibilities, but nothing opened it. Then a thought came to him.

"Mr Roberts, would you be so kind as to get Mrs Shackleton on the phone for me."

The manager sniffed but then proceeded to make the call.

"Mrs Shackleton, this is Giles Roberts, I have Chief Inspector Johnstone for you."

"Mrs Shackleton," the DCI addressed her, "we're trying to access a file on your husband's computer, please can you tell me what your birthdate is…. thank you, we'll be in touch if anything comes to light. Bye."

He went back to the computer and tried 'Dotty080550' and immediately, the file opened.

"Yes!" He beat the air with his right fist.

The DCI began to skim through the file. It contained details of their finances, and one entry threw some light on the cash in the home safe, £6,000.00 – it indicated that it was to pay for silence. Blackmail? If it was, there were no details of who the blackmailer was, nor why someone was extorting money from him. Was this perhaps the reason for his sudden disappearance? It was most certainly a line of enquiry that demanded their pursuit. He continued to scroll through the items in the file, but it was not until he came to the final entry that his pulse quickened – a list of women's names, ten in all, but no surnames nor contact details. Were these women the ones with whom he had relationships? Who were they, and how did he come to know them? The file contained first names only, so how could they possibly identify them, would they perhaps match with client records? Another line of enquiry.

Dani also made a couple of discoveries, firstly a book with the title 'The Perfect Lover' – it was signed inside, 'All about you Leslie xxx', from 'Angela T'. The second find was perhaps even more significant, an unopened letter in the in-tray, the name and address written in roughly printed scrawl.

"Mr Roberts," she asked, "when did this letter arrive?"

"Er...yesterday, no it wasn't, it was the day before. I was expecting Mr Shackleton to come in. We never open anything addressed specifically to him."

"Well spotted Dani," the DCI responded, "we need to open it now, it looks decidedly suspicious. To your knowledge, Mr Roberts, has Mr Shackleton ever previously received a similar letter to this?"

"Well, yes, I've seen a couple previously, but as Mr Shackleton said nothing about the contents, I assumed they were nothing of significance."

He slit open the envelope and drew out the contents. It was one grubby sheet of paper and written in the same printed scrawl was one simple sentence, 'YOU'VE BEEN WARNED, £6K OR SUFFER THE CONSEQUENCES – 8 PM TONIGHT AT THE ENTRANCE TO VALLEY PARK.'

He passed it to Dani to read, "Ah," she responded, "that makes sense."

"Mr Roberts, I'm going to open the other post, we need to know if there is anything of significance in any of them. Incidentally, have you or anyone else in the office ever received similar post?"

"No, I certainly haven't," he responded, "and unless such post has gone to their homes, no member of staff has received anything either."

DCI Johnstone opened the other items of the post but found nothing of a personal nature in any of them, so he passed them to Giles Roberts.

"Mr Roberts, I think we're done for now, but we will be sending in a team to carry out a wider search. In the meantime, we are taking the computer with us

– a detailed examination is necessary to establish whether it can provide anything further to aid our investigation."

"Mr Shackleton was not a computer buff," Giles Roberts protested, "so I see no reason for you to remove it from the office. I'm not sure you have the right to poke into private affairs; it's not as if a crime has been committed."

"Mr Roberts, I think you protest too much – I've already explained that we have full permission given by Mrs Shackleton and the fact that her husband is missing is sufficient reason to take everything seriously. No one knows where he is, so we can't rule out the possibility that a crime has been committed. The content of that handwritten letter is a crime, so don't try telling us how to do our job."

"Huh, Mrs Shackleton has nothing at all to do with the business, she is neither a co-owner nor a director," he responded scathingly "and as for that letter, take it from me, it's nothing. Mr Shackleton, I'm sure he would have shredded the previous ones – he didn't take them seriously."

DCI Johnstone drew close to Giles Roberts and looked him full in the face before replying.

"You take it from me, blackmail is a crime, and we always take it very seriously. Remember, we haven't finished with this business yet, my team will go through it with a fine toothcomb and any nasty bugs will be exposed and removed. By the way, please give me your full name, home address, contact details, email and your age."

Giles Roberts spluttered angrily, reached into his desk drawer and took out a visiting card.

"This gives you all you need to know about me, so please take it and let me get on with my job. I have a business to run in the absence of Mr Shackleton."

"Sorry, it isn't enough," DCI Johnstone insisted, "this is a business card. I asked for full personal details."

This time he reached into his pocket, retrieved another card and passed it over. "Thank you," the DCI responded with a smile, "now your middle name and your age."

"Chief Inspector Johnstone, you're impossible, I have a mind to report you to your senior officer." He then calmed a little, "My middle name is Henry, and I'm sixty."

"Thank you, Sir, that wasn't too difficult, was it?"

The look Giles Roberts gave spoke a thousand words, but he said nothing.

With that, Dani and the DCI left, taking the computer with them. DCI Johnstone was convinced that there would be valuable information lurking around in the computer that was going to prove crucial, something Roberts didn't want to expose.

"What did you make of all that Dani, what was your gut feeling?" he asked once inside the car.

"That man, as you said, protested too much. If there was nothing to hide, he had no reason whatsoever to object to us searching and removing the computer. I glanced across at him at one point when you opened the computer, and he had a distinctly worried look. I would say he was afraid there would be something there for you to find that would incriminate him. Do you think he could be the blackmailer?"

"I'd say that that's a distinct possibility. We need to do a thorough background check on Giles Roberts. I also think we need to move fast on sending a team in to comb through the premises and I think we should remove Roberts' computer too – that'll give him something to protest about."

Before they moved off to return to the station, the DCI phoned ahead to Paul Sheridan.

"Hi Paul, this is DCI Johnstone, will you organise a team to go into Shackleton's Estate Agency on Kerington High Street to do a thorough search. Check all computers and files and talk to the staff, take names and addresses – how long have they worked there and is it a happy place to work? You may encounter difficulties with Giles Roberts, the manager, don't be put off by his pompous attitude – confiscate his computer and pass it to the tech guys. There is also a studio flat above, accessed by a door to the right of the shop door. However, it's locked, and we don't have a key, but we need to gain entry – that too requires a thorough search. Oh, and Paul, today please, it's extremely urgent. See you later."

"Something just occurred to me Sir," Dani began, "that photograph of Leslie Shackleton started it, but then I commandeered this photograph of him and his wife, it was on the shelf beside his desk. Have you noticed how alike they are? I've seen it several times before, couples who've been happily married for a good number of years – they seem to get more and more alike as time goes by. I'm sure it's not fool proof, but I've noticed it many times before. Dorothy said how close she and Leslie were, and I feel their looks are a good indication of the truth of that. Perhaps I'm a bit of a sentimentalist though."

"Hmm, don't dismiss it, I think you may have a point – yes, I've encountered that myself in the past, but I confess I hadn't noticed it in this couple – I need to be more observant obviously. I'm convinced Mrs Shackleton, and her husband were genuinely very close, and she is devastated by Leslie's possible loss. She is certainly going to need someone to draw near to her; otherwise, she is not going to survive."

Back at the office, the DCI passed the computer to the tech department, and then he and Dani set about preparing a case wall ready for the meeting next morning, hoping that by then they would have some positive leads to share. The photographs of Shackleton and his wife took pride of place at the top of the wall, and the DCI noticed how right Dani had been, the couple did share a definite likeness.

CHAPTER 4

THE HOLIDAY HOME

AT 09.00 AM NEXT MORNING, the CID team assembled for a team briefing– Inspector Paul Sheridan and Superintendent Mann were also present. The buzz of chat around the office suddenly ceased as DCI Johnstone walked to the front and called everyone to attention. Everyone looked up expectantly.

"Okay, what do we have? Leslie Archibald Shackleton, sixty-eight years old, has been missing now for six days. He's an estate agent from Kerington and lives in Kerington Mews. The local shop is on Kerington High Street, and he has six shops in the region, employing forty members of staff. A manager oversees each office. Leslie Shackleton was last seen wearing a charcoal pinstripe three-piece suit. He wears a Rolex watch and a wedding ring. Distinguishing marks – an appendix scar, a mole on his upper left arm and a two-inch scar on his right knee, the latter resulting from a climbing accident in his earlier years.

Dani Taylor and I carried out a preliminary search of both his home and business offices. We failed to gain entry to his home computer, so passed it to the tech guys – any news back on that?"

"Yes," Paul responded, "they gained access, but there was nothing significant found – neither in the existing files nor in the history. Sorry, nothing helpful there."

"We did access their home safe," the DCI continued, "and the main thing we found was £6,000.00 in cash. We thought it strange that there was so much cash there, but the reason became clear later. Incidentally, did the search team find anything else?"

Again, Paul responded.

"No, Guv, just the money as you mentioned. Oh, hang on a minute, yes there were copies of their wills, basically leaving everything to each other, but with a few minor bequests."

"Now, when we checked his office computer, we found the explanation as to why the cash was in the home safe – he was being blackmailed, and the cash was the pay-off. Danni found many unopened letters in the in-tray and among them was a hand printed letter. The note inside reads, 'YOU'VE BEEN WARNED, £6K OR SUFFER THE CONSEQUENCES – 8 PM TONIGHT AT THE ENTRANCE TO VALLEY PARK.' It was hand delivered three days ago. The office manager, Giles Henry Roberts, sixty years old, put it in the in-tray along with other personal items of post. The questions we need to ask –

Who delivered it – is there any CCTV of the delivery?

What are the 'consequences' referred to?

Has Leslie Shackleton perhaps been kidnapped and incarcerated somewhere?

Who is the blackmailer?

What does he or she have over Leslie Shackleton?

"We need, as a matter of urgency, to pursue these matters. This investigation has just taken a turn for the worst; it's no longer simply a missing person enquiry. However, I want to make it clear, as far as the media are concerned, nothing's changed – the last thing we need is wild speculation. Outside these four walls, watch what you say and to whom."

"Paul – Giles Henry Roberts, the manager. Background checks please – who is he? Where did he work previously? Check his phone records, bank records and anything else pertinent to our investigation. Does he have any form, big or small? Is he capable of blackmail? Find out what was on his computer."

"Will do Guv," Paul responded.

"Now, on Leslie Shackleton's work computer, we also found a list of ten women's names – just first names, no surnames or contact details. Please be aware; there is nothing hidden here, Mr and Mrs Shackleton had an arrangement, and this is for your ears only – Dorothy Shackleton had a severe accident early in her marriage which left her unable to have a family, but more importantly, unable to have any sexual relationship with her husband. She encouraged him, therefore, to seek satisfaction elsewhere. And other than sex, they had a deeply intimate relationship with each other. However, we need to find out who these women were – were any or all of them women with whom Leslie Shackleton had liaisons? So, who are they, what's their background, were they clients, were they, professional women, do any of them have jealous husbands or boyfriends?"

"Sir," Dani interjected, "we perhaps have one clue. I found a book in his office with the title, 'The Perfect Lover' – it had an inscription, 'All about you, Leslie xxx' and was signed 'Angela T'. I notice there's an Angela on the list, so are they the same person?"

"Thanks, Dani, a good starting point – follow that up, please. What about the search teams Paul, anything back from them?"

"Nothing of significance yet Guv, they've gained access to the studio flat and searches are still ongoing. I hope to get back to you later today."

Dani continued, "Leslie Shackleton drives a blue/grey BMW with personalised plates – LAS 1948. Again Paul, get someone on surveillance cameras – where did he go, has he gone further afield than this area, where is that car now? Send out details nationwide and put out an APB. Anything back from the door to door Paul?"

"Nothing of significance. Neighbours report that they were a lovely couple, though generally kept to themselves. On the morning that Leslie was last seen, a few reported seeing him drive off as normal – he waved as he passed them. We went along the neighbouring streets, but no one there knew him, apart from, that is, one couple who bought their house through him."

The DCI continued, "we need to interview his solicitor, Andrew Hastings of Hastings, Arnott and Gerard – has there been any amendments or codicils to his will? We need to contact his doctor, Dr Barnett in Kerington Rise, and his dentist, Dr Kate Petersfield in Cross Street, Kerington – has he had any recent appointments, hospital appointments and the like. We can't rule out the possibility that he may be seriously ill. We also need to talk to his accountant, Barry Templeton, – he should know the ins and outs of Leslie Shackleton's finances, both home and business."

"Okay, anything else anyone?"

No one responded.

"Right, you all know what's needed, so let's get to it as a matter of extreme urgency – Leslie Shackleton could be in deep trouble."

Everyone jumped to their feet, but before they could go far, Superintendent Mann signalled for their attention.

"Before you do get to your tasks, can I reiterate something DCI Johnstone said earlier, nothing of our suspicions goes outside these four walls for the present. If anyone asks, this is still a missing person enquiry. We don't want the press involved before we're ready to go public and I underline, this is now an extremely urgent investigation. Keep me posted, Bill."

As the team walked back to their desks, the DCI followed one of them, DC Adam Baldock.

"Adam, do a check on known villains who were involved in blackmail – are any living in this area or have any recently been released from prison?"

Next, he went to Dani's desk.

"Dani, will you see if you can make appointments for us to visit his solicitor, doctor, dentist and accountant. If the doctor and dentist can't fit us in urgently, I want to talk to them on the phone. Then check all local hospitals to see if they admitted Leslie admitted recently."

"Okay, Sir, I'll get on it right away."

The DCI then went back to the wall and scanned through all the information displayed. Yes, there was a lot of it, but it told them nothing. Bearing in mind the absolute conviction that Dorothy Shackleton believed that her husband was dead, nothing categorically pointed to that being a fact. There were possibilities of course, such as illness, an accident or perhaps the fulfilment of the blackmail threat that he'd suffer the 'consequences', but it was by no means certain that that was what the warning meant. Anyway, what was the basis for the blackmail – what was he supposedly guilty of? There had to be something else. Were they missing something? Did one of Leslie's liaisons have a jealous partner – a possibility of course. Unless they could identify the ten women, that line of investigation was a non-starter. As he pondered those women's names, the question arose in his mind, where did these liaisons take place, at the person's home? Unlikely. So, further afield, but where? I wonder, did they have other properties where secret liaisons could take place and did they have a garage where he might hide his car? Dorothy might know, and that was worth pursuing.

He picked up the phone and called her, "Mrs Shackleton, DCI Johnstone here..."

"Oh, do you have some news for me?"

"No, I'm sorry, no news yet. I'm phoning to ask whether you and your husband have any properties other than your home and the business premises?

"Yes, indeed we do; we have a holiday cottage in Raton village, near Eastbourne. I haven't been there for years, I'm not much for going out and about these days, but I believe Leslie still uses it."

"Can you tell me; does it have a garage on the site?"

"Oh, most certainly, Leslie liked to look after his car."

"Do you let it to visitors and if so, do you know whether it has been let over the past week or so and whether it's occupied at present?"

"Leslie does let it out, but I can't answer your questions regarding recent lettings, you see East Sussex Holiday Lets' handles that side of things; contact them, and they will answer all your questions I'm sure. Ask for Mr Andrews."

"Thank you very much. I'll give East Sussex's Holiday Lets a call and let you know what we find. Bye Mrs Shackleton."

DCI Johnstone found the number for 'East Sussex Holiday Lets' online and called them.

"Good morning, I'm DCI Johnstone of Barber Street Police in Kerington, London. Please, will you put me through to your manager, Mr Andrews?"

After a short wait, the manager came on the line.

"Mr Andrews speaking, how can I help you?

"I'm DCI Johnstone of Barber Street Police in Kerington, London. We're investigating the disappearance of Leslie Shackleton, who I believe has a holiday home near Eastbourne."

"Yes, of course, Leslie Shackleton holiday let in Ratton Village, I know it well."

"Can you tell me, has it been let over the last week or so and is it let at present?"

"I rather think it's not let at present, but I'll have to check his file. Please hold the line." Moments later, he returned, "right, you say the last couple of weeks or so... no lettings for the last three weeks".

"Do you find that surprising for this time of year?" the DCI questioned.

No, not for this property, because Mr Shackleton requests that we keep certain weeks vacant for his personal use."

Did he advise you whenever he was using the property?"

"No, not always. Providing it was Mr Shackleton specified weeks, we didn't need to know."

"So, what about cleaners going in while he's there?"

"That was all part of his arrangement, cleaners only go in at the end of his time there, before we let it to others. We've scheduled the next letting for next week."

"So, he could have been using it during this period and still be there at present?"

"Absolutely. It doesn't have a landline, so do you want us to check it out for you?"

"No, please don't visit the property, that's something we need to do, but we'll need to borrow a key from you."

"You can borrow a key, by all means, but is Mr Shackleton in trouble?"

"No, he's not in trouble, but his wife has reported him missing, so we need to pursue all avenues. We'll call in, pick up the key and then return it to you as soon as possible. Thank you, Mr Andrews, I do appreciate your help and co-operation. I will get back to you shortly. Bye."

The DCI went over to Dani's desk.

"Dani, have you arranged the visits to Shackleton's solicitor, doctor, dentist and accountant as yet and are any of them for today?"

"We have arranged most visits, but none for today – is that okay?"

"Yes, fine. Are you free for the rest of the day?"

"Can be, do you have something you want me to do?"

"We're going to the seaside, well almost. Leslie Shackleton has a property in Ratton Village near Eastbourne, and at present, it's not let. We need to go and check it out in case Leslie is there. It has a garage too, so his car could be there. Do you have lunch with you?"

"No Sir, I intended to nip out to the sandwich shop across the road."

"Well, we'll both do that and then shoot off – it'll take us a couple of hours or so to get there, depending on traffic. We might be late back, are you okay with that?"

"No problem, Sir, nothing spoiling."

The two of them immediately left the office and set off for Eastbourne via the sandwich shop. Two hours and fifteen minutes later, they arrived in Ratton. It didn't take long to locate the office of East Sussex Holiday Lets. Mr Andrews himself met them.

"Good afternoon," he greeted them "can I help you?"

"You certainly can," the DCI responded as they produced their warrant cards, "I'm DCI Johnstone, and this is DC Taylor. I spoke to you earlier about Leslie Shackleton's cottage; we need to borrow the key please."

"Ah yes, that's no problem."

He went to a secure cabinet in the corner of the office and retrieved the key. "There are three keys, one for the front door, one for the back and the other is for the garage. You will return them when you've finished, won't you?"

"Yes, most certainly. Now can you tell us how to find the property please?"

"I can do better than that, I have a small map, and I marked the property on it. It's about three miles from here and is in a short private road leading to half a dozen cottages – you want number 4."

With Dani navigating, and with the aid of the map, they soon located the private road. The cottage was a few hundred metres along the way, so only moments later they drew up outside. It was a picturesque spot, and it was quite a quaint cottage, it wasn't hard to see why Leslie Shackleton had chosen this as a holiday home. From the road, they could see a well-kept garden, beautifully laid out and bright with colour. It was clear too that the cottage was in good condition. It was chocolate-box with an archway of rambling roses around the front door. There was no sign of life, but that could easily belie the fact that there was someone inside. There was only one way to find out. Both officers climbed out and walked towards the front door. There was a bell, so DCI Johnstone pressed it a couple of times and for good measure knocked hard on the door. There was no response, but rather than immediately using the key, they tried peering in through the windows. They could see nothing, so decided it was time to take the bold approach.

"Okay, Dani, let's see what's going on inside," said the DCI casually. "Stay close, look and listen."

He unlocked the door and pushed it wide open.

"Hello, anyone at home? The police are here; we're here to check that all's well. We're coming inside."

They moved cautiously into the main living area, but there was nothing immediately obvious to suggest that the cottage was in use. Another door led into a beautifully laid out kitchen, and a check of the fridge and cupboards revealed no fresh foodstuffs. There was another door off the living area, and that led to a smaller, cosier sitting room. Everywhere was tidy. They moved next to the staircase and slowly mounted the steps. There were just two bedrooms and a bathroom. The first room had a double bed and various pieces of furniture – again, all was clean and tidy. The bathroom was modern, bright and clean – nothing out of place. The second bedroom was considerably more extensive, but this room was in direct contrast to the rest of the cottage.

"Wow, what do you make of this Dani?"

"I'd say that someone left this room in a hurry and didn't even have time to make the bed properly. Why would anyone leave it like this and yet leave the rest of the rooms in pristine condition? It just doesn't make sense."

"Have you noticed the pillows?" the DCI asked, "They've both been used, so I would say two people occupied this bed."

He moved to the side of the bed and pulled back the covers, revealing a considerable bloodstain, reasonably fresh though dry. "Well, that puts a different complexion on things. We need to get forensics onto this immediately. We need to know whose blood it is; this may well go some way towards confirming Dorothy Shackleton's belief that her husband is dead."

"Do you think there's enough blood there to conclude that someone has died?" Dani asked.

"I'm not sure, but if the person continued to bleed it wouldn't be long before they were, so unless they sought medical attention, I rather think it may well suggest a fatality."

They retraced their steps and exited the front door, locking it behind them. Although they wanted to get things moving urgently, they needed to look inside the garage before they left the cottage. The garage was empty, but just inside the door was another much smaller pool of blood and spots led to where they estimated a door to a car would have been.

"Hmm, was someone rushing the person to a hospital, or removed from the scene? We must check with local hospitals too; did they have a seriously injured patient brought in over the past week? We also have to get the local force to secure the scene and carry out some investigations."

"Presumably we'll have to get on to the Eastbourne division, I doubt very much whether Ratton will have much of a team, though I guess we could get them to contact Eastbourne on our behalf – they'd probably know who to talk to."

"I reckon you're right there," the DCI responded, "let's head back into the town and get Mr Andrews to cancel the bookings for the present, and he can point us in the direction of the local station."

It didn't take long to retrace their steps, and they caught the manager just as he was about to go out.

"Ah, Mr Andrews, I'm glad we've caught you. I'm sorry, but we're going to have to ask you to cancel all bookings for Leslie Shackleton's cottage for the present, we have to preserve it as a possible crime scene and get a forensic team to go through the place."

"Can I ask what you've found, not a body I hope?"

"No, not a body, but all I can say at this moment in time is that we have reason to examine the premises more closely. Do you have a contact number for the local constabulary please?"

"Ah, that is probably not your best port of call. However, I do as it happens to have contact details for your opposite number in the Eastbourne division – I play golf with him sometimes." He searched through his phone, "Ah, here it is, DCI Peter Tomlinson, his mobile number is 07994 282828."

"Thank you, Mr Andrews." DCI Johnstone called the number and waited.

"Hello, DCI Tomlinson?"

"Yes, how can I help?"

"Oh hi, I'm DCI Bill Johnstone from Kerington, London. I'm presently in Ratton at the office of East Sussex Holiday Lets. I'm here following up on a missing person, Leslie Shackleton, he has a holiday cottage near Ratton. We've just been to the cottage, and we're not happy with what we've found, so we need your help to seal off the property and to provide a forensic team urgently. How soon can you get things moving?"

"Can I ask what you've found, is it a body?"

"No, not a body, but evidence of foul play."

"I'll have a team there within the hour."

"That's great. We'll meet you at the cottage. I'll pass you over to Mr Andrews to give you directions. See you later. Bye."

While Mr Andrews was providing instructions, the DCI and Dani set off back to the cottage. When they arrived, they could immediately see that something was wrong, as the front door was open and hanging at a precarious angle. "You have to be joking," exclaimed a frustrated DCI, "someone must have seen us when we visited. I hope they haven't destroyed the evidence."

"Do we go in and check things out?" Dani asked.

"That's very tempting, but in the circumstances, I think we need to wait and let forensics check the place, there could be evidence relating to the latest break-in. Argh, I wish we'd had our team with us, we could have left someone to watch the place while we were away."

Forty minutes later, DCI Tomlinson arrived with three of his men. The DCI and Dani jumped out of the car to greet them.

"Hi, I'm DCI Bill Johnstone, and this is DC Dani Taylor. I'm afraid we have a problem, while we were away someone has broken into the premises, and I fear for the evidence we found. Do we let forensics check things out before we go inside?"

"I rather think we must, but can you tell me what this is all about – what did you find?" They took him aside, "Leslie Shackleton was reported missing by his wife, well, actually she reported that someone had killed him. However, the murder claim was on nothing more than a feeling."

"Oh no, not one of those. Tell me you didn't take the woman seriously."

"That was my initial reaction, but I was persuaded to talk to her, and I found she was not your usual crank. Something told me she might be right, but we have been pursuing it as a missing person only. Just three of us know of the murder claim. Can we ask you to keep it to yourself at present? As for what we found here, the whole place was perfectly clean and tidy until that is, we came to the main bedroom. It was there that we found a blood-soaked sheet and why we called you and your team in."

Before DCI Tomlinson could respond, Dani stepped into the conversation.

"Sir, sorry to interrupt, but I've just noticed something. The garage – unless they've managed to open it with a key – that hasn't been disturbed."

"Well spotted Dani," DCI Johnstone responded. "We've already compromised that as a crime scene, so I think we can again take a look inside."

Sure enough, there was a padlock on the garage with no signs of forced entry. "You know what I think," said DCI Tomlinson, "I think whoever broke into the cottage saw you returning before he or she had had time to break into the garage."

"You could well be right, Peter," Bill replied, "so hopefully everything here is as we saw it previously."

As he opened the door, it was clear that nothing had been disturbed. The bloodstain was visible.

"No mistaking that," Peter Tomlinson remarked, "I suggest we get forensics on that right away, I'm sure you'd like to get a DNA analysis as soon as possible so that you can make a comparison with your guy's."

"Indeed," Bill agreed, "which reminds me, I must contact my team and get them to obtain a DNA analysis for him; hopefully his hair brush or toothbrush will provide some samples."

While DCI Johnstone was contacting base, Dani talked with DCI Tomlinson. "Sir, it occurs to us that this is by no means certainly a murder scene. The blood was in the bedroom and the garage, so that suggests that the victim was not dead – he was still bleeding. Someone may have taken him to a hospital to get him treated, so can you let me have details of hospitals in the area so that I can check whether they've had any emergency involving a patient bleeding out."

"That's a good point DC Taylor, but can I suggest that to save time I get one of my team to do that for you."

Dani agreed. Meanwhile, the forensic team had arrived, so DCI Tomlinson briefed them as to what they needed. One of the forensic team went straight to the garage to obtain a blood sample from the garage floor and to rush it to the lab for analysis. Dani, now left without any specific task, decided to busy herself by patrolling the surroundings of the property. She was working on the theory that someone had been watching when they'd made their first visit. It just might be possible, she reasoned, to find out where the person had been hiding. To one side of the property was a small copse, and that seemed to Dani to be the most likely hiding place.

She strolled along the near side but spotted nothing visible. Inevitably, someone wanting to watch the cottage would be on this side. Yes, of course, they would, but it didn't follow that they would enter on this near side. She stepped out onto the road and began to scan the ground on that side. She'd only gone a few steps when she noticed that the grass had been trodden down and recently. She stepped over the fence and began to follow the trail. She was about two metres from the outer edge, but trees and bushes obscured the view of the cottage. About halfway in, however, a break appeared to her left, and it was there that she found the grass flattened – someone had watched from that spot and restlessly trampled quite an area.

She looked around the ground and eventually found a discarded chewing gum packet, three cigarette butts and even some well-chewed gum. She had an evidence bag in her pocket, so carefully picked the items up, bagged them and slipped them into her pocket. She could see DCI Johnstone looking around, so decided to retrace her steps. She just reached the outer fence when she heard a noise behind her.

Dani turned around and was only in time to see someone wielding a stout stick and swinging it towards her head. Instinctively, she ducked, but it still dealt a glancing blow to her shoulder. Dani almost fell to the ground, but fear for her life took over, and she stumbled away from him and dashed to the fence. It hurt terribly, but with great effort she managed to vault the fence, yelling for help as she did so.

DCI Johnstone came running towards her.

"What happened Dani? Why did you yell?"

The terrible pain brought tears to her eyes.

"Someone attacked me with a stick and smashed it into my shoulder. It hurts like crazy."

"What were you doing in the wood?"

"Gathering evidence. I found the place where someone had been watching the cottage and probably our first visit." She took out the evidence bag and passed it to him, "I found these, and I guess whoever it was watching saw me picking them up."

"Wow, great work Dani, we'll get forensics to check them out for prints and DNA. You really ought to have taken one of the officers with you, but as I said great work. Now, do you need to go to the hospital, is there a chance that something's broken?"

"Thank you, Sir, but no. I'll be alright, though I do feel as though I could do with a good soak in a bath and a good night's sleep."

"I don't think we're going to get back home to-night. We need to book into a hotel. Is that okay with you, do you need to let anyone know?"

"I'll text my fiancée and tell him, we were supposed to be meeting later this evening, but staying on here is fine – do you have any idea where we'll be staying?"

"Peter Tomlinson suggested The George Hotel – they do some great food as well and all reasonably priced – It'll be on expenses of course."

They were there at the cottage for a further two hours, by which time it would have been impossible to get back to London at a reasonable hour. The pain in Dani's shoulder was intense, and by then, it had caused her head to throb too. She wasn't feeling good and desperately needed to lie down and rest. The look on her face said it all.

"Come on, Dani. I can see you're in pain. You need rest and some strong pain killers. Do you have any with you?"

"No, I don't normally need painkillers, but at this moment in time I most certainly do."

"I have some in the car, so let's go and get you sorted."

They left the others and arranged to meet with them again at nine o'clock the next morning. Once in the car, Dani was relieved to rest her head on the headrest, but she was even more relieved when they got to the hotel and found they had two single rooms vacant – both en suite.

CHAPTER 5

THE ROOT OF ALL EVIL?

DANI HAD AN AWFUL NIGHT. Her soak in the bath, together with the painkillers, had eased things, to begin with, but as the night wore on the throbbing had increased, and her head felt as though it was about to burst. Later she had taken more painkillers and managed to slip into a fitful sleep, but at some point, she had rolled over onto her left side and a most excruciating pain shot through her shoulder and down her arm. She was now wide awake, with little likelihood of any further sleep, and yet it was only

3.30 am. She decided to sit up in bed and catch up with texts on her phone. She texted Luke her fiancée and told him what had happened – she just hoped he hadn't left his phone switched on, and it disturbed his sleep. He had indeed left it switched on because moments later she received a text from him.

'You poor luv, wish I was with you to comfort you. Promise me you'll go to the hospital in the morning. Keep me posted. Love you, Luke.'

She spent some time surfing the net, not looking at or for anything. At some point, she did slip into a restless sleep and slept for a couple of hours, only to be jolted awake by her phone alarm at 6.30 am. She crawled out of bed and washed with only her right hand. The dressing was doubly tricky and painful, but eventually, she managed it.

She usually didn't have much by way of breakfast, but she'd skipped dinner last night, so she felt in need of some sustenance. As she entered the dining room, she saw her boss just sitting down at a table and went to join him.

"Good morning Sir, are you happy for me to join you?"

"Good morning, Dani, yes, of course, I am. What sort of night did you have?"

"In a word, terrible, I'm afraid I do need to pay a visit to the hospital, I rather think the damage might be worse than I thought. My shoulder is very black and swollen, and it hurts like crazy. After breakfast, I'll get a taxi and go if that's okay with you?"

"Okay? More than okay, I would rather you had gone last night. You don't need a taxi though – I'm going to take you. I feel responsible for you."

"But you need to get back to the investigations. I'll be fine in a taxi, but thanks for the offer, Sir."

"Dani, I'm taking you. I'll phone Peter Tomlinson and explain the situation, and he can hold the fort until we get back."

After breakfast, having made the phone call, they set off for the nearest hospital with an A&E department. They were there for quite a while, as Dani's shoulder was x-rayed. The x-ray showed fractures to both her clavicle and scapula, but the good news was that the fractures were not displaced. They administered an injection directly into the shoulder and then she was fitted with a sling. The final instruction was to rest it for the next six weeks.

"You didn't hear that Sir, I can't be idle for six weeks, I'd be bored out of my wits. Anyway, I'm right handed, so they haven't rendered me entirely helpless."

"Hmm, I hear what you're saying, but you can't be too careful – no wrestling with villains. We must record the incident when we get back to base. It must go into the accident register."

When they arrived back at the cottage, there was still quite a bit of activity all over the site. Before they exited the car, DCI Johnstone decided it was time to interview Dani about the incident and to write it up in his daybook.

"Dani, tell me the full story surrounding the incident."

Dani did just that – she knew from experience what was required, so she included every detail. When it came to her assailant, the DCI asked her what she could remember about him or her. She closed her eyes to enable her to focus on her memories – it had only been the briefest of glimpses, but some points came flooding back.

"I reckon it was a man. The smell was of aftershave. I'm five foot four, so I reckon he was about five foot nine or ten. He wore a navy baseball cap pulled down over his eyes and a navy hoody over the top. A handkerchief or similar covered his lower face, but from his hands, he was white. He had blue jeans and strong boots on his feet. Slim build, I'd say. There was something else, a tattoo on the back of his right hand...yes, the head of a dragon I think."

"Wow, for the briefest of glimpses, you spotted a lot, far more than the average person. Amazing recall."

"That's Hendon for you, Sir, that was one of the tests we had to undergo. Incidentally, one other detail comes back to me – his hoody had the name 'CHALLENGE' on the front."

The interview completed, they exited the car and joined the others. Everyone looked up as they approached. They saw Dani's sling and immediately gave her a clap. Dani gave a bow and instantly regretted it, as a shooting pain reminded her that the injury was still there. She clutched her shoulder in agony.

DCI Tomlinson approached them.

"You are clearly in pain, Sergeant, take it easy. Rest will help it to heal more quickly, take it from me, I had a similar injury about eighteen months ago, but mine came from a fall when a suspect pushed me down a flight of concrete steps. Thank goodness you had such a rapid reaction, I dread to think how things might have turned out if that blow had hit your head. I don't suppose you had the opportunity to get much of a description of your assailant, but anything would help."

"Peter, believe it or not, Dani was able to give practically everything but his name. I'll write out the details she was able to give and let you have them. Then, of course, you have the items she retrieved from the wood. If we can get a good DNA result from them, I reckon it should be possible to nail him, if only for the assault."

DCI Tomlinson was right about that potential blow to her head. It was one of the thoughts that had crossed her mind numerous times during the night. Why would someone want to kill her? She was only one of a team there that day and, by comparison, only a minor member. Then she suddenly remembered, the evidence she'd retrieved from that vantage point – that's it, he wanted to prevent that from being analysed and used to identify him.

"By the way," DCI Tomlinson continued, "the hospital checks, all negative I'm afraid, nothing that sounds anything like our victim. Forensics got some good results from the door and one or two places inside, including some boot prints on the door and floor. He wasn't too careful this time, but sadly he did remove the sheet from the bed. However, that is not as much a loss as it might have been, they found that some blood had gone through to the mattress, and there were spots right from the bedroom to the garage. We should have a lot to go on. The lab hopes to get back to us later today or tomorrow morning. Are you staying on down here?"

"No Peter, until we get the lab report and have the opportunity to cross reference it to DNA at our end, we don't know for certain that it is Leslie Shackleton's blood. Can I assume you're happy to continue pursuing things at this end?"

"Oh, absolutely. Whether or not it's murder we're dealing with is yet to be established, but at the very least I reckon there's been a serious assault both in the cottage and on Dani, so my gut instinct says they're linked – I'm determined to get to the bottom of what's going on and who's behind it all. As soon as

I get any news, I'll let you know, and I'll send the lab report to you too."

"Great, thank you, Peter, it's been good working with you albeit briefly. We'll be on our way. I think this young woman could do with a rest – though I may have to lock her in a cell to make sure she does."

With that, they parted company, and they set off on their journey back to London. Dani slept for much of the way, and instead of going straight back to the station, he took her to her home.

"You go in, get yourself a drink and stay put for the rest of the day. If tomorrow you still feel groggy, I don't want to see you in the office – make sure you are ready for action before you return. I'll file a report on your attack and advise HR that you need to recuperate for as long as it takes."

Dani was, in fact, glad to be back home and under no pressure to get back into action immediately. Every bump that the car went over as they'd travelled shook her shoulder, and she'd been glad to drift into sleep as the pain was causing nausea. Now Dani made herself a strong black coffee, took more pain-killers and settled back in a chair to relax. Before she could drink her coffee, she had drifted into a deep sleep once more and didn't wake until Luke planted a kiss on her cheek at 7.00 pm.

"My darling," Luke spoke compassionately, "you look awful, go to bed and sleep it off. You'll be cold if you stay here all night. Unless you need help, I'll go, and I'll see you tomorrow. Text me in the morning and let me know how you're feeling. Please don't go to work unless you are really up to it." They kissed, and he left. Dani made herself another coffee and went to her bed. She did have a much better night, but when she woke the next morning, her shoulder ached and felt very stiff. Dani hated doing so, but she phoned the office and told them she was taking the day off. Then she texted Luke and gave him her latest news.

In the office, DCI Johnstone called a briefing and brought everyone up to date on what they'd found at the cottage and what had happened to Dani.

"Okay, what's been happening here while I've been away? James, anything on Giles Roberts?"

"We're still pursuing him. He supposedly worked at an estate agency in Stockport before coming to Shackleton's at Kerington, but they say they've never heard of him, so we can only assume that Leslie

Shackleton didn't follow up his reference. So far, every avenue we've explored concerning his background has come up blank – Giles Roberts, at least this Giles Roberts, doesn't exist. I think it's time to bring him in and challenge him – he has a lot of questions to answer."

"Okay, do just that. What about the DNA checks, have materials gone to the lab and do we have any indication as to when they can get results for us?"

"I'm on that one," responded DC Colin Jenkinson, "we got some hair samples and a toothbrush, and yes, they went to the lab yesterday. They anticipate results later today."

"What about CCTV, any siting of that BMW yet or anything back from the APB?"

"Yes Sir," responded DC Jenny Seymour, "we have CCTV from around his office and on the day, he went missing. We can trace him travelling south, but some cameras are out of action, and we suddenly lose him. There's nothing back from the APB though."

"Ah, it's interesting that he was heading south," responded the DCI, "I suspect he was travelling to his cottage in Ratton Village just north of Eastbourne. Get onto DCI Peter Tomlinson of Eastbourne division and ask him if he could check any CCTV in and around Ratton – tell him exactly what we're looking for and if they pick up any images ask in which direction it was travelling and whether anyone was in the car other than the driver. By the way, who's been cross-checking the ten names against the Shackleton client list?"

"Paul Sheridan offered to undertake that," replied DI Cartwright, "I'll get on to him and get an update."

"Get back to me, James. Adam, did you get anywhere with the check on blackmail artists – any living anywhere near, or recently released from prison?"

"Nothing concrete, Guv, but there is one living in the next parish who is a suspected blackmailer – Jerry Bardon. However, as far as we can ascertain, he has no connections whatsoever with Leslie Shackleton and highly unlikely to be doing business with Shackleton's. He's a rough scruff. We did talk to him, and it seems that he spends most of his time in his local pub and that's a right dive. The landlord confirmed that Bardon is a regular, says he's there every night without fail. I don't think we can take that as an alibi though."

"Okay, thank you. Anything else anyone?"

"What is your thoughts Guv, on what you found in Ratton – is it a potential murder we're looking at?" DI Cartwright asked.

"Too soon to say, James, we don't even know yet whose blood it is, that's why we need the lab results. Even if it turns out to be Leslie Shackleton's blood, it's by no means certain that he's dead, it could just be that he has received a serious injury. I want to urge you all not to speculate and don't voice your inner thoughts outside this room – this is, and I emphasise it, still a missing person case until we get evidence to the contrary. Okay, thank you, everyone. Pursue every avenue – someone somewhere knows something, and we need to find out what that something is. Use your imaginations and turn over a few stones, see what crawls out."

The DCI then called DC Jenny Seymour over, "Jenny, before you go, forget what I said about contacting DCI Tomlinson. I think I'd better do that myself as there are a few things I want to discuss with him, some of which we touched upon when we were together."

The DCI returned to his office and picked up the phone. Moments later – "Hi, this is Chief Inspector

Johnstone from Kerington, London. Can you put me through to DCI Tomlinson...hi Peter, Bill Johnstone here, how's life at the seaside? Peter, I believe we left a photo of Leslie Shackleton with you, and I was wondering whether you could check and see if there are any CCTV images of Leslie's BMW either entering the area or leaving it? It's blue/grey, number Lima, Alpha, Sierra 1948. It would be interesting to see who was in the car if that's at all possible – one person or at least two."

"No problem, we'll get onto that for you."

Fantastic, thanks. The other thing is could your men search the area to see if there is any sign of a body or a newly dug grave – in that thicket, for instance."

"Ah, now there we're one step ahead, we are doing that as I speak and we're also checking with doctors' surgeries.

"Brilliant, good thinking. I'll leave things with you; I hope we both get a breakthrough soon."

"Anything moving at your end?"

"No, nothing positive yet, but maybe today's the day. Thanks again, talk to you soon."

Just then, the DCI's phone rang, and he fully expected it to be Peter Tomlinson calling back, but he was surprised to hear Dani's voice.

"Dani, I didn't expect you to be calling, how are you now?"

Dani explained that she'd seen her doctor and he had prescribed some strong painkillers that were doing a great job of making her feel more comfortable. She was feeling so much better that rather than sitting idly at home, she'd been contacting Leslie Shackleton's accountant, solicitor, doctor and dentist and had persuaded two of them to see them that afternoon and the other two tomorrow morning.

"Dani," DCI Johnstone protested, "you're supposed to be resting, not working. However, I do thank you for what you've arranged, but there's no way I would allow you to come with me."

Dani wasn't about to take no for an answer and begged him to relent, arguing that he had to pass her house on the way to the accountant's office.

"Well, it's against my better judgement, but I'll pick you up – what time?"

"2:15, the appointment is for 2:30. Then the solicitor's appointment is at 4:30. Thank you for agreeing to Sir, I promise I'll rest again after the visits – until tomorrow, that is."

"Detective Sergeant Taylor, you're incorrigible, but I do appreciate your dedication. However, if at any stage you feel it's too much for you, promise me you'll say so, and I'll get you home. I want you fit and well as soon as possible, so remember, you've nothing to prove."

The DCI picked Dani up on schedule.

"How are you feeling now, are you really up to this?"

"Yes, thank you, Sir, it's been much more comfortable since taking the stronger painkillers. I know the effect will wear off eventually, but hopefully, by then it will be time to take my next dose. I'm hopeful that this visit will throw up something useful; we need to know whether someone was blackmailing Shackleton long term. He may not say anything to his wife even if his life were under threat, but his financial dealings might give us a clue."

"Ah, I see we're thinking along the same lines. This business is not something that takes place in one moment; experience tells me it has small beginnings that eventually get out of hand – a few warnings, a few threats and then action. We desperately need those lab results from both Eastbourne and this end – we must determine whether it is Leslie Shackleton's blood. Of course, it may have no connection to the blackmail even if it is his blood."

They arrived at the accountant's premises, and the receptionist ushered them through to Barry Templeton's office.

"Mr Templeton, so good of you to spare us some of your valuable time. I'm Detective Chief Inspector Johnstone, and this is Detective Sergeant Taylor." They all shook hands and sat down.

"So, what's this all about?" Templeton asked, "how can I help you – I think you mentioned my client Leslie Shackleton?"

"Yes, that's right," Dani responded, "his wife reported him missing a week or so ago, and we're trying to trace his whereabouts."

"Well I don't think I can be of much help to you there, I've neither seen him nor talked to him for...two weeks, yes, two weeks ago today. I have an entry here in my diary – Leslie Shackleton, 2.15 pm."

"What was his business with you that day?" asked the DCI.

"I'm not sure I'm in a position to divulge my client's personal information and dealings, they are confidential, you know."

"I fully appreciate that," the DCI responded, "but this is a serious police enquiry instigated by his wife, and if we are to find out what has happened to him, we need all the background information we can glean. Please phone Mrs Shackleton if you need confirmation that we have her full permission to delve into his affairs."

"I fear I must do that Chief Inspector. I can't afford to lose client confidence." He picked up the phone and asked his receptionist to get Mrs Shackleton on the phone and moments later; he was connected.

"Good morning Mrs Shackleton, Barry Templeton here, sorry to bother you, but I have two police officers here asking for information about your husband's affairs, how much am I at liberty to divulge?"

"Anything and everything, Mr Templeton, I want to know what has happened to my husband, so please co-operate."

"If you are sure, I will most certainly help them as much as I'm able. Thank you. Goodbye." He turned to his computer and opened Leslie Shackleton's file.

"Right officers, what is it you want to know? Of course, you asked about his business on the day of his last visit. He said he urgently needed to release £6,000.00, but he didn't want it to show as a specific item on the books, it was to be general expenditure."

"Had he ever requested such an arrangement before?" asked the DCI.

"Hmm, I'm sorry to say he had. Never quite that amount, but four times recently and amounts ranging from £2,000.00 to £4,000.00."

"He never mentioned what the money was for?" Dani asked.

"Never, though I admit I was a little suspicious that perhaps he was being blackmailed, but I didn't pry, it's not my place. However, I can't think of any reason why he might be subjected to blackmail."

"What were his finances like in general?" the DCI enquired.

"Excellent, all his offices were thriving, though I did notice that the Kerington office was slightly down on the others, whereas I would have expected it to be well ahead of the field. Homes in Kerington are not cheap, so it ought to be bringing in the greater returns. Don't ask me why it was like that. I only manage what comes in – I leave the whys and wherefores to Mr Shackleton and his manager, Giles Roberts. He might be able to help you further."

"Were there any entries on Mr Shackleton's file of amounts paid to specific individuals?" Dani asked.

"From time to time," he responded thoughtfully, "well, quite regularly actually – sometimes weekly, sometimes fortnightly. Do you have a reason for asking?"

"Well yes, but can I ask, were the payments to men or women?" Dani pressed him.

"Oh, come to think of it, always women – I don't remember any payments to men. That hadn't occurred to me until you asked. Are you implying what I think you are?"

The DCI stepped into the conversation, "very possibly, but the point is, do you have names and contact details for those women?"

"Hmm, possibly for some of them at least, but for others it was cash payments through Mr Shackleton, and then I only had names. Mind you, if I remember correctly, the contact details I do have are to box numbers only."

"Well, whatever you have, we need to trouble you to provide a list of those names and contact details where you have them – it is important and very urgent. We must talk to them all as soon as possible to find out when they saw Leslie last. I can't emphasise enough the urgency – how soon can you compile it for us?"

"Say at 5.00 pm today? That should be possible."

"We have another appointment when we leave here. I don't think we'll be late, but what time do you close?"

"I normally close at 6.00 pm, but in the circumstances, I'll stay until you arrive."

"Thank you, that's very kind of you. Can I ask you, Mr Templeton, did Mr Shackleton have many transactions in the Ratton or Eastbourne area? And apart from his home and business premises, did Leslie Shackleton have any other premises?" Dani enquired.

"Regarding your first question, yes he did and on a semi-regular basis – he had a holiday home there. As for other premises, he owned a block of garage/lockups on Barnett Street on the edge of Kerington. All but one he let to regular clients. Number 4 he never let to anyone, though I don't know why.

It's quite a rough area compared to the centre of Ker-ington, and I've never really understood why he wanted anything to do with it."

"How long has he owned them and who holds the keys?" Dani asked.

"Mr Shackleton himself holds the keys. I don't have any hands-on involvements – I'm strictly into the financing aspects of things. He purchased the garages in July 2014."

"Can you also provide us with names and contact details for the people renting those garages, please? Are there any other anomalies connected with his affairs that come to mind?"

"Not that I can immediately recall, but I'll go through his account and let you know if anything comes to light. I can certainly supply details of the garage lets. I'll have them for you when you call back later."

"Thank you, Mr Templeton. You've been most helpful. We'll pop back in for those lists, probably around 5.30 pm," the DCI responded.

CHAPTER 6

REVELATIONS

THEY SET OFF FOR THEIR appointment with Andrew Hastings. The solicitor's office was quite near to Shackleton's Estate Agency. They arrived there with time to spare, so sat in the carpark and waited.

"That, I feel, was a very worthwhile visit, Dani. Some things are worth following up – especially those garage lets. They sound rather iffy to me."

"Yes, that's what I thought, it'll be interesting to see what they contain, but I'm rather intrigued by number 4. Why would an entrepreneur like Leslie Shackleton have garages in Barnett Street in the first place, it's a right seedy dump, and why keep one garage free? What did he use it for – storage, but storage of what?"

"Hmm, good question, maybe it has some connection with the blackmail. It would make sense as to why Mr Shackleton had those garages if they're being used for illicit purposes either by Leslie or by others. If something dodgy was going on there, perhaps someone found out and assumed it was all happening with his knowledge or even that he was complicit in their deeds. Mind you, just like you; I can't for the life of me reconcile the Leslie Shackleton we keep hearing about with the criminal world. The more we pursue this case, the more intriguing it becomes. I think there have been things going on that very few people knew about, and that includes his wife."

"Sir, if Leslie Shackleton was paying women for their services, do you reckon they were more likely to be escorts than clients connected with his business? If they were people he'd met in the course of his business, would he be likely to be paying them?"

"Well, good question, though I suppose he could just be saying a big thank you for services rendered. Hmm, I reckon you're more likely to be correct about them being professional women, they're the sort of women who would appeal to someone of his personality – discreet, classy and generally available to be booked in advance."

"It'll be interesting to see whether the list Barry Templeton supplies corresponds with the list of names you found on his computer, including 'Angela T'," Dani remarked.

The appointment time arrived, so they went inside. The receptionist took them straight to Andrew Hastings' office.

"Mr Hastings, thank you for agreeing to see us, I'm Detective Chief Inspector Johnstone, and this is Detective Sergeant Taylor. We won't keep you long, but there are a few points we need to raise with you regarding Leslie Shackleton."

"Yes, Mrs Shackleton advised me that you'd be calling and has authorised me to co-operate with you completely. So, what do you want to know? The fact that he's missing is bad business. I do hope you will locate him soon; it's clear that Mrs Shackleton is devastated."

"Just so," the DCI responded, "we need to know about his will. Mrs Shackleton indicated that she and her husband had written their wills at the same time and that they'd largely left their estate to each other. However, she did say that there were a few additional minor bequests. Is that correct?"

"Yes, it is, Mrs Shackleton left everything to her husband, but Leslie Shackleton left several minor bequests to specified individuals."

"Ah, we need details of those minor bequests please," said the DCI, "do you have both names and contact details? And how many names are we talking about?"

"Yes, I do have full details – there are eight in all. It's highly irregular, but as Mrs Shackleton said full co-operation, I will prepare a list for you. I must urge though, please don't divulge those names to anyone, especially as Mr Shackleton is missing and not deceased. You won't need to contact the individuals involved, will you? It's highly unlikely that they know anything about the endowments."

"I can't promise anything at this stage, though it's highly unlikely that we'll need to mention the bequests unless the case should take a turn for the worst," the DCI responded.

"Do either of the wills have codicils?" Dani asked.

"No, nothing has been added or changed since I prepared the will."

"Would you know if Mr Shackleton had written a new will?" Dani continued, "And would it be valid and supersede the one you hold, what if he'd prepared it himself privately?"

"Oh, my goodness. I sincerely hope Mr Shackleton hasn't done anything like that. However, provided it had been prepared correctly and witnessed correctly, yes, it would be valid, and it would supersede the original. Have you any reason to think that he might have done that?"

"Oh, no," she reassured him, "we haven't found anything to suggest he has. It was just something that came into my mind."

"Phew, that's a relief, you had me worried there."

"Sorry," Dani replied.

"Now, Mr Hastings, a question that might alarm you still further. Are you aware that Leslie Shackleton has a block of garages/lockups in Barnett Street?"

"Well, yes, I represented him during the negotiation for purchase. Is there a problem – what makes you ask about them?"

"Whether there's a problem or not we're not yet sure," the DCI remarked. "Did it not seem at all strange to you that an estate agent who owned a fleet of upmarket shops around the region, should choose to buy six garages/lockups in a...well shall we say, rather run-down neighbourhood? Did he ever say why he wanted to buy them, and do you know what he used the garages for?"

"Providing there is no legal conflict; I see no reason to argue with or question a client's choice. No, he didn't say why he wanted them, and neither do I know what he uses them for – storage would be my guess, but that's his business."

"What about blackmail, whose business would that be?" asked the DCI pointedly.

"Blackmail!" Hastings exclaimed. "Who's being blackmailed?"

It was very noticeable that the solicitor had turned very pale, so the DCI followed it up.

"How would you respond if I told you someone is blackmailing Leslie Shackleton, and I believe he sought your advice about it – what advice did you give him?"

"Detective Chief Inspector, I take exception to your insinuation. He did not, I repeat, did not, consult me about such a matter. Had he done so, I would have advised him to take the matter straight to the police."

"Okay, Sir, I apologise for any offence, but am I wrong in saying that even if he didn't consult you, you somehow knew about the blackmail from another source?"

"This is off the record, you understand, yes I did hear from someone else, or I heard someone else's suspicions. I didn't know anything for certain, and although I tried to contact Mr Shackleton, I couldn't get hold of him, and no one knew his whereabouts. The next thing I heard was from Mrs Shackleton, asking if I'd seen him because he was missing. I assure you I did not have anything to hide."

"Mr Hastings," Dani said, stepping into the arena, "this is not a loaded question, but to your knowledge was Mr Shackleton involved in any business 'grey' areas, anything in the least controversial that would render him a possible target for blackmail or something more sinister – abduction or violence of some kind for instance?"

"I have been Leslie Shackleton's solicitor for a good many years, and during that time, he has been the perfect gentleman, an upright citizen and honest in his business arrangements. However, those qualities took a knock recently when it came to my notice that someone had seen him conversing with a group of men who, shall we say, were none too particular about what they were dealing with, and I did confront him about what I'd heard, but he laughed it off, said it was nothing – they were enquiring about the possibility of storing some equipment in his lockups."

"Did he agree to let them use the lockups?"

"I advised him not to do so, but whether he took my advice I can't be sure – sorry, I just don't know."

"Thank you, Mr Hastings, for all your help. We may need to speak to you again, but that's it for the present. When can you let us have details of the folk Mr Shackleton named in his will to receive minor bequests?"

"Oh, right now if you can hang on for a few seconds."

Hastings turned back to his computer, quickly found what he wanted and printed off a copy of the list of names. He passed it to the DCI who glanced at it and immediately noticed one name Angela Talbot; he showed it to Dani who nodded in acknowledgement."

"Someone you know?" asked Andrew Hastings.

"Not someone we know, but a name we believe we've come across before," the DCI replied nonchalantly. "Anyway, we must be going; thank you again for your help."

They spoke very little until they were back in the car, but once they were there, Dani was first to speak out.

"Do you think Angela Talbot is the same with Angela T?"

"Oh, I don't think there's any doubt," he responded enthusiastically, "it's too much of a coincidence for the name Angela to appear in three places – the computer, the book and now here. However, now we have a name for the 'T'"

"Are her contact details on the list too?"

"They most certainly are – the first real lead we've had into any of the names on that list."

"Fantastic. Now perhaps we can get somewhere, I don't like dead ends."

"Hmm, perhaps not the best choice of words Dani."

They headed back to the office of Barry Templeton, the accountant, to collect the lists of names for the women to whom payments Leslie Shackleton paid and those who were renting his garages. They arrived before 5.30 pm, but the lists had been prepared and left with the receptionist. DCI Johnstone thanked her, and they returned to the car.

"The moment of truth," he said as he slit open the envelope and withdrew a single sheet of paper. "Eureka!" he exclaimed, "Angela Talbot again, and I'm sure many of the others are repeats too."

"What about the lets, any familiar names there?"

"No, I don't recognise any names, but their addresses are all in that same neck of the woods. Ah, one address is care of one of the other addresses. Now that's interesting. I rather suspect they'll be some connection when we pursue them. Anything familiar to you?" he asked, passing the sheet to Dani.

She studied it for a few moments before replying.

"Hmm, I'm not sure. I have a feeling I've come across the name Arnold Broadhurst somewhere before. I'll need to check that out. Now then, don't we know Ali Khan too? I'm sure Paul Sheridan mentioned him in some context recently. I'll have to check with him."

"Before we move off Dani, I want you to be honest with me, how is your shoulder? I've seen you wincing a few times – let me take you straight home, please don't feel you have to keep slogging on."

"Yes, I must admit it is sore, and it hurts like crazy if I forget and move too quickly, but I'm okay to carry on for a while. I want to follow up on Broadhurst and Khan while they're still fresh in my mind. Once I've done that, I promise I'll call it a day."

Back at the station, Dani went straight to see Paul Sheridan.

"Hi Paul," she greeted him, "can you help me? Am I right in thinking that you recently mentioned Ali Khan to me – I can't remember the context, but his name rings bells with me?"

"Ali Khan – now there's a slippery customer for you. You're right. I did bring him in; we suspected him of being involved in drugs along with a few others. All the others had alibis, but Khan's didn't stand up. We didn't have enough to hold him and charge him though, so we had to let him go. Why do you ask?"

"Khan has come up in the Shackleton case. He's listed as renting a garage belonging to Leslie Shackleton – in Barnett Street of all places."

"Barnett Street, you must be joking – Leslie Shackleton owning garages in Barnett Street, it beggars belief. Mind you; it makes sense that Khan would rent a garage in that road, he lives in that area. Do we have reason to do a raid on the garage?" he asked, rubbing his hands together.

"I think it's highly likely," Dani replied, "but that's up to the DCI, though I rather think he'll call on you as you've already had dealings with Khan. Incidentally, do you remember who the others he was involved with were?"

"Hang on a minute, and I'll tell you." He checked his records, "Ah, here we are – Lenny Thomas, Robert Bright, John Porter and Arnold Broadhurst."

"Arnold Broadhurst – that's a name I know from somewhere, but I can't remember where. Anyway, thank you, Paul. See you soon."

"Hey, by the way, how's the shoulder?"

"Could be better but could be worse too. I reckon I'll get there eventually, but I hope it's sooner rather than later. Thanks for asking."

Back at her desk, Dani checked records on her computer for Arnold Broadhurst. He'd figured in an enquiry at some point, and it was bugging her because she couldn't recall when or what for, and moments later, there he was, an attempted burglary that went hopelessly wrong. When the owner's Alsatian confronted him, Arnold fled the scene, but the owner grabbed him – a bodybuilder no less. He faced a fine of £100.00. She remembered him because she was the arresting officer and he was such a puny looking specimen – a drug addict she felt sure.

Dani knocked on DCI Johnstone's door.

"Sorry to interrupt you, Sir, just wanted to bring you up to speed on Broadhurst and the others. Do you have the list to hand for the garage lets – what were the names?"

He found the sheet provided by Barry Templeton.

"Yes, here we are – Ali Khan, Lenny Thomas, Robert Bright, John Porter and Arnold Broadhurst."

"The same as the names provided by Paul Sheridan. Broadhurst was someone I arrested some time back for attempted burglary, I certainly remember him from that incident. Incidentally, but this is only a hunch, I reckon he was a drug addict back then, so

I'm wondering whether that's what all this is about – drugs!"

"Hmm, you could be right, and it could be that Leslie Shackleton inadvertently got caught up with them, perhaps through the garage/lockups. I really can't imagine him willingly becoming involved, though I still can't fathom how it came about that he bought that block in such a seedy area. Someone must have had a hold over him unless I have misread his personality. Anyway, thanks Dani, now please go home, you are looking very grey again – that's an order."

Dani smiled.

"Okay, Sir, you win, but I'll see you in the morning."

DCI Johnstone shook his head and lifted his hands in resignation – she was irrepressible, but deep down, he fully understood her wanting to see the case through to its conclusion. No dedicated copper ever wanted to leave a case part finished. Dani was just such a dedicated officer, and the DCI sometimes wondered if she ever managed to switch off completely, though perhaps Luke could help her achieve that.

True to her word, Dani was in the office on time the next morning. She mainly wanted to be there because she had set up the appointments with Leslie Shackleton's doctor and dentist. They had little hope that either meeting would be as productive as the previous day's appointments; however, the DCI determined that he was not going to leave any stone unturned. Even the tiniest detail would sometimes provide the opening to crack the case.

Dr Kate Petersfield, Leslie Shackleton's dentist, was ready to meet with them when they arrived. DCI Johnstone introduced himself and Dani and explained why they were there.

"You may already know that Leslie Shackleton is missing and has been for more than a week. We are asking all his known contacts when they saw him last and what his state of mind was at that time. How long have you been his dentist?"

"Just over six years. I bought this property, which doubles as my home, through Leslie and the moment I saw it, I knew it was ideal for my purposes. I'd previously shared a practice in central London, but although five practitioners shared the cost, it was getting more and more difficult to support both the practice and the flat I then occupied. I decided to move to this area and never have for one moment regretted the decision."

"When did you see Leslie Shackleton last?" Dani asked, "and how did he seem to you – did he have things on his mind as far as you could tell?"

"It was seven months ago – I see him annually. His teeth were in good condition, so each visit is simply a routine check-up. How did he seem? His normal self, amiable, but we can't chat much with my fingers in his mouth. No, I saw nothing unusual about his countenance."

"Did you ever meet socially?" The DCI asked.

"Oh no, it was strictly a professional relationship between us."

"Sorry to press you on this doctor, but has he ever during the time you have known each other, made an advance towards you?" DCI Johnstone asked.

"Oh, most certainly not. Mr Shackleton was always the perfect gentleman, and he never lingered beyond his appointment. I could never imagine him making an advance towards anyone. When he showed me around this property, he always maintained a discreet distance from me – I never felt crowded by him.

His wife consults my practice too. She is a very different personality, very quiet, reserved, a woman of few words. I would even say she seemed very sad beneath her air of composure."

They thanked her for her time and left the practice, returning to the car in readiness for their short journey to meet with Dr Andrew Barnett from the Kerington Rise practice. Whereas Dr Petersfield's waiting room was practically empty, the waiting room at this practice was heaving. Eight doctors shared the practice, so dealt with many patients every day. They had to wait a short while for Dr Barnett to be free, but then he invited them through to his consulting room.

After introductions, the DCI opened the conversation.

"Dr Barnett, thank you for agreeing to see us. I'm sure you are extremely busy, so we won't keep you any longer than we can help. Are you aware of the fact that Leslie Shackleton has been missing for a week or so now and that we have the task of trying to find out what has happened to him? When did you see him last?"

"Let me get his notes up on my screen – yes, it was three weeks ago today, 2.15 pm to be precise."

"May I ask you the purpose of his visit?"

"Chief Inspector, you must know that patient confidentiality forbids me from divulging such information."

"I fully understand Doctor, but this is becoming more and more serious as time goes by – we fear for his safety."

The DCI responded. "We need, therefore, every scrap of information we can glean, so please help us here – was there anything about his consultation that was serious, perhaps even life threatening?"

"You're putting me in a tough position. It was potentially serious, but not immediately life threatening – nothing likely to cause him to drop dead suddenly."

"Sorry, I must press you. When you say it was serious, do you believe Mr Shackleton's state of mind might have led him to take his own life?"

"Oh, my goodness, no. There was nothing beyond our ability to treat and remedy. Can we leave that line of questioning there please?"

"May I ask," Dani interjected, "did Mr Shackleton seem at all worried about anything when you saw him last?"

"No, he seemed remarkably relaxed. I really can't imagine anything about his demeanour that day that would give cause for concern."

DCI Johnstone stood to his feet, and Dani followed suit, "Thank you, Doctor, we are grateful for your time and for answering our questions as openly as you were able. We'll leave you to your patients."

"Before you go, Detective Sergeant Taylor, can I ask about you...is it your shoulder?"

"Yes, a couple of fractures, a few days ago."

"Hmm, I noticed you wincing a few times and I must urge you to rest more – you really ought not to be working or at least not full days. Chief Inspector, I think you need to put your foot down."

"I'm sure you're right Doctor, but this young lady is as determined as they come, I think I'd have to handcuff her to a bedpost to stop her. Seriously, though, I will do my best, I'm sure your advice is very sound. Are you listening Sergeant?"

Dani smiled and turned towards the door, and the DCI knew they were both wasting their breath if Dani refused to rest; there was nothing they could do about it. They returned to the office and together collated all the things they'd garnered from both day's visits. They updated the evidence board in preparation for the next briefing the following morning, and then Dani surprised DCI Johnstone by telling him she would have to go home, as her shoulder was getting extremely painful.

"Yes, go now," the DCI responded, "thank you for bothering to come in at all, but as far as I'm concerned you resting, and healing is better than slogging on and prolonging the healing process. I want you back fit and well as soon as possible."

"Thank you, Sir," Dani replied, "but before I go, I've had a thought, we should be scouring escort agencies on the net to see if we can locate the source of his 'companions'."

"Good point, yes we'll do just that. Who knows it could throw up some clues? It occurs to me that Leslie Shackleton might well have linked up with other women who were not on the lists we've acquired. He could be elsewhere alive, and well, though having said that, he surely would have seen the missing person bulletins by now – unless he doesn't want anyone to find him of course. Aargh, give us a positive lead someone. Now, Dani, go home!"

HOPE SPRINGS

DANI'S NIGHT WAS FAR FROM PERFECT. She'd timed her final medication for just before she retired so that pain wouldn't prevent her from sleeping. It worked; it worked well, until that is, a vivid dream in which the stick-wielding man confronted her again, causing her to roll over sharply onto her injured shoulder. The pain that she'd felt when he landed that vicious blow seared through her body once again, jolting her wide awake. She gripped her shoulder and gritted her teeth, but the pain was such that falling asleep again would be impossible. It was too soon to take more painkillers, so she got up, made a mug of tea, grabbed her laptop and climbed back into bed. If she couldn't sleep, then she might as well use the time productively. She typed in 'Escort Agencies Kerington London.' She was amazed at just how many sites it threw up, and although she could discount quite a few that were, she felt, too far away, still six remained. She clicked on the first, 'Amorous Escorts', and found that it required her to open an account by providing a name, age and email address. She tried another, 'Glamorous Escorts', and the result was similar. All six required something comparable.

She faced something of a dilemma and wasn't sure what to do. They needed to check it out and no matter who approached the issue, they would face the same problem. It was time to take the bull by the horns – she returned to 'Amorous Escorts' and gave her name as Danny Edwards (her mother's maiden name), aged thirty-eight and her work email address. There was a ping from the right-hand bottom corner of her screen, indicating that an email had arrived at her work address. She was able to access it, and when opened, it welcomed her to the agency, confirmed her details and invited her to enjoy future relationships. It provided a membership number to enable her to access the website, which she now did. Photos of about twenty glamorous women of varying ages appeared. She scanned their names and three correspond with the list they'd already acquired, so she made a note. Dani now went on to access some of the other sites using the same personal details. She had varying degrees of success. One or two yielded nothing, but after accessing five sites, she had located all the names on the list. They were spread over just four of the sites – 'Amorous Escorts', 'Glamorous Choices', 'Ideal Escorts' and 'Exquisite Companions'. Dani felt quite pleased with herself, at least it would save some time the next morning and allow them to pursue the women for details of their liaisons with Leslie Shackleton. Of course, there could still be other agencies, so some general enquiries would always be necessary. It could all be very time consuming and again lead them nowhere – often though, that was the nature of police work, great efforts with little returns.

Dani's shoulder was by now feeling slightly less painful, so she dosed herself with painkillers again and settled down in the hope that sleep would return. Return it did and she slept soundly and dreamlessly until her alarm blared at 6.30 am. She was one of the first of the team in the office that morning, so she printed off the list she'd prepared in the night and mounted it on the board ready for the briefing. Working with one hand was very limiting, but she was getting used to it, though she longed for the day when everything would get back to normal.

The CID team related well together, and often there was banter amongst them that was a welcome relief when faced with complex cases. Just at present though, Dani was the butt of many of their jokes and comments. She took it all in her stride though and often gave as good as she got. There was nothing malicious in their remarks, and Dani knew very well that deep down, everyone cared about her condition and often enquired as to how she was feeling. That morning she was feeling good despite her disturbed night, and she was eager to go with whatever the case might throw up. They were still waiting for that elusive breakthrough, but maybe today would be the day when it came.

DCI Johnstone exited his office carrying papers in his hand and called them to order.

"I have here," he said "lab reports from both this end and from Eastbourne. The blood we found at his holiday cottage did belong to Leslie Shackleton. A report from the scene indicates that he was bleeding profusely, but the trail from the cottage to the garage suggests that he was at that point a walking wounded. There is no way of knowing what happened to him in that garage – whether his assailant bundled him into the car or the boot. However, the Eastbourne team have found CCTV footage of Leslie Shackleton's car speeding northward from Ratton. There is only one occupant, but there is no view that can identify who is driving. Then the car disappears and can't be located again. Now, the lab has analysed the items that Dani found, and they belong to Royston Barraclough, a vicious thug from that area who has a string of convictions for ABH and GBH. He often uses a knife and, it seems, is very handy with a baseball bat – he improvised in his attack on Dani. We have a photo, he looks a nasty piece of work and, despite his slim build, he works out and is very muscular. At present, it seems, he has disappeared off the radar."

"We need to know whether Barraclough has any connections with anyone in our neighbourhood, particularly with any of the five people who rent garages belonging to Leslie Shackleton in Barnett Street. Paul, I believe you know those five and that you've had dealings before with Ali Khan, one of the five. Get search warrants and then take a team, find those five and insist they open those garages for you to search. But, Paul, don't immediately produce the search warrants, tell them that Leslie Shackleton, the owner of the garages, has been located and has given permission for us to access them. See how they react to the news, it might give us a clue as to whether they know anything about Shackleton's disappearance. Only produce the search warrants at the last minute if they still refuse to open their garages. The number 4 garage, incidentally, wasn't let, so access that and see what it contains."

"Next we come to the eight women named on Leslie Shackleton's computer. Shackleton's accountant confirmed the names. They are folk he made regular payments too. Dani has come up with the plausible theory that perhaps they were escorts, that's something we need to pursue."

"Sir," Dani interrupted, "I've put a list on the board – they do all belong to escort agencies."

"Okay, thank you, Dani," the DCI responded with a frown, "er...when did you find that out?"

"About 3.00 am this morning. I was in pain and wide awake, so I decided to use the time productively."

"You're incorrigible, but good work, we now know their backgrounds, and we have contact details for them all, so will you and Jenny pursue them and see what they have to say. We need to know whether he had dealings with other escorts not on the list – sound them out about that. Paul, you were looking into Giles Roberts, have you found out anything more about him?"

"Oh yes, the slippery Mr Roberts. You were right Guv; he most certainly did protest at being 'treated like a common criminal' was how he phrased it. We challenged him about his false reference, and he had no option but to admit it was fake. He had worked in Stockport, but it was as an office clerk alongside an accountant. In his words, 'I knew I could do the job because I'd helped with the accountancy work'. His real name is Brian Palmer, and he originates from Lancaster. When he got rid of the plum from his mouth, he had quite a Lancashire accent. We didn't find anything incriminating on his computer, and he had nothing but praise for his employer. We tackled him about the blackmail letters and to be honest we felt he was telling the truth – he had nothing to do with them. His fingerprints were on the envelope of course, but he'd handled them to put them in Shackleton's tray. He came up with the thought that perhaps someone posing as a customer brought them in and dropped them behind the door. Perfectly plausible."

"Thank you, Paul. Now, regarding the latter point Paul mentioned, James, have someone check CCTV both inside and outside Shackleton's premises, see if you can identify anyone entering, perhaps one of those five who leases his garages or even Royston Barraclough. Get someone on it urgently James. Check with Roberts or Palmer and find out when the first letter arrived and check back to that point in time."

"Dani," the DCI continued, "Leslie Shackleton's attacker may have brought him back here, so please check hospitals in the area and then arrange checks on CCTV for his car or any other tell-tale signs. Okay, anything else anyone? Right, go to it – we have many avenues to pursue – something or someone is going to point us in the right direction. Keep me posted. No matter how insignificant it might seem, run it by me and let's decide together how to interpret the signs."

Paul immediately set about acquiring the necessary search warrants and, once received, assembled a team of a dozen officers. They already had contact addresses, so he briefed them about the mission and the tactics DCI Johnstone instructed them to use. They delayed the mini raids until early the next morning, to ensure the operation was as successful as possible. The last thing they wanted was to afford someone opportunity to alert the others so that they went to ground. Ideally, they needed to contact all five at the same time. Therefore, at precisely 6.30 am next morning, they set off for their designated homes in the hope of catching their quarries before their day began.

Sergeant Paul Sheridan was overseeing the operation and was standing by with additional officers to step in if anyone needed support. The officers went out in pairs: PC Jeff Orpington with PC Jenny Holmes to visit Arnold Broadhurst; PC Peter Jones with PC Barry Kenneth to visit Ali Khan; PC Ravi Ahmed with

PC Annie Tranter to visit Lenny Thomas; PC Jess Peters with PC Joel Temple to visit Robert Bright and PC Andrew Peake with PC Martin Williams to visit John Porter. All the visits were coordinated and worked perfectly in respect of Broadhurst, Thomas and Bright, but Khan and Porter were not at home. It was just what Paul Sheridan didn't want because now the element of surprise with those two was lost.

The officers followed the instructions. A not so bright-eyed Robert Bright responded to their hammering on his door.

"Alright, alright I'm coming, this had better be important..." his voice tailed off as he saw the uniformed officers standing there, then his courage renewed, "what do you lot want?" he snapped.

"Good morning Mr Bright," responded Jess sarcastically, "would you like to throw on some clothes, we'd like to visit your lockup together."

"Get lost, I haven't got a lockup and even if I had you'd need a search warrant to see inside."

"Now Mr Bright," she continued, "that's a porky you're telling. You rent a lockup from Leslie Shackleton, and he has permitted us to view it."

"It's not up to him. I decide who sees inside while I'm paying him rent, he has no right to give you permission. Get a search warrant and things might be different."

"Oh, so you do have a lockup? Had you forgotten for a moment?" she quipped.

"By the way, we forgot to tell you," PC Joel Temple joined in, "we do have a search warrant, so do as the lady say. We don't want to take you wearing just your underpants."

He muttered a few expletives and went inside, Joel followed to make sure he didn't bolt out of the rear door. Meanwhile, the visit to Lenny Thomas went much the same as it had done with Bright. However, Arnold Broadhurst responded somewhat differently when told that Leslie Shackleton had given the police permission to visit the lockups. He looked decidedly shocked, even stunned.

"He...he...can't have," he stuttered, "I don't believe you, no it's not possible."

"He can't have – it's not possible," PC Jeff Orpington repeated, "why can't he and why is it not possible? Are you trying to tell us something – what did you think had happened to him?"

"C...course not, I'm just saying he can't have because it said on the tele last night that there was still no news of his whereabouts." He responded, having recovered his composure, "you're just trying to trick me into letting you look inside my lockup. Well hard luck, it didn't work. Get a search warrant or get lost."

Finally, Jeff produced the search warrant, "Mr Broadhurst, we do have a search warrant for your lockup, so be a good boy and come with us."

A while later the three teams arrived at the block of garage/lockups. The opening of the doors was co-ordinated, as they wanted to observe reactions when the three saw each other. In the event, there was no reaction, no indication of recognition. They opened all three garages simultaneously, and so revealed the contents – boxes. Boxes piled high in all three.

Upon entering Lenny Thomas's lockup, PC Ravi Ahmed instructed him to open some of them. Some contained cigarettes, some spirits, some expensive wines and others household gadgets. They noticed that he was avoiding some boxes, so PC Ravi Ahmed instructed him to bring them to the front.

"It's only more of the same," Lenny protested, "it's stocks I've bought to provide a service to local shops and pubs. It's all legit; I'm sure I've still got the receipts somewhere. Let's go back to my pad, and I'll dig them out for you."

"In a few minutes, Mr Thomas," said Annie calmly. "Let's just check a few more boxes before we do so."

At this point, he let rip a stream of obscenities and lashed out at Annie, but she was too quick for him, and before he knew it, she had his arm up to his back.

"Stop – you're breaking my arm," he yelled, "I'll have you for police brutality."

"Feel free," she responded calmly, "but before we take you to the station to make your complaint, open those three boxes."

She released his arm, and he proceeded to co-operate. The boxes contained bags of white powder, dozens of them.

"Er...which shops and pubs do you supply? Have you got receipts for those too?" she asked sarcastically. "You'll be telling me next; it's just flour. Lenny Thomas, I am arresting you for possession and intention to supply drugs and stolen goods. You don't have to say anything, but it may harm your defence if you fail to mention when questioned something you later relay on in court. Anything you do say will be taken

down and may be given in evidence. Do you understand?"

He said nothing in response, and so they handcuffed him and led him out to a waiting car. It was
much the same scenario in the other two garages and
so Bright, and Broadhurst was also arrested and
taken in for questioning. They seized drugs and
goods worth millions of pounds in the raids. All the
garages had heavy-duty padlocks, but when the
sharp-eyed Jenny Holmes watched Arnold
Broadhurst open the lock on his garage, she noticed
that there was another similar key on the keyring.
Therefore, as they exited his lockup, Jenny instructed
him to try the other key in the padlock on the number
4 garage. It opened immediately, revealing Leslie
Shackleton's car parked inside. They called a SOCO
team to secure the whole site and to carry out a close
examination of all they'd located. Although they had
search warrants for the other two garages, they
needed to find Khan and Porter first. They needed
them to be there to open the garages themselves; otherwise, the two men could claim that the police had
planted whatever the garages contained.

Paul Sheridan called DCI Johnstone.

"Hi Guv," he began, "we've found the car, it was in the number 4 garage. Yes, SOCO is here, and we're securing the whole site. We didn't get hold of Khan and Porter, which is a shame, but at least we can prevent them from getting at anything they've stashed in them. I didn't tell you, all the garages contained cigarettes, booze and drugs – cocaine or heroin I reckon, worth millions. Yes, I've requested that SOCO focus on the car and that they get us some results urgently. I'll see you back at the shop."

CHAPTER 8

CONNECTIONS

WHILE THE REST OF THE TEAM were on the dawn raid, Dani and Jenny Seymour were working in the office. Dani didn't like desk work, her love was pursuing things out in the field, but she knew very well that at present, her boss would not risk her tangling with villains.

She was far from idle though, as she and Jenny were busying themselves in following up the escorts with whom Leslie Shackleton had associated. Eliminating them from their enquiries was essential, though of course, they could never be sure that there was no connection with his disappearance. It was always possible that an association had angered someone somewhere and what had happened was an act of retribution – because of all that blood, a cruel act of revenge.

Dani and Jenny took two agencies each to follow up. It was impossible to contact the women directly, so it had to be through the agencies. No doubt the arrangements were deliberate; otherwise, clients could bypass the agency, thus avoiding paying their cut of the proceeds.

Dani made the first contact with the Amorous Escorts Agency.

"Good morning, this is Kerington police, and I am Detective Sergeant Dani Taylor. You will no doubt have heard via the media that we are seeking to find a missing estate agent, Leslie Shackleton. We have come across records that show that he had liaisons with three of the women attached to your agency and we must talk to them urgently – they may have information that can aid our enquiries."

The woman on the other end of the phone was immediately on her guard, "I'm sorry, we make it an agency policy not to divulge anything about our clients' business with our ladies. Such information is strictly private, and even I don't know what passes between them."

"Very admirable I'm sure," Dani responded, "but this is a police enquiry. We are now very concerned for Mr Shackleton's safety, so we could pursue this formally and request to see your records and bring all your escorts in for questioning or ask for your full co-operation voluntarily. One way or the other, we need to speak to all the escorts with whom Leslie Shackleton had a relationship. There may be others, but we know of three – Angela Talbot, Deirdre James and Martine Solomon. Please ask them to call me so that we can arrange an informal interview. Also, may I have your name please?"

"Well if I must I must, my name is Charlene Masters and I will contact the girls immediately and pass on your message. Goodbye."

"Hmm, not a happy bunny," Dani remarked, closing the line, "have you had any joy, Jen?"

"Ideal Escorts seems to be permanently engaged, and at Exquisite Companions, the conversation went pretty much as did yours. A Madame Avril

Bartholomew will ask Amie Warburton and Denise Parton to call me back at their convenience."

"Well get her; Madame Bartholomew had better pull her finger out and get her girls to do the same. Also, Jen, check the phone number for Ideal Escorts with directory enquiries just in case their website is not up to date."

"Yes, will do, I'm just hoping they haven't closed down."

When Dani phoned Glamorous Choices, they could not have been more helpful and co-operative. The owner, Gail Johnson, said without any hesitation that she was extremely concerned when she heard that Leslie Shackleton was missing, especially as Andria Herbert had reported that Leslie had seemed distracted, even worried about something at their last meeting. At the time, they had assumed that it was something to do with his wife.

"I need to talk to her urgently. Please ask her to call me. Incidentally, was it only Andria that Leslie ever met with?"

"Oh yes, he was never interested in any of the others. I hope you find him unharmed. He was a charming man. I'll contact Andria immediately; I'm sure she'll not delay in getting back to you."

How right she was – no sooner had Dani put the phone down when it rang, and it was Andria. Dani asked her to come into the station and ask for DS Taylor, "If you are free and can come right now, that would be extremely helpful. Thank you. See you shortly. Bye."

Her colleague Jenny Seymour was on the phone when Dani finished and was having a hard time with someone on the other end.

"Ms Heinrich, I don't think you grasp how serious this case is. Mr Shackleton has been missing now for over a week, so every second count. I would hate to think that you are obstructing us in the execution of our duty because if you are, I need to warn you that it is a serious offence. Hear what I'm saying if you continue to refuse to co-operate; we will charge you with obstruction and then get a court order to search your premises and records. If you want to avoid such action, please ask Sally Turner and Pat Hastings to contact us immediately. Thank you."

"A little cussed Jen?" Dani asked with a smile.

"Aargh! You're not kidding, a real job's worth. Anyone would think we were trying to steal her girls. She seemed to be completely unconcerned about Leslie Shackleton. I think she got the message though."

"Jen, are you free to help me? I was going to phone round the hospitals now, but I have Andria Herbert on her way in, would you make a start on that for me?"

"Sure, no problem. I rather suspect there'll be no joy. I have a suspicion that Leslie is not going to be found alive."

Dani didn't need to respond, because just then the phone rang to inform her that Andria Herbert had arrived.

"Will you show her to the interview room please and I'll be right along."

Dani walked into the interview room, came face to face with a gorgeous and well-turned-out woman, the sort of woman any man would be proud to have on his arm.

"Andria, thank you so very much for coming in, please have a seat. It is an informal interview, but can I urge you to be as open as you can be, the tiniest detail might be important in our search for Leslie Shackleton. How well did you know Leslie?"

"Quite well, he was a lovely man, kind, gentle and very open. We met together quite a few times, and we talked, dined out together and sometimes went to shows."

"Sorry to ask you this, but was there a sexual relationship between you?"

"No, never – it was a subject he never mentioned."

"Did that surprise you?"

"Not really, I am an escort, not a prostitute. My work pays better than that of sex workers, with fewer risks. It is, in fact, quite a glamorous profession."

"You told Gail Johnson that the last time you met with Leslie, he seemed distracted or worried. Tell me what you noticed or what he said – or perhaps it was something he didn't say?"

"One of the great things about Leslie was his conversational skills, but that night he was hard work – monosyllabic responses. He seemed as though his mind was elsewhere. I did challenge him about it, but his answer was garbled. He said something that sounded like 'leeches, bleeding me dry,' but he wouldn't elaborate – simply changed the subject. He was not a good company, so I made excuses and went home by taxi."

"Officially you are employed by the agency, do clients pay you through the agency or direct?"

"Oh, always through the agency, we get a percentage of the payment, and the rest goes to Gail and her support staff."

"Am I right in thinking that sometimes you received payments direct too? I am not trying to trick you with this question, and I will not tell Gail."

"You're right, Leslie was very generous."

"Finally, was there anything that night that suggested Leslie was in danger?"

Andria thought long and hard before answering.

"Come to think of it, maybe there was. When we were walking along the street, Leslie kept looking around, glancing back over his shoulder. He seemed distracted. It never occurred to me at the time that he was fearful, but now I rather think he was."

"Andria, thank you for your time and for being open with me. It is remotely possible that I might need to speak to you again, do I need to contact you through the agency?"

"No, I'll give you my mobile number – for your eyes only please."

Dani returned to the office and went to talk with her colleague.

"How did that go, Serge?" Jenny asked.

"Well, nothing conclusive, but she did say that she thought something was amiss with Leslie when they met last. She said he was normally a great conversationalist, but that night he was distant, and his mind was elsewhere. Significantly, she said his eyes were everywhere, looking over his shoulder. All she could get out of him was something like 'leeches bleeding me dry.' To me, it all fits with what we've previously discovered. Anyway, how have you got on?"

"Nothing from the hospitals that corresponds with the injuries we anticipate Leslie was suffering from and certainly no one with his name, though of course, he could have been there under a false name. Charlene Masters of Amorous Escorts rang, the three women will be in to see you at 10.00 am tomorrow. I must say she sounded like a real dragon, she was very shirty."

"Hmm, doesn't surprise me, she never wanted to co-operate in the first place – I had to threaten her with a search warrant and seizure of her records. What about your enquiries, any joy there?"

"Yes, the two from Ideal Escorts are coming in at 11.30 am tomorrow, and the two from Exquisite Companions are coming in at 4.00 pm. I hope we can..." Her voice tailed off when DCI Johnstone yelled across the office.

"Listen up everyone, Khan and Barraclough have been spotted on our patch. Uniform saw them jumping into a blue Ford Transit in Station Road. They got a partial registration, Kilo, Romeo, six, four, four, but passing traffic then obscured their view before they could get the rest. Running it through the computer suggests that the plates are false. Traffic is following it up, and they're scouring CCTV all around the area. Barraclough is a priority; he has some questions to answer."

"Yeah, I've got some questions for that thug too," Dani remarked angrily to Jenny, "and I know what I'd like to do to him."

The whole case was progressing painfully slowly, oh yes, they had a few possible leads, but nothing concrete, nothing to get their teeth into, nothing that gave them confidence that they were nearing a conclusion. Although the likelihood of finding Leslie Shackleton alive was growing increasingly slim, there was still no definitive proof that he was dead. All that blood, though; could anyone survive losing so much.

"Hmm, I'm getting to the point of believing that Dorothy Shackleton was right from the start, her husband had died at 4.10 pm that Wednesday afternoon," she said to herself.

She banged her desk with her fist, causing others in the office to turn in her direction. "Sorry," she responded, "just letting off a bit of frustration." She leaned back in her chair, "Now come on, girl think," she told herself, "there's just got to be something." Who was her chief suspect? Royston Barraclough of course, but what would be his motive? Barraclough lived in the Eastbourne area, and Shackleton's cottage was nearby, but what would connect them – perhaps not what, but who? Ali Khan, of course. Ali Khan was probably conspiring with Lenny Thomas, Robert Bright, John Porter and Arnold Broadhurst and what were they involved in – fags, booze and drugs. Whose garages were they using? Those belonging to Leslie Shackleton. The fact that someone blackmailed Shackleton was in no doubt, but who was the blackmailer? Probably one of the infamous five and maybe, just maybe, Shackleton was refusing to co-operate any longer and threatening to go to the police. That would be a motive for silencing him and who better than Royston Barraclough to do the dirty deed. That still did not explain the connection between Khan and Barraclough. Unless."

Dani picked up the phone and called Paul Sheridan.

"Paul, it's Dani. Did you do a background check on Ali Khan when you had dealings with him the first time?"

"Yes, fully checked."

"What can you tell me about him?"

"Well his parents lived in Southampton, and he got involved in a gang, and they were constantly involved in gang wars, street fighting and muggings. A string of minor convictions led to his parents moving him to live with relatives in the Eastbourne area. More convictions and a spell in prison followed. Eventually, he disappeared off the radar, and then he surfaced here."

"Thanks, Paul, you've confirmed my suspicions and given me a probable earlier link between Khan and Barraclough."

That, she felt sure, was that. Okay, Khan had moved away from the Eastbourne area, but that didn't mean that he'd severed ties with Barraclough. It was extremely likely that Barraclough was the connection for the drugs, cigarettes and booze found in the garages – probably smuggled in through Southampton docks. Could they prove that somehow?

It was time to bring in her boss. She knocked on DCI Johnstone's door.

"Sorry to disturb you, Sir, but is it a convenient moment for me to run some things by you?"

"Yes, sit down Dani," he responded, pointing to a chair, "so what's on your mind – have you solved the case?"

"I wish, but maybe what I've come up with will be an aid to achieving that." She went on to explain her thinking and explained how Paul's background check had provided a possible link between Khan and Barraclough. Finally, she described her theory that the gang smuggled the goods through Southampton docks.

"Do you think you could contact Customs and Excise to see if they have any ongoing investigations into illegal imports?"

"Goodness me, Dani!" DCI Johnstone exclaimed. "Barraclough may have cracked your bones, but I reckon you may have gone a long way to cracking the case. Where on earth did all that come from? Thank goodness we didn't lose you when that thug attacked you. That's a fantastic deduction, and I will most certainly contact Customs and Excise. I'll phone them right away and get back to you shortly."

It was, in fact, an hour or so later that DCI Johnstone called Dani back in. "Customs and Excise have just called me back, you were right, there is an ongoing investigation, and Royston Barraclough is one of their suspects. However, they believe he is only one small cog in a gigantic wheel. They are convinced there is an extensive network and they're biding their time in the hope of smashing the whole network – even identifying the source too. They're pretty convinced they know how the stuff is coming in, but the distribution network is proving tricky to trace. The information we provided has interested them greatly, and that's largely down to you for joining the dots. It does mean, of course, that we likewise must pursue the network at this end. We need to find out who it is they're supplying and who's the mastermind behind it all. I'm equally sure that our five, plus Barraclough, are only the couriers, they must have receivers who then distribute it around the country. We could have stumbled upon a massive operation and all because Mrs Shackleton reported her husband's murder based on a 'feeling.' I'll never dismiss 'feelings' again. If she's proved to be correct, then it's just incredible."

Dani nodded in agreement, "Both Jenny and I have meetings with some of the escort women in the morning. I don't know what you think, but I believe we need to follow them through just in case there is something other than the link with the smuggling ring. Do you agree?"

"Most certainly, we can't afford to discount any possibilities at this stage. We could miss something vital if we do. No, pursue them and let's eliminate them from our enquiries. Have you contacted all eight between you?"

"Yes, but tomorrow 'Angela T', or Angela Talbot, is one of the three I'm seeing. I want to get her on her own and find out whether there was something different, something unique, about her relationship with Shackleton. That book I found seemed to suggest that perhaps they did have a more intimate relationship."

"Yes, I agree, press her hard on that point and find out where they met."

"Hmm, that's something that's been bothering me. We're certain that Leslie Shackleton was not at his cottage alone, so what happened to the other person? Were they caught up in the violence too, because there was no trace of anyone else and that to me suggests they may well have either escaped or end up dead? Could we be looking for another body besides Leslie Shackleton's?"

"That is a distinct possibility. We've never located a diary, and I know of a few business people who didn't keep a diary. He doesn't strike me as a modern guy who would use his phone alone as a diary. No, I'm convinced there's a diary somewhere, but where is anybody's guess. So, there is no knowing who might have been at the cottage with him, there have been no other reports of missing persons, and surely someone would have missed them after all this time."

"Could he have been seeing someone from the Ratton/Eastbourne area? We'll contact the escort agencies in that area to see if he did have an account down there."

"Hold your fire for a while on that, let me check with Peter Tomlinson to see if they have any missing person reports that coincide with the date of Leslie Shackleton's disappearance. I'll get on to him right away and get back to you."

Dani returned to her desk. She had nothing pressing to do, so she decided to go on the net and search for escort agencies in the Ratton/Eastbourne area. Time was of the essence, so a bit of research now could save time later. She found a definite five and, using the identity she'd used locally; she set up provisional accounts with them all. It was not long until her computer emitted those pings, confirming receipt of emails. It was just four of the five, but that was a start, she could start checking the moment her boss gave the word. If he didn't have a name, then it would mean her having to contact the agencies direct – always tricky when they insisted on client confidentiality. However, she would cross that bridge when she came to it. A while later, DCI Johnstone emerged from his office and walked towards Dani's desk.

"Nothing doing on that score, there were no missing person reports in our time frame. The nearest two were before the event, and they were both males."

"I thought that might be the case. I've already identified five possible agencies, so it will be a case of finding out whether Leslie Shackleton was a client on their books and whether he had a date booked for our time frame."

"Dani, I know you've done the preparatory work, but how would you feel about me asking Peter Tomlinson's team to check with the agencies for us? The day is almost over, and I think it would be more profitable for you to focus on the agency women in the morning. I don't undervalue the importance of those interviews; something tells me that Leslie Shackleton's liaisons were focused here and not down there. Are you with me?"

"Sure Sir, I suppose it makes more sense for them to pursue things that are on their patch – let them have the agro instead of us."

What now? Dani thought to herself. There was no way she was going to sit and twiddle her thumbs if indeed she could have done so with her arm in a sling. What was pressing? That diary. She too was convinced that he must have had one, so where was it? Could someone have removed it, and why would they have done so? Unless of course, there could be damaging information in it. That still left the 'who, the where, the when and the how'. One thing having her arm in a sling did not affect was her capacity to think, reason and weigh the possibilities. That was going to be her plan for the rest of the day unless anyone interrupted the process.

CHAPTER 9

A HIDDEN GEM

THE WHEREABOUTS OF LESLIE Shackleton's diary, if indeed there was one, was bugging Dani. It was not in his cottage, not in his home, not in his office and not in his flat. His car – was it in his car? They hadn't been able to search when they found the vehicle because Dani and the investigating team needed 'scenes of crime officers' to do their stuff before they could touch anything. But surely, SOCO could at least tell her if they had found one there. She picked up the phone and made the call. Dani explained what she wanted to know and why, but they were able to tell her categorically that there was no diary.

"Argh," she growled as she replaced the phone, "dead end after dead end."

She has faced so many frustrations, with only the occasional bright spot. Her thought process had to be kick-started into operation again, and she was determined to find a way out of this maze. People don't usually take a diary with them everywhere they go, so where might it be if he hadn't taken it with him? I wonder? She whispered under her breath and picked up the phone once again and called Paul Sheridan.

"Paul, when you and your team searched Shackleton's flat, did you find a safe?"

"No, and there was no obvious place for one."

"You didn't. Now please don't get me wrong, I'm sure your team was diligent during the search, but I'd like to see the place for myself, are you available to drive me there now?"

"Nothing is happening at this end, so yes."

Okay, see you in the carpark in a few minutes."

She grabbed her jacket and shouted across to Jenny.

"Jenny, Paul and I are going to Leslie Shackleton's flat to follow a hunch – we probably won't be long."

A while later they were heading towards Kerington High Street when a thought came to Dani.

"Hey Paul, I assume you have a key to the flat because we couldn't get in when we were there last."

"Yes, indeed I have," he laughed, tapping his pocket, "we plods are quite resourceful, you know. We had to break in when we visited before, so repairs have been carried out and a new lock fitted. If Leslie Shackleton should return, he'll not be able to get in. Do you think he will be found alive? I hear they found a lot of his blood at his cottage."

"Yes, quite a lot both in the bedroom and the garage. Between you and me, I don't hold out much hope for his safe return. By the way, about his cottage, have you got anywhere in the search for Khan and Barraclough, or Porter for that matter?"

"A few reported possible sightings of the blue van, but only patchy CCTV coverage, so now we're no further forward. We've put out APBs, so we're hopeful we'll get a real lead soon. Porter – nothing, absolutely nothing. I reckon he heard of the three arrests and he's gone to ground somewhere. The hope is that he gets brave or desperate and sticks his head above the parapet and then we'll get him."

They arrived at the estate agency and parked in the carpark behind. Paul unlocked the door from the road to the flat, and they mounted the stairs, which turned left at the top and led them into the flat itself. There was a comfortable lounge area with a kitchen-diner off it and beyond was a reasonably sized bed-room with a double bed. En suite facilities were off the bedroom. Apart from essentials, there was little by way of furnishings. It didn't give the impression of being a place to bring his lady-friends, more a man-flat, a place to chill at short notice.

"In his office at home the safe was hidden behind part of the bookshelf, but there's no chance of that here," Dani said glancing around the room.

"Behind pictures?" Paul suggested, moving to-wards a couple on the lounge wall, but they concealed nothing. Dani meanwhile, checked behind the one picture on the bedroom wall, but again to no avail.

"Do you think there might be something in the kitchen – behind units, for instance?" Paul asked.

"I guess it's possible," Dani answered casually, "but hang on a minute, Paul, I have a thought." She began scanning the floor, occasionally tapping the floor with her foot.

"Ah, I see what you're after, you think there may be a floor safe. Good thinking, but as the whole floor is carpeted it will have to be at the edge of the room, and I think we would have to pull the carpet back. I reckon it must be under a piece of furniture somewhere. I don't think that 'somewhere' is in here, so let's try the bedroom."

There were only two options, the bed or a small chest of drawers, and they opted for the latter. It was in fact on casters and moved quite quickly.

"Bingo!" Dani exclaimed triumphantly. "Look, you can just see two slits in the carpet." She set to and peeled back the carpet, the underlay and finally a loose board, revealing a small safe beneath.

"A combination lock," Paul remarked, "we don't know the combination, so we're stuffed."

"I'm not so sure," Dani reassured him, "we're all creatures of habit, so I guess that the combination will be the same as his home safe – if I can remember it that is. It was something to do with birthdays, yes, that's it, Leslie's birth date in reverse – 48-08-16. I remember it because it was almost my dad's birth date in reverse, except that his was 1946." She turned the dial to the numbers, making sure she lined them up carefully, and as Dani lined up the final '6' there was a distinctive click, and she was able to turn the handle and open the lid.

It was like finding the hidden treasure, especially as there on top was a leather-bound volume that said '2017 DIARY' – a hidden gem. Dani carefully lifted it out as if it were some delicate and rare object. It had a built-in bookmark, and consequently, it opened at that marked place. There was a ring around one day, Tuesday 24th May, and the entry read, 'Pick up Angela T (Cottage)'.

"Well there's our answer, Leslie Shackleton was at the cottage with Angela Talbot. She's supposed to be coming in to see me in the morning, hardly likely unless she did make her escape. I wonder if she has a mobile phone."

"It all raises a lot of questions," Paul remarked, "we seem to get more questions than answers. You don't think Khan and Barraclough have abducted her, do you?"

"Always possible, I suppose, but I sincerely hope not. Barraclough is a nasty piece of work by all accounts, so I wouldn't wish my worst enemy into his hands."

Dani decided to leave studying the diary's contents until they were back in the office and turned her attention back to the safe. She noticed several handwritten envelopes in there.

"Have you got gloves with you, Paul? If so, can you grab those envelopes? If I'm not mistaken, those are the other blackmail notes – they had not been destroyed." Further down there were a couple of bundles of banknotes (she estimated about £200.00 or so) and some letters with very feminine handwriting. The letters, they decided, might offer additional clues, so they took those with them too.

"That I must say, was a good visit," Dani said with a note of satisfaction, "thanks for coming, I reckon we make a good team."

Back at the office, Dani knocked on DCI Johnstone's door and, as she entered, held up the diary for him to see. Initially, the significance didn't register, but then the penny dropped, and his mouth opened wide in astonishment.

"Leslie Shackleton's diary," - "where on earth did you get that?"

"Paul and I just went to Shackleton's flat. I had a hunch there might be a safe somewhere, and we found it under the floor beneath a chest of drawers in the bedroom. It wasn't just the diary we found – we also the other blackmail letters and some personal letters that I feel sure were from his lady friends. Paul's having the blackmail letters analysed for prints, and I have the personal letters on my desk. Anyway, the crucial point we found was a diary entry for Tuesday 24th May – 'Pick up Angela T (cottage)'. She was there with him, so we must find out what happened to her. She supposedly was coming in tomorrow morning, but I don't think that will happen."

"Fantastic work Dani, but you're right, the fact that Angela Talbot was with him is worrying. I'll get Peter Tomlinson and his team on it right away – she could be dead or in hospital injured."

"Equally," Dani interjected, "she could have been abducted by Khan and Barraclough, and that's a fearful prospect everyone needs to be aware of as we seek to apprehend them. I don't think for one-minute Barraclough would think twice about using her as a lever to get what he wants – she could be in grave danger."

"Search that diary from cover to cover Dani, see what else it gives us."

That was just what Dani intended to do. Her hopes were high, but she knew very well that those hopes could well come to nothing. She grabbed herself a coffee and, although it was already late in the day, she did not intend to go home until she'd completed her task. For the most part, the entries were simply appointments with potential buyers or with his lawyer or accountant. She was particularly pleased to note that some were for dinner dates or shopping sprees with his wife. She noticed too reminders to buy a card and flowers for Mrs Shackleton's birthday and their wedding anniversary – both events were to be celebrated with a grand meal out. Romance in their relationship had not ceased, despite the difficulties. Almost every week there was an entry with just a woman's name, each one Dani recognised as being on the list they discovered. Most disturbing were five entries recording receipt of the blackmail demands, all but the last followed two days later by 'Make Drop'. They knew that the last one was for £6,000.00 and that money was still in the safe – he never made the drop. That presumably precipitated the violent attack at the cottage.

The rest of the diary was relatively empty, with only the occasional forward appointment. At the rear of the journal were pages for notes and it was here that Dani found a further list of those eight names, but this time they had mobile numbers alongside. It was a most welcome find – direct lines to all the women could prove invaluable, saving time and speeding operations.

Although theoretically, Dani was seeing Angela Talbot the next day, she had grave doubts that it would happen. As if on cue, the phone rang, and Dani lifted it to her ear.

"Hello DS Taylor here."

"This is Charlene Masters, it's about Angela Talbot, I can't get hold of her, and nobody has seen her."

"Did you know she was going with Leslie Shackleton to his cottage at Ratton?"

"Yes, she did tell me her plans, but normally she would have reported back to say that she was free. However, no one has seen or heard from her since."

"Hmm, I understand," Dani responded, "I promise you we will look into it. Okay, leave it with me, and we'll get back to you as soon as we have anything positive to report. Thank you. Bye."

That was timely, but no surprise. It confirmed their suspicions and Leslie's diary entry. However, Dani now had a mobile number. She had to try it in the hope that she could get into direct contact with Angela. She pressed the number in, and it began to ring – she connected, but no one spoke, though she could hear breathing.

"Hello Angela, this is Detective Sergeant Taylor, are you okay?"

Initially, there was no response, and then a male voice said harshly. "Bitch!" and the line went dead.

Although the person who had struck her with that stick had never spoken, she instinctively knew that the voice at the other end belonged to the same person, Barraclough. That, to Dani, was the worst possible outcome, proof that someone at least had her phone and most likely Angela too. What sort of state was she in if she was with Barraclough? Dani decided to pass the information to DCI Johnstone, but he'd gone, it would have to wait until morning. No, she decided, she'd text him anyway, although probably there was little if anything he could do. Still, that was up to him to decide.

Dani left the station by the main entrance and, unexpectedly, Luke met her. "Hey, you, this is a lovely surprise," she said as she climbed into his car, "I wasn't expecting to see you until the weekend, you haven't got the sack, have you?"

"Nope, I'm here because my favourite girl deserves some TLC. I've booked a table at Nanjose for 7.00 pm, so do you feel up to that and do you want to slip home first?"

"You bet I'm up to it, the very thought of Nanjose makes my mouth water. How on earth did you manage to get a table, it's usually sold out weeks in advance?"

"Just goes to show how right it was – when I called them, they'd just had a cancelation, so I was straight in."

"Fantastic, but yes I'd like to pop home first and freshen up – I think I need to wear something smarter too. Wow, this is exciting." Nanjose not only served fantastic Latin American food but also had a dance floor with a bar off it, the ideal place to end a romantic evening.

Luke was a solicitor in the city, and due to the pressure of work, he often worked late. He lived in a flat very close to his office. Today he'd left his clerk in charge so that he could spend some quality time with Dani. They would be getting married in September, but both were considering their future – they didn't want to spend their married life apart, so one of them would have to move. The latest thinking was that Luke would try to move to a practice in or near Kerington, as setting up home together in central London would be extremely expensive. Anyway, Luke decided to avoid mentioning work and their future home for this evening, he wanted it to be as memorable and relaxing as he could make it. It was, in fact, a truly wonderful evening, and although they talked much throughout the evening, nothing in the least controversial was on their agenda. That night Dani slept better than she had any night since her beating and the next morning, she woke up alert, and almost pain free and raring to go.

DCI Johnstone called his usual morning briefing.

"Okay everyone," he began, "let's have your attention, we have some things to share, and there have been several developments which you all need to know. Firstly, I have the lab results on Shackleton's car and the garage where we found it. The car had a massive pool of blood on the rear seat, and we have confirmation that it belongs to Leslie Shackleton. Their assessment concludes that the total blood loss suggests that the victim would not have survived. They also found evidence in the boot that suggested someone was there – there were scratches in the paintwork caused by sharp-heeled shoes - probably high heels and human hair, not yet matched. I am now officially upgrading this enquiry to one of murder. Because of this, I can tell you that Mrs Shackleton reported her husband's disappearance as a murder, but because there was no evidence to support her claim, we treated him as a missing person. Regarding the interior of the car, there is DNA evidence, obviously Leslie Shackleton's, but also at least two other people. One could well be Angela Talbot's, but there are prints on the wheel, door handles and other parts that they've not been able to identify. However, they can confirm that they've not found any DNA belonging to Barraclough, so who drove that car back from Ratton?"

"Could it have been one of the infamous five Guv, particularly Khan or Porter?" asked DI Cartwright.

"No, that was my first thought too, but we have their prints on file, so they've been eliminated. Whoever it was, the same prints were found at the garage at the cottage and number 4 in Barnett Street. Anyway, thanks to Dani and Paul, they found Leslie Shackleton's diary in a safe in his studio flat, and it makes quite interesting reading. It confirms much of what we suspected, but also provides us with some additional information – phone numbers and the like. Also, in the safe were the other blackmail demands he received, which I believe you, Paul, have sent to the lab."

"That's right Guv, and they've promised to try and get us results later today or tomorrow morning. I did read the contents before passing them to the lab, and they were demands for varying amounts of money. What I noticed was the first one was slightly different, because it said it was payment for him or her, the blackmailer, keeping quiet about the drugs. What that means I'm not sure, was he taking drugs, storing drugs, distributing drugs through his offices, turning a blind eye to what he knew was going on, or what? We need to pursue that aspect of the black-mail."

"Yes, I agree. James, interview Bright, Thomas and Broadhurst again, see if you can elicit anything that will throw light on the blackmail, they were involved somehow. It's got to be pretty strong evidence; other-wise, I'm sure Shackleton would have called their bluff, and it's possible that latterly he did – he didn't pay the final demand, so maybe that's why he was at-tacked. Okay, what else? Probably the most vital information provided by the diary is that Angela Tal-bot was with Shackleton at the cottage, a fact that puts a new complexion on the case. Where is she? What does Angela Talbot know, what did she see? Is Angela still alive, or is she perhaps in the hands of whoever drove that car? It is possible that she escaped and is in hiding. We need to tread carefully, do noth-ing that might endanger her life. In connection with this, Dani, tell them what happened."

"Yes, I obtained Angela's mobile number from a list in Shackleton's diary and decided to give her a call. Someone answered, but initially, no one spoke. I said who I was, and a male voice said 'Bitch' and hung up. I somehow got a feeling it was Barraclough, but

I'm by no means certain because when he attacked me, he said nothing. The point is though, someone has her phone, but do they have Angela too?"

"Dani, you mentioned something about finding personal letters in the safe too," DCI Johnstone said, "did you discover anything from them?"

"No, Sir, they were from his womenfolk, thanking him for wonderful nights or wonderful weekends or his generous gifts. There were a few juicy bits too. I couldn't see anything worth pursuing though. They were comparatively innocuous. All the women were from the list we already had, no one new."

"DCI Johnstone clapped his hands together hard.

"Come on, folks. We must step up a gear. We must locate Barraclough and Khan. They're key figures in this. Who do they know, who do they mix with, where do they hang out, what pubs do they frequent, what family do they have? Ask around, press those three we have in custody – they know them, they operate together, they lease adjacent garages, they can give us answers – pit one against another if necessary, get them singing. I... WANT... ANSWERS!" he yelled, "go and get them."

He then added, "Paul, hang on a minute, will you."
Paul came over.

"Push hard to get me DNA and prints from those blackmail letters, hassle the lab, tell them I'm hassling you. The other thing is, did you get anywhere with the CCTV from the estate agency, did you spot anyone dropping a letter behind the door?"

"Ah, yes, but it's a very grainy picture, the tech guys are trying to clean it up enough for us to perhaps identify whoever it is. It's someone wearing a hoody, but we couldn't even say whether it was male or female."

"Push that too. We now have dates for receipt of the other letters, Dani can give you details, so get someone to trawl past tapes for images of those drops. Do what you can, Paul, upstairs are demanding results."

DCI Johnstone then went over to DI Cartwright's desk.

"James, I know everyone is doing their best on this case, but we have to rack it up a few notches. Upstairs are screaming at me, they say it's hanging on too long. Get every member of the team involved, asking questions, pushing doors, pursuing known criminals. Are our fugitives holed up with family or friends? Where is that blue van? Stress the urgency to everyone and let's make some progress. Yes, another thing, who was driving Shackleton's car and who was in that boot? Get some samples for DNA from that Angela woman – Dani could do that for you. I'm away for the rest of the day, some ridiculous conference, so take charge until I get back."

DI Cartwright immediately assigned Dani the task of securing samples from Angela Talbot's flat for DNA testing. She had Angela's address, but as there was no way she could drive at present, DI Cartwright assigned PC Jenny Holmes to be her driver. "It's flat 3 in Coniston Mansion, Clarkson Mews, do you know it, Jenny?" Dani asked.

"Yes, funnily enough, I've been there before, it was a disturbance, some bloke trying to get into one of the flats, but the occupier phoned us for help in getting rid of him. I remember he was extremely abusive, the woman in the flat was a 'bitch', I was a 'bitch' – he was eventually arrested and charged with violent and abusive behaviour. He received a suspended sentence and was bound over to keep the peace."

"Jenny, when was this and did you remember his name?"

"It was about six months ago, yes it was November last year. His name... I remember it didn't fit his character... Simon Goodfellow. Why do you ask?"

"I said in the meeting, I tried Angela Talbot's phone number yesterday, and a male voice simply said 'Bitch!', so your experience rang bells for me."

"Dani, the more I think about it, the more I am convinced that we were called to Flat three. I'll check my passbook when we get there, and I'm sure it will all be in there."

AN UNESPECTED ENCOUNTER

IT WASN'T A LONG JOURNEY, so before long they drew up outside Coniston Mansion, Clarkson Mews. Jenny took out her passbook and began to thumb through the pages back to November 2015.

"Yeah, there we are, it was Flat 3, and it was Angela Talbot, a professional escort. She had, a few weeks previously, accompanied Simon Goodfellow to a private function, but after a few drinks, his true personality began to emerge. The woman hosting the event told him no more drinks and to go home, and he became abusive and called her a 'stupid bitch' for everyone to hear. They evicted him, and Angela called a taxi to take him home. She refused to go with him, so she too was a 'bitch'. After that, he hounded her daily and eventually turned up at her flat. The rest you know."

"Thank goodness you came with me today," Dani said, "all that you've just shared is, I'm sure, entirely consistent with what this case is all about. It throws some new light on the subject, and I think you've opened up an entirely new line of investigation."

"I rather think I'm going to get it in the neck for not making the connection earlier," Jenny remarked worriedly, "sorry."

"You've nothing to be worried about, how could you have made the connection before today, you neither knew about Angela Talbot's connection with Leslie Shackleton, nor my call to Angela's phone. No, I rather think you've done us a big favour. I'll call James and get him to check on Simon Goodfellow."

Dani called the station, but James Cartwright was out, so they left a message on his desk. Dani and Jenny left the car to go into the block of flats. It was a somewhat upmarket complex with a door security system to keep out unwanted visitors, so how Simon Goodfellow had managed to gain entry was something of a mystery.

"Er...how do we get in and into the flat?" Jenny asked.

"Oh, I didn't tell you, I've arranged with Charlene Masters from Amorous Escorts for someone to meet us here and let us in."

Dani pressed the buzzer for Flat three and without anyone answering, the door lock released, and they went inside. Flat three was on the first floor. They ascended via the stairs.

The door was slightly ajar, so they knocked and walked in.

"Hello, it's the police, anyone there?"

"In the lounge," said a quiet voice. Dani and Jenny moved straight ahead towards the lounge area, and then suddenly a man wielding a knife jumped out behind them, and before they could react, he pushed them violently forward into the lounge.

"Sit down," he ordered, "and don't try anything, I'm not afraid to use this; it's already had practice."

"Who are you, and what do you want?" Dani demanded.

"Oh, I know who he is," Jenny responded, "this is Simon Goodfellow."

"Shut your mouth bitch – yeah, and I know you, you're the bitch copper that arrested me in this very spot last year. Well not this time, copper, this time I hold the trump card."

"Don't be stupid Simon, you're not going to get away with this," Jenny said confidently, "the station knows we're here, and if we don't report in, they're going to come looking."

"Just put the knife down," Dani added, "Jenny's right, you're going to be in deep trouble if you persist in this madness. Put the knife down and let's talk."

He moved towards Dani and slapped her hard across the face, "I said shut up bitch, so button it, there's plenty more where that came from and worse if you don't."

The slap hurt and brought tears to Dani's eyes, but it also caused anger to bubble up within her – this creature was not going to get the better of them, though at that precise moment she was at a loss to know what her next move would be. While he had that lethal weapon in his hand, she wanted to do nothing to provoke him further. He was already in an extremely volatile state, partly induced, she felt sure, by drugs. Had he knifed Leslie Shackleton over his infatuation with Angela? Had he stabbed him more seriously than he'd intended and had it forced him to dispose of the body?

That thought set her mind racing. Was Leslie's body somewhere in this flat and did he have Angela captive somewhere too? Thinking about it, what happened to the person from the agency, was she also in the flat? Dani looked towards Jenny and noticed that she glanced down towards her side. What was it she was trying to say? It then dawned on her it was her radio, she needed Dani to distract him.

"I know what you said, but I desperately need to go to the loo," Dani said.

"Cross your legs. You're not going; I want you where I can see you. Now shut up, I need to think."

"Look, I'm sorry Simon, but I do need to go – I can't hold on, please be reasonable."

She fully expected him to come over and slap her again, though this time she'd be ready for him. However, he didn't.

"Stand up bitch and give me your phone." She handed it over, and he pushed her towards a door on the corridor.

"In there and leave the door open."

He stood in the corridor where he could watch Dani and Jenny at the same time. His glances towards Dani just gave Jenny enough time to reach down to her radio and move the switch to the transmit position. Now any conversation would automatically go through to the station, providing he didn't think to remove her radio from her.

"Simon, I completely understand that you resent me arresting you last year, but I was only doing my duty, and it was Angela who asked for our help. I have nothing against you; I'm sure deep down, you're a nice guy. Talk to us; we might be able to help you. I wondered how you managed to get into Angela's flat, wasn't it locked? Do you know where Angela is? Did she let you in?"

"Just quit your babbling, I can't think when you're rabbiting on like that. I'm not your friend, so don't try appealing to my better nature. Just shut up. And you," he growled, speaking to Dani, "get yourself out here now or I'll come and drag you out."

"I'm doing my best," Dani responded, "but it's not easy with just one hand." She flushed the toilet, washed her hand and did as he said. As she walked back towards the sofa where she'd been sitting, Dani pretended to stumble and reached out for a dining chair for support, she grabbed it and swung it with as much force as she could towards Goodfellow. It smashed into the hand with the knife and sent it flying across the room. Having just one right hand and arm hampered her significantly, but Jenny sprang to her side, grabbed his arm and thrust it hard up his back before he could respond. Dani grabbed Jenny's handcuffs from her belt and snapped them onto his free arm, thrusting that up his back to join the other. They locked the second cuff into place. Once secured, Jenny banged the back of his legs, causing them to buckle and sending him crashing to the floor. Lying on his stomach on the floor he was helpless, but it didn't silence his mouth, he yelled and rained a barrage of curses on them.

"Oh, be quiet you foul-mouthed yob," responded Jenny, "you're in no position to threaten us now. Simon Goodfellow, I'm arresting you for kidnap and imprisonment, threatening with a lethal weapon, striking a police officer and resisting arrest. I caution you – you don't have to say anything, but it may harm your defence if you fail to mention when questioned something you later relay in court. Anything you do say may be taken down and given in evidence. Do you understand?" He never stopped yelling and cursing throughout Jenny's cautioning.

"Oh, do be quiet, Goodfellow," Dani yelled back at him, "nobody's listening to you."

Dani went along the corridor to a door opposite the bathroom, which she assumed was the bedroom. She cautiously opened the door, pushed it wide and looked inside. Across the bed with arms and legs tied was a well-dressed middle-aged woman with tape across her mouth. Dani went inside and removed the tape from the woman's mouth.

"I assume you are from the agency, here to let us in. I'm Detective Sergeant Dani Taylor."

"Yes, I'm Charlene Masters. Do you know that vicious brute who attacked me?"

"Yes, we know him, Simon Goodfellow, but we have him safely handcuffed in the lounge. Was there anyone else here – was Angela Talbot here?"

"No, I thought you knew she was missing, I thought that was why you needed me to let you into the flat."

"Yes, that's right, but we suspect Goodfellow's behind her disappearance and maybe Leslie Shackleton's too."

All the time they were talking, Dani was untying Charlene and once loosed, Charlene rubbed her limbs to get the blood flowing again, and they went into the lounge. Goodfellow was still lying face down on the floor, and Jenny was on her phone. Charlene walked over to Goodfellow and kicked him hard in the ribs, "take that you evil pig; that's a thank you for your treatment of me."

He winced with pain, and then the cursing started all over again.

"Shut your foul mouth," said Charlene forcefully, "otherwise, I'll give you one the other side to match."

"Now Charlene," cautioned Dani, "we can't allow you to attack our prisoner; let's leave the law to take its course."

"I've called for transport to take him back to the station, they should be here shortly," Jenny said. "Do you want to get your samples for DNA, and we'll keep an eye on chummy here – he's not going far yet, but I suspect he'll be going out of circulation for quite some time."

Goodfellow started his cursing all over again, swearing vengeance on every 'bitch' present – oh what he would do to them once he was free, he was extraordinarily graphic and disgusting. Before Jenny could stop her, Charlene was true to her word and landed another kick to his ribs on the other side. It didn't improve his temper, and Jenny was glad when the door alarm buzzed, and it was their colleagues with the van to collect the prisoner. It was in fact PCs Jeff Orpington and Peter Jones, both quite well built and equal even to the bad tempered Goodfellow. He didn't go quietly but continued his tirade against the women, all of whom were bitches of the highest degree. Dani collected Angela's hairbrush and toothbrush and bagged them ready for lab analysis. While they were in the flat, they had a quick look around and checked drawers, cupboards, wardrobes, etc., but found nothing of interest.

"Are you okay for getting back, or can we give you a lift?" Dani asked of Charlene.

"Thanks for the offer, but I'm fine. I have my car outside. I can't thank you enough for turning up when you did. I was fearful for my life with that knife-wielding maniac."

"Yikes, the knife!" exclaimed Dani, "I forgot to pick that up and bag it, thanks for reminding me. Without the knife, he could deny everything."

They finished their task and left Charlene to secure the flat once more. Once in the car, Dani spoke up, "Jen, thanks for your quick thinking and reaction back there, I don't think I could have held him with just one hand for much longer. Do you think base got to hear what was going on? If they did, it could help us when we interview him."

"I hope they picked it up, it wasn't long though, your action with that chair put paid to any further discussion. Having said that, though, I did leave it on while Goodfellow was yelling and cursing on the floor. Fortunately, I'd turned it off before Charlene put in the boot – or in her case a quality shoe."

"Yes, I'm glad she got that in before we could stop her, he deserved that and more," Dani responded with a gleam in her eye.

Jenny coughed, "well actually she did get another kick in, she was too quick for me to be able to stop her. I shouldn't think he'd have the nerve to bring an assault charge against her, but he's the sort who'd sue his grandmother for her pension if he thought he could get away with it. You know, it beats me why someone like Angela would go as his escort to a private function – in fact, it beggars belief that he'd be invited to such a function in the first place."

"Hmm, I know what you mean, but I suppose Angela doesn't know what her clients are like until she meets up with them for the first time, it's a precarious profession. I suppose it can be glamorous sometimes, but I bet there are more occasions when it's less than glamorous. I'll stick to policing; at least we know that often we're dealing with rogues and villains."

Back in the office, Dani immediately reported to DI Cartwright all that had happened at Angela's flat and that at the same time had fulfilled the original point of the visit – samples for DNA testing, that she'd passed to the lab.

"Paul I'm concerned that we still haven't found Angela. If Goodfellow knifed Shackleton and drove his body back in the car, and if it was Angela in the boot, where is Shackleton's body and what has he done with Angela?"

"Hmm, good questions – we do need to focus on finding out from Goodfellow what he knows, somehow we have to get him talking. You didn't mention the knife; did you bring that back with you?"

"Oh yes, I forgot to mention that – that too is with forensics. I'm hoping they might find traces of blood from Shackleton, though my guess is he'll have made a good job of cleaning... How stupid am I?" Dani said suddenly stopping mid-sentence, "I thought that Goodfellow would have taken Angela back to her flat, but of course he'll have taken her to wherever he's staying, and that's something else we have to find out, though I doubt if he'll be very forthcoming. Who's going to interview him?"

"Who arrested him?" asked Paul.

"Jenny Holmes, and then Jeff Orpington and Peter Jones brought him in."

"Well, why don't you and Jenny do the initial interview and I'll watch through the window. I can step in later if necessary, but you two get things underway. Don't forget to get your reports in too. You know that upstairs are sticklers for their paperwork."

"We'll do a preliminary interview this afternoon, but we need Angela's lab results to confirm whether she was in the boot of the car before we can pursue the kidnap and unlawful imprisonment. We have his attack on Charlene Masters and his assault on me, but I feel we need to pursue these charges along with the more serious crimes. Oh, I almost forgot, it was obvious he was very high on drugs, so we need him to come down before we interview him formally. Do you agree?"

"Most certainly, get the forensic examiner (FME) to give him a look over. Warn him, though, that he's going to be remanded in custody awaiting lab reports and the influence of drugs. See how he responds. Does he have a solicitor present? Do you know?"

"No, I don't know, but I expect custody will have advised him of his rights if he was lucid enough to understand."

Later that afternoon, Dani and Jenny went to the interview room where Simon Goodfellow was already waiting. He sat with his elbows on the table and his head in his hands, looking a picture of misery – obviously coming down from his drugs.

"Simon," Dani addressed him, "this is only going to be a preliminary interview, as we're awaiting a forensic report which should be with us tomorrow morning. We also need to give time for you to get the influence of drugs out of your system. Are you able to continue with a brief interview now?"

"Yeah, let's get it over with," Simon responded.

Dani turned on the recorder.

"Interview commencing at 6.30 pm, those present are DS Dani Taylor and PC Jenny Holmes.

"Would you give your full name for the tape please Simon?"

"Simon Anthony Goodfellow."

"Thank you, Simon, I now want to repeat the caution which was given earlier. You don't have to say anything, but it may harm your defence if you fail to mention when questioned something you later relay on in court. Anything you do say may be taken down and given in evidence. Do you understand?" Jenny said.

He nodded his head.

"No Simon, for the tape, do you understand the caution?"

"Yeah, okay."

"Has anyone explained to you that you have the right to have a solicitor present and do you want one?" Dani asked.

"Yeah, somebody said something about it – no, I don't need a solicitor, I ain't done nothing wrong."

"So, you're waiving that right, is that correct?" Dani added.

"Yeah, I just said, so didn't I? My head's aching fit to bust."

"Do you want to stop and see a doctor?" Jenny asked.

"No, let's get it over with," he responded, "I need a good sleep."

"So, will you confirm your date of birth and your current address please?" Dani asked.

"Yeah, 18-12-83 and my address is Flat 3 Coniston Mansion, Clarkson Mews, Kerington."

"That's Angela Talbot's address, are you saying you live there too?"

"About to, we're an item now."

"You're telling us that you and Angela are an item and yet she had you arrested a few months back for harassment and violent behaviour towards her.

Hardly the sound basis for a mutual relationship now," responded Jenny.

"Think what you like; I apologised to her, and we made up and..." he shrugged his shoulders, "we're together, and that's it. I've promised to kick the drugs too."

"Okay Simon, we'll leave it there for now and reconvene tomorrow, interview terminated at 4.36 pm," Dani said, switching off the recorder. Dani and Jenny went back to the office and Goodfellow back to the cells.

"Well, despite his drug induced state, that was one very cool customer," Dani remarked to Jenny.

"Hmm, too cool for my liking. I don't buy Goodfellow's claim that he and Angela are now an item and are going to be living together. Although I've never met Angela, I get the impression she is one classy woman and where she lives is a very classy flat in a very classy area. Chalk and cheese – he's a yob, a slob and a drug addict. No, I don't buy it."

"Seems extremely unlikely to me too Jen, but sometimes there's no accounting for taste. It'll be interesting to hear how he develops his story tomorrow. I hope forensics come through on the DNA checks;

we need to know whether that was Angela in the boot and what they found on the knife."

DCI Johnstone returned late in the day, and after he'd had time to settle, Dani knocked on his door.

"Have you got a few minutes, Sir?" she asked.

"Yes, if it's someone talking sense," he responded, "I've had a day listening to a load of top brass spouting nonsense that won't make a scrap of difference to how we operate, and yet they say it will improve our performance. These people get so out of touch with reality. Sorry Dani, not a good day, but you don't want to hear me moaning. What can I do for you?"

"Nothing Sir, just wanted to let you know about our day, though I expect James will bring you up to speed."

"No, he's been called out on an urgent job, so if what you have is pertinent to tomorrow's briefing, I need to hear it, so fire away."

Dani shared the days happening with him, culminating in the fact that they now had Simon Goodfellow in custody.

"He's claiming that he and Angela Talbot are in a relationship and he is at the point of moving in with her."

"You're joking! No way, they're chalk and cheese. Have you done a full interview with him with a solicitor present?"

"No, not yet. Goodfellow is under the influence of 'spice' at present, and we're awaiting a report from forensics on the samples from Angela and the knife he was wielding. He doesn't want a solicitor."

"Push forensics, Dani. We only have twenty-four hours to charge him before we must release him. If you have enough evidence to charge him with a more serious offence we can apply for an extension, so keep me posted."

She started to leave the office.

"Oh, and Dani," he called after her, "let me know when you're going to interview him again, I'll be very interested to hear what that joker has to say."

Dani went straight for her phone and called the lab. She explained the urgency and they gave an assurance that the results would be available first thing next morning. She spent the rest of the evening writing reports, the aspect of policing that was the bane of everyone's life. They knew that records were essential, especially as the case progressed, but all too often, they were very time consuming amid busy schedules. Dani decided to stay on for a while that night, as she felt she needed to get her mind fully in gear for that interview next day. She made notes – questions to ask, details to be clarified and history to be uncovered.

She had just finished her notes when Jenny Holmes entered the CID office. "Oh, hi Jenny, are you okay? Do you need to talk?"

Jenny came over to Dani's desk and grabbed a neighbouring chair.

"Yes, I'm okay really, but thanks for asking. I've been mulling things over, trying to get things clear in my mind about this case. I don't believe for one minute that Goodfellow and Talbot are an item, but I rather suspect that he's going to prove a slippery customer and he'll have an answer for everything. What do you think are our strongest lines of attack?"

"Ah, that's the million-dollar question. We need to listen carefully to Goodfellow's every word – even the most slippery customer will slip up or have inconsistencies, and we must pick up on those and exploit them. He might well get flustered if we're snappy in our responses and it's then that he'll make mistakes. I'll take the lead, but feel free to jump in at any point.

Regarding our strongest lines...hmm...that knife, the DNA in the boot and his links with Shackleton's cottage – why was he there?"

"Do we know where he lived before, he moved here?" Jenny asked.

"No, I don't believe we do, so that's something we need to pursue. Which reminds me, I asked Paul to do a check on Goodfellow. I must ask what he found out. We don't even know if he has a record."

At 9.00 pm they realised how late it was and decided to call it a day. They needed their sleep and needed to be alert when they faced Goodfellow next day. "I'll take you home Serge, I've got my car, and you're not far out of my way."

"Are you sure, Jenny? I can easily get a bus – I've become quite used to public transport since I acquired this," she said, pointing to her shoulder.

"Nonsense, come on, I'll save you bus fare – every penny counts you know." Dani clasped her colleague's shoulder. "Thanks, Jenny, you're a real star and please, when we're alone, call me Dani."

INTERROGATIO N

IT SEEMED THAT NO SOONER had Dani arrived home than she was on the bus back to work again. She'd slept well, the pain in her shoulder had all but disappeared, except for occasions when she turned over in bed and lay on it. She was looking forward to the day, the interview with Simon Goodfellow was something she felt might well open some serious information that would lead to the final cracking of the case of Leslie Shackleton's disappearance.

It was bizarre that Leslie Shackleton's disappearance had almost become swamped by so many other lines of enquiry and especially the drug aspect. Today though, she hoped that the forensic reports would greet her as she entered the office, she anticipated getting crucial evidence in the interview that would follow. There was nothing on her desk, but she was not surprised by that, so she went over to James Cartwright's office. He wasn't there, but neither was there any report on his desk. The only hope now was that DCI Johnstone had it, but he was not yet in his office, and she wouldn't go and look without him being present.

Just then, Jenny walked in and went to her desk.

"Morning, Jenny," Dani greeted her. "I was just looking to see if the forensic report had come through, but unless the Governor has it, it hasn't come as yet."

"I sincerely hope it does come. Otherwise, we're stuffed. We don't want to run out of time with Goodfellow, if we have to let him go, I doubt if we'll find him again."

While they were still talking, DCI Johnstone walked into the office and made his way towards his own office. He glanced across the office and saw them, "Hey Dani," he called, holding up a folder, "you might be interested in this."

Dani went over to him, and she went into his office. "I met someone from the lab in the corridor, and they gave me the report. I think you're waiting for." He opened it up and skimmed through it – "I think you're going to like it."

He passed it to Dani, and she too skimmed through it.

"Wow, yes!" she exclaimed. "Angela's DNA in the boot. The knife – only Goodfellow's prints and traces of Leslie's blood. I rather think Simon Goodfellow has got some explaining to do."

"I don't think he'll be able to talk his way out of this," DCI Johnstone said, "so go for it, I reckon you have some strong evidence. Let me know when you're ready to start."

Dani went and passed on the glad tidings to Jenny and then called custody to instruct them to move Goodfellow to the interview room. Then, having informed DCI Johnstone and DI Cartwright that they were about to start interviewing, they went along to the interview room.

"Good morning Simon, I hope you had a reasonable night and that you're free of the influence of drugs now – how do you feel?"

"I'm okay, a banging headache, but the doc gave me painkillers, so hopefully they'll kick in soon."

Dani turned on the reorder.

"This is the continuation of the interview with – please state your full name."

"Simon Anthony Goodfellow."

"PC Jenny Holmes."

"DS Dani Taylor. Simon, I must remind you, you are still under a caution," Dani said, "and I must ask you again, would you like a solicitor present?"

"The answer's still no. I don't need defending when I've done nothing wrong."

"Okay Simon, I want to pick up where we left off yesterday. You said you and Angela Talbot are an item and that you're in the process of moving in with her, where did you live previously?" Dani asked.

"Near Eastbourne, I lived there with my mum."

"What's her address and when did you leave there?" Dani asked.

"46 Victoria Street, Lyneham, Eastbourne – can't remember the postcode. I left there six days ago."

"Why did you leave then?" Jenny asked.

"Huh, I got fed up with mum nagging me about the drugs and a few days before that I'd made it up with Angie and she invited me to come and live with her. I didn't need to think about it. It was the best offer I've ever had."

"So, where's Angela now?" Jenny continued.

He shrugged his shoulders, "I'm not sure actually. I don't intend to stop Angela doing the escort work. It pays good money, that's why I didn't object to her going to the cottage with Shackleton."

"But you drove Shackleton back in his car, why didn't Angela come with you?" Dani asked.

"They had a terrific bust up, I reckon he tried things on with her that she objected to – anyway, he said she'd left and that she was making her way home. I was surprised that she didn't turn up, but I supposed she'd stopped off somewhere. She has friends all over the country."

"Simon, I have to ask you to think about the answer you've just given," insisted Dani, "isn't it true that when you came back, Angela was locked in the boot?"

He frowned and shook his head.

"What are you talking about, of course, she wasn't in the boot. If she'd been with us, she'd have been up-front with me. What makes you think she was in the boot?"

"We found signs that someone with high-heels had been in there, and then we found DNA belonging to Angela. So, I say again, am I not right in saying you put her in the boot?" Dani persisted.

"Of course not, that's rubbish. I wouldn't mind betting that Shackleton put her in the boot when they'd fallen out. Angie said he could be quite moody and violent."

"Did you think that Shackleton had harmed Angela in some way?" Dani asked.

"Yeah, I suspected it, but I had no way of being certain. It seemed strange that she'd leave to make her way home."

"So, tell us how you came to be driving Shackleton's car," Jenny asked.

"Well, I knew Angie was at the cottage with him, and I was nearby, so I called round to see if I could see her and..."

"Hang on a moment, Simon. You said you called at the cottage when you knew that Angela was with a client. Are you in the habit of calling on her when she's with clients? You said moments earlier that you didn't mind her continuing her profession, but I think you were jealous and wanted her for yourself. You resented her being with him didn't you and using that knife was your way of finally ending the relationship. You knifed Shackleton, didn't you? We've experienced your nasty temper. You can't help yourself. That's how it was, wasn't it, Simon?" Dani suggested.

"No, no, no, of course, it wasn't you stupid bi–...woman. Stop trying to make something out of nothing. Yes, I went to the cottage, but only in the hope of seeing the woman I love if she was there, but I could see no one, so I went closer and heard terrible groaning. It was then I knocked on the door, and I heard someone calling for help. I went inside and there he was, on the kitchen floor and the knife was nearby. He was bleeding heavily, and he asked me to drive him to a hospital in Kerington."

"Are you sure he was in the kitchen, Simon, and not upstairs – did you go upstairs?" Jenny asked.

"No, he was in the kitchen and lying in a pool of blood – I didn't go upstairs at all."

"You didn't bother looking for Angela, and yet you say you were hoping to see her. If you didn't go upstairs, how do you know she wasn't up there?" Jenny questioned.

"I...er...yes, yes I did look upstairs, but there was no one there nor anywhere else."

"What did you see upstairs, did anything stand out for you?" Dani pressed him.

He shook his head slowly.

"No, I thought it was particularly tidy, the beds in both rooms looked as though they hadn't been slept in, the bathroom was clean and tidy. There was no sign of Angie's stuff anywhere though."

"Okay Simon, back to the kitchen where you say Leslie Shackleton was lying in a pool of blood," Jenny said, "what would you say if I told you forensics didn't find any traces of blood in the kitchen, but plenty in the main bedroom in the bed that was left unmade?"

"Can't understand about the bed, but they wouldn't have found any in the kitchen, because I cleaned it up."

"You took the time to clean it up when a man was bleeding to death? Where was he while you were doing this cleaning and why did you bother cleaning it up anyway? Incidentally, how did you clean it up, what did you use?"

"What does it matter what I used, I cleaned it, and Shackleton was leaning against a wall outside while I was doing it."

"Simon, it does matter why you cleaned up and what you used," persisted Jenny, "we need to get things straight in our minds. So please tell me why you bothered to clean and what you used."

"You're just trying to confuse me. Instinct – instinct said it was a horrible mess and needed cleaning. You're right, I shouldn't have bothered, but my mum was a stickler for cleanliness, so instinct said I ought to do it. I only used soap, water and a mop – the mop was outside the back door."

"That wouldn't have removed traces of blood Simon," Jenny explained, "Forensics would have seen it on the floor and the mop. There was nothing. I believe you're lying, trying to cover yourself. Did you find them in bed together and did you lose your temper and stab him there in his bed?"

He banged hard on the table, jumped to his feet and yelled at them.

"Stupid bitches, you're just trying to pin his murder on me. I never touched him, I found him in that bloody state – yes he was in bed and not the kitchen, but he was on his own."

"Sit down Simon and calm down," Dani ordered him. "So why say he was in the kitchen, why not tell us the truth from the start?"

"Because I know how you coppers think, if I'd said it was the bedroom, you'd have jumped to the conclusion I'd killed him there."

"But you already told us he was alive and asked you to drive him to the hospital in Kerington. Which hospital was it?" Dani asked.

"The Valley Hospital I think it's called."

"What did you do with him – was he able to walk and did you go in with him?" Dani persisted.

"He could walk with me supporting him. I took him to the door of A&E and yelled for help. A bloke came with a wheelchair, and we got him into it. I left, I can't stand hospitals, and even the smell makes me feel ill."

Dani pursued the matter.

"Simon, again I have to ask, what would you say if I told you that we'd checked all the hospitals around the region and no one of Leslie Shackleton's name or description of his injury is listed."

Again, he shrugged his shoulders, "I can't help it if their records are wrong, I know I took him there."

"So, you say, Simon, but the evidence for what you're claiming doesn't stack up. I suggest you've concocted that story to cover up the reality of what happened. We don't doubt that Shackleton was in the car when you drove back and the blood on the rear seat suggests he was still alive, but bleeding profusely. I suggest that you were so angry that you decided to put paid to Leslie Shackleton for good, so you've hidden him away somewhere to bleed to death. That, Simon, is murder. As for Angela, she was in the boot, you put her there, and you did so because she knew what you'd done and refused to go along with it – probably threatened to report your action to the police. Have you dumped her alongside Leslie Shackleton?"

Once again, Goodfellow slammed his first down on the table, stood up and made a grab for Dani.

"You stupid, stupid bitch, do you want to join them where I've supposedly dumped them? Why would I do anything to harm the woman I love and

who loves me – I DON'T KNOW WHERE THEY ARE!"
he yelled, "Get that into your thick heads and stop trying to blame their deaths on me."

"Ah, so you know they are dead do you, otherwise
why would you say we're trying to blame their deaths
on you? I wonder how you would know that if you
were not responsible or had some hand in it. Come
on, Simon, start telling the truth and let's get it over
and done with."

"Are you deaf, or are you just plain stupid? You
know I didn't mean they were dead, it's you two
who're inferring that. I just told you, I DON'T KNOW
WHERE THEY ARE! Just get that into your thick
skulls and stop playing games with my head."

"Okay Simon, calm down," urged Jenny, "let me
ask you, why were you in the Ratton area that day?"

"I told you I lived with me mum in the Eastbourne
area and I'd been to her house to collect my gear to
take it to Angie's and, to be honest, I didn't just go to
the cottage to see Angie, I went in the hope that old
Shackleton would give me a lift. Carrying all my gear
on public transport was a nightmare, so I thought
he'd perhaps do me a favour, especially as Angie was
with him. It was a bit of a shock finding him in that

state, but it worked out fine for me when he asked me to drive him back to this area. I dropped him off at the hospital, then took my gear to the flat and then put the car in his garage as he asked me too."

"How did you get into Angela's flat?" Dani asked him.

"Angie had already given me the keys and the code for her alarm, though actually, I expected her to be there, as Shackleton said she'd left him the day before. I don't know why she didn't get back unless Shackleton was lying, and he'd done something to her."

"That doesn't quite add up though Simon," responded Dani doubtfully, "if Angela or someone else had stabbed Leslie Shackleton, he'd hardly be in a state to do something to her and then dispose of her body. You said yourself; he was only able to walk with your support. We're certain Shackleton was knifed in the bedroom, that being the case, he'd have the added problem of negotiating the stairs carrying her body or forcing her to walk. She could easily have eluded him in his state. Which brings us back to the more likely scenario, you knifed Shackleton, and you forced Angela, probably at knifepoint, out of the cottage and into the garage, where you locked her in the boot of the car. Then you went back for Shackleton and dragged him out to the car. We know he was in the garage because he left a pool of blood on the floor – probably while you struggled to hold him and open the car door at the same time. That's how it happened, wasn't it Simon?"

"Cobblers, absolute cobblers. You're determined to pin something on me and yet you're not even sure of the facts. How do you know anything has happened to Angie? Yes, you might be certain she'd been in Shackleton's boot, but nothing to prove that I put her there and you never will prove it because I didn't. Neither do you have any evidence that I knifed Shackleton? Everything you have is circum...circumstantial, nothing concrete."

Dani was quick to respond to his accusation.

"Ah but Simon, I believe we have very credible evidence that you knifed Shackleton. We have a knife that has Shackleton's blood on it, a knife that only has your fingerprints on it, the same knife with which you threatened us in Angela's flat. That knife, Simon, you said had been used once and could be used again."

"So? I agree with all that you've just said, I too believe that it's the same knife that slashed Shackleton, but I found it on the floor and picked it up. Yes, it has my prints on it and no one else's, but if the other person were wearing gloves, of course, there'd be no prints. Okay, I did wrong in taking the knife from the scene and most certainly wrong to threaten you with it, but that was the drugs. I was drugged up to the eyeballs, and when I'm in that state I do stupid things, and that's why I've promised Angie that I'll kick the habit, but I need her help. Charge me with threatening behaviour and resisting arrest – even charge me with spoiling a crime scene and carrying an offensive weapon – I'll plead guilty but stop trying to stick things on me that you have no evidence for."

"We haven't finished yet, Simon, so don't get too hopeful, these crimes won't simply go away. Tell me," Dani said, "do you know someone by the name of Royston Barraclough?"

The mention of Barraclough's name brought a flash of recognition to his face, but then it disappeared. "Royston Barraclough? No, no, I don't think so. Should I know him? Where does he come from?"

"Your old neck of the woods – Ratton and East-bourne area. The point is he was interested in Shackleton's cottage at the same time as you were there. He was in the nearby thicket, watching the cottage from behind the trees. Did you agree to operate together?"

Goodfellow laughed, "Is he the one who did that to you?" he asked, pointing to her shoulder.

"What makes you ask that Simon? Am I right in thinking that you now recall Royston Barraclough after all – do you recognise his handiwork? You think that his level of violence is funny, is that because you approve of violence, especially violence against the police and most especially when they are bitches?"

"As if I'd think such a thing," he responded in a somewhat sarcastic tone. "You're harping back to my drug-induced outburst against the two of you at the flat. I'm not really like that. I know you were only doing your job."

"Are you the placid individual you'd have us believe?" Questioned Jenny. "Were you that good-natured person that night when Angela called us to her flat because of your vile and abusive behaviour? Were you docile when you fought the officers to the station and then in the station itself? Were you placid throughout the night when you yelled and kicked and screamed abuse at all and sundry? Don't plead drugs. You were displaying your true nature – a vicious thug just like Royston Barraclough. I believe you're thugs in common."

"Well, for your information, I don't know him. Yes, I met a guy in the wood near the cottage, but I didn't know his name, but if that was Royston Barraclough then that's that. We talked; briefly, he said he had a score to settle with the guy in the cottage and was awaiting his opportunity. I asked him to hang on until I'd got my girl out, and he agreed. Well you know the rest, somebody had beaten us both to it."

"Somebody had beaten you both to it," Jenny repeated, "so you're admitting that both your intention and Royston Barraclough's intended to do serious harm to Leslie Shackleton? Was Barraclough wearing gloves?"

"What? No...no he wasn't wearing gloves – what are you on about? Stop twisting my words. I didn't go with any intention of harming Shackleton. You twist everything I say. I can't vouch for Barraclough. He said he had a score to settle, but I didn't ask him what he meant by it."

"Which of you had the knife in the first place? Did you go in together? You conspired together, didn't you?" Jenny pressed him.

Once again, he banged on the table, "HOW MANY MORE TIMES, WHY DON'T YOU LISTEN! I didn't know him, we'd never met before, and we didn't go in together, I found the knife on the floor – HAVE YOU GOT THAT, STUPID BITCH?"

Dani stepped back into the questioning.

"Hmm, Simon, you have got a temper, haven't you, did it get the better of you that day? Was Shackleton taunting you about Angela, was he telling you what a fantastic relationship they had? Do you know what she gave him and said about him? She gave him a book, 'The Perfect Lover' and inside it said, 'All about you Leslie xxx', from Angela T. That's how she saw their relationship. How did it make you feel, were you angry when you saw them together and did you lose it? I'm sure you didn't mean to harm him, but seeing them in bed together made you see red, and you lashed out as a reflex reaction."

Dani's scenario made his hackles rise. Again, with a thump on the table, he blurted out.

"He had no right to be there with my girl, he deserved what he got, but then she attacked me, kicking, screaming, scratching and biting, so I had to give her a slap."

"So, you're admitting that you physically attacked both Leslie Shackleton and Angela Talbot – you knifed Shackleton and slapped Angela, is that right?" questioned Dani.

"No, I did not like knife Shackleton, someone else did. I smashed his stupid face a bit, but that's all. I admit I slapped Angela hard, she was hysterical, but I hit harder than I'd intended, and she went out cold."

Dani continued to press him, "when you say someone else knifed him, to whom are you referring?"

"No comment."

"Come on, Simon, don't start the no comment routine. You've come this far, so clear your conscience, tell us everything, it'll be better for you in the long run. At present, you're looking at ABH at the very most, but that could become conspiracy to murder – if Shackleton is dead. Tell us exactly what happened and who did what and why." Dani encouraged him.

"Yeah okay. I wanted to go into the cottage alone, but Barraclough insisted he go in with me. We could hear the action in the bedroom, so we crept up the stairs. I kicked open the bedroom door, and there they were locked in each other's arms, both starkers. I went over and smashed him hard in the face a couple of times, by which time Angela was screaming blue murder, so that's when I slapped her hard and she went out cold. Barraclough then pushed me aside, grabbed Shackleton by his thingy, his plonker," he said, pointing to his groin, "and slashed it off completely. Shackleton then started screaming for help, so I hit him again, and he too went out cold. Barraclough calmly wiped the knife on the bedclothes, removing all traces of his prints from the handle. He then threw it on the floor and legged it, yelling at Shackleton, 'that'll teach you for threatening to squeal.'"

"Let me get this straight, Barraclough cut off Shackleton's penis and what did he do with it?" Dani asked.

"I heard him flush something down the bog, so I guess that was what he did with it."

"This is bizarre. So then, what happened next?" Jenny asked, shaking her head in disbelief.

"I dressed Angie as best I could, tied and gagged her and then carried her down and put her in the boot. Shackleton was coming around by the time I got back, so I helped him dress and told him I wanted him in the car. He pleaded with me to call for an ambulance, but I told him I'd take him to a hospital. With my help, he managed to stumble to the car, but he was pouring blood. I got him into the rear seat and then went back into the cottage. I picked up the knife, thinking it might confuse any investigation if the weapon wasn't to hand. Then, using Shackleton's keys, I locked the cottage, backed the car out and locked the garage. I set off to drive here, but after just a few miles Shackleton started making gasping noises and suddenly keeled over. There was no pulse. He was dead."

"Simon, why should we believe it was Barraclough who mutilated Shackleton and not you? Let's face it; you'd blame anyone rather than admitting your guilt. As yours were the only prints on the knife, I'm inclined to think it was down to you."

"Look, I know I've lied up until now, but I swear to you I'm levelling with you in this. I've always relied on my fists - I hate knives. I promise you, Barraclough had the knife, and he didn't hesitate to use it, he even seemed to enjoy using it."

"So, if all this is true," Dani said, "why didn't you come clean from the start, why waste so much of our time?"

"The truth? I was scared stiff. Barraclough threatened that if I said a word about him, he would get me and do the same to me – he meant it too, but I've now realised I'll be safer locked away, though please, not with him. If you catch him, please make sure I'm not banged-up with him, he'll get me for sure. He is an evil monster."

"Now, this is important, Simon, which day and what approximate time did Shackleton die?" Dani asked

"Day, time, er...I can't remember. No, wait a minute; it was a Wednesday, sort of mid-afternoon, say around 3 or 4 o'clock."

"Again, this is important, Simon," Dani asked, "what did you do with his body, where did you dump it?"

"It's in a derelict building, an old warehouse, it has an empty tank in the basement, and I dropped him in there with some corrugated sheets to cover him. I can't tell you where it is, but I reckon I could show you."

"And what about Angela?" Jenny asked, "Don't tell me she's dead and dumped there too."

"No, she's alive, but she's in the warehouse as well, but on an upper floor in an old office – it was carpeted."

"But you left her there still bound and gagged and without food and drink?" Jenny questioned. "What if we'd kept you in custody, how long do you think she would have survived in that state? If you cared about her as you say you did, why on earth didn't you take her straight to the hospital or even back to her flat if she wasn't injured?"

"I'd have told you where she was if you'd locked me up, I'm not a monster. I do still care about her, and that's why I was at the flat, I was proposing to take her back there, but then that woman turned up, let herself in and we came face to face. She started screaming, so I had to silence her. I tied her and gagged her and left her on the bed where you found her."

"What were you planning to do with her?" questioned Jenny.

"I don't know. I hadn't thought that far because you two came on the scene."

"Well Simon," Dani warned, "I can tell you that you will be charged with manslaughter at the very least, but possibly an accessory to murder. There will be other lesser charges – GBH, kidnap and false imprisonment and possibly a few others besides. However, the most urgent thing at present is for you to direct us to where Leslie Shackleton and Angela Talbot are. So, interview terminated at 12.35 pm. We have to arrange suitable transport and scene of crime officers to accompany us to the site, so you'll be taken back to your cell in the meantime."

CHAPTER 12

MISSING

DANI AND JENNY LEFT THE INTERVIEW room to return to the office, and as they entered, DCI Johnstone and DI Cartwright met them.

"Fantastic work you two and an excellent result," DCI Johnstone said. "I've contacted CPS and asked them to consider the evidence and advise what charge we bring against him, and SOCO is standing by to accompany us to the warehouse – if Goodfellow can indeed find it. So, let's get moving, Angela Talbot's in grave danger."

The convoy set off from the station, Goodfellow was under guard in the car that led the procession.

"Simon, have you any idea what road the warehouse was on?" Dani asked.

"I think it might have been Brick something, but I'll know it when I see it."

"Okay – Brick Street, Brick Lane or Brick Road – which one?" Dani suggested.

"I... I... I don't know, it might have been Brick Street – I don't know this area, but I think it's one of those you said."

"Okay Peter," Dani said to Peter Jones who was driving, "go along Corporation Street and turn right into Brick Road, from there we'll see Brick Lane off to the right and Brick Street off to the left."

A while later as they turned into Brick Road, Goodfellow suddenly sat up and looked around.

"This looks kind of familiar, yes, turn left, turn left!" he yelled urgently, "this is it, it's on the right a bit further down – there, the one with the iron sheeting on the front."

Goodfellow, handcuffed to Sergeant Paul Sheridan, led the way into the derelict building. A considerable amount of vandalism was patently evident on the interior, with debris strewn every-where. They made their way to a staircase that led to the basement and there Goodfellow pointed out the tank where he'd dumped Leslie Shackleton's body. They then left the SOCO team to it and retraced their steps to the ground floor and from there made their way up to two flights of stairs to the second floor. It was amazing that Goodfellow, even though he was well built, had been able to carry Angela all that dis-tance. The office that Goodfellow pointed out was in the centre of the floor, so they made their way there. They flung the door wide open, and it was immedi-ately apparent that Angela was no longer there.

"Where is she, Simon?" Dani demanded, "Are you sure this is the right floor and the right office? Where exactly did you put her?"

"Just there, in that corner – this is the right place. Angela must have escaped, either that or someone saw me bring her in and took her away."

Just then, one of the officers who had been in the basement came rushing up to them, "There's no body in the tank. SOCO can see that the sediment in the bottom has been disturbed and there are even foot-prints both in the sediment and on the floor nearby.

The galvanised sheets have been thrown to one side, and there are drag marks on the floor too."

"You have to be joking," DCI Johnstone retorted, "why would anyone steal a body? I can understand they would take a live woman, but a dead body? There's no possibility he was still alive and has climbed out is there?"

"We asked that Sir, but SOCO says no chance, they believe at least two people moved the body."

DCI Johnstone turned to Goodfellow.

"Think, man," he demanded angrily, "did you see anyone when you brought them inside? Could anyone else have been in the building and watched you?"

"No, I saw no one, I made sure that the coast was clear before I moved either of them. Why would anyone else be in the building, and why would anyone take them?"

"Use your head man, why do you think anyone would take an attractive woman? I do not doubt that drug addicts and all sorts used this place. For your sake, I hope no harm comes to her. Otherwise, you'll be facing more charges."

Just then, Jenny walked towards the corner of the room where Simon said he'd left Angela, she bent down and retrieved an earring.

"Do you recognise this, Simon?" she asked.

"If it's engraved with an 'A' then it's Angela's, I told you this is the place where I left her. I didn't want any harm to come to her – you have to find her."

"If you hadn't dumped her here, she wouldn't be in any danger," Jenny said accusingly, "you'd better pray we do find her and quickly before anyone can abuse her in any way."

"We need to get this whole site sealed off and searched," responded DI Cartwright, "there must be half a dozen derelict premises like this, and she could be in any one of them or none. I'll call for backup. Get him back to his cell, Paul. He's caused enough problems."

"Sir," Dani addressed DCI Johnstone, "I've been thinking, there's one person I can think of who'd perhaps want to remove the evidence, Royston Barraclough. If it were Barraclough who mutilated and murdered Shackleton, he'd most likely take the opportunity to dispose of the body elsewhere. Which leaves Angela...what would he do to her?"

"Yes, I think you might well be right, but how would he know Goodfellow had dumped them both here?" the CI responded.

"Hmm, I was thinking about that too and the only things I can come up with are either he was keeping an eye on Goodfellow all the time, after all, he had threatened to kill him if he squealed, or someone in the building saw it all happen and somehow got the news back to him. To my mind, probably the former rather than the latter."

"Does Barraclough know anybody around here to solicit help from?"

"You know Sir, I reckon there's a network operating, and they all know each other, the five who leased the garages, plus Goodfellow, Barraclough and probably lots more – drugs and illicit imports being the connection. We know that Khan and Porter are still on the loose, so one of them could be his accomplice."

"Hmm, you may well be right. We must step up the quest to find them, somebody somewhere knows their whereabouts," growled DCI Johnstone, "if we must drag every villain in off the streets and interrogate them, we'll do it. They are NOT going to escape justice – they're laughing in our faces."

Everyone set off back to the station, leaving the SOCO team and the search teams to finish their tasks. They still hoped that forensics would come up with something useful, but in the meantime, CID needed to work out a plan of campaign that intensified their efforts to find not only Khan, Porter and Barraclough, but now, once again, Leslie Shackleton and Angela Talbot. In one sense, the latter two were the most urgent, with Angela top of the list. If she was still alive, she was in great danger, who could tell what they might do to her.

DCI Johnstone called his team together, including Paul Sheridan. Just as he was about to start, Superintendent Andy Mann walked in and asked to address the gathering.

"Chief Inspector Johnstone has brought me up to speed on this case, and I want to emphasise the extreme urgency that we must adopt in solving the latest debacle, the loss of Leslie Shackleton's body and the loss of Angela Talbot – dead or alive. The press is all over this now, I don't know who's been talking to them, but they seem to know as much as we do about the whole case. On the matter of the leak, if I find out who's been opening his or her mouth, a head will roll.

We're now a laughing stock, and the cry is for resignations. I know that's a stupid stance, but we have to prove now that we are more than capable of solving the matter and in double-quick time. From now onwards, everything we glean stays within these four walls. If the press knows our business, then you can bet your bottom dollar the perpetrators do too, and that always enables them to stay one step ahead of us. Thank you. Chief Inspector, back to you."

"Thank you, Sir. Right, I want ideas, theories and suggestions to flow from each of you. Who has snatched Shackleton and Talbot? Why remove them from the warehouse? How did they remove them? Where have they been taken and what do they intend to do with Shackleton's body – are they wanting to dispose of it and if so, how or where? What plans do they have for Angela Talbot and are those plans for her dead or alive? Did anyone witness the removal of Shackleton and Talbot from the warehouse? I want every known villain or addict in the district questioned. If someone saw Goodfellow there, then it's likely he or she saw the two bodies removed. Paul, CCTV again, it's probable that they used a van to carry them – what van, whose van, what make and colour?

Was it the blue Ford Transit Kilo, Romeo, six, four, four? Everyone, I want friends, neighbours and relatives of Khan, Porter and Barraclough questioned – pile on the pressure, somebody will crack eventually. Any immediate thoughts or ideas from anyone?"

Just then, Paul Sheridan's phone rang.

"Sorry, Guv, I have to take this."

" Hello, okay, yes bring them all in, but tell them it's not an arrest, we want their help with our enquiries. I'll see you later."

Paul turned to the Chief Inspector, "that was the search team Guv, they've rounded up some squatters and druggies from the warehouses, and they're bringing them in. Hopefully one of them will have spotted something."

"Thanks, Paul, feel free to go and see to that, and the CCTV search, and I'll fill you in on anything else we gather here this afternoon. Oh, before you do go, did you get anything on the CCTV of deliveries to Shackleton's Estate Agency and the letters themselves?"

"Yes Guv, you should have received a report. We did see the same hooded figure on each occasion going into the shop, and he was holding an envelope in his hand, but when he exited, he had nothing. We didn't see him drop the envelope, he just looked at the properties on a display board and then left. We never got a good view of his face, but we're sure it was a male figure, it could have been porter, but not Khan, he was too white. Forensics found a thumb print on one envelope and a finger print on another – the same prints were on the padlock on Porter's garage, so I reckon he was the blackmailer."

"Good work, Paul, thanks."

Paul left the meeting, and DCI Johnstone once again called for thoughts and ideas.

"Sir," Dani spoke up, "it occurs to me that the reason why we've not been able to locate the blue van is that it's no longer blue. I think it's likely they've resprayed or repainted it and probably fitted it with fresh false plates, so we need to keep open minds regarding looking for that van."

"Good thinking, thanks you Dani, link with Paul on that will you. Anything else anyone?"

DC Adam Baldock spoke up, "Guv, you asked about disposing of Shackleton's body – if it was Barraclough who mutilated him, he'd want to destroy the evidence. I know the most obvious way of disposing of him would be by burying, but a permanent way is by burning, such as in a cremation. Do you think they might be able to obtain access to a crematorium?"

"All things are possible in the villainous fraternity – check it out, Adam."

"Guv, we haven't considered the wider network for the drugs and smuggled items," DC Jenny Seymour said, "do you think that's worth pursuing?"

"Jenny, we need to smash that network anyway, but they may well be up to their necks in this, fearing their whole empire could come crashing down if we delve too deeply. Follow it up, Jenny."

"What about mobile phones Guv?" questioned DC Colin Jenkinson. "If we could somehow gain access to their phones via the phones belonging to Broadhurst, Thomas and Bright, we could perhaps identify more of their network members."

"Fantastic, now you're thinking Colin, link with Jenny, see what you can dig up between you."

No ideas were forthcoming, so DCI Johnstone closed the briefing.

"Okay everyone, go to it, we need answers, and we needed them yesterday. Let's show the press that we know what we're doing and we're not just sitting on our backsides all day drinking coffee. Be always alert though, these villains are ruthless, and they'll stop at nothing. They're not going to love us, but they are going to hate us. What we've already recovered from the lockups used by Broadhurst, Thomas and Bright are worth millions on the street, so they're not just going to roll over for us. Keep me posted please."

Dani once again stayed on late that evening. It was her best time to think, a time when fewer people were around and fewer distractions. She had joined the force to defeat villains, not for them to beat her, and at this moment in time, she felt they were getting the upper hand. There had to be some way of short-circuiting the laborious slog that things were becoming. Something within her told her that they were missing something, something vital, and therefore she had to think. While she was pondering, a call came in from SOCO.

"CID, Dani Taylor speaking."

"Hi, we've completed our examination of the site on Brick Street and thought you would like to know our findings. The tank in the basement, two sets of footprints, one size 11, deeply patterned soles, corner missing from the heel on the right boot, traces of paint, dark green acrylic enamel. The other set was size 10, again deeply patterned, and the right one had a crack across the centre."

"Anything from inside the tank?" Dani asked.

"Yes, there were traces of dried blood belonging to Leslie Shackleton."

"Any prints?"

"The only recent ones were Goodfellow's."

"Was there anything from the office on the first floor?"

"There were scuff marks on the carpet, probably made by high heels and there were traces of size 11 footprints again and specks of green acrylic paint."

"Well, thank you for all that and such good service, it's very much appreciated. Please, will you let us have your written report as soon as possible."

"Most certainly, it will be with you tomorrow."

Well now, Dani reasoned, they could be almost certain that the van had been resprayed – green acrylic, but was it done professionally or was it a DIY job? She guessed that it was professional – it was a big job and needed doing quickly, but was it someone in the trade who did the work in someone's garage, or a paint shop? Dani favoured the latter. Again, it was a big job on quite a large vehicle. It would take space and all the right equipment and conditions. She needed to search for local paint shops, vehicle repairers or garages with spray facilities. It could be a big task, and there could be many such places. However, her thinking was that they were more likely to use backstreet establishments – the backstreet traders were more likely to prefer cash-in-hand. By this time, it was getting quite late, so the search would have to wait until morning.

She left the building and walked to the bus stop. It was a frequent service, so a bus came along within a couple of minutes. The journey typically took fifteen to twenty minutes, depending on the traffic. It was dark outside, and the light inside the bus made it challenging to see out clearly, but about ten minutes into the journey, while they were stationary at traffic lights, a dark green Ford Transit drew alongside the bus in the next lane. Her heart leaped – was that the van they were looking for? It pulled away slightly more quickly than the bus, so Dani was able to read the number plate – KP64 2RZ. That was the place to start, though she knew it was extremely likely that it was false – if, of course, it was the same van.

She was on a high when she got home and felt that it would be difficult to sleep in that state. She might have been inclined to have a glass of wine to help calm her excitement, had it not been for the fact that she wasn't supposed to drink alcohol alongside her pain-killers. Instead, she decided to read, not a novel or biography, but rather a textbook passed to her to help her prepare for the Inspectors exam at some point soon. It was quite a hard slog, but it did the trick, and before long, she found her eyelids drooping. Now was the time to settle down and let sleep take over. Moments later, or so it seemed, the alarm clock sounded, and it was time to start the new day. She immediately remembered the task for the day and felt good about it. Somehow, she knew something was going to come from it, maybe even that long-awaited breakthrough. "Oh, please, please, please," she breathed.

Paul Sheridan was waiting at her desk when she walked in.

"Hi Paul, you're an early bird, couldn't you sleep? Mind you, I was coming to see you, so I'm glad you're here. Did you want me?"

"Yes, I wanted to let you know that a traffic camera on Corporation Street picked up a green Ford Transit heading in the direction of the Warehouse about 11.34 pm the night before last and then coming away again at 2.38 am. Unfortunately, the camera didn't get the full plate, just KP64. Do you think it could be the one we're looking for, resprayed?"

"I'm certain, and by the way, the full number is KP64 2RZ."

"What, how did you know, have you seen it somewhere?" asked a bemused Paul Sheridan.

"Yes, it drew up alongside the bus as I was travelling home last night, but that was on London Road," responded Dani with a laugh. "Unfortunately, I couldn't see the driver and as far as I could see there was no passenger unless there was someone in the middle seat." She went on to explain her theory regarding backstreet paint-shops and garages. "What do you think, shall we give it a whirl?"

"You bet – two possible sightings can't be ignored, and if we can find out where they resprayed the van, we'll be halfway to finding out who carried out the removals from the warehouse," Paul responded excitedly.

"Er...of course we need to check the number to make sure it's not genuine before we start," Dani said cautiously.

A check on the police computer was all it took, and they had their answer.

"The number's genuine, but it belongs to a Peugeot 308, registered to someone in the north of England. I rather think they've 'borrowed' the number."

"Any thoughts as to where we start?" Paul questioned.

"Hmm, I've been wondering about that. If my theory is right and it's a backstreet place that did the respray, then they're unlikely to be advertising in Yellow Pages or any business directory, so what if we try an online search and perhaps the local free newspapers? They may well want to advertise, but at the lowest cost possible. It'll be a starting point, and if we draw blanks there, we can widen the search field. Does that seem reasonable to you?"

"Absolutely. Tell you what, we have all the freebies through our door, and they tend to stack up. I'll nip home and grab what we've got. I should be there and back within forty-five minutes. Are you happy to do the online search if I do that?"

"Yeah go for it, Paul, perhaps your hoarding habit will pay off."

While he dashed off, Dani set to work on the computer. She did various searches – 'Spray-shops', 'Accident repairs', 'Garage repairs' – all near Kerington. The searches threw up quite many suggestions, but she was able to reject quite a few as being irrelevant to what they were looking for, and fifteen local possibilities emerged, and all were on the less salubrious side of the region.

Three drew her attention. One was on Brick Road, one on Station Road, just a few streets away, and the third were on River Lane, just beyond Station Road. She'd just finished when Paul walked in carrying a pile of newspapers – he got a cheer from the rest of the office and a few derisive comments.

"You can laugh," he remarked, "we've finished our work, so it's time now for a coffee and a read."

"Well said Paul," she laughed. "I've done what I can, and there are about fifteen possibilities, but three, in particular, interest me greatly." She showed him her list.

"Hey, you may well have hit on something there. Let's look through the papers though and see what they offer in their classified sections."

Paul was the first to spot something.

"Ah, one of your three favourites, Auto Paintmatic, Station Road. Hmm, there are one or two other possibilities. Anything in yours?"

"Yes, another one of my three, Respray Technologies, Brick Street. Yeah, like you, one or two further possibilities."

By the time they'd finished they had narrowed it down to six distinct possibilities, so they then set about arranging them in visiting order.

LINKS IN THE CHAIN

"I DON'T KNOW ABOUT YOU, Paul, but I have a good feeling about this. Do you think we should focus on these six ourselves and if we draw a blank, get other members of the team to follow up the other possibilities?"

"Ye...s, maybe. No, I tell you what, let's get two more of my officers to make a start on the others, we can always recall them if we hit the target. I'll get Jones and Tranter onto it. I'll go and call them and brief them."

He left, taking the list of nine further possibilities with him. As it happened, both Jones and Tranter were in the station for refs, so he was quickly back with Dani, and they set off to their first port of call. They got to Respray Technologies on Brick Street only to find the building boarded up – the company had closed down. So, it was on to Auto Paintmatic on Station Road. Here they were preparing a car for a respray. It was an accident repair, as it had been fitted with a new front wing and door panel. Two men were in the paint bay and a third in the makeshift office. He was a rough and ready type, and a respray would have done him a world of good.

"Hi there," Dani greeted him, "we're from Kerington Police Station, I'm DS Taylor, and this is Sergeant Sheridan." They showed their warrant cards. "Have you recently had a blue Ford Transit in for a full respray, changing it from blue to dark green?"

"No, nothing like that in recent months, in fact, no green resprays for as long as I can remember, it's not a popular colour."

While Dani was talking to him, Paul was looking through the window into the paint bay and suddenly said, "Excuse me Mr...?"

"Sheppard, Bob Sheppard," he responded.

"Well Mr Sheppard, I don't know much about vehicle spraying, but just enough to know that unless you have excellent extraction equipment, you tend to get a lot of overspray. Now unless I'm mistaken or colour blind, I reckon the last vehicle sprayed in that bay was sprayed dark green. Look through this window with me and tell me I'm wrong."

He got up from his desk and moved towards the window.

"You're right, that's green, somebody's been moonlighting, I reckon. Let me call those two in – Lenny, Barry - come in here; please, NOW!" he yelled.

They looked up and saw Paul in his uniform, and one of them made a dash for the outside. Paul anticipated it and, despite his size, grabbed the man before he could get clear of the premises. He hauled him into the office, while the other man walked calmly in.

"This is about that van, isn't it?" said the second man, who turned out to be Barry, "I knew it was dodgy when you said the boss told you to do it late that night. We didn't even prepare it but sprayed over the blue paint."

"Shut your mouth, Barry," snarled the other man, "do you want to get us killed?"

"What's been going on, you two?" Sheppard demanded, "whose van was it, and why didn't you tell me about it?"

"I'm sorry," Dani said, "but I'm going to have to ask you to accompany us to the station to help us with our enquiries."

Dani called for transport, and while they were waiting, they ascertained that it was a family business and Sheppard was uncle to Lenny and Barry Tyler who were brothers – offspring of his sister and brother-in-law.

When the van arrived, they were loaded on board and driven to the station. As neither the uncle nor his nephew Barry was unperturbed by being taken in for questioning, they were first to be interviewed. Sheppard, it appeared, really didn't know anything about the nocturnal happenings. Yes, the lads had keys to the premises and did sometimes do little jobs for friends, cash in hand, but a full respray was out of the question as 'a job for a friend.'

It was Barry's turn next.

"Barry, how did you come to be doing such a big respray job?" Dani asked.

"We were in the pub, The Foresters, one night and this bloke comes in, walks over to our table and sits down. He then asked if we'd like to earn a couple of grand. I didn't like it, it sounded dodgy to me, but Lenny said yes and asked what we had to do. The bloke said he knew we did spray painting and he had a Ford Transit that he wanted respraying. Lenny laughed at him and said something to the effect, 'A couple of grand for respraying a Tranny, you have to be joking. It'll cost that to prepare it and half as much again for the paint.' Then the bloke said, okay, four grand. Well, I was amazed, he agreed to pay us four grand, and he'd supply the paint. I still didn't like it, but Lenny wouldn't turn down that sort of money, so he said we'd do it. I didn't like what the bloke said next – no one was to know we were doing it and if we said anything to anyone, we could say goodbye to our futures – he pointed to a knife in his belt. We didn't prepare it, just washed it and then sprayed over the old paint. So not even uncle Bob knew about it, though if he'd looked, he'd have seen the green colour on the walls."

"Was he on his own the whole time and did he never give his name?" Dani enquired.

"I asked his name, but he said it was better if we didn't know. I never saw anyone else with him."

"Had you ever seen him before or do you know where he lives?" Dani questioned.

"No, I didn't know him, and as far as I know he hadn't been in the pub before, so how he knew he'd find us there, I don't know, though I suppose someone must have told him and even pointed us out. I certainly don't know where he lives, nor anything about him."

"What did the bloke look like?" Paul asked.

"Tough looking, muscular, a bit of a bruiser, about five foot ten tall, red tee shirt, blue jeans and a pair of boots with thick soles."

"Any distinguishing features?" Paul pressed him, "Hair colour/style, a motif on his tee shirt, rings, piercings or anything else?"

"Now you're asking, brownish hair, I think, and quite short. He did have something on his shirt, yes, small skull and crossbones. He had a tattoo of a tiger on his left bicep, but I don't remember any rings or piercings."

"Were there number plates on the vehicle?" Paul asked.

"Yes, but we took them off before we sprayed. He said he didn't want them, as he wanted to fit new ones, so I dropped them into the bin outside."

"Thank you, Barry," Dani said, "you've been very helpful. We don't want to keep you longer than can help, but we have one more interview to conduct, and that's with your brother."

"Good luck with him," Barry remarked.

Before they continued, Paul sent an officer to retrieve the old plates from the bin. Then it was soon apparent why Barry had said what he did, Lenny had an entirely different personality.

"Lenny, tell us about this spray job you did, how did it all come about?" Dani asked.

"No comment," he responded.

"Lenny, you're not under caution, we're not recording, so you don't have to respond with no comment," Dani reminded him. "I can't see that you've committed any crime, so there's no need for you to be cautious. So, the sooner you tell us what you know, the sooner we can release you. Where did you meet the guy, who asked you to do the respray?"

Again, came the response, "No comment."

"You've been watching too much television, Lenny," Paul chimed in, "you're not wanted for murder or any serious crime, as my colleague says we don't believe you've committed any crime, so we can release you once we've got a few answers. Just saying 'no comment' makes me wonder if you have something to hide, so answer our questions. Look, we know from your brother that the man threatened what he'd do to you if you opened your mouths, so the sooner we can take him off the streets the sooner everyone will be safe and especially you and your brother. If you fear for your lives, we can give you police protection, so please tell us what you know."

"Do you promise police protection if I do talk? Because without that promise it's no comment."

"Yes, we promise," Dani reassured him.

From that moment on, he answered all their questions and almost everything corresponded with his brother's answers. The only difference was he had seen him before.

"Just a couple of days before he came to us at the pub, I saw him on Corporation Street talking with two other guys named Ali Khan and John Porter. I vaguely know them, our paths crossed some months back – they tried to get me into drugs, but I don't want that muck. They said they could get me pretty much anything I wanted, fags, booze or electrical goods. I told them I wasn't interested. Our business may not look much, but our uncle is great, and the work pays quite well. I won't jeopardise the family business for the sake of cheap muck and rubbish."

"Do you know his name or where he lives?" Dani questioned.

"I think I heard the name Roy…no, I think it might have been Royston or something similar, but I don't know his surname. My guess is he lives with one or both of the other guys, Khan and Porter."

"I guess you don't know where they keep the van, do you?" Paul asked.

"No, but it must be nearby because I saw it before it was resprayed, and I've seen it since. It has new, different plates – KE56 4EU. I have got a good head for number plates."

"Fantastic, thank you, Lenny," Dani said, "you've been most helpful. We'll join the others now and see about setting up a safe house for you and your brother."

They all came back together, and Dani explained the position and informed them of the plan to put them in a safe house until they'd caught the man who'd threatened them.

"Does that mean these two wouldn't be able to work?" Bob Sheppard questioned.

"Well, strictly speaking, yes it does mean that," Dani replied, "it would be difficult to protect them outside the safe house."

"Nah," Bob Sheppard said, "they can't do that. No, they can come and stay with us until you've done the business, the wife and I will make sure they're safe, and they can come to work with me in the car."

"Thanks, Uncle Bob," Lenny said tersely, "but it's our lives that are on the line, and I'm not sure you can stop that thug if he comes calling – he's a mean so and so."

"Quit fretting lad, I can protect you, I have a few tricks up my sleeve, so if he does come after you, he'll regret it. You're coming to us, and that's settled. We'll go and pick up your stuff and then it's home with me."

"Look, are you sure of this Mr Sheppard? We can provide accommodation for the whole family if you'd prefer it. If this man is who we think he is, he will stop at nothing – he doesn't make idle threats," Dani warned.

"Thank you, but no thank you. Between us, we're more than capable of protecting ourselves and whether we like it or not we have to make a living. We have customers who depend on us and orders we have to fulfil their orders. Don't be concerned about us; we'll be alright."

"We can't force you, but the offer remains if you change your minds, so please don't take risks and don't take the law into your own hands; call us if they come calling," Dani concluded.

Paul, immediately following the interviews, got in touch with his two officers, Jones and Tranter, and instructed them to abort their trawling of the other possible spray shops. They then returned to the CID office to bring the boss up to date. They still didn't know where Barraclough was, nor what had happened to Shackleton and Talbot, and that was of great concern to them. The longer this went on, the more they feared for the outcome. They could, of course, put out the details of the van, which they were convinced remained local, and they remained hopeful that a traffic camera would pick it up and lead them to their base. It was highly unlikely that Shackleton's body would be wherever they were 'holed up', so that was another question – where had they disposed of it?

DC Colin Jenkinson met them as they walked into the office.

"There you are, Serge. We've got something. We checked the mobiles belonging to Broadhurst, Thomas and Bright and we've found what we believe is a number for Barraclough. It didn't specifically have his name but was 'ROBA' – a bit of a coincidence if it's not him. We're having it checked with his service provider at present, and we're also trying to establish his location. I'll let you know when we get something back."

"Thanks, Colin," Dani responded, "keep on it, it may well be the vital link we need. That's good news, eh Paul? All we need now is for him to use his phone at the same time as we pick up the van on a traffic camera. For once I hope he does use his mobile while he's driving. Are your guys still monitoring the traffic cameras?"

"They'd better be, it's more urgent than ever now. I told them to particularly focus on the areas where they've previously been spotted. I'm hoping they think that we don't know they've changed the colour and fitted new plates, so will be a little braver. In the circumstances, I guess it's best if the Tyler's are still working, if the place was suddenly closed Barraclough might get a bit suspicious."

"Hmm, you're right, it's a good thing that Bob Sheppard refused to move to a safe house," Dani agreed, "though I can't help being concerned for their safety if Barraclough gets a whiff that the Tyler's have talked to us."

Later that afternoon news came through from traffic that they had spotted the van on London Road. Dani immediately spoke to DI James Cartwright, and he arranged for transport to despatch two unmarked vehicles to the area to locate the van and follow it wherever it took them.

They had orders to keep watch, but not to immediately apprehend, hoping that it would lead them either to where they were living, where he parked the van or to where Shackleton and Talbot were. Sometimes breaks between one traffic camera and another failed to reveal if a vehicle turned off the main thoroughfare, so this made it difficult for officers to locate a moving car. That was so in this instance. The cars sped to London Road, but the van had failed to turn up at one of the cameras, so now it was a case of the traffic cops driving around the area in the hope of spotting it somewhere. Although they looked long and hard, it had simply disappeared, so they concluded that it had been parked away somewhere in that area. Refusing to give up though, they continued to search the area in a bid to identify all potential hidey-holes. The question was, were Shackleton and Talbot on the same premises? The body of Leslie Shackleton would by this time have severely decomposed, so the smell would be more than most people could stand. It was, therefore, more than likely that it had been buried or deposited somewhere.

Paul ordered his men to carry out urgent searches of rubbish dumps, household waste disposal sites, canals, lakes, rivers and wooded areas. The problem was the region of Broxton, stretching from Brick Street and beyond, was an old industrial area, so was a rabbit warren of roads, alleyways and passages. There were countless old warehouses and business premises, some were still operational, but many were long defunct. Scattered throughout this vast estate were homes, years earlier these had housed families

of workers from the businesses. Amazingly, a few occupants still lived there, and they knew the region like
the back of their hands. The police suspected that
many criminals operated from such homes and most
likely used the empty warehouses to stash their ill-
gotten gains. They suspected that Barraclough and
his cronies lived here somewhere, and their van was
hidden in the area too. This maze was also the ideal
site for disposing of a body – where to start looking
would be the question. Their only hope might be that
a squatter might come across it and report it to the
police.

CID had discussed how they might have permanently disposed of the body and cremation was one
theory. That to Dani's mind was unlikely. It would be
too difficult to arrange and conceal. No, there had to
be another solution. Dani had to have another of her
thinking sessions. She left the office and went into a
local park, found an unoccupied shelter and sat
down. It was a peaceful spot, and few people were
around – Dani now was free from distractions. She
didn't believe they'd had time (nor possibly inclination) to bury the body, so what other means of
disposal had she ever heard of? Perhaps dumping the

weighted body in deep water but again, it would require time and inclination. She thought dropping the body into a well could work. Hmm, possible, but unlikely now.

"Come on," she ordered herself, "think!" Then, quite out of nowhere, quicklime popped into her mind. Yes, she'd heard of that being used to quicken the decomposing process, but round here? Surely not. However, it was a thought that wouldn't go away, and so she took out her phone and Googled the question, 'Uses for quicklime'. It came back with several uses, one of which attracted her attention, 'For use in the manufacture of aerated concrete blocks.' Broxton was an industrial area, so did it have a concrete block manufacturing company? She felt quite excited as she pursued another search. Back came the result, 'Barfield Brick Company, Crofton Road' – closed 2014. When they closed, did they remove all traces of their production methods? It was certainly worth checking out.

Boyed up, Dani returned to the office and sought out DI Cartwright.

"Guv, I have a theory as to where they either might have disposed of Leslie Shackleton's body, or intend to do so. Can I run it by you?"

"Sure, go for it," he responded enthusiastically.

"Well, I was thinking about ways of disposing of a body quickly and efficiently. We'd suggested cremation at the briefing, but I think that's too complicated to achieve and especially quickly. I came up with weighting the body and dumping him in deep water, but again I think it's unlikely around here. They could bury the body, but that takes time and effort, so doubtful. I think it's unlikely they'd dump it in a disused warehouse, as a druggie or a squatter could easily discover it. Then, I don't know why I thought of quicklime. You know as the Nazis did during the war. So, I looked up uses for quicklime, and one that struck me was in the process of manufacturing aerated concrete blocks, and it so happens there used to be such a plant, Barfield Brick Company on Crofton Road. It closed in 2014, but it occurs to me that they may well have left materials on site and perhaps one of the gangs knew about the plant as it's on their patch. What do you think? Is it worth a look?"

"Hmm, it's a long shot, but I guess it could be a possibility. Have you spoken to the DCI about it?"

"No, I brought it straight to you, is it worth us sounding out the boss?"

"Yeah, let's go, we've nothing to lose and plenty to gain if your theory's correct."

DCI Johnstone had no hesitation in sanctioning the search of the premises.

"Do you know who's responsible for the site now? Is it up for sale or what? Find out Dani please, if we can avoid a search warrant it's all to the good."

Dani searched with the land registry and found that the council had served compulsory purchase orders on all the businesses and homes in that immediate area, as they were planning to build homes for first-time buyers on the site. Having secured the information, Dani contacted the council to ask for permission to enter the site. The official she spoke to said that at present the site had not been sealed off and that they knew it was the haunt of squatters and drug addicts, but they were too numerous and evasive to control. Clearance of the whole site was imminent, ready for building work to commence. Regarding the police search of the site, they would send someone along to meet with them and to ensure they could gain access. DI Cartwright was unable to accompany Dani to the site but suggested that DC Jenkinson go with her. They travelled to Crofton Road and were soon able to spot the sign that said, 'Barfield Brick Company'. The council worker was waiting for them.

"Hi, I'm Tom Harvey," he greeted them, "I believe it's this firm's premises you want to visit, is that right?"

"Yes, that's right," Dani replied. "I'm DS Dani Taylor, and this is DC Colin Jenkinson. As I understand it, they used to produce aerated bricks or blocks and that they used quicklime in the process. What we want to see is if they left any quicklime on the premises. We're pursuing a possible murder, and we want to check whether the perpetrator has sought to destroy the evidence by immersing it in quicklime. Have you visited this site before?"

"No, not this one. I've been past many times, but as this firm closed quite recently, it was reasonably secure. As always though, squatters and drug addicts have demolished the doors, so it's no longer secure. We'd do something about it, but in the next few weeks, the bulldozers will be moving in to clear it all. Anyway, let's go and see what was left here."

They went inside and entered the filthiest environment imaginable. Everywhere was thick with cement dust, and it was difficult to believe that anyone would have wanted to work in such alien conditions. Had they known what it was like, all of them would have worn protective footwear and clothing. It was immediately clear from footprints in the dust that others had been here before them. One set of prints particularly interested Dani, distinctive tread patterns, with a corner missing from the heel on the right footprint – the same prints seen at the warehouse where Goodfellow had initially left the body.

"Please make sure you don't tread on the distinctive footprints in the dust, nor those alongside them, they're evidence," Dani said.

They followed the prints, which led into the heart of the plant, and there they found a series of large pits in the floor. Most only contained dried sludge, but one was half-full of water that was bubbling and giving off strong fumes. The three of them covered their nose and mouth with their handkerchiefs.

"That, if I'm not mistaken, has been recently filled and I suspect the bubbles are given off by quicklime that has been thrown in too. This is what I suspected, but the question is, is there a body in there also?"

Nearby Dani found a couple of long paddles, obviously there for use in stirring the sludge. She put one to use now in delving into the depths, but it appeared that there was at present nothing more than the water and the lime. It was a gruesome thought that they intended to drop Leslie Shackleton's body in there next."

"We need to get out now if our vehicles are spotted the whole plan will fail and we'll not catch the perpetrators. Mr Harvey, we'll have to ask you to leave, because we'll be setting up a surveillance operation and everyone must be out of sight if this is going to work. We'll give you a call when we've finished."

They all moved out, leaving everything as they'd found it and while Tom Harvey went back to his workplace Colin moved the car out of sight, and Dani called DCI Johnstone and explained what they'd found.

"Can you arrange for a backup team to come and join us here Sir, I have a feeling they could be back tonight, and they may well have Shackleton's body with them this time."

There was no hesitation, he immediately agreed to assemble a team and despatch them to the premises, adding that he would accompany them himself. A firearms team would be at the ready nearby in case Barraclough, and his cronies were armed and resisted arrest.

"It's not that I think you're incapable of handling the situation Dani because I think you're more than capable," he said, "but you're far from being operationally fit at present, so if we have to go in hard, I want your shoulder protected."

CHAPTER 14

MURDER REVEALED

WITHIN THE HOUR, EVERYONE was in place. Four officers, including Dani and DCI Johnstone, hid around the pits on the inside waiting to pounce. Other officers, including some in cars, were stationed nearby outside the building. The firearms unit were in the building across the street. The vehicles were to be used to block the road to prevent escape by anyone who managed to get back to their car. Once Barraclough was inside the firearms unit would exit the building and standby outside the entrance to

Barfield Brick Company. All they now needed was for the flies to come into the web. It could be a long night, as Barraclough would want to be sure that the fewest number of people were around, though some such as squatters and addicts were often nocturnal in their habits.

DCI Johnstone had issued orders that there was to be no communication except from him to the team. All mobile phones were to be off or silent; everyone was always to remain in position and alert. Such stakeouts were tedious, and officers in these situations longed to be able to move around to relieve aching limbs. All they could do was think their thoughts and this Dani did to good effect, thinking about Angela Talbot – where was she? Was she still alive and how would they find her if such as Barraclough refused to divulge her whereabouts? She was always local, of that she was confident, so once the threat of Barraclough was removed, someone somewhere would surely want to salve their conscience. Then, of course, there were the drugs, if they could get Khan and Porter, they would be able to gain access to the final two garages, although that would not satisfy Customs and Excise, who wanted to smash the whole drug ring, as no doubt the drugs unit would too. Well, as far as she was concerned, getting millions of pounds worth of drugs off the street was a big step in the right direction. It was times like this when officers became convinced that their watches had stopped, every minute seemed like an hour. Waiting was one thing no officer enjoyed – action was what everyone craved.

However, time did pass – 11.00 pm, midnight, 1.00 am – then at 1.50 am the sound of an engine broke the silence. It was quiet and distant, but it had stopped outside.

"Stand by," came the whispered voice of DCI Johnstone.

It was at this point that nerves tensed, hearts began to race, and any feelings of tiredness disappeared. Everyone's muscles were like coiled springs; ready to shoot into action the moment DCI Johnstone gave the order.

A vehicle door closing rang out in the stillness of the night, and then someone pushed open the factory door. Two figures appeared in the gloom, half-carrying half-dragging a third. Surely Shackleton was not still alive. Alternatively, could it be Angela Talbot?

Dani questioned in her mind. As they came closer, it became clear that it was a male figure – it had to be Shackleton. They approached the edge of the pit, and at that moment, DCI Johnstone gave the order.

"Go, go, go!"

All the officers sprang into action as one, quickly surrounding the two figures. They dropped the body on the floor, scared out of their wits by the sudden activity.

"Okay, okay," they yelled, "we're not going anywhere."

Someone shone a light on them, but neither of the two was known to them – Barraclough was not there. Pangs of disappointment flowed through Dani, how she'd hoped that that vicious thug would be there and taken off the street. Then a thought popped into her mind – the van, was he still in the truck? She immediately radioed to the officers outside, "check the van, but be careful, Barraclough may still be in there and could be armed."

Moments later came the reply, "negative, the van's empty."

Dani went over to check the body on the floor and was shocked to find it wasn't, in fact, Leslie Shackleton.

"Sir," she said, displaying her disappointment, "this is not Shackleton. He's about the same age and build as Shackleton, but there's no blood on him and judging from the marks on his neck this man was strangled with a ligature of some sort."

DCI Johnstone moved to her side, "are you sure?" He too looked closely, "You're right, so who on earth is this and who murdered him?"

The officers were going to haul the two men back to the station, but DCI Johnstone shouted after them.

"Hold on a minute! Hey, you two, who is this man and who murdered him?"

"We don't know," responded one man calmly, "we were just told to dispose of his body in this pit – we know nothing about his death. We owed a lot of money to the guy who told us to dispose of the body, but I don't know his name; he promised to cancel our debts and pay us a grand each to get rid of the body, it seemed too good an offer to miss. We knew about this place as we've often dossed in the office, so it seemed ideal."

"Well I for one don't believe you don't know more, but we'll find out at the station. Caution them and charge them with murder and attempting to dispose of a body illegally – take them away."

In the event the two turned out to be serious drug addicts, Noel King and Rory Chandler, who indeed had become seriously in debt to Barraclough. Their story held up, so the charge against them was illegally attempting to dispose of a body.

DCI Johnstone called SOCO. They urgently needed information on this latest victim – who was he, where did he come from, who killed him, and did he have any connection with the Shackleton case?

"Don't be too disappointed everyone," urged DCI Johnstone, "all in all that was a good night's work, at least we took two more of the gang off the street. I know we wanted Barraclough, but his turn will come. Anyway, I suggest you all go and get some sleep and reports can wait until morning. Thank you all."

When everyone else had gone, Dani spoke to DCI Johnstone, "I must admit I am disappointed Sir, because I'm deeply concerned for Angela Talbot. I hate to think about what that animal might be doing to her."

"Yes, I know what you mean, and that's on my mind too, but at least we can focus on Barraclough now and hopefully rescue Angela at the same time. We will get him, Dani. I believe we're getting close. What's bugging me is this body – I believed it was going to be Leslie Shackleton. Now suddenly we have a second murder on our hands, but at least we have the body this time. Everything about Shackleton's death is just secretive – we think we're getting somewhere and then the rug's pulled from under our feet. I begin to wonder if we've got to the truth with anyone, it's as if there's a gigantic conspiracy to confuse us – and it's working. Barraclough could well be the perpetrator of both murders, of course. Anyway, come on, I'm taking you home, you're looking exhausted, and I suspect that shoulder's aching again."

"You're right, it does ache rather, but you don't have to take me home, I can get a bus."

"Nonsense, not at this time of night you're not. For all we know, Barraclough could be near, and he could have been watching everything that's been going on, so you'd be very vulnerable on your own. One woman in his hands is more than enough. I want you solving crimes not being the subject of a crime, so now it's an order, get in."

She was grateful for his kindness. It speeded her arrival home considerably. When they got there, he waited until she was safely inside the door before pulling away. As he moved off, he glanced into his rear-view mirror and just for a moment thought he saw a shadowy figure emerge from a front garden and move towards Dani's flat. He pulled into the side of the road and cut the lights and engine. He had to satisfy his mind, so he walked back towards the flat and cautiously peered into the entrance to the block. Someone was there and pressing a door buzzer. He heard a woman's voice say 'Hello' and then the figure responded, "This is DCI Johnstone. I forgot something, may I see you for a moment?"

DCI Johnstone raced up the short approach and spoke as he did so.

"This is DCI Johnstone, and I want a word with you." Just as he spoke, the door lock released and the figure made a lunge to get through the door, but the DCI was too quick for him, grabbed his shoulder and dragged him backwards. There were two steps to the door, and the person fell backwards down the steps and fell slowly onto his side on the tarmac path. However, he was quick to recover, sprang back to his feet, and as he did so, he dragged a long-bladed knife from his belt and made a slash for DCI Johnstone's face. Self-defence was a strong point with the DCI, so as the blade flashed towards him, he sidestepped, grabbed the outstretched arm and yanked and twisted it at the same time. His assailant did a half somersault and again landed on his side, at which point he knew he'd met his match, so rose to his feet and ran as fast as he could away from the property.

The door opened, and there stood Dani with a hockey stick in her hand. "What on earth was all that commotion about?" she asked.

"You had a visitor – you almost let Mr Barraclough into the building."

"You're joking, I thought it was you at the door, but how did you come to be here? I thought you'd left."

"I spotted him in my rear-view mirror, so I walked back and only just in time I might add. Anyway, you're not staying here, and you're not going out to play hockey."

She looked at the hockey stick and laughed, "It's my walking stick, I don't want you thinking it's a lethal weapon. Thanks for what you did, but I'll be okay now."

"No, you won't, I'm not taking any more risks with you, I'll have Luke on my back if I do. Get some things together and come with me, you can have our guest room until we have that creature behind bars."

She stopped protesting and decided to do as he said. She invited him in, and as she turned, she came face to face with many of her neighbours, awakened by all that had been happening and had come out to investigate.

"Sorry to have disturbed you all, we had a potential vicious intruder, but this man, my boss, Chief Inspector Johnstone, saw him approach our flats and stopped to foil his intentions."

"The man I spotted is a wanted criminal," responded the DCI, "someone we have been trying to apprehend all evening, that's why we're so late. I think you can rest easy in your beds now. I'm sure he'll not be back."

"So, are you a police officer too?" asked one of Dani's neighbours.

"Yes, I'm Detective Sergeant Dani Taylor. It's amazing, we live in such proximity, yet we so rarely meet and get to know each other. We really ought to have a get together sometime, but for now, I'm sure we all need a good sleep. Sorry, we disturbed you."

Dani led the way to her first floor flat, leaving the neighbours to speculate about their intentions. Dani went into her bedroom to pack a bag, and the DCI looked over her bookcase. "You have quite a highbrow taste in literature," he remarked as Dani emerged.

"Yeah, I like a good challenging read. It keeps my brain active. I do occasionally read novels, but I never keep them, I usually pass them on to charity shops."

They left the building to go to the car, and Dani felt sure she noticed a few curtains twitching. It didn't bother her. She knew that it was all very innocent. When they reached the Johnstone home, there was a light on in the kitchen. When they got inside, his wife, Kate, met them in the hallway.

"Oh hi, I was just getting a cup of tea, something disturbed me – I thought it was you coming in, as it sounded like the door rattling."

"How long ago was that Kate?" Bill asked.

"About five to ten minutes ago, but I couldn't see anyone around, so assumed it must have been a fox or something. Anyway, sorry, Dani, isn't it?" she welcomed her. "Are you okay? Bill told me about your injury – what a good job that thug missed your head."

"Darling, Dani too has had a potential unwanted visitor tonight, so I suggested she come and use our guest room until we can catch the villain. We know who he is, but he's proving elusive. Is that okay with you?"

"Oh absolutely, it's good to have it in use again. It's been idle since Sarah, our daughter, left home and then married. It's all ready, and it's very late, so let's go up – unless you'd like a drink before you go Dani?"

"Just a glass of water if I may, I'm blushing and a bit uncomfortable, so just water and painkillers will keep me going until morning, and that'll soon be here."

"Not early Dani, so no alarm, we'll knock on your door when it's time to get up. Just sleep well, we have a busy day, but later."

It was in fact 9.30 am when the knock came on her door. She looked at her watch and immediately panicked. She knew the boss had instructed her not to set her alarm, but 9.30 am was ridiculous. She showered and dressed in record time and then rushed down to the kitchen.

"Good morning, Dani," Kate greeted her.

"Did you sleep well?"

"Too well, I think. I'm sorry I'm so late – I'll be getting the sack."

"Only if your boss gets the sack too," laughed Kate, "I'm sure he'll be down soon. Right, breakfast, what would you like? Fruit juice, cereal, yoghurt, toast, full English – what do you normally like?"

"Fruit juice would be great and a round of toast, please. Has your husband not emerged yet?"

"No, he hasn't so don't feel pressured, sit and enjoy your breakfast. How do you like your toast, white or brown? Marmalade, preserve or Marmite? Tea or coffee?"

"Goodness, Mrs Johnstone, you're spoiling me. Er... brown toast, marmalade and coffee if I may."

"No problem, and by the way, please call me Kate, Mrs Johnstone makes me feel old."

They chatted amiably while they ate, and eventually, Bill emerged.

"Good morning –look at you two putting the world to rights. Sorry I'm rather late, but I haven't been languishing in bed, I've been on the phone with our beloved superintendent. He knows we're going to be late in and he completely understood when he heard about our nocturnal experiences. I've brought him completely up to date and talked to James and asked him to hold the fort until we get there. They're carrying out the post mortem on the body from last night as we speak, and they've requested that we call in before we go into the office."

It was about 10.45 am before they set off for the mortuary. Dani and DCI Johnstone talked as they travelled.

"I reckon that what Kate heard last night was Barraclough once again. I'm going to arrange for regular patrols and checks for both our properties. The more Barraclough is out and about though the better; we've then more chance of spotting him and getting him off the streets."

"I've been thinking about how we can apprehend him, and it occurs to me that if he's watching us and waiting for an opportunity to attack, I'm willing to offer myself as bait."

"Oh no, we're not going there Dani. Thanks for the offer, but no thanks. He's a devious, vicious and cruel thug and I would not risk anyone's life to get him. We'll wait until boldness gets the better of him and he starts making mistakes, which I've no doubt he will if we give him time. I really can't understand what he thinks he'll achieve by attempting to attack such as you, what good will it do him? It only makes us even more determined to get him and lock him away. There is nothing he can do that will make us give up our quest to ensure he's convicted and put away, preferably for the rest of his life."

They arrived at the mortuary and joined the mortician. "Good morning Shan, what do you have for us? By the way, have you met DS Dani Taylor? Dani, this is Dr Shan Fitzgerald"

"I've certainly seen you Dani, but we've never been formally introduced – do you mind me calling you Dani?"

"No, not in the least, please do."

"Well, you keep bringing me bodies and this one is especially interesting. Firstly, though, the man died from strangulation, as you probably noticed, and I would say the ligature was no larger than five millimetres in diameter. Judging by the depth of the groove, I'd say he was killed in one of three ways, simply by someone powerful, or by someone using a wire-twisting tool, or by hanging. If it was the latter, it was not full body weight, as that would probably have displaced the vertebrae in his neck. Before his death, he had been severely beaten, kicked and stamped on. He has a broken nose and jaw, several broken ribs and boot marks on his chest, stomach and right thigh. At some point in his past, he suffered severe burns to his back and left leg. Now I said this body was especially interesting and that is because his DNA is extremely close to that of Leslie Shackleton, in other words, he is a very close relative and, if you want a guess, I would say his brother."

"Brother!" Dani and the DCI exclaimed simultaneously.

"Yes, I would say so, it is highly unlikely that the relationship was any more distant."

"Well, that's incredible Shan, we didn't even know he had a brother. Thank you for your speedy response, I think we need to pay another visit to Mrs Shackleton – she never mentioned a brother. Let me have your report as soon as possible, please."

"Of course, as always, we don't sit on things down here you know," she responded with a wink to Dani.

"Yeah, yeah, yeah, whatever," the DCI laughed.

As they walked back towards the CID department, Dani raised the question that was uppermost in her mind.

"Sir, this can't be just coincidence, there has to be a connection. I can understand why Barraclough would murder Leslie Shackleton, but why would he want to or need to murder his brother too?"

"Hmm, that question was going around in my mind too. There must be a connection, but I can't think what that might be unless they were both somehow mixed up in the drugs business. I know it's unlikely that Leslie was directly involved in drugs, but was he inadvertently drawn in because of his garage lets? I wonder if they blackmailed him into buying those garages somehow so that they could use them for their illegal purposes. I also wonder if he felt he was in danger of being implicated in their criminal activities and wanted out, so threatened to expose everything," reasoned the DCI.

"Yes, that makes sense, but where would his brother fit into all that, unless of course, he too threatened them? Well I suppose there are other possibilities, for instance, he could have tried to avenge his brother and fallen victim too, or he could have been part of the initial conspiracy to kill his brother. We need to know what their relationship was like and only Mrs Shackleton can answer that."

"Yes, that's going to be our next port of call. I have a few things to sort out, but that shouldn't take more than half an hour, so will you phone Mrs Shackleton and make sure she's available for us to visit? Arrange for about an hour."

Dani returned to her desk and phoned Mrs Shackleton.

"Hello, Dorothy?"

"Who is this, please?"

Oh, sorry, this is DS Dani Taylor from Kerington Police Station, is Dorothy there, please?

"Please hold for a moment, and I will call her."

Moments later, Dorothy came on the line.

"Hello Dorothy, it's Dani Taylor."

"Have you some news for me?" Dorothy asked.

"No, sorry, we still haven't found your husband, but there have been some developments, and we need to talk them over with you. Would it be convenient for DCI Johnstone and me to visit you in about an hour?"

"Yes, that will be quite convenient, so I will see you later."

Dani just had time to deal with several emails and make a few notes for later before DCI Johnstone came over to announce that he was ready. Dani took the opportunity while they were travelling to check on a few points with her boss.

"By the way, Sir, it seems that Dorothy Shackleton has a visitor and in fact, she answered the phone, but I don't know if she's staying, or whether she's a neighbour. Anyway, I wanted to ask, as we're certain that her husband is dead, are we going to share that with her? I don't mean the gruesome details, just the facts."

"Yes, I think we need to prepare her for the final revelation that will come when we locate his body. You're right, not the gruesome details. She doesn't have to know that unless she asks anything definite, but even then, I think we can be slightly evasive. I think she's a very perceptive woman though and she senses when things are being withheld, so we have to be ready for whatever comes."

"Another thing, I don't believe we've ever mentioned the garages to Dorothy, do you think it might be an idea to ask her if she knows why Leslie bought them?"

"Good idea Dani, it can't do any harm, and it might throw up something useful. There must be a reason why he would buy such a pig in a poke. It doesn't make sense for an estate agent of his calibre. Yes, let's sound her out."

A DREADFUL SHOCK

NO SOONER HAD THEY PRESSED the doorbell than the door opened, she'd seen them arrive.

"Hello, Dorothy," Dani greeted her, shaking her hand, "thank you for agreeing to see us at such short notice."

"You're both enormously welcome. You've been so kind in tolerating the fancies of an eccentric old woman," she replied gratefully.

"You're not eccentric Dorothy, and neither are you particularly old, it's just that life has dealt you some painful blows – you have every reason to feel aggrieved and very weary."

"Thank you, Dani, you're most kind, but talking of painful blows, I notice that you're carefully holding your left arm, has something happened to you?"

Dani put her hand to her shoulder.

"Yes, I'm afraid so. I encountered a thug who attacked me with a stick and broke my shoulder in a couple of places. We've arrested him, though, and my shoulder is healing."

"Oh, my word, you police officers have a lot to contend with. Sorry Chief Inspector, I'm neglecting you – when women get together, you know…" she remarked with a laugh.

It was good to see her laugh, something they'd seldom seen.

"Mrs Shackleton, I do know only too well, when my daughter was at home, and she and my wife were together I ceased to exist."

They went to her sitting room, and she ushered them to sit down.

"Tea or coffee?" she asked.

"Thank you, Mrs Shackleton," DCI Johnstone replied, "but don't go to a lot of trouble for us."

"Oh, it's no trouble," she responded, "I have my sister-in-law staying, and she's offered to make it for us. So, is it coffee for you both? Milk, no sugar?"

They both acknowledged her, and she passed on the information to her visitor in the kitchen and then returned, sat down and looked at them expectantly.

"We wanted to bring you up to date with where our investigations have led us," DCI Johnstone began, "we believe that sadly your initial feeling was correct and that your husband is dead. We believe we know the perpetrator, but to date, we haven't been able to apprehend him. Neither have we been able to locate your husband's body. I suppose we believe that when we find the perpetrator, we'll find Leslie's body too."

"Tell me, how do you know the perpetrator if you've neither found him nor my husband's body? I don't understand."

"There was a third-party present when the attack that eventually killed your husband took place. We have him in custody, and he testified to what happened. The perpetrator fled the scene taking your husband with him – at that point, we believe, he was still alive, but in due course, he died from his injuries. We're still pursuing his assailant."

Just then, the coffee arrived and was placed on a coffee table in the centre of the room.

"This is my sister-in-law Jean. Jean, this is Detective Chief Inspector Johnstone and Detective Sergeant Dani Taylor."

They all shook hands.

"Do you live locally, Jean?" Dani asked.

"Oh no, I live in the States and have done for more years than I care to remember. My husband and I moved there in the hope of enjoying a new life together, but then almost ten years ago, he very tragically lost his life in a motoring accident – a gas tanker went out of control and hit him head on, and the whole lot erupted in a gigantic fireball. There were three men in the car, and they were badly burned that it was nigh impossible to identify who was who."

"That must have been traumatic for you Mrs...sorry I don't think you gave your surname."

"No, it's Shackleton, Jean Shackleton. I was married to Leslie's brother Peter."

"Oh indeed," responded DCI Johnstone, "did he have other siblings?"

"Just one, a sister," Dorothy replied, "and she lives in Scotland. She married a Scot and moved to the small fishing village where he lived. They have four children – two boys and twin girls. I never see them, though they do phone very occasionally."

"Did you and your husband have a family?" DCI Johnstone continued.

"No, we didn't," she replied sadly, "we weren't blessed in that way."

"Dorothy," DCI Johnstone said, "do you mind if Jean joins us for a while? I need to ask her something."

"Of course not," she replied, "sit down, Jean, dear."

"Jean," he began hesitatingly, "may I ask you more about your husband's death? I believe the three bodies were burnt beyond recognition that it was nigh impossible to identify them. How did they eventually identify Peter's body?"

"Two things, his watch and his mobile phone. Those were the only two things that partially survived and differed from his companion's belongings. Not very conclusive, but sufficient they said. It was his car."

"Do you have a photo of your husband, Jean?" Dani asked.

"No, not with me I'm afraid – do you have one Dorothy? It will be quite old, of course, if you do have one."

"Yes, I'm sure I do, just bear with me for a moment." She disappeared out of the room, but returned moments later carrying a photo album. "I'm sure there's one in here." She flicked over a few pages before announcing triumphantly, "Ah, there, that's the one."

She passed the album around, and when DCI Johnstone and Dani had seen it, Dani nodded to her boss.

"Jean, what I am about to say may shock you somewhat," the DCI continued, "but it seems that your husband didn't die in that crash. I'm not saying he wasn't in the car, but we're sure he didn't die there."

Both Jean and Dorothy looked at him, baffled.

"Whatever do you mean Chief Inspector?" Jean managed to say, "no one could have survived that terrible inferno. But what makes you so certain he didn't die?"

"Well, sadly I have to inform you that we believe we have your husband's body at the mortuary and if it is, then he only recently died."

"No, no, that can't be so...it...it...you must have made a mistake. How could he possibly have survived that accident and what happened to him? No Chief Inspector that can't be right – I need to see the body you have, I'll prove that it's not Peter."

"Mrs Shackleton, Jean," Dani interjected, "you can certainly view the body, but the DNA test proves that he was very closely related to Leslie and the mortician says he can't be any more distant than a brother. This man has suffered extensive burns at some point in his past, so we agree he was probably in the crash vehicle. How he got out alive and what happened to him afterwards, we can't explain."

"This is beyond belief," Jean said, "if it was not Peter, we had a funeral service for, then who was it and what must that guy's family be thinking? How soon can I view the body?"

"We can take you when we've finished here if you'd like to, I'll phone ahead and let the lab know we're coming." DCI Johnstone responded.

"Thank you; you're very kind. I'll go and get ready while you talk to Dorothy."

She left the room, and they turned their attention to Dorothy. Dani took the initiative, "Dorothy, do you know anything about the six garages belonging to your husband in Barnett Street?"

"Barnett Street? Oh no, he wouldn't be interested in any properties in that area, he only dealt in upmarket properties. Goodness me, that's an awful slum area. However, I do remember him saying he was under pressure from a client to buy some garages, promising that he would get an excellent return on them as it was shortly to be redeveloped by the council. It hadn't occurred to me that it would be in Barnett Street, but I suppose it would make sense. I don't know who the client was though."

"I rather think we do," Dani said.

"Going back to Peter, Dorothy, how did Leslie and Peter get on before Peter emigrated?" the DCI enquired.

"Ah well, there you've hit on it. Peter was older than Leslie and, as I think I told you, Leslie took over the business from his father. That's was their father's choice; he decided that Leslie was the one with the business acumen. Peter, their father said, was too flighty. He was probably right at that time; however, their father ought, for the sake of harmony, to have invited both to take over. Peter was outraged, and even though Leslie asked him to join in running the business, he refused and said he'd show everyone that he was more than capable. He was right, he set up a business in America, and it was doing very well, and then tragedy struck – or so we thought."

"So, what happened to his company after the accident?" Dani asked.

"He left everything to Jean in his will, but she wasn't interested in it, and so the directors bought her out. The business is still thriving, and that's what's puzzling me. Why, if he wasn't killed, didn't he come back after the accident – back to Jean and back to the company? Where has he been all this time? I have a feeling that something was going on that none of us knows about."

"Hmm, and we know about your feelings, Dorothy, they tend to be on the mark," Dani responded.

At this point, Jean returned, and they all stood. "Would you like me to come with you, Jean?" Dorothy asked.

"Would you Dorothy? I think I might need your support. Is that all right, Chief Inspector?

"Most certainly," he replied, "and we'll make sure you're returned here afterwards."

They went straight to the mortuary where they found that Shan, the mortician, was ready and waiting for them. There was no knowing how Jean would respond when she viewed the body.

"Just tell us when you're ready," DCI Johnstone said in a calm voice, "there's no rush."

"Thank you. I'm ready," Jean said with a weak smile.

Shan drew back the sheet to reveal his face and shoulders, and Jean stepped in close while clinging on to Dorothy's arm.

"Oh Peter, Peter, where on earth have you been? Why didn't you come back to me? There's no doubt. It is Peter. I'd been trying to convince myself that it couldn't possibly be."

Tears were gently rolling down her cheeks, and Dorothy produced a tissue and passed it to her. "Can we spend a little while alone with him?" she asked.

"Of course, take as long as you need," DCI Johnstone responded, "Dani will remain outside the door and when you're ready just come out, and Dani will arrange transport to take you home."

Dani was glad to have a few minutes alone. It gave her time to think about this whole perplexing business. What was the relationship like between Leslie and Peter? Had it soured to the point where Peter wanted revenge, where he wished his brother ill? Dani had a feeling, just the feeling Dorothy might have. With Leslie and Peter, blood was thicker than water. It wasn't logical for her to think that – how could she possibly know? She didn't, of course, but until something came up to change her opinion, she was going to work on the assumption that Peter was just as much a victim as Leslie. That still didn't begin to solve the key issues – how did Peter escape from that inferno, where was he treated, why didn't he return to his wife and business, what was Peter doing in England and how did he fall foul of - was it Barraclough? So many questions and some weren't going to be easy to resolve. However, she did now know where she was going to start – she needed some more answers from Jean.

She didn't have to wait long for Jean and Dorothy to emerge. Jean, it had to be said, looked more bewildered than distressed. She had done her mourning years previously when she thought she was going through the loss of her husband.

"That must have been quite a harrowing experience for you Jean and indeed very confusing for you both. Are you all right?" Dani asked.

Jean nodded. "Yes, I'm all right really, it just seemed so impossible for him to be lying there when I'd laid him to rest years ago. Yes, harrowing and confusing."

"Will you allow us to provide you with some tea? I have a few more questions to put to you before we take you home. Do you feel up to that?"

"You are most kind Dani, I'm sure we'd both love some tea, and please feel free to ask all the questions you need to, anything to help us get to the bottom of this awful mystery."

Dani took them through to the soft interview room, a room generally reserved for children and people of a nervous disposition. On the way, she asked for tea and biscuits to be brought through. It was a comfortable room with soft furnishings and tastefully decorated. In one corner it had a bookcase and a box of toys for children to play with while being asked questions. Today was different; it was merely a place to relax and talk. No sooner had they taken their seats than the refreshments arrived. Dani poured the tea, passed it around and then followed with the biscuits.

"I'm sorry to have to ask these questions now, but the sooner we can get started in our investigations the sooner we can get some answers for you. So, Jean, do you know the date when you and Peter moved to the USA and where you lived together?"

"Yes, we moved in July 1986, and after a very brief spell in a flat in New York City centre, we moved to a lovely home on Staten Island, where I still live. My husband's company was on the industrial estate on the Island, and they were involved in research into tropical diseases. The company was SyroTech. I'm sure the name has significance, but what I never asked."

"Do you remember the date of the accident and where it happened?" Dani asked.

"Only too well, it's etched on my mind. It was November 8th, 2005. They'd been to visit a similar research establishment in Manhattan and were returning along the Hudson River Greenway when the gas tanker, travelling fast in the opposite direction, suddenly swerved across and hit them head on. They didn't stand a chance, the police said, it was as though someone had dropped a bomb on that scene. There were many secondary collisions, as vehicles slammed on their brakes to avoid ploughing into the burning wrecks. Fortunately, no one else was seriously injured."

"As we know, Peter had severe burns, do you know which hospital he would have been taken him to?" Dani asked.

"Hmm, I think it would be Hudson State Hospital, but I don't know that area well. However, the police said that no one got out alive, so as far as they were concerned no one was taken to hospital as such, though I suppose the bodies could have been taken to the morgue there."

"How was the relationship between Leslie and Peter? Dani asked gently, "I understand he was put out by being overlooked by his father but did it permanently sour their relationship?"

"Well, they were never bosom buddies," Jean replied, "but they did keep in touch albeit intermittently. Once he'd established his company he was satisfied, Peter had proved his point, so was happy to be friendly towards Leslie. Yes, there were occasional phone calls both ways, and from time to time they'd talk online. There was certainly no hatred."

"Two final questions," Dani said, "can you think of any reason why Peter would not return to you and his company? Also, why he might have come to England?"

Both women shook their heads.

"Not the slightest idea," Jean answered, "it's strange and rather hurtful."

"Thank you both very much for staying on, I think that's all the questions for now, so when you've finished your tea, I'll get one of the drivers to take you home."

There were now clear avenues to pursue. For one reason or another, no one noticed Peter Shackleton's escape from that terrible collision, and he didn't feature beyond the crash – why? How did he get clear without anyone noticing? He was on fire, so surely that would have been noticeable? Did he go to the hospital? With burns like his, he must have received medical treatment. Where did he go beyond any treatment and probable hospitalisation? Someone must have pressed him for the cause of his burns – why didn't the police know? What was his state of mind? If they believed that Peter Shackleton had died in that accident, how did he manage to get new official documents and were they in his real name? Somehow, they had to ascertain when he left the States, the flight he was on and the name he used to travel.

"We have to talk to the state police and enquire about the accident and inform them of the mix-up," Dani muttered under her breath.

That also begged the question, if it wasn't Peter, who was it they'd buried or cremated? Who was in the car that day, were they all from SyroTech? Has no one reported a missing person?

Dani went to DCI Johnstone to give her report about the interview and all the questions on her mind related to the case.

"There is so much about this that isn't right, and questions we need to ask. Someone somewhere has messed up, and it needs sorting."

"I agree," he responded, "it's an absolute fiasco. Is your passport up-to-date?"

"Er...yes Sir, what do you have in mind?"

"We can't sort this out over the phone and via the internet alone; we need to talk to people face to face. I'm proposing that we fly out there and do what we can to get it sorted. James can hold the fort while we're away. You do have the new passport required in the States, don't you?"

"Yes, I've only just renewed it, Luke and I were hoping to holiday in Florida later in the year. Will you make the necessary arrangements with the state police and Hudson State Hospital? And what about booking tickets and hotel?"

"Leave all the arrangements with me. I'll clear it with upstairs too and then we'll see if we can get a flight out the day after tomorrow, is that okay?"

"Perfectly. I'll inform Luke. I don't want him making a surprise visit and finding out I'm not home, and I'll also get my bags ready. How long do you think we'll be away?"

"That, I'm afraid, is a bit of an unknown, but let's say five days."

CHAPTER 16

OVER THE POND

IT WAS AN EARLY START ON the day of the flight, departure was at 8.35 am, and check-in from 4.35 am. However, check-in and seating had been pre-booked, meaning they didn't have to start quite so early, it was just a case of going to drop-off and then on to security checks. They had just over an hour until boarding, so they went for breakfast and afterwards browsed the bookshop. Armed with their selected reading, they sat and read until their gate number came up.

Throughout the nine-hour flight, they did all the usual things – read some, talked some, slept some and people watched. Neither of them was particularly interested in the available movies, so mid-flight food was a welcome diversion. JFK airport was bustling, and consequently, it took quite a while to pass through passport control and luggage reclaim. They'd booked hire car, and it was ready and waiting for them as they exited the airport concourse.

"Dani, you're the navigator for our journey. If you look in the glove compartment, you should find a map and a zip code for the Holiday Inn Express, Madison Square Garden, so if you could punch that into the satnav, we can get underway. It didn't take long for Dani to punch in the details and the satnav sprang into life. She liked maps, so she followed their progress on the map, the journey taking them along Hudson River Greenway, close to Hudson State Hospital and then turned off into Manhattan district. DCI Johnstone was a confident driver even in a left-hand drive automatic car.

Once ensconced in the hotel, they washed and then went down for dinner. They chatted amiably over the meal, but Dani was ready for a good sleep when they parted company and retired to their rooms.

"Breakfast at 8.30 am Dani, is that okay with you? We have an appointment with the chief of police at 10.30 am."

"Yes, that's fine, it'll be good to get things moving. Goodnight!"

She took a couple of painkillers before getting into bed and then slept solidly until her alarm call at 7.30 am. The breakfast choice was extensive, but though Dani restrained herself somewhat, her boss didn't hold back. They left fully prepared for the day. Shortly afterwards, they were on the road and heading for the police department. On arrival, they checked in at the reception desk.

"Hi, I'm Chief Inspector Johnstone, and this is Detective Sergeant Taylor, we're from London, England, and we're here to see the chief of police, Arnold Ogilvy."

"Oh hi, yes he's expecting you. May I ask you to sign in on our visitor's book and I'll give you your badges – this shows you're on the premises in case of any incident. Then if you'd like to take a seat, I'll inform him that you've arrived." They didn't have time to get comfortable before the same desk officer asked them to follow him as he escorted them to the chief's office. Oh, how the other half live – his office was large, grandly furnished, with a massive mahogany desk. He welcomed them and invited them to sit in some comfortable chairs that would not have looked out of place in a luxury home. He sat in the third chair opposite them. He ordered coffee, and they chatted until it arrived.

"So, what can we do for you? What's brought you from England? It must be something important."

DCI Johnstone outlined the case of Leslie Shackleton and explained how his sister-in-law, a widow, still lived on Staten Island, though was visiting Leslie's wife at present.

"This brings me to the purpose of our visit; do you recall a terrific accident on Hudson River Greenway in November 2005?"

"Whoa, don't I just! A gas truck hit a saloon head-on, and the whole thing erupted in a gigantic fireball, killing the three passengers in the saloon, but the truck driver escaped and fled the scene. I don't think anyone knows who he was and why he left the scene, but he's never been found. Terrible day. So, what about it? Is there a problem?"

"Well, one of the passengers in the car was Peter Shackleton, brother to Leslie, the victim whose murder we're pursuing. Peter was pronounced dead following that crash, only identifiable by his watch and mobile – his cell phone. However, he has recently turned up dead in the London area, killed by strangulation. His wife has identified the body, and there's no doubt it's the same guy because he has the marks of severe burning on his back and leg. Somehow, he got out of the wreckage without anyone knowing and that begs the question, who was the guy with Peter's watch and cell phone?"

"This is very worrying – something happened in that car, and we need to get to the bottom of what it was. I attended that scene, but Sergeant Judd Templeton led the team on site, and he liaised with the emergency teams. Let's get him in here." He put in a call, and a few minutes later, the sergeant knocked on the chief's door.

"Come in Judd – this is Chief Inspector Johnstone and Detective Sergeant Taylor, they're from the UK."

They all shook hands, and Chief Ogilvy then explained the situation.

"You're joking," Judd said, "there's no way anyone got out of that wreck alive. Everyone in that car was dead before the gas ignited. The truck had completely flattened the body of the vehicle down to the wheels. Human body parts were scattered."

"What happened to the bodies afterwards?" Dani asked.

"Initially they were taken to the hospital morgue at Hudson State Hospital. Later they were transferred to the coroner's department."

"So, no other hospital was involved?" Dani pressed him.

"No," Judd insisted, "we always try to use the nearest hospitals."

"Sorry," Dani persisted, "I understand what you're saying, but could Peter Shackleton have taken himself to another hospital – or somehow been taken?"

"Not anywhere near if he were badly burned, he'd be in agony and desperate to get treatment. I don't think he could have taken himself anywhere, someone must have transported him, but I can't imagine how that could happen without someone seeing him."

"Is it possible for us to visit the site of the accident, Sergeant Templeton?" DCI Johnstone asked.

"Sure, no problem, I'll get one of the officers who were with me that day to join us, and we'll shoot off. Is that okay Chief?"

"Yeah, do that, get back to me if you find anything." The chief responded.

"Okay, come with me," the sergeant invited them. On the way down, he motioned to another officer and collected the case notes. He introduced Officer Shane Tyson to the others, and then they descended to the garage and piled into a car. Officer Tyson drove across the city to the Hudson River Greenway. They drove for about five minutes and then pulled onto the hard shoulder.

"This is the spot," Templeton announced, "a spot I'll never forget – I had nightmares about it for days."

They climbed out, and DCI Johnstone asked them to describe the scene as they found it.

"The gas truck made a sudden swerve about a couple of hundred yards back there," Templeton said, pointing up the highway, "then he straightened as if he was trying to get back over, but they collided head-on, and the saloon went between the front wheels and completely under the truck. Nobody could have survived it."

"Was one of the victims in the driver's seat?" Dani asked.

"Yeah, one in the driver's seat, one in the front passenger seat and one behind the driver. The other seat was empty."

"Perhaps a silly question when you have a mangled wreck," Dani said, "but was it possible to tell whether any door was open when the two vehicles collided?"

"Not a silly question Ma'am, because that puzzled us. The nearside rear door had been ripped off and later found a few feet away from the wreck. Is it significant? Do you have a theory, Ma'am?"

"Yes, someone was in that spare seat just before impact, but opened the door and rolled out. Peter Shackleton was, though, sufficiently near to still be caught by the explosion and it badly burned his back and leg. It was Peter Shackleton."

A questioning look spread across Officer Tyson's face.

"Why Peter Shackleton? How would you possibly know that?"

Dani explained further.

"Although Peter Shackleton was said to be one of the victims, he wasn't, because we have his body – he was killed by strangulation in London."

The officer shook his head at the incredulity of the situation.

"How did we come to get it so wrong?"

"May I ask a question?" DCI Johnstone interjected, "who identified the watch and cell phone as belonging to Peter Shackleton?"

"Well," Sergeant Templeton began, "as there was only one passenger in the rear seat and the cell phone was by his side, we assumed that it belonged to him. It had one print on it still visible, and it was Shackleton's print. The watch, though partially melted, had enough print to enable identification of the make and model – Shackleton had that make and model. From what you've just revealed, I reckon the latter was just a coincidence – they happened to have the same watches."

"So, regarding the three victims in the car, who was the third man if it wasn't Shackleton?" Dani questioned.

"You guys have blown our open-and-shut case sky-high. We have to reopen it," the sergeant announced.

"Were DNA tests carried out on the three victims?" DCI Johnstone asked.

The sergeant opened the case file.

"Tests would have been carried out, and the report should be here somewhere...ah, yes, here we are. Victim one, the driver, Conrad Jameson, victim two, the front passenger, Arnold Sanderson, victim three, the rear passenger, Peter Shackleton."

"Can't be," DCI Johnstone protested, "we have his body, and he died only recently. There must be another explanation. Tell me, do you know whether SyroTech had another missing employee then? Did anyone ask who went on the visit that day?"

Again, the sergeant thumbed through the file.

"You know, I don't think anyone specifically asked that question, but surely they would have said if a fourth employee hadn't returned."

"I think we need to visit SyroTech tomorrow and start asking some questions." DCI Johnstone said. "Something's not right."

"We'll join you if you don't mind," the sergeant insisted, "it's our mistake, and we need to rectify it. My guess is, we had the remains of three people, and no one thought to check the roll count with SyroTech.

Mind you, and they have questions to answer – why did no one register a missing person – not them, nor family? Surely someone missed him being around?"

"Hmm, that's one of my questions too," Dani agreed, "but I've been wondering – there's no chance it was a deliberate smash is there?"

"Wow, Ma'am, you sure do come up with the questions. There's no reason to suppose that it was, but none of us knows the intention of the driver. Do you have a reason for asking?"

"I'm just juggling thoughts for why no one seems to have missed him and wondered whether someone wanted Peter Shackleton and the others dead. I may well be barking up the wrong tree, but the chief says the tanker driver escaped and fled the scene – have you located it?"

"Let me check the file. The tanker driver should have been Selwyn Davison – his firm, Bulk Transfer Services, confirmed his name."

"But was the DNA from the cab of the tanker compared with that of the real Selwyn Davison?" Dani pressed him.

"Hmm, most surely should have been I'd say, but we'd have no reason to suspect it wasn't the guy it was supposed to be. You're going to ask for a check ain't you Ma'am?"

Dani raised her eyebrows, tilted her head and smiled, "who could resist that look? I'll get somebody on it right away."

He immediately relayed the request back to the station, emphasising the urgency.

"Send the results to me when they've got them."

"Okay guys, what next?" the sergeant asked, "back to the station, or is there anywhere else you need to go?" Then he added, "we'll help you in any way we can."

"Well, we intended to go to Hudson State Hospital," DCI Johnstone replied, "but we can make our way there if you have other things pressing."

"I guess your visit is to do with that guy Shackleton, so it might be best if we're with you. They might not take kindly to you asking questions. They don't have many options with us – we want their co-operation, not protocol."

"Great, thanks, your presence would be appreciated, and I'm sure you know the way and probably who we need to talk to, so we're in your hands."

Forty minutes later, they were at the hospital and walking into the emergency department. Sergeant Templeton introduced himself at reception and announced he urgently needed to talk to them about a case on the police file. The receptionist made a call, and a senior official invited them to his office.

"How can I help you?" he asked, "I'm Jethro Tullington, clinical manager."

"Mr Tullington, with respect, are you a hands-on guy down there in the ED?"

"It's Dr Tullington; I am a qualified physician. I don't have hands-on these days, but I'm sure I can answer any questions you may have."

"I doubt it, but heck, let's give it a go. Do you remember the smash on Hudson River Greenway in 2005 when a gas truck and a saloon collided head-on?"

"I remember it, yes, but I wasn't here that day," he responded.

"In that case, Doc, you can't help us. We need to speak to the senior guy who was on duty down that day. Can you get him or her to come here right away?"

"I...I...I'm not sure that I can, the person may not be on duty, I'll have to check the roster." He retrieved a file from his cabinet. "Do you happen to know the actual date and time?"

"November 8th, 2005 was the date," Dani immediately answered, "but I don't know the time."

"Late afternoon," the sergeant added, "about 4.00 pm."

"That would be...ah, yes, Dr Grace Bellamy and you're in luck, she is on duty today. I'll page her." He picked up his pager and put out a call. Moments later, the phone rang as she responded. "Grace, are you free to come to my office? I have the police here, and they need some information."

When she arrived, and introductions were over, Dr Tullington addressed her, "Grace, these officers want information about the accident on Hudson River Greenway in November 2005, do you recall it?"

"Oh yes, it was tragic, and everyone involved died as I understand it, we only had minor injuries to attend to – a few shunts as drivers slammed on their brakes – there was nothing serious."

DCI Johnstone nodded to Dani.

"Dr Bellamy, did you have a patient in that same afternoon with severe burns to his back and leg?"

"Wow, now you're asking, it was a long time ago, but let me think for a moment. You know, I think I do recall such a patient. It was much later when a guy came in with his clothes melted to his body and yes, his leg. He said he'd mistakenly poured gasoline on a fire in his garden and thought it was kerosene and the flash hit him as he turned away. I thought at the time that it was a bit odd, as he was wearing a suit, but we don't give our patients the third degree."

"Would you know his name? Presumably, you will have records?"

"Yes, I can find that out for you, but may I ask what it's all about?"

"That guy," Sergeant Templeton interjected, "supposedly died in the crash and now it seems he's turned up dead in the UK."

"You think he was in that smash but got out alive and turned up much later here? Well, that would make sense of the suit, but how did he get here? He must have been in terrible agony. I'll go and retrieve his records."

Five minutes later, she was back.

"Okay, let me see what we have. Ah, name John Doe. It's all coming back to me now, he claimed that the trauma had caused him to lose his memory and that does happen sometimes, so we treated his injuries, and he was in the burns unit for six days. He was then discharged and told to see a doctor regularly until the burns healed."

"So, no address for him?" the sergeant asked.

"No, not as such, but his records show that he intended to go to the homeless hostel on Hudson Boulevard until he regained his memory."

"What did he do for clothes?" Dani asked, "Presumably his were destroyed."

"They sure were, but my guess is he had money, and a member of staff did some shopping for him. We wouldn't record that information, of course."

"Thank you, Doctors," Sergeant Templeton said, stretching out his hand for theirs, "that's been very useful."

They all followed his example and left.

"Sergeant Templeton, is it possible for us to visit that homeless hostel that was mentioned?" DCI Johnstone requested, "I'd like to know if he did check in there and what name he used. I don't buy that loss of memory. I reckon he was content to let everyone believe he died in the crash because he was running away from something or someone. A change of name would be partway to a change of life, and if we can find out what name he used, it might tell us who he was when he came to England."

"Boy, you Brits believe in using your powers of reasoning, but I guess I see where you're going with it. So, yeah, we can go to the hostel, it's not far from here."

It took less than five minutes to drive to the hostel and, using their police authority, and they parked outside the building despite it being a restricted zone.

"It'll not take long here, so I reckon we'll not disrupt the traffic flow too much," he laughed. "Stay with it Shane, and you can absorb any flack."

The sergeant knew the guy on the desk in the hostel – he was a former offender but had been going straight for many years.

"Grady, my man, good to see you earning your keep still – how're things?"

"Great Serge and as far as work is concerned, I'm staying alive. What can I do for you? I'm sure this is not a social visit."

"That's true, just a bit of history if you can help us. Do you keep all back records of people using the hostel?"

"Yeah, we sure do – how far back do you want to go?"

"November...14, 2005."

"Woah, that is way back, but I think we can help you. Just give me a couple of minutes."

He disappeared into a back room and reappeared carrying a book.

"Let's see if we can find what you want. November you said...okay. August, September, October, November 14. What am I looking for?"

"How many signed in that day, say from late morning onwards?"

"Not many that day as it happened because we were full, and we sent folk on to River Street. We don't take newcomers in until after 10.00 am, so the first was a John Channing, then a Conner Fairchild, nothing then till 2.00 pm when Jeff Birchall came in. After that, we took in a further five in the early evening, and that filled all the available rooms."

"Do you record any special needs or features?" Dani asked.

"Er…yeah, John Channing had a limp and asked for a room on the ground floor, and he also requested a doctor to visit him. Fairchild, he was a black guy and asked to see a priest. Birchall…"

"No, that's okay, I reckon we've found our man. How long did Channing stay?" Dani asked.

"Just a couple of days, then he signed out, and he mentioned a flat on Cross Street. He also stated that he was going to England just as soon as he could get his passport renewed."

"Woah!" the sergeant exclaimed. "That I think is your question answered guys, he probably went to the UK soon afterwards."

"How easy would it be for him to get a passport?" DCI Johnstone asked, "would he have the necessary paperwork and registration, or whatever is required?"

"No, definitely not, but that wouldn't stop him. If you know the right people and have the cash, you can get one. It wouldn't stand up to scrutiny, but he might get away with it. We can check with the airlines from that date and see if he booked any flight. Could be quite a task, but we can do it. Let's go back to the station and see what we can find out."

When they arrived at his office, Sergeant Templeton found a report waiting for him on his desk.

"Boy, that's been quick," he said, noting that it was the DNA report on Peter Shackleton versus the guy in the smash.

"Hey, listen to this, the DNA is largely a close match to that of Peter Shackleton, but there is a slight difference. They suggested his son. Did he have a son?"

"No, apparently not, well not according to his wife, but of course he could have played away somewhere."

"The son of a gun!" the sergeant exclaimed.

"Quiet," DCI Johnstone said, "and with him, it must have been many years ago, that son was well and truly grown up. It seems very strange to me if the car that crashed belonged to Peter Shackleton, why wasn't he driving? What was going on there, and how did Peter manage to roll clear? Also, what was Shackleton junior doing in the car anyway? Something about this whole business smells to me."

"Are you sure that the other people in the car were from SyroTech?" Dani asked.

"We were, but I have a feeling you're going to cast some doubt on that now Ma'am," the sergeant responded with a shake of his head.

"No, no, not necessarily," Dani laughed, "just thinking aloud. May I ask more questions?

'Fire away,' the Sergeant replied.

'How were the bodies identified? If as you say they were burnt, and we've already found out that there was a mistake with the identification of Peter Shackleton as the man who died in the car, so what about the others? Were DNA tests carried out?"

"That's what's puzzling me, DNA tests are carried out as a matter of routine and yet there's no lab report in the file. I'll call the lab and check with them," he answered.

He immediately made the call.

"Hi, do an urgent check for me please, case ZH21-HUDSON-2005/11 – was a lab report issued and did it include DNA? ... It was, and it did. Thanks, copy it to me urgently please – Judd Templeton."

Ten minutes later, it arrived, and the sergeant studied it carefully.

"Yeah, everything was carried out correctly. We compared DNA samples from the remains with samples taken from the victim's homes. The sample taken from Shackleton's home did differ slightly from that taken from the remains. Why the report was not in the file, I don't know, unless someone deliberately 'misplaced' it, realising that the discrepancy would raise suspicions. If that's the case, what could the alleged perpetrator be hiding and does that mean we have a bent officer? I don't like this one little bit."

"I don't think we can get much further today, so tomorrow, our visit to SyroTech, do you want us to come here or will you pick us up from the hotel?" DCI Johnstone asked.

"We'll pick you up about 9.00 am; it's on our way. What do you hope to find out there?"

"Well, for starters," DCI Johnstone answered, "I want to know what their relationship is with the company in Manhattan, what company it is and whether Shackleton's son has any connection with either company. It would be good to find out what they know about the backgrounds of Shackleton and his colleagues. Some questions need to be asked and answered."

THE UNVEILING

ALMOST ON THE DOT AT 9.00 am next morning, Judd Templeton, with Shane Tyson driving, arrived at the hotel where DCI Johnstone and Dani Taylor were ready and waiting. It was an hour's drive to their destination, and they arrived with time to spare for a 10.30 am appointment.

The meeting took place in the boardroom with Constance Hewitt, research director, and Howard Carson, managing director. After introductions, DCI Johnstone jumped straight in.

"Tell us, please, about your employees lost in that accident in 2005."

"That was a terrible blow to our company," Constance Hewitt said, "and set us back several months, as Arnold and Conrad were two of our top researchers and no one was able to continue on the work they'd been doing. Peter, of course, was an enormous loss too, as he was very much the driving force of the company. I took over his role, but he was way ahead of me, and I've been running to catch up ever since."

"What were they doing in Manhattan? What company were they visiting?" Dani asked.

"SyroGenics was the company they were visiting and, as their name suggests, they were researching similar work to us. We were considering working together on one aspect of research into dementia. We'd both been working on this for some time, but coming at it from different directions, so we were looking into pooling our resources. We'd both recently experienced partial success, so we reasoned that together we could have achieved the breakthrough we were pursuing."

"Did you hear anything from your people after they left SyroGenics for the return journey?" Dani asked.

"Yes, and that's the strange thing, we got a text from Peter that said, 'Disaster! Talk later.' SyroGenics were the ones who initiated the idea of working together, and they were pushing to persuade us to send a delegation only days prior. Since then they've refused to talk to us, so we've no idea what went wrong."

"Hmm, interesting. Well, we have some information that might multiply your concerns," DCI Johnstone announced. "Peter Shackleton didn't die in that crash – he was in the car, but we have reason to believe that he rolled clear before the impact. He was badly burned, so must have been very close, but he lived to tell the tale – except, of course, he didn't tell."

Hewitt and Carson both looked decidedly shocked and bewildered.

"Not killed," Howard Carson exclaimed shaking his head, "but there were three bodies in the wreckage, so what are you saying?"

Sergeant Templeton continued the story.

"Your employees Sanderson and Jameson were in the wreckage, but the third guy was not Peter Shackleton. As far as we can ascertain, the third guy was likely Peter Shackleton's son – their DNA comparisons were close, but not exact. That point was somehow missed or not followed up at the autopsy."

"This doesn't make sense," Constance Hewitt responded, "if he was alive, why didn't he come back? He loved his work and what about his wife? He was always praising her; they were devoted to each other. Are you sure about this? Surely, there's some mistake?"

"No, Ma'am, there's no mistake," the sergeant reassured her.

"So, where is he? Was he so badly injured that he couldn't return to work?" she persisted.

"I can partly answer that," DCI Johnstone interjected, "no it wasn't his injuries that prevented his return, though we're at a loss to know what went wrong. By one means or another, he changed his name to John Channing and travelled to the UK, but he turned up dead recently, murdered."

"Aw gees!" Howard Carson said with raised eyebrows, "you've got be kidding, why would anyone murder him? He was the nicest guy you could wish to meet. Why the UK and why John Channing? I can't believe it."

"So, you can't think of any reason he was on the run? And what could his grown-up son be doing in the car?" There was a short pause, then he asked quietly, 'Why do you think Conrad Jameson was driving Shackleton's car?"

Both men looked extremely bewildered. The news of Peter Shackleton/John Channing's demise in the UK was so surreal, and it made no sense whatsoever.

Dani broke the silence that had descended on their meeting.

"Who were your contacts in SyroGenics?"

"There were three guys as I remember it," Constance replied, "Jacques Sompater, Peter's opposite number, Jerry Bushall and Kate Ford."

"Woah, did you say Jerry Bushall? Are you sure? Did you ever meet him, and do you know what he looks like?" Sergeant Templeton asked.

"Well, yes, I'm sure that was his name," Constance responded, "and yes, I met him once at a convention. He's about five eleven, and I'd say 210 pounds, dark hair, slightly balding and has a tattoo of a bush on the back of his left hand."

"The son of a gun!" Sergeant Templeton exclaimed. "That's the guy I'm sure. You Brits have a saying I think, 'Poacher turned gamekeeper', except in his case I can't believe he has turned. That guy was a hardened drug user, well known as a pusher and violent with it. Call it a suspicious mind, but I reckon that guy's up to his same old tricks and using Syro-Genics to legitimise his business."

"Do you think Peter Shackleton found out what was going on through his son who perhaps worked there?" Dani asked, "or maybe Bushall got heavy handed with the SyroTech delegation, trying to force them on board with drug production in the two companies?"

"That sounds quite feasible Ma'am," Sergeant Templeton replied, "I think my men need to make a surprise visit to that company."

"Sergeant," Dani began tentatively, "was there anything in the report on what they thought was Peter Shackleton's remains that suggested that he'd experienced recent violence?"

"You'll appreciate, Ma'am, that the bodies smashed on impact and subsequently incinerated. Any additional trauma would have been difficult to detect. Anyway, let me look at the report again."

He'd brought the report with him, so he opened it and began to read. "No...not...really, broken bones, but that could have been from the crash and a cracked skull – again, it could have been caused by the impact."

"You have a theory Dani," DCI Johnstone interjected, "I know that look. What's on your mind?"

Dani looked at him and smiled.

"Hmm, you may well be right. We were wondering, weren't we? Why was Peter in the rear seat and not driving? Well, what is more, natural than for a parent to tend to their injured child – I believe that was what he was doing. His son had probably suffered a violent attack, and most likely Bushall was the perpetrator if he is the thug you say he is, Sergeant Templeton. Is there any way we can find out whether Peter's son did work at SyroGenics?"

"It's a bit of a problem, Ma'am, when we don't even know his name," the sergeant said, shaking his head.

"Hang on a minute," DCI Johnstone broke in, "do you have a missing person list? Think about it, even if we don't know who he was, somebody somewhere must be missing him. Did anyone file a missing person report about the time, or soon after, November 8th, 2005?"

"That's a good point; I'll put in a call to the station and find out – shouldn't take long."

The sergeant left the room.

"Sorry, you don't want to hear all this police business I'm sure," DCI Johnstone said to the SyroTech leaders, "and I'm sure you've got a company to run."

"It's quite intriguing listening to you all," Howard Carson responded, "but I guess we should leave you to it, there may be things that it's best we don't hear. You're welcome to stay on here – can we send coffee in for you all?"

"That would be very kind," DCI Johnstone replied, "but we'll try not to commandeer your boardroom for too long, we don't want to interfere with your business in any way."

"You're not intrusive at all, we rarely use this room, so take all the time you need. Shout if you need anything, we're only next door." With that, they left, and next moment the coffee arrived.

Five minutes later, the sergeant returned.

"Well, it appears you could be right about missing persons, there were, in fact, two rounds about then, one on the 10th and another on the 14th. The one on the 10th was a Chester Clinton, and the one on the 14th was a Jez Campbell. Officers are checking these two as I speak, attempting to get DNA samples. It's a longshot after all this time, but if someone's kept some momentum, we could be in luck."

"So, what are you proposing regarding the Syro-Genics firm?" DCI Johnstone asked.

"A team is going in unannounced this afternoon; they have warrants to search the premises and to seize anything suspicious. I have a feeling they would be fortunate and unearth a significant black-market drug operation. I hope we can tie Bushall in to it all. It's just a pity we can't pin anything on him regarding Shackleton's son, but who knows."

"We are going back to the UK the day after tomorrow, but we are keen to hear how things go at SyroGenics and to know whether you get DNA from the homes of either of the two missing persons. Will you keep us posted?" requested DCI Johnstone.

"I sure will, and in case we don't see each other again before you leave, thanks for coming, I appreciate your input and you, if I may say so Ma'am, you've got a very sharp mind, and I could do with you on my team."

"Believe me, Sergeant, and I appreciate her tremendous attributes. I especially value her brilliant mind, without Dani's reasoning we would often struggle, so you may covet her, but there's no way I could do without her."

"I think it's time we were leaving gentlemen," responded the embarrassed Dani.

Back at the hotel, both DCI Johnstone and Dani immediately went to their rooms. Dani did want time alone to ponder the day's activities and see if she could make anything of it.

It seemed incredibly unlikely that events in America could have any connection with what was happening in the UK, yet she had a nagging belief that somehow, there was a connection. Was it just coincidence that three members of the Shackleton family died mysteriously? Oh yes, she was fully aware that officially Shackleton junior had been killed in that horrific collision, but had he died from wounds inflicted back at SyroGenics before the crash happened and is that why Peter was happy to abandon his son before impact?

That was another question – what was SyroGenics producing? She was confident that research was just a cover, and ideally, the police raid would clarify that. Ah, a thought – to where were they exporting their wares? Did it include the UK? Is that the connection between America and the UK? It was essential to ask Sergeant Templeton to get that checked out by his team. She paused in her thinking to call the sergeant and very soon he'd wholeheartedly agreed with her reasoning and promised to prime the team immediately.

Back to her thoughts, she found herself focusing on Peter Shackleton and the likelihood that his son had revealed the true nature of SyroGenics' business. Did they threaten to blow the whistle and did that led to an attack on Shackleton junior?

"Hmm," she wondered out aloud, "I'm still not convinced that the smash wasn't deliberate – rather a drastic way of silencing them though. But how could they have engineered it? No, perhaps I'm wrong on that score."

One thing was sure, whoever wanted to silence them knew very well that Peter hadn't died in the crash, but they weren't able to locate him and deal with him before he fled to the UK. They certainly caught up with him in the UK, and that to Dani was proof that there was a link between the two countries. Her thoughts returned once more to the crash, as she couldn't help but think that it was too much of a coincidence that the accident was a chance happening, but that brought her back to the question, how could anyone engineer it? Hmm, perhaps a homing device planted on the car. Did Peter expect an attempt on their lives so was therefore primed for action? Was her thinking too far-fetched?

Once more, Dani called Sergeant Templeton.

"Sorry Sergeant, it's Dani again, hi. Do you remember we talked about the DNA of the tanker driver? Did you ever get an answer?"

"Nothing yet Ma'am."

"Could you check it out please and get back to me?"

About ten minutes later, the sergeant called back and broke the news.

"The lab only has DNA results for the occupants of the car, and there is no report for the tanker driver. The transport company are certain that it wouldn't be Selwyn Davison as he was their most reliable driver – he'd been with them for twenty years. However, they haven't seen him since. My team are looking into this matter again. We can't recheck the tanker; it's gone for scrap, and that was a big mistake on our part."

Dani was once again deep in thought when a knock came on her door. She assumed it was her boss and went to open it, but as she did so, a man dashed straight at her brandishing a long-bladed knife. Since the attack by Simon Goodfellow, Dani had been brushing up on her self-defense moves, so as he came at her, she dived to her right and at the same time lashed out with her left leg against the attacker's shins. He fell heavily and, in the process, stabbed the knife into his left shoulder. Before the assailant could recover, she leaped to her feet and then knelt on his neck and shouted for help. DCI Johnstone's room was just across the corridor. His response was swift, and together they were able to secure the attacker.

"Dani, you seem to have a knack of attracting attackers, but this time you did very well to defend yourself and turn the tables on him."

The man was bleeding profusely, so they applied a towel to stem the flow and called the police and medics to the scene. Sergeant Judd Templeton was one of the officers who came, and he took one look at the assailant and recognised him immediately.

"Officer Janson, why am I not surprised? Well, this time you're on the receiving end, you're under arrest for attempted murder and dereliction of duty." Meanwhile, the medics treated the wound and then took him to the hospital, accompanied by another officer to guard him.

"I am so sorry Ma'am," Sergeant Templeton addressed Dani, "are you okay? I hope you haven't damaged your shoulder again. As you will have gathered, that was the bad egg I talked about, and very soon he would be on the receiving end of my anger, and he'd better start singing if he doesn't want to be locked up for the rest of his life. I hate corrupt officers, but hopefully, he'll realise it's in his interest to cooperate. Again, I'm sorry ma'am, we don't normally treat our visitors that way."

"Don't let it bother you, Sergeant, I'm not hurt, and he allowed me to practice my self-defense," Dani said with a laugh.

After the sergeant left, Dani and her boss went down to the restaurant for dinner, and she brought him up to date with her thoughts and the information provided by Sergeant Templeton.

"I'd been thinking about that terrible crash, and you know it now seems pretty certain to me that someone planned it. I called Sergeant Templeton, and he confirmed that no one had seen Selwyn Davison since the incident. Although it seems unlikely that he was driving that day and obviously, they can't check for DNA in the tanker's cab, as they've scrapped it. So, whosoever drove the truck remains a mystery."

"This whole case seems to get bizarre by the minute – it makes you wonder just how many victims there are out there. Still, Selwyn Davison is a problem for the local police; we have enough bodies of our own. It sounds to me as though that mind of yours has been working overtime again. I expected you to take time to rest, but I guess I should have known better. Did you have any other thoughts?"

"Nothing significant. I was thinking about Peter Shackleton and wondering why anyone would want to murder the three, well four, men in the car and it occurs to me that they somehow found out about an illegal drug connection in SyroGenics and most likely from Shackleton's son – we need to know whether he worked there. Anyway, why the murders? I reckon they were going to pull the plug on SyroGenics and put paid to a very lucrative side to their business."

"Yes, I'm with you on those thoughts. We do need to know how the raid goes, that might tell us whether the son did work there. We also need some joy on the DNA of the two missing persons from around the time of the crash. We can tie up some loose ends if we can get that information. I was also wondering why the two companies were considering joining forces, and the only conclusion I can come to is that it strengthens the illusion that SyroGenics is entirely legitimate."

"Hmm, that's very likely," Dani agreed. "Incidentally, I also asked Sergeant Templeton to check where SyroGenics export to – I'm betting the UK is a major customer."

The next day they had nothing planned, so decided to do the tourist thing – to see the sights, visit a few places and generally relax. They had an early flight back to the UK the next morning, so that evening they needed to pack and get a good night's sleep.

Sergeant Templeton had their contact details and promised to call with any news. It was a most enjoyable day and included a boat trip on the Hudson River, and that was relaxing as it included a meal on-board.

Soon after 4.00 pm, they were back at the hotel. A little later, they were sitting in the lounge, and DCI Johnstone's phone indicated that a text had arrived. It was from Judd Templeton and said, 'Raid successful, illegal drug op, six arrested including Jerry Bushall – pleading innocence! Phone link with a Jenson Luxton (holder of truck Licence – possible tanker driver - pursuing). Exports – many overseas, major = UK – London Pharmaceuticals. Obtained DNA – both missing persons, Chester Clinton match – worked SyroGenics. Phone later.'

Dani punched the air and yelled.

"Yes, result!" causing many to look in her direction. "That is fantastic news, don't you think?" she said in a more restrained voice.

"Absolutely, the best, thank you, Judd, you've come up, trumps," DCI Johnstone replied triumphantly, "we can return to the UK happy people – lots of loose ends tied up and some answers to our questions. Now, all we have to find out is when Peter Shackleton's alias John Channing travelled to the UK, where he lived, whom he knew, and who killed him. I reckon we know why – a massive drug operation."

LONDON PHARMACEUTICALS

LATER THAT EVENING, THEY SPOKE to Judd Templeton and thanked him for all his help and co-operation and he, in turn, expressed his appreciation for the way they'd helped to clear up a massive drugs operation. They bid their farewells, and after a couple of celebratory drinks, Dani decided to call it a night and went to her room.

Dani felt more relaxed than she had in a long time, and her mind was free from her normal thinking state. She sent a quick message to Luke, 'Flying back tomorrow morn. Missing you, love you loads.'

She didn't wake until her alarm call at 5.45 am. She showered, dressed and carried her bags down to reception. Her boss wasn't there but arrived moments later. The drive to the airport was uneventful, and once they'd checked in, they intended to go through to have breakfast, but before they could do so, pandemonium broke out after them as a loud gunshot rang out.

Instinctively, they dived to the ground and shuffled towards whatever cover they could find.

Other passengers were screaming and running in sheer panic, but DCI Johnstone yelled for everyone to hit the deck.

Two more shots rang out, the bullets ricocheting from the floor near them. Then two further, much louder, shots rang out, and it was all over.

Security had stepped in, and the gunman shot. He was not dead but severely wounded – they rushed him to hospital for emergency treatment.

Thanks to DCI Johnstone's timely warning, there were no injuries, though a number required treatment for shock.

"It has to be said," DCI Johnstone remarked calmly, "they don't give up, they're pursuing us to the last, but why us I don't know."

The police held them for questioning for about an hour. DCI Johnstone then asked them to speak to Sergeant Judd Templeton, who immediately vouched for them, and when the officers took their statements, they could leave. They missed breakfast, but they caught their flight. It was a relief to board the plane, and soon they were airborne and winging their way home.

There was an enormous feeling of joy for Dani as she walked into her own space once more. She'd missed the familiarity; here she felt free and able to do her own thing. She was looking forward to going back to work on Monday, and as tomorrow was Sunday, she would have the whole day to unwind.

Dani looked around her kitchen, wondering what she might have for dinner and it was then that she found the fridge and the cupboards fully stocked. Inside the refrigerator of all places, she found an envelope, which she quickly opened. It was from Luke – a lovely welcome home – he had done the shopping for her, but the most exciting thing of all was the final sentence, 'I've got a new job with a firm located in Kerington Mews, so I'm moving there permanently – I hope you can cope with my presence every day.'

What a fantastic welcome home it was. She'd cope with him, oh how she'd love having him there. Just then, the door buzzer sounded, and she tentatively answered it.

"Hello?"

"Hi, I wondered if you had anything to celebrate and whether you needed help in doing so?" A voice answered.

"Luke!" she yelled, "Yeah, come on up. You are just what I need."

They talked long into the night, making plans, sharing news and enjoying each other's company. The weekend was over far too soon, but the consolation was that in just a few weeks he would be starting his new position and then they could focus on sharing their lives, especially as Luke was suggesting they bring their wedding date forward. Dani liked that suggestion; she liked it very much.

When her colleagues saw Dani in the office, there inevitably came the jibes, "Did you enjoy your holiday?"

Not to be phased, she was quick to answer.

"Fantastic, I can recommend it – did you get my postcard?"

James Cartwright brought the situation back to reality when he asked, "we saw on the news that there was an incident at the airport, someone with a gun, did you see anything of it?"

"Not a lot," Dani replied, "we were lying low on the floor, but we heard the bullets ping close beside us."

"You're joking. You were there when it happened?" James questioned.

"Well sort of, we were the targets, and the boss was great in yelling at folk to hit the deck. Security shot the gunman, and he's now in hospital. I expect the boss will fill you all in about our 'holiday', it was quite eventful, and that attack was not the first, but I'll leave him to bring you up to speed."

As if on cue, DCI Johnstone came out of his office and called everyone to order. "Okay everyone, let me tell you all about our little holiday as you seem inclined to call it. It was extremely profitable and has clarified a lot of things." He went on to share chapter and verse of their activities, highlighting all that they'd discovered and especially everything appertaining to their ongoing investigations about Leslie and Peter Shackleton.

"Okay," he continued, "Dani, will you follow through on London Pharmaceuticals, as you're familiar with their supplier in the States. James, will you organise a trawl of the airlines from the States from the 15th of November 2005 and see if you can identify when either Peter Shackleton or John Channing arrived in this country. Another line of enquiry that needs to pursuing is electoral rolls, James; you're in charge of that – where was Peter Shackleton or John Channing living? We also need to know whether he knew anyone and his purpose for being here. It may be that he wanted to expose the massive drugs trade and those responsible for killing both his son and his colleagues. Anything to add Dani?"

"Yes, one thing, those involved in the whole setup are ruthless, violent and extremely dangerous. They have killed many people already, and they have nothing to lose if they kill again, so watch your back and don't take unnecessary risks. Busting their network means they've got everything to lose business wise and they'll do anything and everything to preserve it."

"Dani is right, you've seen what has happened here, well in America it was even more violent and we, Dani especially, experienced first-hand the extremes to which they're prepared to go. So, don't underestimate the enemy. Okay, let's go!"

Dani immediately set about her allotted task – investigating London Pharmaceuticals. She fully expected that the name would be merely a front whose purpose was to deceive any casual onlooker into believing that it was a bona fide company. In the event, she found that such a company did exist, listed in a region to the south of Kerington in the borough of Bakerston – 147 Chery Lane. Dani vaguely knew the area, it was a commercial region, but upmarket compared to some. The website listed it as distribution depot, servicing pharmacies across the whole of London and the southeast.

"Hmm," Dani thought to herself, "surely that can't be a distributor of illegal drugs, sounds too genuine to me, but I suppose that's how they mean it to sound."

Dani made for her boss's office and knocked on his door.

"Sorry to bother you, Sir, but I've just looked up London Pharmaceuticals, and their website shows their location as 147 Chery Lane, Bakerston. It looks genuine, but I suppose it would. What do you think, phone them or pay them a surprise visit?"

"Most certainly the latter, that way it's possible to study faces and body language. Jenny Seymour can drive you there unless she's out or tied up elsewhere, is that okay with you? I wish I could join you, but I have a meeting upstairs. I get the impression they think it's time we wrapped everything up. Sometimes I think the powers that be forget what it's like at the coalface – perhaps they'll have a few magic wands we can use," he muttered sarcastically.

"Jenny will be fine, Sir. She's an excellent colleague and very alert. We'll go just as soon as she's free. Thanks."

Jenny had just finished what she was doing and was delighted to be able to get out of the office for a while. Like Dani, she preferred to be able to get hands-on with cases. Sometimes background checks, though essential, could be monotonous and frustrating, especially when after the hard slog, someone else did the follow through.

"How are we going to handle things today, Serge?" Jenny asked as they travelled towards their destination.

"Come on, Jen. It's Dani when we're on our own. I think we must improvise. We'll see if we can get to meet whoever is in charge and ask about their past association with SyroGenics. We need to particularly read body language, see what they do say and even what they don't say. They're not going to admit to any dodgy dealing, but we need to ask whether anyone in the company could handle illegal drugs without anyone else knowing about it."

"So, do we ask to see literature – invoices, delivery notes, distribution dockets and the like?"

"Yes maybe, if we can. We can't demand to see anything without a warrant of course, but if they volunteer the information, that's all good. Don't be afraid to jump in if anything occurs to you. You may see or think of things that I don't."

It took thirty-five minutes to reach Chery Lane, and London Pharmaceuticals was hard to miss, its bold sign stood out prominently as they turned into the road. There was a decent carpark on the premises, so they were soon able to enter a spacious and well-decorated reception area, beautifully laid out with potted palms and other plants. It was very welcoming.

They approached the reception desk, where two immaculately dressed receptionists were waiting to greet them. Both officers produced their warrant cards and asked to see an executive of the company.

"Ah, you need to see Dr Christina Bolland, I'm sure she will be able to answer all your questions, but if she can't, I'm sure she'll know who can. Please have a seat for a moment."

It was only a moment, and then one of the receptionists escorted them through to a very comfortable office. After introductions, Dani explained the reason they were there.

"We are part of an investigation team working on the murder of Leslie Shackleton, the estate agent from Kerington – no doubt you've heard about it or read about it in the press."

"Indeed, I have," Dr Bolland responded, "dreadful business, but didn't I hear of a second more recent murder? Do you think there's a serial killer on the loose?"

"No, no, it's nothing like that, but we do believe they're connected, and drug-related. Please, could you tell me whether you purchase any of your drugs from American drug manufacturers?"

"I'm sure we do because we purchase a tremendously wide variety of drugs as you can well imagine, and we source the most commercially viable suppliers possible. The NHS is our biggest customer, and you know how the government have reduced budgets recently, so we try to obtain the best possible deals wherever we can. Is it one particular drug you're interested in?"

"No, not one particular drug," Dani answered, "rather it's one particular supplier, SyroGenics of New York."

"I'm sorry, I've never heard of such a company – are they new?"

"I have no idea how long they've been in business, but they're certainly not a new company, and they were looking to enter into a joint enterprise with SyroTech – is that a company you've heard of perhaps?"

"Ah, yes, SyroTech from Staten Island – yes I've visited them on more than one occasion. Now let me see, whom did I meet? Yes, Peter, Peter Shackleton.

Oh, Shackleton – is he related to the murdered Shackleton?"

"Sadly, yes, his brother," Dani explained, "he and some of his colleagues were involved in a terrible accident as they returned from a meeting with SyroGenics, three people died, but Peter escaped though with serious injuries."

"Oh, my goodness, I must get in touch with him, he and his wife Jean were very kind in entertaining my colleague and me when we were over there."

"Sorry Doctor, that won't be possible, Peter has since died, and Jean is staying with her sister-in-law in Kerington at present."

"That is awful. How did he die? Was it his injuries?"

"No, it wasn't anything to do with his injuries, it is yet another death we're looking into, and he died in this country, in fact, it was the second victim you alluded to, however, that's why we're enquiring about SyroGenics."

Dr Bolland suddenly jumped to her feet and went to a bookcase to the right of her desk. She selected a book and returned to her desk.

"This is the ultimate guide. It lists drug manufacturers, suppliers and outlets. Now this American firm, SyroGenics did you say?"

"Yes, spelt like SyroTech, but capital G, then lower case 'e, n, i, c, s,'" Dani said.

"Hmm, okay...Syro...no SyroGenics, only SyroTech. It just isn't listed, I don't think it can be genuine," Dr Bolland concluded, "do you have a specific reason for asking us about this company?"

"The American police raided SyroGenics and uncovered a massive illegal drug manufacturing process. In the course of their investigations, they checked their distribution list, and London Pharmaceuticals was their major UK outlet."

"No way," Dr Bolland protested, "this company would have far too much to lose to allow even a sniff of anything illegal. Every single one of our customers is a major retailer and highly reputable."

"Is it possible that someone in your organisation could be intercepting incoming illegal drugs and forwarding them to local outlets unbeknown to you and your colleagues?" Jenny asked.

"No, because everything we receive is barcoded and that registers origin - the supplier, contents, batch number and our unique order code. Anything received from a fake source would not scan, so would automatically trigger an alarm. It must be that way, and we must be meticulously careful that what we receive is what we've ordered and that there can be no possibility of cross contamination. That's the electronic side of things, but then our staffs unpack the goods, and the three checkers manually ensures everything is perfect. They looked at different aspects of the consignment."

"And there is no possibility of anyone bypassing the system, by removing something before it goes through processing?" Jenny pressed her.

"Well...er...I hadn't thought about it from that perspective – yes, potentially someone could, I suppose. You have me worried now."

"Do you have any CCTV coverage of the receiving area?" Dani asked.

"Yes, indeed we do, we have cameras everywhere in our office premises monitored by security guards day and night. Would you like to view the recordings?"

"That would be very helpful, but is it possible just to see the recordings from the camera covering the receiving bay?"

"Oh yes, every camera is independent. You won't need to sit through hours of recordings. It's possible to fast-forward between deliveries. Let's go to the control room now."

Dr Bolland led them past the laboratories, various offices and the storage room. At the farthest end, they came to the receiving bay and overlooking the bay was the security control room with its banks of monitors. Two men were in the office, but Dr Bolland explained that there were three security guards in total, two were always in the office, and the third patrolled the premises both inside and out. The two guards glanced round as they entered and then swiftly returned to scrutinising the screens.

"Bob," Dr Bolland addressed one of the men, "we want to view goods inward for say last Thursday please."

Bob extracted a recording from a rack and slotted it into a monitor that sat on a desk to one side. Dr Bolland operated the controls and expertly fast-forwarded through times of inactivity and allowing them to view the handling of all receipts. It took a comparatively short time to finish the day shift and then it showed the night shift. There were only two-night deliveries – nothing appeared untoward. Dr Bolland was just at the point of changing to another day when Dani stopped her.

"Doctor, please will you rewind to the second delivery please?"

They watched the process through a second time, and Dani noticed something.

"Back again please – there," she whispered, "the guard received a call on his mobile just before the consignment was received. Can we see the recordings from last week Wednesday? Fast-forward to the night deliveries, please. Okay," she said, "nothing there, what about Tuesday?"

They repeated the process for each day, but found nothing – "Okay, what about the previous Thursday?"

She inserted that recording and forwarded to the night shift and that night, and there were three deliveries.

"Please rewind to the second delivery and observe," she whispered, watching the screen intently before the vehicle pulled into the unloading bay, the same guard received a call.

They repeated the process for Thursday night shifts, and everyone revealed the same guard and the same phone call.

"Thank you, gentlemen," Dani said. "Sorry to have disturbed you. We'll leave you to it now."

Dr Bolland looked a little bewildered by Dani taking the initiative, but a wink from Dani persuaded her to go along with it. Once they were clear of the security office.

Dani explained, "sorry if that took you a little by surprise, but I believe we've found out how illegal drugs are brought into the country through your company."

"I don't understand what you saw that makes you think anything illegal is taking place? I didn't see anything untoward," Dr Bolland said curiously.

"Every Thursday evening the same guard was on duty in the receiving bay, and during that evening, just before one particular delivery, the guard received a phone call," Dani said, "I think that phone call may be significant."

"Do the security guards always receive incoming goods?" Jenny asked.

"Yes, that's part of their role," the Doctor replied, "only security touches anything until it's passed through security checks, and then the drugs pass into the storage bay."

"Is it possible for security to bypass the scanning process on an incoming package?" Jenny continued to question.

"Well supposedly not, but now you have me worried that someone has found a way. However, theoretically, even if someone has found a way to bypass the scanning, which incidentally is by machine, it's not a hand scanner, so there's no way anything can get into the system without going through the scanner. For instance, if anyone attempted to carry an item through a door, an alarm would sound. If an operative were to attempt to carry a water bottle or lunch box through, the alarm would sound."

"It sounds foolproof I have to admit," Dani said, "but I believe something is going on and I'd stake my reputation on it having a connection with SyroGenics. What we witnessed on those recordings was too regular to be just coincidence and innocent. That security guard, I'm sure, was part of some elaborate process. By the way, do you know his name?"

"Yes, it's Patrick Jennings, he's Irish, and has been with us about twelve months now. All our employees are police-checked before they're taken on."

"Dr Bolland, does Patrick Jennings always work the night shift?" Jenny asked.

"Yes, he does. We have a team who permanently work the night shifts. Believe it or not, some prefer nights to days – I can't understand that myself, but there's no accounting for people's preferences."

"Before we go, may we quickly see what happens once items have cleared the scanner?" Dani requested.

"Yes, of course, it's through this door here." She pressed the door lock code and led them into a sizeable room where goods were unpacked, and the contents checked against their order code.

"At this stage, we double check that our supply complies with what we ordered."

"Is this operation carried out overnight too?" Dani asked.

"Oh no, it wouldn't be profitable to employ anyone this side of the scanner during the night. Whatever comes in waits here till the day shift comes on."

"So, goods stand here overnight...does security have access to this room during the night?"

"Yes, of course, they have access to all areas and are required to check all areas day and night."

"Okay...so Patrick Jennings, for instance, could come in here after the goods have come in overnight and what...could he send a particular package through the rest of the system undetected?"

"Oh, my goodness! Well yes, I suppose he could, the system doesn't cater for a rogue security guard – but of course, we're still not certain that he is rogue. Your line of enquiry is deeply worrying and distressing. I thought we ran a tight ship, but now I'm not so confident. All this because an American company named us as its main customer. We do need to resolve the issue, urgently; otherwise, we're going to have to suspend trading until we've sorted it and that could cost us millions of pounds. Did you say the American police raided SyroGenics and did they close them down?"

"Yes, they did carry out a raid," Dani responded, "but I can only assume that the police have closed them down completely and, of course, they could have other bogus companies or branches. No doubt the American police will be pursuing such connections."

"Do you ever get mismatches?" Jenny asked the doctor, wishing to distract her from her worries.

"Extremely rarely, but yes it can happen, and if it does, then it is sent through to the returns department where they talk to the supplier and arrange for its return. Returns must have barcodes, which the supplier forwards to us online. The incorrect or faulty goods are then re-packed, and arrangements made with a carrier to collect and return them. All correct goods go through to stock control and eventually to distribution. Our whole company is highly sophisticated and rigorously controlled throughout – it has to be, as our customers have to be able to trust us."

"Quiet," Dani said, "I fully appreciate you have an excellent procedure in place, but I fear someone has breached your security. I could be wrong, of course, and I hope for the company's sake that I am, but a little niggle tells me I'm not. I rather think Patrick

Jennings is feeding packages containing illegal drugs through your company's system himself, even down to labelling."

"Oh dear, I suspect you could be right," Dr Bolland said in a worried tone.

"Please don't breathe a word about our suspicions to anyone," Dani said, "we don't want to forewarn any guilty party. We need to talk to our superiors now and decide how to proceed, so we'll leave you to get back to your work, and we'll be back in touch with you very soon."

Back at the station, they shared the details of their visit with DCI Johnstone and DI Cartwright, explaining what they'd seen on the CCTV recordings and the procedure within the organisation for receiving deliveries and processing incoming goods.

"So, what's your gut feeling about the company? Are they complicit with any illegality or have people breached their security?" DCI Johnstone asked.

"The latter, wouldn't you say Jenny?" Dani asked.

"Oh yes, Doctor Bolland came over as entirely genuine and extremely worried about any possible breach of security, or any connection with illegal drugs for that matter. She was entirely open and helpful."

"So, what's your theory for illegal activities in the company – how are drugs getting through?" DCI Johnstone questioned.

"Well, I believe it begins with the security guard, Patrick Jennings. He has found a way to bypass the mechanised security check on incoming shipments, though how he does it, we don't know. Beyond the scanner, which is supposed to authenticate goods coming in, is the room where goods are unpacked and checked against company records. They send mismatches to despatch, who supposedly report errors to the supplier and arrange to return them. In practice, I believe that Jennings, who has access to all departments overnight, is pushing the package through the system himself and finally labelling it for despatch to rouges like Barraclough, though under what name I don't know."

"Hmm, sounds feasible," DCI Johnstone said quietly, "do you have any ideas on how to investigate this further?"

"Is it possible to put some of our people alongside theirs to watch how things are done?" DI Cartwright asked.

Dani shook her head.

"No, though that would have been the ideal way – the rooms are too small for that. I think the only way is to do it through their CCTV system, but I don't think the security guards can investigate because we can't be sure who's involved in the scam. Ideally, we need to put our people in to watch the monitors and, if their system allows it, zoom in on the operatives as they perform their tasks – especially Patrick Jennings as he does whatever he does to bypass the scanner. Though I don't know how we could get our people in to replace theirs."

"Could we get our people to pose as engineers from the manufacturers of their system to go in to check that everything is working to its optimum?" Jenny suggested.

"Ah, now there I think you have the beginning of an idea, Jenny," the DCI enthused, "we could get someone from the manufacturer to go in with us to watch the monitors. An expert would know what they see, whereas we might not. Contact Dr Bolland, Dani, and see if she is agreeable and get details of the company that installed their system – we need someone available to help us. It was Thursday evenings you said it always happened, is that right?"

"Yes Sir, always Thursday nights, actually in the early hours of Friday morning."

"Okay, go ahead and keep us posted," the DCI instructed.

THE ROUTE EXPOSURE

WITH THE HELP OF THE DI, Dani set up the surveillance at London Pharmaceuticals for the coming Thursday night. A representative of the company 'Total Security Systems' was part of the team and was one of the original installation engineers. Dr Bolland had arranged for all of them to go in at four o'clock in the afternoon on the pretext that they were there to check that the system was working correctly and to adjust where necessary – a requirement demanded by the insurance company and not far from the truth, as the insurance company was always demanding upgrades.

The difficulty Dr Bolland had was what to do with the two security guards in the office while leaving Patrick Jennings still operating outside. The last thing she wanted to do was arouse any suspicions. Eventually, she came up with the idea of giving them the night off (fully paid) and offering Patrick Jennings a future night off in lieu. All were happy with the arrangements.

The team that went in consisted of Dani Taylor, James Cartwright and Joel Temple. While the engineer from Total Security Systems, Lucas Jenkins, went into the receiving bay to talk to the security guard there and to watch the scanner in operation, Dani, James and Joel, posing as engineers, stood alongside the day shift security guards in the office. They questioned them intelligently about the working of the monitors, alarms etc. – asking if they ever had problems, such as screens blacking out, alarm failures or even false alarms. They asked how often system checks were carried out, alarms tested, and system malfunction tests pursued.

"Very occasionally a screen will go blank for a few seconds," one of the security guards said, "but then the picture returns as normal. We've also had occasional false alarms, but they are rare. Generally, the system is good and works well."

They recorded everything, as the data would be useful for compiling a report for both the installation company and the insurance company.

Shift changes took place at 6.00 am and 6.00 pm – each shift working 12 hours, three days/nights per week. The company closed on Sundays, so security was minimal and outside only. Security guards operated on a rota, having an extra shift every few weeks. The day the surveillance team were working only Patrick Jennings arrived and Joel Temple, posing as an engineer, met him to put him at his ease.

"Hi, you must be Patrick, I'm Joel. As you are aware, we're carrying out a full check of the system, so as far as you are concerned, do what you normally do, and we'll be monitoring the system from the control room. Are there any problems with the system from your perspective, anything you feel needs adjusting?"

Patrick Jennings had quite a broad Northern Irish accent, which was very noticeable as he replied.

"No, I've never noticed any problems, the machine works well, and I've never heard any complaints from others either."

"That's great, thanks, I'll leave you to it. Have a good shift."

It was 2.10 am before any activity, and then a courier arrived at the gate and Patrick opened it for the driver to enter the receiving bay. The engineer observed as Patrick fed a package into the scanner, but he did nothing to arouse any suspicions.

Dr Bolland had come into the office to supervise the surveillance and stood watching the screens herself. James Cartwright spoke to her.

"Dr Bolland, why do you have night deliveries?"

"As you may well imagine, some drugs are very popular and sometimes very urgently required, so we need to have them on the premises so that they can be processed and shipped to our customers very early next morning. There are many days when drugs are in and out in a matter of an hour or so. We have to run a very slick operation."

The screens in the control room monitored all activity throughout the company, so Patrick Jennings appeared as he patrolled the outside of the premises. The site was comparatively small, so it didn't take him long to complete his tour, and then he made a quick sweep of the offices. He looked in on the control room and was surprised to find Dr Bolland there.

"Oh, hello Dr Bolland," he said, "I didn't expect you to be here. Surely you're not doing a double shift?"

"No Patrick I'm not, but I felt I ought to be here to oversee the system check, so tomorrow and Friday I'm not going to be in the office, I'm going away for a long weekend."

"Good idea, I think I'll follow your example when I take my day in lieu."

Just then, his phone rang. "Oh excuse me. I rather think that might be another delivery on its way. Sometimes drivers phone ahead so that we're ready and they are no delay."

The monitor covering the receiving bay picked him up, ending his call and opening the gate. Dani addressed Lucas Jenkins, the engineer.

"Right Lucas, this could be it, watch closely and see if he does anything differently when he puts it through the scanner."

Jennings had his back to the camera when he received the box from the driver and placed it on the roller conveyor at the entrance to the scanner. He signed the driver's delivery note and then reopened the gate for the vehicle to turn and drive away. Then, he returned to the scanner and, still with his back to the camera, seemed to turn the box around, push it along towards the scanner and then press the button for the scanning process to begin. In the office, the results of the scan flashed onto one of the screens. It said the package was from 'Lelland Pharmaceuticals' and the contents 'Candesartan tablets.

"Is that a bona fide delivery, Dr Bolland?" asked Lucas Jenkins.

"Well, yes, the delivery is from one of our suppliers and one of the drugs we purchase from them, so it all looks genuine."

"But is it your unique order number?" James asked.

"It certainly looks genuine, but that would be checked in the morning by the day shift."

"Dr Bolland," Dani said urgently, "can we go through to the room beyond the scanner before Patrick Jennings comes through please?"

Dr Bolland led the way, and Dani went straight to the box that had just come through. It looked quite normal at first, but then she noticed that the label with the barcode had curled slightly at one corner. She peeled it back and revealed that there was another barcode beneath.

"That, I would say, is how the scam works – Jennings places a false barcode over the original."

"So, what happens then?" James Cartwright asked.

"Ah, that's the bit I don't know," Dr Bolland replied, "I do know he'll come in here soon, so we need to go and watch the screen for this room."

Dani replaced the false label, and they all left the room. About twenty minutes later, the screen showed Jennings entering the room. He began moving boxes away from the scanner exit. To anyone watching, Jennings was tidying the room ready for the day shift, but as they watched closely, he placed the box in question on the conveyor to despatch. He glanced around the room as though checking that everything was in order and turned towards the door. Just then, the screen went blank for about four seconds and then returned to normal. Jennings had gone, and a sharp-eyed Dani noticed that the box had gone too.

"Whoa," Dani said, "how did he do that?"

"Do what?" James asked, "Do you mean the screen, blackout?"

"Well yes, but move the box too, it's gone," she remarked, a puzzled look on her face. "Lucas, is it possible for someone to cause a camera to blackout?"

"Well...er...yes, theoretically I guess so – some signal jammer would do the trick, but I've never come across anything like that. Do you think Jennings caused it then?"

"Yes, I do, and it was just enough time to deal with the box. What would Jennings do with it, Dr Bolland?"

"Simple, a quick push would send it through to despatch, but it would need to have a proper label for the despatchers to deal with it."

"So, could he have swapped the labels at that time?" James Cartwright asked.

"Maybe he could," Dr Bolland responded, "he seems pretty adept at sleight of hand. Anyway, we need to see whether he goes into despatch now."

He didn't. Instead, he returned to the receiving bay with a cup of tea and a sandwich. He was a very cool customer. While he was consuming his snack, they went to despatch and found the box. Sure enough, the guard had changed the label, and in fact, it now had a return label on it addressed to SyroGenics, 245 Westminster Road, Newham, London E3. They made a note of the address. Maybe, just maybe, it would lead them to Barraclough and the heart of his little empire.

"So, what do you suggest now?" asked Dr Bolland, "It's clear that Jennings is committing a crime in laundering drugs through this company and I want him off these premises as soon as possible. That man is putting our name and our future in serious jeopardy, so please remove him immediately."

"We will gladly, Dr Bolland." James Cartwright answered, "he has many questions to answer. He doesn't come over as a hardened criminal though, I rather think he is a victim somewhere down the line, so hopefully, he'll talk to us once we get him back to the station."

James called for transport for a prisoner and then went down and arrested Jennings, cautioning him as he did so. The moment James arrested him, his eyes filled with tears.

"Thank goodness that's over with, I hated doing it, but I had no choice."

"Save your confession for later when we're back at the station, and then I hope you will unburden yourself. Patrick, do the right thing, and it will be to your advantage."

Transport was not long in coming, and they whisked Jennings off to the station. Meanwhile, James went back to talk to Dr Bolland.

"Well, he's on his way, but I have to say he was quite relieved, he's obviously got himself into deep water and didn't know how to get out. It may not count for anything as regards your company's reputation, but I do believe he may yet make some restitution. Can I recommend that you update your system, Doctor? You need more cameras that view departments from different angles, and you need to talk to Total Security Systems about upgrading the CCTV cameras. From our point of view, I want to thank you for allowing us to disrupt the running of your security system, but to cover you until the day shift come in, I will stay and watch the monitors and Lucas has agreed to stay with me."

"That's very kind of you DI Cartwright, but I can't let you do that. I have a couple of colleagues who are on call, and I can contact them, and we can cover everything between us."

Having snatched a few hours' sleep, James and Dani didn't turn in at the office until after lunch. They'd taken with them the box of drugs that Jennings had attempted to pass through the company. The box was evidence against Jennings, though neither James nor Dani felt that he would need the evidence to make him talk.

"Tell us, Patrick," James Cartwright said when they interviewed him later, "how you came to be involved in the drug scene and passing illegal drugs through London Pharmaceuticals."

"I started using class 'B' drugs when I was about fifteen, but my supplier kept pushing me to try something stronger, so eventually I gave in. I've never injected, and I couldn't take to snorting, but swallowing pills has never been a problem. What was a problem though was that I began to want more stronger pills. I couldn't pay for my habit, so I borrowed more and more money. I owed thousands of pounds, and I still do, because the interest increases faster than I can pay it off. Anyway, along comes this guy and he says he's the one I owe the money to, and he comes up with the idea of me passing the drugs through the company. I hated doing it. I loved my job, and I loved the people, but he said I either do it or he would hurt my family."

"Do you know the name of the guy you owe money to?" Dani asked.

"Yeah, it's Barraclough, Royston Barraclough. He's a right thug, and I'm no match for him. Anyway, he never comes alone. He's always got two of his cronies with him – I think one's called Khan and the other's Porter – those two fancies themselves when they're with him, but Barraclough is both the brains and the brawn I reckon."

"Do you know where any of them are living?" James Cartwright questioned.

"I don't know for certain, but I remember one time one of them mentioned Broxton, though I don't know exactly where in Broxton."

"What do you know about the address the box of drugs was meant to go to – 245 Westminster Road, Newham, London E3?" Dani said.

"I know nothing about that address at all; Barraclough simply sends the labels to me."

"When did you first start to launder the drugs through London Pharmaceuticals?" James said.

"This week is the sixth week, and it's just been one box each week, but I get the impression that the contents of each box are worth many thousands of pounds on the street."

"Do they feed your habit now?" Dani asked.

"No, no, they don't, I've kicked it completely, and I'm never going back to it either, even though they put me under a lot of pressure to do so. I will completely change my life if I can get rid of my debt; it's a millstone round my neck. If my girlfriend waits for me, then I'm going to ask her to marry me. I know I've completely blown it with London Pharmaceuticals, but I'm still going to ask them to consider taking me back again – a forlorn hope I know, but I live in hope."

It was a comparatively short interview because Jennings pleaded guilty to the charges against him of laundering drugs. After consulting with the CPS, they charged him for the offence. For his safety, they remanded him in custody. In normal circumstances, bail would not have been out of the question, but here there was a serious threat of reprisals by Barraclough.

Next on their agenda was an investigation into SyroGenics at their supposed London address. It was something Dani was anxious to investigate, so the first port of call was to check with Companies House. As she suspected, there was no such listing, and this, she felt sure, was a clear indication that it would just prove to be a front for the drugs ring to receive supplies. She passed the information to James Cartwright.

"Are you free to come with me to pay them a visit?"

"Sorry Dani, I'm not at present, but if Jenny is free, why don't the two of you go? How are you going to play it? Because someone will certainly be there – you can't just turn up and waltz in there, it could be dangerous."

"Yes, that's true, but what I thought was perhaps we could watch the place for a while and observe activities in and around the premises. I'm taking a camera, so we can get pictures of everything and anyone who shows. Perhaps a raid could come later, but we need to know how the land lies."

"That sounds reasonable, but please be careful and be safe. Call for backup if things go wrong or if anything is kicking off there."

Jenny was delighted to be going out again, especially as it was with Dani. They had a great rapport and understood how each other's minds worked.

"Where to boss?" she asked in a friendly tone.

"Well, supposedly SyroGenics is at 245 Westminster Road, Newham, do you know the area?"

"Hmm, vaguely, but we have satnav. SyroGenics, that's the company in the States, isn't it?"

"Yes, but the London address is what was on the parcel we confiscated at London Pharmaceuticals. I don't know what to expect, but I rather think it will be a front for the drugs ring. We're only going to observe, to see how the land lies, and then later we'll need to carry out a full-scale raid."

It took about an hour to get there through the London traffic, but as they turned into Westminster Road, they noticed it was a thriving district in the Docklands Area. They drove slowly along the road, and suddenly Dani spotted a sign on the front of a building, 'SyroGenics'.

"Wow, I'm amazed!" she exclaimed, "I didn't expect it to be that sort of place, but it looks quite legitimate."

"Hmm, it's quite a nice building, nice sign and in quite a good area, are you sure it's not a legitimate company?"

"No, it isn't, well, not if the American company was anything to go by and we certainly know that Jennings was helping them by laundering illegal drugs through London Pharmaceuticals. Anyway, Jen, let's go and turn around and then park on the other side, about where that lamppost is, and then we'll have a good view of what's going on."

From their position on the opposite side of the road, they could see the whole of the building, but it was quiet, and Dani was concluding that the place was deserted and that their surveillance was going to prove fruitless. However, they didn't have to wait long before a small van came along and stopped outside SyroGenics' premises. Interestingly, the van had the same logo on the side, "Boy they've gone to a lot of trouble to make the company look legitimate. No one would suspect that it was anything other than genuine," Dani said, snapping away with her camera.

"Maybe it is genuine," Jenny suggested, "but they have this side-line in illegal drugs – it could be that Barraclough has coerced them somehow."

"Hmm, I don't think so Jen, there's no such company listed. Come on, whoever you are, get out of the van, let's see who you are."

"I think he's on his mobile," Jenny responded, peering through the windscreen.

Just then the driver's door opened, "Ah, here we go, turn this way – yea, Barraclough, I thought it would be you," Dani said triumphantly.

She continued to snap away as he walked towards the entrance. He pressed a bell and moments later the door opened, revealing Ali Khan. They stood there talking, and it was apparent that Barraclough was not happy. Dani opened her side window a little to see if she could hear anything – there were loads of expletives and something about 'not delivering goods'. Khan replied, but his voice was inaudible, and then Barraclough's booming voice responded, "Jennings is a dead man." He turned and climbed back in the van and drove away at top speed.

"Oh dear, I'm afraid we've upset Mr Barraclough, he was expecting a delivery that didn't arrive and now, no doubt, he's gone to pay Patrick Jennings a visit."

"Dani, these people don't know me, how about I go and pay them a visit on the pretext that I'm looking for a job – I might get to see inside?"

"Tempting Jen, but no. James distinctly said 'no risks' and I think he's right, we don't know what or who's the other side of that door – these are ruthless thugs. So, thanks for offering, but I think it will be better to set up a raid for another day."

They stayed in position for another hour or so and were on the point of thinking that nothing else was going to happen when the door opened again, and this time both Khan and Porter emerged. Both looked extremely serious, probably rattled by Barraclough's diatribe. He was not a man they want to mess with, and there was no knowing on whom he would vent his fury. They left, striding along the pavement away from Dani and Jenny.

"Tell you what Jen, it could well be that there's no one there now, so we could take a sneak peek around to see how the land lies behind the building."

They made their way across the road and entered an alleyway that ran to the side of the building. It led to a small yard at the back, and there was little sign of upkeep, with weeds growing in profusion and rubbish strewn everywhere. Unlike the front of the building, the rear looked very dishevelled, with broken guttering, dirty brickwork and boarded-up windows. There was a rear door, but that didn't look as though anyone had used it in years.

"I think we can say that this place is just a front in more ways than one," Dani remarked derisively, "tell you what Jen, we will press the bell now – I think it's unlikely anyone's in, but if someone does answer, I'll ask if Luke Frazer works here."

"Who's Luke Frazer?" Jenny said with a frown.

"Come on, Jen, Luke – my fiancée," Dani replied with a laugh.

Ringing the bell produced no response. People were only there when they were expecting deliveries.

"My guess is, this place is yet another storage place for their drug stocks, and it could be quite a profitable raid if we could catch Barraclough, Khan and Porter here. Anyway, we'll have to see what the boss thinks," Dani said.

James Cartwright was out when they arrived back at the office, and DCI Johnstone had company. Dani and Jenny returned to their desks, but moments later DCI Johnstone called Dani into his office.

"Dani, this is CI Charlesworth of the drugs division. He is deeply concerned that you were in danger of compromising their operation today. It appears they have a surveillance team watching the premises you visited today."

"Yes, we do," CI Charlesworth remarked officiously, "and you very stupidly went up to the building, round the back and then pressed the bell. What on earth did you think you were doing?"

"Excuse me, Sir, but we were doing our job. For a start, no one informed us of any operation by the drugs team, so how could we know to keep clear? Additionally, Sir, I think we know the people involved better than anybody and our enquiry ultimately is about murder, which I think eclipses a drugs operation."

"Sergeant, I think you are treading on dangerous ground with your remarks. Remember, I am your superior, and I expect greater respect."

"Jerry, you are not superior to me, and I agree with DS Taylor, your department was in the wrong by not informing us of your operation. Also, we reserve the right to pursue these people. We know that Royston Barraclough has committed at least one murder, but possibly more, and he is probably holding a woman captive somewhere, so there's no way we're drawing back from the case. We will keep you informed of our operation, and we fully expect you to keep us informed of whatever operations you are carrying out. It is extremely likely that we will be carrying out a raid on those premises, if DS Taylor's report tells us what I think it will, so if your people want to be part of that raid fine, but remember, Barraclough is ours if he's on the premises. Now, if you don't like any of that, then I suggest you take it up with Andy Mann – we are working to his instructions."

"Bill, we are working for the same team you know, you don't have to be heavy-handed. Yes, we'll co-operate with you, but we expect the same courtesy."

"I have no problem with that," DCI Johnstone countered, "but please be aware, I am fiercely protective of my team when they're doing their job."

Charlesworth got to his feet and reached out his hand firstly to Bill Johnstone and then to Dani.

"Thank you both, I think that's been useful and cleared up a few issues." With that, he left the office.

"Cleared up a few issues indeed," DCI Johnstone snorted, "pompous ass, he's only interested in scoring points. You may have been a bit direct with him Dani, but by golly, I was with you all the way. Anyway, how did you get on at SyroGenics?"

"Well, we were surprised to start with, as the building looked quite legitimate. It had a well-produced sign and clean-looking frontage, but that's where it ended. The rear was just the opposite, very run down. More to the point though, Barraclough turned up in a van that again looked genuine, even to the logo on the sides. He was not happy and as far as we could hear it was because he thought Jennings had let them down – "He's a dead man" were his words. We also saw Khan and Porter. Yes, we rang the bell, but only to ascertain if there were others after that Khan and Porter left. If we can time it right, I think a raid is in order."

"Hmm, I agree, but we need to time it so that Barraclough is on the premises too, so how do we guarantee that?"

"Sprats and mackerel come to mind," Dani suggested, "what took him there today was the hope that there was a delivery, so perhaps we should guarantee that delivery and that way entice him there. We have his drugs, and we could arrange to deliver them, wait for him to turn up and strike."

"Yes, it's a tempting idea, but we are going to get some stick if we lose that evidence. Oh, come on, nothing ventured, nothing gained. I'll clear it with Superintendent Mann, we need to keep him in the loop, and then I suppose we'd better invite the drug squad to the party."

THE SECRET UNWRAPPED

SUPERINTENDENT MANN APPROVED the plan, and everything was set up for the following day. An officer, posing as a courier, would deliver the goods the next morning. As the drug squad's surveillance team were already in position, they would radio in when the drugs arrived and then radio in again when Barraclough came. DCI Johnstone didn't like being dependent on the drugs team but felt he had little option – both sides needed to work together harmoniously.

"I just hope Khan and Porter are there when the courier arrives," a concerned Dani said to her boss, "this isn't going to work if they're not. They normally receive the delivery on a Thursday, so they won't be expecting it."

"That could foul the whole operation. I suppose we don't by any chance have a phone number for any of them?"

"No Sir...well, hang on a minute, maybe Patrick Jennings had a contact number on his phone. Dani dashed down to the basement to check his personal effects. Fortunately, his phone was charged but looking down his contacts list, but there was no number for either Barraclough, Khan or Porter. There was only one other option, Jennings himself. She went along to the custody suite and asked to see him, and the custody officer escorted her to his cell.

"Patrick, we need your help, how do you contact Barraclough to let him know that a delivery is on its way?"

"I just text 'YES' to a number – it's 7984."

"Thank you, Patrick, that's another tick in your favour."

She returned to DCI Johnstone and told him what she'd found out.

"Good work, Dani. Okay text him and let's see if it works."

Forty minutes later, the surveillance team called to say that Khan and Porter had just turned up and gone inside the building. On the strength of that, the officer posing as a courier arrived on a motorcycle and rang the bell. Porter answered, signed for the delivery and immediately went back inside. The question was, would Barraclough turn up and could the team make a successful swoop? DCI Johnstone and his team were by this time poised and ready to surround the building to prevent anyone from escaping. The call came through that Barraclough had just driven up but was again sitting in his van and talking on his phone. DCI Johnstone planned to swoop the moment Barraclough went into the building, but CI Charlesworth had different ideas and decided to go in immediately.

"Go, go, go!" he yelled, and his team sprang into action, sprinting towards the van and the building. The moment he heard the shout from Charlesworth, Barraclough also sprang into action. He started the engine and, with tyres screaming, he drove away at high speed. The car that DCI Johnstone was in turned into the road at that precise moment, DCI Johnstone saw the van shoot away and ordered the driver to give chase, but Barraclough had a head start on them. He was quickly out of sight. The roads in that area were a rabbit warren, so despite their searching, neither he nor the van was anywhere in sight.

"The blithering idiot," growled DCI Johnstone, "Charlesworth's a glory seeker, and he just couldn't wait to go in as planned, so now we've missed catching Barraclough – goodness knows where he'll go to now."

They drove back to SyroGenics where Charlesworth and his team were congratulating themselves on a job well done.

"Two arrests and a drug haul worth millions of pounds," he gloated.

DCI Johnstone took him to one side and laid into him.

"What the blue blazes did you think you were about? You knew the plan, and yet you couldn't wait for us as arranged. Don't you realise what you've done? You've lost our main quarry. I told you we had to catch Barraclough, and he's most likely responsible for two murders, and the life of a woman is in his hands. Your idiotic impulse may well have put that woman's life in jeopardy. You haven't taken drugs worth millions off the street, those drugs were a plant, a sprat to catch a mackerel and you knew it."

"Come off it man, we had a good result, and it's just sour grapes with you because you didn't get to call the shots. You shouldn't have been involved in the first place, this was always our operation, and we've achieved our goal."

"Achieved your goal – how can you say that when you missed catching the main man behind the operation? You think you achieved your goal, but at what cost? You just don't get it," DCI Johnstone responded angrily, "anyway, I want Khan and Porter, they're part of our investigation, so be aware, you haven't heard the last of this – we will be interviewing them."

With that, DCI Johnstone walked away, leaving Charlesworth smirking outside the building. DCI Johnstone felt certain that Superintendent Mann would have something to say about Charlesworth's action because he was under pressure from above to clear up the murders urgently. The press was making a meal of the fact that nothing seemed to be happening, not in their eyes anyway, though the force knew differently.

It was a very complicated case, a double murder, a missing person and a widespread drug ring, all intertwined. Charlesworth had set them back considerably because Barraclough was a key element and very nearly in their grasp. The arrest of Khan and Porter was a significant step in the right direction, but in DCI Johnstone's mind, the fact that they'd failed to arrest Barraclough along with the drugs put a dampener on the whole operation. While Barraclough was at large, it could be guaranteed that his operation would spring up somewhere else. Drugs was a lucrative business on the scale at which they were operating, so there was no knowing where the centre of operation would emerge next.

DCI Johnstone was correct in his estimation of Superintendent Mann's reaction to CI Charlesworth's premature move on SyroGenics, he was furious and immediately sent for the offending officer. Mann wasn't one for raising his voice unduly, but that day Charlesworth's dressing down was audible throughout much of the station.

"Your stupid, idiotic action has set us back considerably. Royston Barraclough was within touching distance of arrest, but your ridiculous point-scoring action allowed him to escape. You knew very well what the arrangements were and although there was no obligation for you to be involved in the operation DCI Johnstone was willing to share the action with you, but that was on the understanding that he called the shots. He's your colleague, man, and you abused his trust in you."

"Sir, I must protest most vehemently, you were not there, and in my estimation, there was a danger of the whole operation compromised by the fact that DCI Johnstone's team had not turned up. I had no choice but to act. My officers attempted to apprehend Barraclough, but he was just too quick for anyone to prevent him from leaving."

"That is precisely my point. The plan was to WAIT until Barraclough left his van and went into the building. Your action was disgraceful, and I will not protect you if the top brass call for an investigation, which I've no doubt they will. Now get out of my sight, but know this, you haven't heard the last of it."

Charlesworth still had a smug look on his face when he passed through CID to return to his own office. He even didn't accept any wrongdoing on his part. His demeanour was that of someone who felt that in the long run, he'd be exonerated. After all, his team had arrested two wanted men and taken possibly millions of pounds worth of drugs off the street.

Khan and Porter were charged with drug offences, and DCI Johnstone demanded that his team should now conduct interviews with them. He designated James and Dani to carry out the interviews and James set the ball rolling as the first interview was with Ali Khan.

He further cautioned him and then began the interview.

"Mr Khan, you are already facing a long sentence for drug-related offences, so it will be in your interest to co-operate with us in our investigation. We know that Royston Barraclough has committed at least one and probably two murders and we have photographic evidence that you associate with him, so unless you can convince us otherwise, we are inclined to charge you with being an accessory to murder."

"You can't do that," Khan protested, "I ain't killed no one. I'll hold my hands up to the drug offences, but you ain't fitting me up with no murder."

"Okay, then the best thing you can do is to start talking. Who killed Leslie Shackleton and then his brother Peter?"

"I'm saying nothing, Barraclough will kill me if I open my mouth."

"Right Sergeant, charge him with being an accessory to murder."

"No, stop – let me talk to my brief," Khan leaned across to his solicitor and having done so responded. "Listen," he continued, "if I tell you what you want to know, I want an assurance of police protection – I don't want to find myself in prison with Barraclough, he's a maniac and will stop at nothing."

"We'll make a note of that, and you will be protected," James answered.

"Barraclough killed them both. I wasn't even in the area when he killed the first guy, but he's always boasting about what he did to him – Barraclough cut off his tool," he said, pointing to his groin, "and he bled to death."

"What has Barraclough done with the body?" Dani asked, "where is it now?"

"I don't know exactly," Khan answered, "except that it's something to do with Bob Bright – I heard him talking about it one day."

"Bob Bright," Dani questioned, "do you mean the Robert Bright who's in custody on drugs charges?"

"Yeah, that's him, but I don't know what the connection is."

"Okay, well let's now talk about Peter Shackleton, what happened to him?" James asked.

"I don't know no Peter Shackleton, is he something to do with the other guy?"

"Yes, his brother – ah, perhaps you know him as John Channing – does that ring bells?"

"Channing, yes, I've heard of him. Yeah, Barraclough did for him because he was threatening to expose the whole organisation. Came in from America spitting blood and threatening murder, so Barraclough got in first – tied an electric wire around his neck and hoisted him over a door."

"Were you there when he did it?" Dani questioned.

"No, but I walked into the building soon after, you know, the building where we were arrested, and he

I FELT HIM DIE

was still hanging there, it was horrible. Barraclough said he'd do that to anybody that crossed him, and I believe he would – he's deranged. I hate that guy, but once he's got you, there's no getting out – everybody's scared stiff of him."

"Has anyone asked you about the garage you rented from Leslie Shackleton, the one in Barnett Street?" Dani asked.

"Yeah, that bloke Charlesworth, he's taking us there tomorrow morning. I don't like him. He's a right self-opinionated idiot."

"How did you and the others come to be involved with Barraclough in the first place?" Dani asked.

"We all had a drug habit, and we all got into debt with Barraclough. That's how he recruits people, he feeds their habits and then presents them with a bill they can't pay. He then demands that folks work off their debt, except that nobody ever can – he won't let them."

"What do you know about Angela Talbot?" Dani asked.

"I know who she is, but I know nothing about her except that she's a posh prosy."

"So, you don't know where she is?" Dani pursued the matter.

"No idea, I didn't know she was missing."

"And you've never heard Barraclough say anything about a woman he's holding, or worse, killed?" Dani pressed him.

"No, sorry, nothing at all."

"Okay, Mr Khan, thank you for your co-operation," James said, "I've made a note of your concerns regarding reprisals, and we'll make sure we give you protection."

The interview with John Porter followed a very similar pattern, and he eventually agreed to co-operate and offered the same information. These two were minor players and were almost victims themselves, albeit of their own making.

"Well," James said, shrugging his shoulders, "I don't think we have further else, except that we now have two testimonies regarding Barraclough's guilt, though only Peter Shackleton's case would stand up in court, the other is hearsay."

"Don't be despondent Guv," Dani said reassuringly, "we have to pursue every avenue, and we do have a slight lead – Khan said that the body of Leslie

Shackleton was connected to Robert Bright. We need to talk to him and see what he knows."

"Yep, good point Dani, will you pursue that line? Pay him a visit in prison if necessary."

Dani retrieved the case notes for Bright to check his home address, but unfortunately, it merely said, 'No fixed abode'. No next of kin was listed either, so the only option was to talk to him. She contacted the prison and arranged to visit next morning. Fortunately, he was local, so once again, Jenny did the honours by driving her there.

It proved to be a fruitless visit, and he was not forthcoming with anything useful, merely insisting that he'd stayed with friends and that he had no family. It was back to basics, time to think things through and hope that something came to mind that would give them a decisive lead. One point that did immediately come to mind was whether anyone had found out when Peter Shackleton went to the UK and where he'd been living. She made a mental note to ask James about it when she got back to the office.

She went straight to see the DI when she arrived back and reported her fruitless visit to see Bright.

"By the way Guv, did you ever find out when John Channing arrived in the UK and where he was staying?"

He picked up a sheet of paper from his desk.

"Funny you should ask that I've just received this report. He came to the UK on the 12th, but despite extensive enquiries, they couldn't find out where he was living. My guess would be a guest house or a hotel. Did you ask for a reason?"

"No, just dotting I's and crossing T's. I think we've already discovered why he was here and what connection he had with Barraclough. I think it's certain that somehow Barraclough had Chester Clinton murdered in that horrendous road smash, probably because he opposed the manufacture and distribution of illegal drugs and threatened to expose SyroGenics for what it was. He and the delegation from SyroTech – which included Peter Shackleton – were all supposed to die, but of course, Peter Shackleton or John Channing, as he called himself, escaped and vowed to avenge his son by destroying Barraclough and his evil empire. Unfortunately, though, Barraclough landed the first lethal blow. I know some of that is speculation, but I reckon if we could prove his motive, that wouldn't be far from the truth. I think Barraclough controls a bigger empire than any of us have ever considered."

"Well Dani, you convince me – yes, I too believe Barraclough wields great power and influence and that on a worldwide scale, far greater than any of us even know. We must get him and soon before he can wreak any more havoc and ruin more lives. What we've achieved so far, both here and in America, must have hurt him greatly and that makes him even more dangerous – he's a wounded animal. I think it's time for you to get that thinking hat of yours on again," he said with a grin. "We desperately need something to go on."

As the day ended for them, Dani determined to use her evening to do some thinking. Even though it was work-related, she enjoyed it and found it relaxing.

So, after a quick meal, Dani settled back in an armchair with a small glass of wine by her side. She was not much of a drinker, but a small glass of red – well, it touched a spot. Her mind didn't just focus on Barraclough, even though he was an urgent priority, but especially on Angela Talbot and Leslie Shackleton. For Dorothy Shackleton's sake, she desperately wanted to find the body; she was a dear lady who needed closure.

"Angela, Angela, where are you? What has he done with you? Please, God, let her be alive and keep that monster at bay," she pleaded quietly. Somehow and for some unknown reason, she felt that Angela was alive.

Barraclough's van, she suddenly thought, that could help track him perhaps. No doubt he'd have painted over the logo, but it seemed unlikely that he would get rid of it, as it was comparatively new. They knew the vehicle's registration, and they even had photos showing it. He might have had changed the plates, of course, but it would be worth circulating a description and its primary colour, surely, he wouldn't have had it resprayed in such a short space of time.

First Dani decided to set that in motion the next morning. She ran the idea past both the DCI and DI and both agreed it was worth a shot, they had nothing to lose.

Mid-morning a call came in from an officer on the beat to say that he'd seen the van on London Road. Traffic then picked it up on a street camera and was able to follow it to Westminster Road in the Dock-lands area.

"The cheeky blighter, he's surely not going to the SyroGenics premises?" the DI said, "he'll not get in if he does, it's been sealed off."

A car had been despatched to try to intercept him before he left the area again, but when they arrived near SyroGenics, he was nowhere in sight. They cruised the area and eventually spotted the van parked close to one of the docks. They parked out of sight, and four officers approached on foot. There was no one in the truck, and there was no sign of Bar-raclough anywhere around. They hid nearby, and half an hour later, a man walked out of a nearby cabin and towards the van. They waited until he had climbed into the truck and then rushed him. He looked at them in utter shock.

"Hey, what's going on," he yelled, "what do you want?"

"Who are you?" one of the officers asked, "I'm Larry Warner, so who are you?"

They all produced their warrant cards.

"We're police officers," one of them replied, "what are you doing in this van?"

"I'm going about my lawful business. Why? What's wrong? This is not a restricted zone, and anyway, I have business here."

"Whose van is this?" one of the officers demanded.

"It's mine. I bought it this morning. It was going cheap, and it was just what I needed. I've got insurance cover if that's what you're concerned about and it has eight months' MOT."

"Who did you buy it from?"

"The guy said his name was Dave, and he worked for SyroGenics. He told me the company gave him the van instead of severance pay – it seems the company has closed down. It was parked on the side of Yeovil Street, the guy had just parked it and put the 'for sale' sign on it. I bought it there and then – would you believe it, he only wanted six hundred quid for it. I painted over the logo – it's only water-based gloss paint, so just a temporary fix."

"And you had that amount of money on you?" the officer asked sarcastically.

"No, of course not, but there was a branch of my bank just around the corner, so I went and withdrew the cash."

"What did the guy look like?"

"Not one to argue with, all muscle and tattoos, but average build with dark brownish hair swept back and to one side. I should say his nose was broken at some point, and it's healed bent to the right. He was wearing a white tee shirt with a dragon logo, and blue jeans and black trainers."

"You seem to have noticed a lot, Sir, are you sure you hadn't seen him before?"

Larry Warner laughed.

"No, I hadn't seen him before, but my main job is recruitment, so I notice things about the people I meet, it helps me to assess them. It's not my only work. I also run an outdoor clothing and equipment shop on the High Street called 'Fair or Foul Supplies', hence the need for a van."

"Okay Sir, sorry to have bothered you, feel free to be on your way."

After he'd gone, one officer rang CID and told them what had happened.

"It wasn't Barraclough, he's sold the van, and it was the chap that had bought it that we located. He described the man he bought it off, and there was no doubt, it was Barraclough. Sorry."

It was a very frustrating time for CID and Dani felt it. Every avenue they explored led to a dead end. There had to be a solution, an open road somewhere, a way of tracing Barraclough and finding Leslie Shackleton and Angela Talbot. The latter especially bugged her a lot – what was she going through? How was she being treated? Was she still alive? Shackleton's body must be seriously decomposing by now. Surely no one would keep a putrid body anywhere near them, so had it been dumped or...what, frozen? Yes, that was the most likely scenario and if that were true, then finding it would be nigh impossible. Surely something positive had to come along soon.

It so happened that later that day a dog walker was walking his dog in a small copse near the river in the Greenwich area when he saw a man dump something substantial into the river and then drive off in a filthy, rusty, grey van down Gypsy Lane towards the main road. He managed to get a partial registration – Golf, Tango, Romeo 6. He thought it was a Commer van.

"Did you get a description of the man?" the officer taking the call asked.

"About average height, very muscular and had tattoos," he said. The officer passed the information to

CID, and immediately DCI Johnstone called his team to attention.

"Listen up, everyone. There's just been a reported sighting reported to us of someone, probably Barraclough, dumping a heavy object into the river at Greenwich. According to the eyewitness, the approach to the river is along Gypsy Lane. He was driving an old Commer van, and we have a partial registration – Golf, Tango, Romeo 6. It's a dirty and rusty grey vehicle. Jenny, organise SOCO and a dive team to meet us there. James, Dani and Ravi with me."

It took about fifty minutes to drive there, as they encountered roadworks en route. Gypsy Lane was challenging to locate, as it was nothing more than a dirt track; however, with the help of a local, they found it and drove along to the river. It wasn't hard to see where the van had been. It had reversed to the river's edge, tyre tracks showing in the damp earth. "Don't tread on those tyre tracks," the DCI yelled, "we might need to take impressions of those."

Just then, the SOCO team turned up, closely followed by the dive team. SOCO immediately got to work on the tyre tracks, while the dive team started kitting up and getting their equipment ready.

"Sir, there's a bloke with a dog just over there by the wood, shall I see if it's the same bloke that reported the incident to us?" Ravi Ahmed asked.

"Yes, do that Ravi and, if it is, see if he can tell us anything more about what he saw. Get his name, address and phone number, we may need to contact him again."

Two divers gently lowered themselves into the water. It was quite fast-flowing at this point and the water level raised due to recent heavy rain. Ropes attached them to their colleague on the bank, so there was no danger of the current sweeping either man away. It took just a matter of minutes for them to locate the object. The object was immersed in approximately ten feet of water, and the difficulty would be lifting the heavy object clear and up a further four feet of the embankment. They slipped webbing slings beneath the object and with everyone pulling together and the divers pushing from below they were eventually able to hoist it onto the bank. It was the right shape and length for a body, but the suspect had wrapped the body in black plastic and weighted with stones, it was impossible to determine who or what was inside. It was now down to the SOCO team, and they needed to preserve everything, as anything might well be useful in identifying a suspect, or later used as evidence in a trial.

It took quite a long time to remove coverings, as strong cord tied everything together. Undoing the knots was made more difficult due to their soaking in the water. Eventually, they were able to remove the final covering and reveal the body; there was no doubt, it was the body of Leslie Shackleton. The body was well preserved and displayed no signs of decomposition. Despite his time in the water, his trousers showed the symptoms of massive bleeding in the groin region.

"We can do no more here," one of the SOCO team announced, "we need to get him back to the mortuary and carry out a full post-mortem. I think, though, you know some of the answers already."

The CID team was much relieved. It had been a long, drawn-out investigation, which shed loads of frustrations along the way.

"I'd like to say we can relax for a while now," DCI Johnstone sighed, "but that won't happen until we capture the elusive Mr Barraclough – oh how I'd like to get him off the street."

"Of course, Sir," Dani interjected, "we still must find Angela Talbot too, and we don't know where she is and whether she's alive or dead."

"Oh, how right you are, of course, it would be so easy to forget her amongst all the rest that's going on. Anyway, first things first, we need that post-mortem report."

ABDUCTION

IT WAS A FULL TWENTY-FOUR hours before they received a message that the mortician had something for them. DCI Johnstone and Dani went down to see what she'd discovered.

They arrived at the mortuary, and the DCI greeted the mortician.

"Good morning, Shan, what do you have for us?"

"Well, let's deal with the injuries firstly," she replied. "The man has multiple fractures to his jaw; his left cheekbone has been shattered, his left eye socket smashed, and his eyeball burst. You probably know that someone removed his penis and there are deep cuts to the inside of his thighs, which on the left has severed the main artery. He died from traumatic shock and severe loss of blood. His killer kept him in a deep freeze for some time, so it's difficult to pinpoint the time of death, but it's not in the last few days."

"I think we know from his wife exactly when he died, but hers is not scientific evidence, just a feeling – she 'felt him die' and can pinpoint it to the exact minute. However, we do have the evidence of Simon Goodfellow – he was present when Barraclough used the knife that did the damage."

"Wow, as you say, Mrs Shackleton's testimony is not exactly scientific, and it wouldn't stand up in a court of law, but we could take her date and Goodfellow's testimony as an indication of when the killer inflicted the fatal wounds. My report, therefore, will reflect that information."

"That's good enough for me. Is there anything else?"

"Yes, at some point, he was taken out of the freezer and laid on the ground; as a result, he picked up debris from his surroundings. I found grass, pine needles and, most especially, ceramic clay of all things. Wherever he was it was outside, and at some point, in time, ceramic clay had been present there. You may well be looking for a site near an old ceramic work, although it could equally be a home industry."

"You're not saying the clay was quarried locally, just scattered on the ground – is that it?" DCI Johnstone asked.

"That's right, not a quarry, but yes a scattering – not necessarily a considerable amount, but probably a significant quantity."

"Thank you very much, that's extremely helpful. Will you let us have your report as soon as possible, please?"

"Later today, unless anything unforeseen crops up."

"Should we let Dorothy Shackleton know now, Sir?"

"Yes, indeed, give her a call and ask if we can visit a little later."

Dani called her and asked about visiting and immediately Dorothy knew the purpose of the visit. When they arrived, she welcomed them as usual and took them through into the lounge.

"You've found him, haven't you?" she asked tearfully.

"Yes, we have Dorothy," Dani replied softly, "earlier today we recovered his body. We will need formal identification, but we believe it is Leslie. We are so sorry."

"Well, I knew all along it was only a matter of time, but I'm glad it's over. Did my Leslie suffer?"

"Sadly, we believe he would have," Dani replied slowly, "but it may not have been for long."

"Oh, poor Leslie. Do you want me to come and identify the body Sergeant?"

"At some point yes, but only when you feel up to it Dorothy."

"If it's convenient for you, I'll come with you now," she said.

Dorothy carried out the identification with her typical dignity, asking for a few moments alone to finally weep over him. Afterwards, they returned her home, where Jean, her sister-in-law, was due to come and stay again. It was good that they could grieve together and be there to support each other. Surprisingly, Dorothy never asked why Leslie's body had not commenced decomposition.

On their return to the station, they went straight to the office and Dani immediately set to work researching local businesses and crafts producing ceramics. There were no full-scale businesses, so she turned her attention to home industries. Here she had more success. There were three listed, though none still operational. One was of interest – a small operation called 'Kitchen Crafts' and the premises were at 63 Jardine Road. It closed in 2008.

"Bingo!" she yelled.

Everyone looked round and grinned.

"It's okay, Serge," one of her colleagues said with a grin, "you're the only one playing."

Jardine Road was in the right area, not far from the industrial heart of the region. Who lived there now was a matter of priority, she needed to find out, and that involved the electoral register.

A call to the local council office should provide that information, she reasoned. She gave them a call.

"Oh hi, my name is Detective Sergeant Dani Taylor, and I need information from the electoral register concerning an ongoing murder investigation. Yes, it's 63 Jardine Road, Broxton."

"That property, along with most others in the area are empty," came the reply. They are all due for demolition shortly."

Thank you. Just one more thing, presumably there is no electricity on the site?"

"Not at that property, but there is one dwelling, next door, in fact, that someone is still living in – it's number 65."

"Can you tell me who lives there, please?"

"Yes, it is a James Bright, and at present, he is refusing to leave, but a compulsory purchase is due to be activated in the next few days. The occupant will have to leave and be relocated to a flat not too far away."

"Thank you. You've been most helpful," Dani said, putting the phone down.

"Hmm, all very interesting," Dani said to herself, "Just a coincidence that the cottage industry was at number 63 and someone with the name Bright still lived at number 65? I think not."

An elated Dani Taylor looked round, hoping that DI Cartwright was at his desk, but he wasn't.

"Anyone knows where James is?" she called across the office.

"Called out on a job," came a response, "said he didn't expect to be back until late."

Dani turned instead to DCI Johnstone's office; he was there still. She approached and knocked on his door.

"Come in Dani," he called, "what can I do for you? Tell me you've got some good news."

"Er, well, maybe, possibly a big step towards it. This morning Shan mentioned ceramic clay on the body, well I researched business and cottage industries in the area, and one attracted my attention – it was in Jardine Road, 'Kitchen Crafts'. It closed in 2008, and the place is now vacant, awaiting demolition. Next door, however, is still occupied because the resident refuses to move – his name is James Bright."

"Bright, that's the name of one of the men who leased the garage isn't it, are they related?"

"Well I don't know for certain Sir, but I'd stake my pension on it, it's too much of a coincidence for them not to be related. Anyway, Sir, that house would probably have electricity and maybe a chest freezer, but even if it didn't have a freezer, they could have taken one in next door and run an extension cable from

James Bright's house. I could be completely up a gum tree, but I'd like to pursue it. What do you think, Sir?"

"By golly, I think you could well be right. Could it be that Mr Barraclough is also using those premises? Let's go through and look at the map."

"There's Jardine Road," Dani said, pointing at the map, "so...the houses in question would be about half-way along, about...here."

"Hmm, so those houses are back to back with those on Carney Road. Okay, I think we'll mount an operation in the early hours tomorrow, and we'll need to station officers on Carney Road before we move in on both properties. I hope Mr Barraclough is getting his beauty sleep when we get there, though in his line of business nocturnal activities are a norm. Is James out?"

"Yes," Dani responded, "apparently he's been called out on a job and won't be back until late."

"Okay, I'll set things up with Paul Sheridan, we'll need about six of his team and six from CID. Will you talk to the guys here, including James, we need everyone here and ready by 5.00 am. I'll get a firearms team out too. We'll strike at 5.30 am. Warn everyone to wear stab vests and to be aware that Angela Talbot may be on the premises."

Raids such as this were both exciting and scary at the same time. Going in hard and fast gets the adrenalin pumping, but on the other hand, what lay on the other side of a door was a complete unknown. When it was someone with the reputation and track record of Barraclough, it was like dealing with a ticking time bomb. He was extremely likely to explode, and another murder would mean nothing to him. Dani had a real fear that he would use Angela Talbot as a human shield or as bargaining power. The police didn't give in to that sort of manipulation, but it was tough to put someone's life at risk. How she hoped that the early morning raid would catch him napping – quite literally, that would be the best-case scenario.

At 5 o'clock the next morning, the whole team was poised and ready to go. Everyone knew the assigned positions, and they knew what was expected of them. Dani would have loved to be part of the frontline team going in hard, but due to her incapacity, she was one of the officers taking up a position in the passageway linking Carney Road with Jardine Road. Barraclough was not the sort to come quietly, and it was quite likely that at the first sound of the team entering the premises from the front, he would attempt to escape through the rear. Dani and her fellow officers were there to cut off such escape roots; effectively, they had both premises surrounded.

By 5.25 am, everyone was in position awaiting that final instruction via radios from DCI Johnstone. Suddenly that familiar call came.

"Go, go, go!" At that point, the frontline team moved as one to both buildings. Front doors were battered open, and the calls went out.

"Armed police, stay where you are."

Number 63 Jardine Road proved to be empty, but at number 65 there were two occupants, one of whom leapt from an upstairs rear window and moved at speed over fences and rear gardens. He was undoubtedly very athletic, but the final fence bordered a passageway between the properties, and as he dropped into this a specific officer was waiting there with baton drawn and whacked him behind his legs, bringing him crashing on his face to the ground. Instinctively, he reached for a weapon in his belt, forgetting that he was only wearing boxer shorts. His arm then shot out to grab her ankle, but she jumped heavily onto his arm with one foot and at the same time fixed her other foot firmly on his neck. He screamed and cursed, though it was more in rage than in pain. Another officer joined Dani and quickly cuffed him, arms behind his back.

"Mr Barraclough, I presume? I've been waiting a long time for this," a triumphant Dani said, "Royston Barraclough, I'm arresting you on suspicion of murder. You don't have to say anything, but it may harm your defence if you fail to mention when questioned something you later rely on in court. Anything you do say will be taken down and given in evidence. Do you understand?"

Leaving out the expletives, he said very little, but his cursing grew louder and louder, and the term 'bitch' occurred as almost every other word. It was water off a duck back to Dani, she'd been called many things during her career, and he didn't appear to be coming up with anything new.

"Take him away, Andy," she instructed, "and find him a nice comfortable cell, I think he needs to have a little more sleep, he's a bit crabby."

Dani now walked round to the front of the buildings where the other officers were congregating. DCI Johnstone turned to her.

"Dani, was that down to you? Did you manage to apprehend Barraclough?"

"Well, yes, sort of, but with the help of Andrew Peake."

"I deliberately placed you in what I thought was a relatively safe position, and what do you do – how on earth did you manage to get him?"

Dani explained what had happened, and everyone was in fits of laughter.

"No wonder his cursing could be heard in the next county, not only was he bettered by a woman but a one-handed woman at that," the DCI laughed, "very well done to both you and Andrew."

"Was anyone or anything else in the house – Angela Talbot, a freezer?"

"No, Angela wasn't there, and that's worrying. James Bright was, and he was scared out of his wits by Barraclough. He's an older man, and I'm sure has nothing to do with anything that's been going on. Robert Bright is his grandson. Porter brought Barraclough into James' home, and he told him

Barraclough would kill them both if he didn't let him stay. We'll talk to James again later in the day when his nerves have had time to settle. He may know something about Angela's whereabouts. However, you were right, there was a chest freezer in number 63, and an extension lead went into number 65, so I reckon your reasoning was correct, the freezer was used to preserve Shackleton's body. It was empty, but there were bloodstains on the ice. We need to get SOCO to give the premises the once over, but I'll be shocked if Barraclough's prints aren't everywhere. Okay everyone, back to the station, I think it's time for some breakfast. Thanks to you all."

Dani was desperately concerned about Angela, though she knew she was not responsible for her being missing and it wasn't for want of trying that they'd failed to locate her. She didn't expect for one moment that Barraclough would come clean and tell them everything; he was one of the 'no comment' brigades. He was so angry that he would do everything in his power to make their investigations as difficult as possible. Nothing was going to be easy. She fully expected him, if he said anything at all, to deny the murder of Leslie Shackleton and in fact to blame it on

Goodfellow – she had grave doubts that he would even admit having been at Shackleton's cottage. The only real hope they had was to find Angela safe, and well, she was the only one whose testimony they could on about what happened – or could she? Goodfellow said that he'd slapped her so hard that she'd passed out, so when Barraclough carried out the reprehensible deed, she couldn't have seen it. This case was one headache after another. Anyway, first things first, where was Angela? What would Barraclough have done with her – assuming she was still alive? Oh, how she again needed to think.

Just then, DCI Johnstone came over.

"You look as though the weight of the world is on your shoulders, are you okay? You ought to be elated?"

"Yeah, health-wise I'm reasonably okay, I did twist my shoulder a bit when I swung to whack Barraclough. Perhaps I need to wear my sling again for a while. However, that's not my problem, the truth is I'm desperately concerned for Angela Talbot, I can't get her out of my mind, and I can't see how we are going to locate her. I don't believe for a minute that Barraclough is going to tell us, I'll be amazed if he says anything – unless it's to say it was all down to

Goodfellow. I have another of those feelings that we're missing something important, and I need time to think."

"Look, I know you," he remarked, "you've got one of the most brilliant minds I've come across. Grab yourself a coffee, go and find a quiet place and think it all through. We're not going to be interviewing until this afternoon, so don't worry too much."

"Thank you, Sir," Dani responded gratefully, "I won't take longer than I can help. I hope whatever comes to me would be quick. I'll only be across the road in the park if I'm needed."

She then took her boss at his word, grabbed a coffee and headed once more for the nearby park. There were more people around today, but she located a secluded bench, surrounded by trees on three sides, with the third side providing an open view across a small lake. On a non-working day, she would have been content to sit here with a book, read and admire the scenery, but today she didn't have that luxury.

She sipped her coffee for a few moments as she leaned back in the seat.

"Now mind," she said to herself, "get busy, you've work to do." She closed her eyes so that not even the beautiful landscape would distract her, then suddenly strong hands thrust a wad of chloroform-soaked material over her nose and mouth. She could hardly breathe and fought with all her might with her one good hand to wrench herself free. Slowly though, she felt herself drifting into deep unconsciousness as blackness descended.

She awoke later with a splitting headache, her shoulder hurting, from what she assumed was a dreadful nightmare. It was pitch black, and slowly as her senses returned, she realised that her bedroom was never pitch black, as there was a street light just outside. Dani attempted to lift her hand to brush her eyes, but realised her right arm was tied, as too were her ankles. Her left arm was free but trying to move that sent staggering pains through her shoulder. Now the full realisation came to her – it wasn't some dreadful nightmare, it was for real, someone had abducted her.

She wanted to yell for help but realised that tape covered her mouth.

"How could I have been so stupid as to let this happen?" she blamed herself. "But how could I have foreseen such a thing? Because, you idiot, someone had already tried it the other night. You assumed it was Barraclough, but it wasn't. The boss said it was him though and he saw him, how could he have made that mistake?"

She listened for sounds that might give her a clue to where she was, but except for deep breathing, she could hear nothing. She supposed her abductor was asleep nearby.

Dani was not one to surrender to her circumstances. Her mindset was that of prisoners of war, and it was her duty to escape and to continue to fight. It was time, therefore, to bite the bullet. It was going to hurt like crazy, but she couldn't cry out even if she wanted to. Getting her arm out of the sling was no easy matter, but by rubbing her arm against her body, it might slide out. She ignored the pain and continued to twist and rub simultaneously. It was working, and remarkably, soon it was free. Now all she had to do was turn her body, leaving her feet where they were and reach with her hand towards the other wrist. As she stretched out her arm, the pain in her shoulder was excruciating, and at one point, she felt she was in danger of passing out, so had to stop for a while. She concluded she was trying to do too much too soon, and Dani needed to gently exercise it for a while and attempt to free it – full healing was still some way away, and she had hurt it again a few times recently.

While she was gently exercising her arm and shoulder, she slowly lifted her hand and drew back the tape from her mouth and then the blindfold from her eyes. She could see that the room she was in was dirty and sparsely furnished, and she was lying on a bare, badly stained mattress on a bed frame. She looked over in the direction from which the deep breathing was coming, expecting to see her attacker, but instead, she could see another woman, likewise tied to a bed. The realisation hit her, this was probably Angela Talbot, and she was still alive.

Dani thought of speaking to Angela, and although she wouldn't be able to reply because of tape at least Angela would know she was no longer alone, but at that moment she heard footsteps coming in their direction. Dani was concerned that whoever it was would see her arm was out of the sling and tie her other hand to the bed. She quickly reapplied the tape to her mouth and eyes and then did her best in the short time available to attempt to reinsert her elbow into the sling, but only succeeded in drawing her arm beneath the sling.

She heard the door being unlocked and opened, and a voice yelled, "wake up my beauties, it's time to earn your keep."

Both mumbled their response through their taped lips.

"Oh dear," the man scolded, "are you only going to grunt at me, that's not very polite – oh, I forgot, your lips are sealed."

The next second, he roughly yanked the tape from their lips.

"There, is that better? Are you going to be more friendly now?"

"Who are you, and what do you want?" Dani demanded.

"Ah, she speaks. Who am I? Well, we have met, but we weren't properly introduced, though I think you'd remember me. What do I want? Your cooperation and for someone very dear to me to be released from your friend's clutches."

"If we've already met then there is little point in leaving the blindfold in place. Take it off, and we can talk properly."

"Anything to oblige a lady." He roughly snatched the tape away from her eyes.

Dani blinked a few times as though seeing the dim light for the first time and then looked up at the man standing over her.

"Royston Barraclough, but...how come...how did you escape from custody?"

"Oh, my darling Dani – I think that's your name – you're a little off beam. I didn't escape from custody, because I've never been in custody. We ought to have been introduced when I called on you at your flat, but your boyfriend interfered. Let me put the record straight, I'm Shelton Harvey, though by rights it should be Shelton Barraclough – Royston is my twin brother. We were separated at birth and Malcolm, and Charlotte Harvey adopted me. My brother and I only recently met each other after many years, and now you're trying to separate us again."

"Shelton, I don't understand why I'm here," Dani said, "and who's that?" she asked, nodding towards the other bed.

"Tut, tut, Dani," he responded sarcastically, "you know very well who that is, it's my dear friend Angela. You are a tease; you knew who she was, didn't you?"

"No, not for sure – remember, I've only just found out she was there. I couldn't have seen her because of the blindfold even had I been conscious. Anyway, I ask you again. What do you want?"

"I want my brother and you two are going to help me get him released."

"How do you propose to arrange that? I can't simply ask and expect them to do my bidding. He's on a murder charge, so even you must realise that's a serious offence. No one's simply going to let him go."

"Oh, I do realise that, so we'll offer a little persuasion. I'm sure the police would want you both back in one piece, so we'll tell your colleagues, if they don't cooperate, they'll get you both back one little bit at a time – one finger from each, then another, then another and if we run out of fingers we'll start on toes. You must admit that might be quite persuasive, and I guess you'll both be hoping they get the message and quickly. That's why I invited you to my little party, Dani. They might take risks with other people's lives, but not one of their own, I'm sure."

"You're sadistic just like your brother. He likes cutting off body parts."

"Hmm, true," he laughed, "and it was a little naughty, but you must admit it is quite effective, it does get people's attention. Maybe we'll put that to the test soon. Oh, I almost forgot, would you like a little drink? I only have water, I'm afraid."

He picked up a bottle of water and gave each of them a drink and then he produced his mobile phone.

"Okay ladies, time now for a photoshoot. It will straight go to your pals at the office Dani, so be careful, be polite and be cooperative. I want you to say, 'We are both well, and this man wants Barraclough released, or you will receive our digits one by one until you do.' Got that? Nothing more and nothing less. Right, go!"

Dani coughed and then spoke.

"We are both well, and this 'B'– this man wants Barraclough released, or you will receive our digits one by one until you do."

"Thank you, you almost slipped up there," Barraclough said, "but corrected yourself just in time. Now we await their response."

CHAPTER 22

ESCAPE TO VICTORY

BACK AT THE OFFICE, THE DCI was getting slightly agitated. Dani hadn't returned, and it was time to conduct the interview. Her phone was dead, so they couldn't get hold of her.

"I don't like this one bit, Dani is normally so reliable. I think we have to send officers to search for her," he said to members of the team.

"Jenny, you know Dani well, what coffee does she drink – is it from the canteen?"

"No Sir, she always chooses Costa cinnamon latte from the kiosk by the park."

"Jenny, take two officers with you and check if Dani was there earlier and what she ordered. Then search the park – check secluded spots especially, as she was there on my instructions to think. Check bins near seats, see if you can find her coffee cup and any trace of her."

Jenny and two of her colleagues went as directed to look for Dani or any trace of her having been in the park. They enquired at the kiosk as to whether she'd been there that morning and they confirmed that she had and had purchased her usual cinnamon latte. They'd last seen her heading towards the lake. The three set off in that direction too, intending to split their search once they'd reached that area. They moved off in different directions and very soon, Jenny came across the seat where Dani had been sitting and saw a cup with coffee still in on the bench. She called the others to meet her where she was.

"I reckon Dani was here and that this is her almost full cup of coffee – that's cinnamon latte I'm sure. Let's take it back for analysis."

"Hey, look at this," Peter Jones said, pointing to a rag behind the seat, "do you think this might be something to do with her disappearance?"

He carefully picked it up and sniffed it.

"Take a sniff at that, what do you detect?"

"Chloroform!" they exclaimed simultaneously.

"Someone has kidnapped Dani," Jenny declared, "let's get these things back to the station and let the boss decide what to do."

Meanwhile, Barraclough having left them alone, Dani decided to renew her efforts at escape. Firstly, she partially removed the tape from her mouth and eyes and then spoke quietly to Angela.

"Angela, can you hear me?" Angela turned her head in her direction and nodded.

"Has that brute hurt you at all?" She shook her head.

"I'm going to try to get free, but it's not going to be easy – I just hope he doesn't return for quite some time."

Angela this time did a thumb up sign with the thumb of her right hand which was able to do despite her wrist tied to the bed frame.

"Now girl, grit your teeth time – you can do this," she told herself. As before, she twisted her body and reached with her arm at the same time. The whole process put terrible stress on her shoulder, and the pain brought tears to her eyes. That, though, was nothing if she could get to the knot that secured her right wrist. She rolled and stretched many times, each time getting nearer the knot. One last mighty push and she got her hand on it. However, that was but the start. Undoing knots without seeing it is a problem within itself, but her fingers were quite skilful, and after feeling around the knot for a few minutes she was able to determine which strand to attack. She had to take numerous rests and felt sure she was not doing her shoulder bones a world of good, but necessity dictated in the circumstances. At the next attempt, she found that the cord he'd used was quite stiff and that worked to her advantage because she found she could push the loose end towards the knot and wriggle it a little until the knot started to come undone. She was fortunate that he'd not pulled the knot too tight, and moments later her arm was free. Freedom was a lovely feeling, but now the exertion on her shoulder told its tale.

Dani needed to rest for a few moments but dared not take long in case Barraclough returned. Then with renewed strength, she started on her feet, and it was much more comfortable, as she was able to sit up and shuffle towards them. After just a few moments she'd released them, and now went over to do the same for Angela. It took very little time to free her and after a short time spent rubbing her cramped limbs, Angela was able to stand. She immediately hugged Dani and thanked her profusely. It was time now to plan how they were going to overpower Barraclough.

Back at the station, DCI Johnstone was horrified when he saw what the three officers had found in the park and immediately sent them for analysis.

"I rather think someone has abducted her," he said to Jenny, "but I can't think for the life of me who'd be responsible. But I have a feeling that very soon someone's going to be in touch with us."

Then, right on cue, there was a ping from his computer, indicating that something had come in. He opened what turned out to be a short video clip. It showed Dani lying on a filthy mattress on the bed and then she coughed and spoke, "We are both well and this 'B'– this man wants Barraclough released, or you will receive our digits one by one until you do." That was all, no instructions.

"Do you take that seriously, Sir?" Jenny asked.

"I think we have to. Whoever 'he' is who has them – I presume the other is Angela Talbot – is probably quite capable of carrying out such a threat, especially if he's anything like Barraclough," he responded with a perplexed look on his face.

"There's something about what Dani said that puzzles me, it was the emphasis she put on the 'B' – it was as if she was almost pretending that she was going to say 'bastard', but I don't think she was, that's not a word I've ever heard her use. I think she was trying to convey a clue as to the identity of her captor. 'B' – who would that be? Who would we instantly recognise whose name begins with 'B'?"

"If we didn't have him in custody, I'd have said Barraclough," Peter Jones replied, "but it can't be him."

"Whoa, that's a point Peter, was a background check done on Barraclough and did it include family?" DCI Johnstone asked.

"I'm sure there was a check, I'll see what's in the file." He brought up the file on the computer and scrolled through it.

"Here we are, all the usual checks on his past record and I think...yes, family – he has a sister in

Florida, uncle and aunty in Gateshead – his parents are both dead."

"No, siblings?" DCI Johnstone asked.

"No, not really...well that's not strictly true, he was a twin, but his brother was given up for adoption. It says, 'Unable to trace details of adoptive family' and that's it, Sir."

"And that I feel sure is it. The 'B' that Dani referred to was Barraclough, the twin brother, and that's why he's desperate to have him freed. This is not good. I fear it may be that as twins, they share the same temperament. It concerns me greatly that he may not think twice about carrying out his threat. I hope he contacts us again before doing so."

Meanwhile, Dani was busy contemplating their next move. There was nothing they could use in the room as a weapon, but then it occurred to her that the single chair in the room would certainly stop him in his tracks.

"Angela, do you think you could wield that chair as a weapon? I couldn't easily do it with just one hand."

"If you mean could I use it against that maniac, I reckon I could even use the bed. What do you have in mind?"

"Your bed's behind the door, so the first thing he sees when he enters is my bed. If you waited behind the door with the chair and I was to be sitting on the bed looking as though I was trying to untie my ankles, I'm sure his reaction would be to come to re-secure me, and that would be your opportunity to attack. What do you think?"

"Oh yes, let's do it, anything to get out of this place and away from his vile and evil threats – I like my fingers and toes where they are, thank you."

They sat and talked in whispers for about an hour before they heard footsteps approaching. Angela jumped up, grabbed the chair and hid behind the door. Dani climbed back on her bed and dangled the ropes from her ankles. She reached down as though trying to untie them and then they heard the key turn in the lock.

"I'm coming, my beauties, it's time for you each to make a little sacrifice."

As he opened the door, he immediately saw Dani sitting on the bed and rushed towards her.

"Hey, hey, my lovely, where do you think you're going..."

That was all he had time to say because Angela dashed over and brought the chair crashing down across his head and shoulder. He collapsed like a sack of potatoes - he was out cold. Blood oozed from a gash on his head, and he was going to have a headache and some good bruises across his shoulders. Dani hadn't meant for her to hit him quite so hard but guessed her ferocity was due to pent up anger and fear. What she had gone through during her time in captivity she alone would tell, but at the hands of Barraclough, it was certainly not going to have been pleasant – he wasn't the most desirable company.

"Quick, Angela!" Dani yelled, "grab the cords he used on us and let's tie him up tightly." She didn't need telling twice, between them they tied his hands together behind his back, and then they secured his ankles together.

"Let's be sure he's restricted," Dani suggested, "we'll tie his legs to his hands, he'll not get out of that."

They only just finished in time, as he regained consciousness. He tried to move, but quickly realised he couldn't – the captor had become the captive. He was not in the best frame of mind and vented his anger with tirades of cursing and abuse. Angela was not in the mood for his torrent, so aimed a vicious kick where it hurt him most. She was about to do it again, but Dani stopped her.

"Enough, Angela, he'll get what's coming to him."

She searched his pockets until she located his phone, intending to use it to call for transport for her prisoner, but then realised she had no idea where they were.

She dashed down the stairs and through the derelict ground floor to the street. She ran to the end where the street name sign was located. She quickly called the station and briefly outlined their situation, requesting transport for her prisoner.

"It's Barnett Street, about one hundred yards along on the left. We'll be waiting. Thanks."

She now messaged her boss. "Sorry Sir, I'm running a bit late, but I was rescuing Angela Talbot and arresting Shelton Harvey Barraclough! I'll be back shortly."

Dani arrived back in the office to rapturous applause, much to her embarrassment. The DCI heard the applause and went to the door of his office.

"Detective Sergeant Taylor, I want a word with you," he said in his fiercest possible tone.

Dani entered his office in a bewildered state, whatever had she done wrong?

"Sergeant, are you trying to put the rest of the force out of a job? I sent you out to think and what do you do, you almost clear our books of outstanding crimes."

An enormous smile creased his face. "You are an absolute wonder, I don't know how you do it, but I congratulate you. Now, sit down and tell me everything."

"Thank you, Sir. I must admit you had me going there. I thought I was going to get a roasting."

"Sorry Dani, it was a bit insensitive after all you've been through, but if I had roasted you that lot out there would have lynched me. Please tell me all that happened."

Dani gave him blow for blow, reliving the whole ordeal. Throughout he was shaking his head at the wonder of it all.

"Are you okay? Did he harm you in any way and has it done any further damage to your shoulder?"

"It's very sore, but that's because it was the first time I had it stretched. No, Barraclough didn't harm me, or Angela for that matter, but the knife he was carrying when he came in that last time Barraclough told us meant business – he was going to carry out his threat to cut off fingers and toes one by one and send them to you."

"Ah, that's a point, your deliberate mistake in presenting his message wasn't lost on us – that was a stroke of genius – but do you know, the background check on Royston Barraclough failed to flag up the fact that he had a twin brother at large? We knew he had one, but never fully pursued it. Does this Shelton look anything like Royston?"

"Two peas from the same pod. That person you chased off from outside my flat was Shelton, he said as much."

"Is Angela still at the station do you know?"

"She was, she agreed to give a statement there and then, very brave of her, but she preferred to do it while everything was still fresh in her mind and to get it out. I guess Barraclough will need hospital treatment, Angela didn't hold back when wielding that chair. I hope she doesn't get into trouble for injuring him."

"I shouldn't think that in the circumstances he'd have the nerve to try and bring charges against her.

What she did was self-defence in the most traumatic of circumstances. You were both under threat of mutilation by that animal, so I think he would have great difficulty persuading a court that he was the victim."

"I hope you are right, Sir, I hate to think how traumatised Angela was in captivity by that creature and, as you say, his threat of mutilation was genuine."

"Don't let it worry you and now I think you both should go along to the hospital to be checked over, trauma has a potent effect on people, and I am concerned as to whether you have done any damage to that shoulder. No arguments Dani, please go along now, I'll get Colin to drive you both."

Just then, a knock came on the door, and Superintendent Andy Mann strolled into the office.

"Sorry to interrupt you, but I've just been hearing of the exploits of this young woman, and I wanted to add my thanks, congratulations and best wishes – you are a credit to the force and this department especially. You're supposed to be resting that shoulder and wrestling with villains is not part of your therapy I'm sure, but again, thank you for taking the risk you did. I'm sure your efforts will not go unacknowledged."

"Thank you, Sir," Dani responded.

Superintendent Mann left the office, and the DCI turned to Dani.

"Wow, praise indeed when the chief comes to thank you; it's good to know that even he notices and acknowledges excellent work. Now go and get yourselves checked out – and Dani, take some time off if they tell you to rest it more."

"Thank you, Sir, but resting's not my style, well not if I can help it. I'd rather be here. Anyway, we haven't finished yet. We have to smash the rest of the drugs ring."

"Get thinking, and you'll solve that before bedtime," he teased her, "but keep out of the park."

Dani and Angela were not the only ones to visit the hospital that afternoon, Shelton Barraclough did indeed have to go to be checked over. He was complaining of a splitting headache and blurred vision. They treated him and carried out a head scan. The diagnosis was a touch of concussion and bruising. They assured him that all would soon clear and prescribed him painkillers. A night's sleep in a cell would work wonders for his physical condition, but nothing would improve his temper; he didn't like being locked up and made his feelings known very audibly. Most of his venom was against the 'bitches' who attacked him – he'd sue them for actual bodily harm.

There was quite a wait at the hospital, especially for Dani, as they wanted her to have another scan of her shoulder. Therefore, as was her habit, she took the opportunity to think things over. Were Royston and Shelton Barraclough, together with Goodfellow, merely the muscle of the organisation or were some of them the brains? Folk like Broadhurst, Khan, Thomas, Bright and Porter were simply receivers and distributors, but who was the mastermind, the controller, the brainpower?

The question was, was such a person on their patch or elsewhere? They'd no doubt hurt the organisation by finding and seizing their stocks, but they'd by no means took them out of business. More muscle could be found, and plenty more could be recruited as receivers and distributors. The lure of massive financial gains would sway many weak-minded folks to join their ranks. The ultimate masterminds both in the UK and overseas were the responsibility of Customs and Excise and drug squads, but anyone operating on their patch was fair game, providing the local drug squad didn't warn them off. How could such a controller be located? Mobile phones – those mobile phones belonging to all eight of those taken into custody. The likelihood was that all of them would have contacts in common because all would be subject to the directions given by the controller. That was something Dani was now determined to pursue when she returned to the office. She was like the proverbial terrier with a rat, she just couldn't let things lie – and in her mind, they'd already stirred up a whole nest of rats.

Remarkably, the scan revealed that the bones were knitting well; the extra exertion had done no damage whatsoever. The doctor suggested that for much of the time, she could dispense with the sling and only use it if the pain became excessive. That truly delighted her, and although she realised that she was not yet ready to wrestle with criminals, she did feel that day was drawing near. Angela popped by the x-ray department to see Dani. Angela herself had been instructed to take things easy for a while, and trauma counselling was offered if she needed it.

"I don't think I need counselling though," she told Dani, "the opportunity to kick that so-and-so, where it hurt, was enormous therapy for me. Thanks again for your rescue Dani, I'll never forget your bravery and kindness. I think I'm due a change of career, something less stressful – an air steward comes to mind, but I might be too old."

"Go for it, Angela. You'll never know until you try. Good luck for the future wherever life may take you. Oh, by the way, before you dash, did anyone take your statement?"

"Yes, a DC...Seymour, would it be? She took it. I thought it best to get it done while everything was still fresh in my mind."

"Yes, Jenny Seymour, great, I'll talk to her when I get back to the station."

Back at the office, Dani found Jenny and asked her about Angela's statement. "Yes, I've got it here," she said, "Angela said that although she was knocked out by Goodfellow, she came around and pretended to be out still – she didn't want another beating. When Barraclough attacked Leslie Shackleton, she says she was squinting and can testify to all he did to him. She's willing to stand up in court if needed."

"Thanks, Jen, that's brilliant."

Next, she ran her thoughts past the DCI. He shook his head in amazement. "Dani, you are a glutton for punishment. I understand your line of thinking, but there doesn't have to be a local controller, though I guess you're right in thinking that someone somewhere must have a finger on the pulse. I've no objections to you pursuing it, so just run it by James and see what he thinks. He may well appoint someone to work on it with you."

James Cartwright was at his desk, so Dani did just as the boss had suggested. He was quite enthusiastic about it and offered to help her himself. Their next port of call, therefore, was the evidence room. In this room, they had to take every care that nothing could be contaminated, removed or mixed.

So, for the search, they wore protective clothing to cover all parts of their body, including masks and gloves. Each worked well apart from the other and opened one bag at a time, taking out just mobile phones. It was quite a job listing contact names and numbers from each of them and took a few hours to complete. The last one James checked belonged to Ali Khan, and here he found the battery was flat. It was frustrating, but then he realised it was the same make as his own and he had a charger cable in his desk drawer.

James phoned through to the office and asked a colleague to find it and bring it through to the evidence room. It soon arrived, and he found that it fitted, so was able to plug into a power socket. He waited a few moments and then turned it on, now he was able to access Khan's contacts. They both breathed sighs of relief when they completed the job. Now they had to cross-reference the eight lists, looking for shared connections. They found that all eight had numbers for each other, and all eight had one contact name and number in common –listed 'Father'. It was a fictitious name because there was no way they could have the same father.

"This was your idea, Dani," James said, "are you happy to pursue the number with the service provider?"

"Yes, sure," she responded, "I just hope it doesn't turn out to be a pay as you go."

In the event, it was not a pay as you go phone and Dani managed to get the service provider and the name of the account holder – Peter Smith. His registered address was 1044 Mile End Road, Watley – the next borough to Kerington. Dani was in no doubt that Peter Smith would turn out to be a fictitious name but, most probably, the address was genuine. Dani now returned to DI James Cartwright to share the data she found.

"What do you think we should do now Guv?" she asked. "I'm very tempted to phone him and say that someone gave me his name as a possible source of new stocks, could he help, but I don't want him tracing the call back to me."

"Hmm, I might be able to help there, it just so happens that I have an old pay as you go phone in my drawer and that wouldn't be traceable. Mind you, I think perhaps I should make the call, I don't want to appear sexist, but I doubt if there'd be many women asking about stocks. Would you be happy with that?"

"It makes sense, and you've got quite a deep macho voice, so I think you'd sound more convincing."

"Okay, but not here, we need to go where it's quiet with no phones in the background – let's try the park."

"Huh, I'm not sure it has the attraction it once had, but at least we can find a quiet spot."

They sat at the bench where the attack on Dani took place, but at least it was off the beaten track. James now punched in the number.

"Hi, is that Peter and is it safe to talk?"

"Yeah, who's that?"

"Okay, I'm Arnie. A friend passed your name to me, said you'd provide stocks of - snow and crystal – two kilos each? What price?"

"180 grand the lot and no arguments."

"Yeah, no probs, sounds about right. How soon and where?"

"Tomorrow noon, 108 Pallson Street – just for a first meet before we have a deal."

Well, okay, if it must be, it must be, but I can't afford to run out of stocks, so no messing or I go elsewhere. Tomorrow noon it is."

"I thought that might happen," Dani said, "they're unlikely to trust a stranger. Do you think it's safe to go? I think we have to run it past the boss, and I reckon you need backup if you're going to step into their domain, it could be dangerous if they smell a rat."

The DCI was not overly enthusiastic, though he recognised that if they were to get more dealers off the street, they had to take risks.

"I think you need to wear protection and a wire, and you certainly need backup nearby. These people are very suspicious of strangers and won't think twice about removing you if they think you're a threat."

"I agree about backup, but no protection or wires Sir, they're bound to frisk me all over, a wire could be an even bigger risk. I'm happy to go in without any wires or anything. I reckon I can be quite convincing."

"Okay, James, if you're sure, but get out of there if you think things are getting too hot," DCI Johnstone said, "we'll need to get the backup team in place well in advance of the meet, so I'll organise that, you just concentrate on your strategy – they're going to ask you some awkward questions, so think it through well, know how you're going to convince them."

Next morning DI James Cartwright arrived at the office in an almost unrecognisable state. He was wearing old dishevelled clothes, his hair was unkempt, his boots were dirty and worn, and dark stubble covered his usually clean-shaven face.

"Good grief Guv," Dani exclaimed astonished, "you look like a drop-out and your eyes, what have you done to them? They're red, and you've got dark bags beneath – are you on drugs?"

"Well if you think that," he replied, "hopefully Peter Smith will think so too. My wife is the artist behind this look. She's a make-up artist in the East End. I reckon she's good at her job, don't you think?"

"Wow, you're not kidding, it's brilliant," Dani responded enthusiastically.

There were many double-takes that morning as the team came into the office and saw the DI, his appearance was compelling. When the DCI saw him, he congratulated him on the effort he'd made to look the part.

"All we need to do now is make sure we play our part by putting the backup in place. I wish we could move in and arrest whomever you meet there and then, but we have to wait until they have the drugs before we move in, so that will have to be at a second meet."

ALL IN THE LINE OF DUTY

By 10.45 am, the backup team, including members of the drug squad, was in place, well ahead of time. It was important that Smith and his cronies didn't spot any of the backup team getting into position. Pallson Street was one of the many streets that were part of the redevelopment site, so all the properties were vacant.

Dani stationed herself in a strategic position where she could watch proceedings through a pair of binoculars. She also had a camera with a long-distance lens; they needed photos of the meet if possible, to produce as evidence. It was, as always, a long wait.

Eventually, mid-day came and went, but there was no sign of the contact. At nine minutes past the hour, a motorbike came on the scene and stopped outside number 108. James walked towards it, and at the same time the rider and his passenger moved to meet him. Both the motorcyclists wore helmets and scarves across their faces. Dani was afraid they were not going to remove their gear, in which case she wouldn't be able to photograph their faces. However, at the last minute, they did, and she snapped away. Then one of the two went right up to James, and her thought was that he was going to offer his hand, but instead he punched James hard in the stomach causing him to bend double, he then hit James on the back of his head with his helmet. The other man moved in and frisked James thoroughly all over.

Satisfied that he was not carrying a weapon, nor concealing a wire, he now shook hands.

"Sorry about that Arnie, but you understand we can't be too careful in our line of business."

"Huh, there's careful and being bloody-minded," James replied, "hit me again, and you'll regret it. If that's the way you treat your customers, I'm inclined to take my business elsewhere."

"No, no, no, you don't want to do that, you want the gear, and we've got it. Anyway, tell me something, how come I haven't met you before?"

"Not that it's any of your business, but my usual supplier got pulled, though I've not been operating in this area for long. My previous market got a bit hot, so I headed for cooler climes, but now it's getting a bit warm here. Anyway, enough talk, are we in business or not?" James asked, impatiently.

"Yeah, yeah man, keep your shirt on, we aren't talking peanuts, and I had to be sure. Tomorrow, same time, same place. Tommy here will bring the gear, and you bring the readies."

"No deal, you bring the gear – I only deal with the genuine article, I don't want your puppy running off with the proceeds and you thinking I stuffed you."

"He wouldn't dare do that Arnie, but for you, okay."

As he turned to leave, James deliberately dropped his wallet, which Peter Smith picked up.

"Hey Arnie, you might need this, you shouldn't go throwing your money away, there are unscrupulous people around here," he laughed, turning to leave.

Once well away from the others, James dropped the wallet into a plastic evidence bag he'd concealed nearby before the meet – the wallet would be suitable for fingerprints.

The team reassembled back at the office.

"Well done James, you handled that well. Are you okay after that punch and hit on the head? Do you need to be checked over?"

"Yeah, I'm fine Sir, it was a bit sore at the time, but I'm okay now, and there's no need for a check-up – I've got a thick skull. Can someone take this down to the lab to be checked for prints?" he said, handing over the wallet.

"That was a stroke of genius James," Dani remarked, "that was one you'd prepared earlier. I also need to look closely at the photographs I shot, but I reckon I've come across the one who calls himself Peter Smith before, although his name was not Peter Smith, I'm sure."

They would have to repeat the whole process the next day, but this time the intention was to swoop on them and catch them in possession of the drugs. The hope was that they'd not only get the dealers but also locate their stash and get it off the streets. Dani's photos, she hoped, would enable her to identify at least one of the men and trace an address for them. Smashing drug dealerships was notoriously difficult because they tended to spread their stocks around so that if someone found one stash, other stashes would be safe.

Dani now set about uploading the photos from the camera to the computer. She desperately wanted to enlarge them to identify the two men, but especially 'Peter Smith' as he called himself. It was a swift process to get them onto the computer, and now she began to look for the best shots that showed full faces. There were four great ones of 'Smith' and three of 'Tommy'. She was now absolutely convinced Peter Smith was not Peter Smith but was she felt sure Ethan Roberts, someone she'd previously had dealings with, and Tommy was more difficult. She vaguely recognised him but couldn't put a name to him. Paul Sheridan was the best bet. He would know if anyone did. She printed off three copies of each of the men and went off to find Paul. He was on the front desk and, as luck would have it, there was no one else there at the time.

"Hi Paul, will you take a look at these two photos please, who do you think they are?" she asked.

"Sure. Oh my," and Paul laughed, "there's no mistaking those mugs, Ethan Roberts and Lucas Evans. Right beggars they were, but that must be what, five years ago? Don't tell me they've surfaced again – it'll be nothing good if they have."

"Spot on Paul. I recognised Ethan Roberts straight away, he was the first one I ever arrested, and that was for possession of Cannabis. I recognised Lucas Evans, he was someone else's collar, but if I remember rightly, he too was arrested for possession."

"He most certainly was Dani, and it was me who arrested him. They only got suspended sentences though. What is it this time?"

"Would you believe it, Roberts is the local big-wig dealer, and Evans is his sidekick. I took these photos on a stakeout this morning. We're hoping to get them both tomorrow. James Cartwright is posing as the buyer – 180 grands' worth."

James whistled.

"Woah, that's a big wad, quite some operation. Are they mobile?"

"Yeah, a motorbike, or at least that's how they travelled today. So, thanks Paul, we'll no doubt, see you tomorrow."

Dani returned to the office and found the DI in the DCI's office. She knocked on the door and entered.

"Am I interrupting Sir?"

"No, not at all, we were just wondering how things went with the photos."

"That's why I've come to see you both. When I saw the enlargements of the photos, I instantly recognised Peter Smith as Ethan Roberts, my first collar. I also recognised Tommy, but couldn't put a name to his face, so I've just been to see Paul Sheridan, and he instantly named him as Lucas Evans, someone he arrested."

She handed them copies of the photos.

"My goodness, it was fortunate that I had nothing to do with their arrest," James remarked, "it would have been very tricky, to say the least, if they'd recognised me. Anyway, thanks Dani, you've done a great job with these."

"Actually Guv," Dani laughed, "I don't think they would have recognised you, we hardly did – we wondered what drop-out had wandered into the office."

"You wait until tomorrow when this has grown a bit more," he responded, rubbing the stubble on his jaw.

"Anyway," the DCI intervened, "let's talk about tomorrow because I don't believe it's going to be a walk in the park. It won't surprise me if they have an armed backup, they'll not be taking any chances with £180,000.00 worth of drugs, nor with the cash from the sale, but neither will we. That money never leaves our sight, so make sure everyone understands that."

"What am I carrying it in Guv?"

"We have an old and battered bag. It needs to fit in with your image. Now the plan is to have everyone in position well in advance as we did today. The firearms team are going to surround the scene should they start shooting for any reason. When Roberts and Evans arrive, and I'm expecting their backup team at the same time, then we'll block off the roads well away from where you're doing business, just in case they try to run. We can't let them escape us, taking the money with them."

There was much to be arranged in preparation for the operation, but all was completed by mid-morning. Having to be in position well in advance of the drop, meant that everyone had time to feel the build-up of nervous anticipation, Time stood still, and the deadline took ages. Everyone was on tenterhooks, as the hour approached - what lay ahead was the question in their minds. Because it was an area due for demolition and redevelopment, everywhere was quiet, few vehicles passed along the roads and even fewer pedestrians.

Surprisingly, few squatters used the buildings, and that may have been because it was a long way from civilisation, fewer people meant fewer folks from whom to beg. A while later, a car dropped James off on the outskirts of the area, and he made his way to the meeting spot. Had he not known differently, James would have said he was utterly alone and very vulnerable as he walked to the meet site, but he knew his colleagues and the armed response team are watching his every move. James needed to see that he had backup he could depend on – there's no honour amongst drug addicts, they are generally only interested in themselves, so he and his colleagues had to be primed for any eventuality. Even so, James knew only too well that he was in front of the queue if Roberts and his associates decided to double-cross him and start shooting.

He glanced at his watch numerous times, but it wasn't until almost a quarter past the hour that he heard engines approaching. It was, he estimated, more than one vehicle. When they came into view, there were, in fact, three motorcycles, with two riders on each. Roberts had brought backup, just as the DCI had predicted. They halted their bikes a short distance away, and while Roberts and Evans approached carrying a bag, the other four surrounded them on the periphery of the area. James noticed that all four had guns drawn.

"Good grief, Peter, you're not very trusting, are you? Why all the firepower and muscle?"

"Can't be too careful Arnie, you never know who or what you're going to encounter. There's too much at stake here to take chances," he said, pointing to the two bags. "Show me what you've got."

"Huh, tell you what, you show me what you've got," he countered.

"Okay," responded Peter, "let's both of us place our bags on the floor, and we'll let Tommy open both together."

James sniffed loudly, indicating his unease.

"Right, but try anything, and I promise you, you're dead men."

"You're in no position to make threats Arnie. My friends won't hesitate if I give instructions."

"That's it, the deals off, stick your drugs where the sun don't shine, I don't deal with crooks."

He started to leave and immediately, Roberts called him back.

"Arnie, Arnie, don't be so touchy. Come on. I'm not here to play games, let's clinch the deal. Let's both place our bags on the floor and open them together."

They did just that. Both opened their bags and moved to allow the other to see. "Can I examine your contents, Arnie?"

"Sure, if I can check yours."

They moved to each other's bags and at that moment, a motorbike roared out of an alleyway and shot along the road towards them. Roberts then pushed James' bag further away, and the pillion passenger leaned over, grabbed the bag of money and they were gone in an instant.

"Why didn't your goons stop them?" James demanded. "Ah, I see it now, they were with you, and now I suppose you're just going to walk away with the stuff."

"You're not as thick as you look Arnie, but no money, no deal. Perhaps we'll see you around."

"I'm sure I will and probably much sooner than you think."

They picked up the bag and walked towards their bikes. The four on the periphery pocketed their guns, and they too walked towards their bikes.

James dashed into a nearby property, and once he was under cover, the shout, "go, go, go!" rang out from DCI Johnstone.

"Armed police throw away your weapons and lie flat on the ground – NOW!" he yelled.

One man grabbed his gun and let off a round at one of the officers, wounding him in his hip. He fell to the ground clutching at the wound. Another of the armed officers immediately let off a round at the man on the ground and hit him in the shoulder. After that, there was no more resistance. The officers moved in and cuffed them all. James emerged from his shelter and approached the group, and Roberts saw him coming.

"You're not going to get away with this Arnie you b..."

"Now don't be so touchy Peter, or should that be Ethan? I think we've already got away with it and you're soon going to be put away for a long time."

"Huh, but we got your money, and that will come in mighty handy, not least for the best defence lawyer."

"Er, do you mean those two on the motorbike, those two coming this way? Hmm, my colleague seems to be carrying something – oh, it's the bag with the money in it. Sorry to disappoint you, Ethan."

There followed a stream of insults and curses, some of which he seemed to have invented on the spot especially for the officers before him.

"Oh, take them away and charge them," the DCI responded, "he's hurting my ears."

Just then, a shot rang out, and James fell in a crumpled heap to the ground with blood pouring from his side. Dani, noticing from where the bullet had come, immediately dashed into a nearby property and out to the rear. She moved along to the back of the property where the gunman was and waited.

Meanwhile, the firearms team advanced towards the buildings on that side of the street and slowly along in the direction of the gunman.

Shots continued to ring out and pinged off the road very close to where the police officers were lying. Then the firing ceased, and Dani tensed, anticipating that the gunman would exit in her direction.

Moments later, he dashed out, and Dani sprang out and karate-chopped him across the throat. The force of her chop and his forward momentum caused him to leave the ground and then fall slowly on his back.

He was choking and winded, so Dani took the opportunity to roll him over and cuff him.

She kicked his gun out of reach and then called for help. Seconds later, officers arrived and took him away, bagging his weapon in the process. James was now her worry, so she dashed back to the front of the buildings where paramedics were already tending to him.

"Is he okay?" Dani asked worriedly, "Is it a serious wound? And what about Joel's injury?"

"Fortunately, only fairly superficial wounds to both," the paramedic assured her, "flesh wounds, but clean."

"We'll live, Dani," James said, "these things are all in the line of duty," he laughed and then regretted it, as the pain seared through his side.

"Well, we got the guy who shot you, so that's one more creature off the street," she reassured him, "and hopefully he'll be out of action for quite some time."

Processing all the prisoners was a lengthy process and took the rest of the day to complete. Then there were reports to write – the aspect of policing that was the bane of every officer's life. It was late into the evening before any of them could relax and eventually go home.

The next day interviews were the order of the day, but few of those interviewed were willing to co-operate. Both gunmen had little option but to plead guilty, though beyond that they employed the 'no comment' response. The one thing the police desperately needed were the addresses of the properties of those arrested; they needed to search for evidence of involvement in the drug scene and possibly stashes of drugs. For all the police knew at present, there could well be others involved, but that was something they hoped would become clear in due course.

Later, prisoners processed, and reports written, Dani took the opportunity to mull over the case to date.

The long-running and far-reaching saga that had begun with an elderly lady's 'feeling' was ending. Initially, they'd considered that what she'd 'felt' was so bizarre, that the inclination was almost to dismiss it out of hand – how could any credible investigation be launched based on a 'feeling'? It was only because a station sergeant saw something convincing in that lady's demeanour, that he was able to persuade his senior officer to take on the case. Little did they realise just how far the case would take them, but initially it was very simply an unsubstantiated murder, so secret that it took an inordinate length of time for them to be convinced that murder was behind Leslie Shackleton's disappearance – they still had no body. It was inconceivable that they would, in the course of their investigations, reveal not one, but five murders and all of them committed to cover a massive, multi-million-pound drugs ring – a drugs ring stretching to the USA and beyond.

As that eventful day ended, Dani once again felt that need to pause and ponder the events of this drawn-out case. So, what better place to think could she find but that local park. Yes, it had dealt its tranquillity a blow when she Shelton abducted her from there, but surely such threats were over now that both Royston and Shelton Barraclough were in custody. Therefore, a somewhat buoyed up Dani stepped outside the door of the police station to go to the park. However, as she did so, her eyes were immediately drawn to a man on the far side of the road, and she did a double-take; it was Barraclough! As Dani gazed in utter bewilderment, he pulled a gun and fired three shots, sending Dani sprawling backwards by the impact of the bullets. She fell to the ground in a crumpled heap, a pool of blood quickly forming around her.

Paul Sheridan, who was on the front desk, heard the shots and through the glass-panelled door saw Dani hit the ground. He rushed out, immediately saw the vast pool of blood and called the ambulance. By this time, several officers had gathered, and one rushed to inform DCI Johnstone.

The DCI, disregarding the blood, knelt by her side.

"Dani, Dani, can you hear me, squeeze my hand if you can."

He felt a slight grip on his hand.

"Dani, hang in there, the ambulance is coming."

Dani then gave a little cough.

"Barraclough." she whispered, "Check..." and then her voice trailed off.

The paramedics stepped in and sought to stem the gushing crimson flow. A drip was quickly set up to counter the massive loss of blood.

In a matter of seconds, she was in the ambulance, which raced at speed towards the hospital with a police escort. They rushed her straight into theatre, where they had to perform surgery to remove three bullets. One had lodged partially into the right upper heart chamber, another in her right lung and the third in the muscle of her right arm. To say that she was in a serious condition would be a massive understatement – she was critical, in grave danger. The next few hours would be touch and go, and she had lost so much blood that her vital organs were starved of oxygen. She was in theatre for six hours, and during the operation, she lost output five times. Each time the surgeon administered heart massage from the inside, and they employed electric shock treatment too. Dani was deteriorating fast.

Blood was pouring out as quickly as they were pumping it in, but eventually, the surgeons were able to seal off the wounds. By this time, her body had just about reached the point of shut down. From the theatre, she went to ICU, where she had twenty-four-hour monitoring by specially trained nurses.

Dani's parents were both dead, and her only family were a sister and brother. Her sister was part of cabin crew on long-haul flights with a major airline, and her brother was a consultant engineer located in the Middle East. They informed both of Dani's condition, but neither was able to get back immediately. Luke, though, did. He handed things to a colleague and came at top speed to be at her bedside.

A senior nurse spoke to him as he arrived.

"I have to warn you, Mr Frazer, Dani is extremely poorly, and it's highly unlikely she will survive until morning."

Luke was devastated, but all he wanted now was to be at her side. She couldn't die; they had so many plans and such a great life ahead of them. No, he would support her, encourage her, urging her to hang on and fight for survival. Oh, how he loved her, needed her and longed for them to be with each other, yet here she was teetering on the brink, with a desperately poor prognosis.

The sight that greeted him as he entered the room was frightening – so many machines, so many tubes and so much activity from the nurse in charge.

"Can I sit with her, please?" he asked.

"Of course, you can, are you her fiancée – Luke is it?"

"Yes, and I want my lovely fiancée back – we must help her."

The nurse smiled weakly and passed a chair to him. Luke sat on one side as the nurse worked on the other, twitching knobs, adjusting flows, continually making notes. Luke held Dani's hand and gave it a gentle squeeze.

"I'm here, my darling, so let's be strong together. You are strong. You can do this. You can't let that evil coward win. Fight, my darling, fight and let him see that he failed to defeat you."

Luke continued to talk to her about their wedding plans, their honeymoon in the Bahamas and their plans. He spoke gently, but encouragingly, stroking her hand, kissing her forehead.

At three o'clock in the morning, pandemonium broke out – Dani had gone into cardiac arrest. The nurse ushered Luke out as the crash team went in to attempt resuscitation. They were there for quite some time but eventually left, and Luke went back in.

The nurse looked very grave, "Luke, I have to tell you, Dani's heart has suffered severe shock, and her pulse is extremely weak. The prognosis is not at all good. Her heart will likely give up the fight at any moment. Sorry, but there is little we can do except allow the machines to maintain her life for as long as her organs continue to function. Keep talking to her, help her to fight."

Luke didn't need telling twice; he once more took up his position at her side and held her hand.

"Now Dani Taylor, this is not the girl I know, love and admire. You don't just lie there. You use that very agile mind of yours to focus on what your body needs to regain its strength. You do not give up. You fight and fight and then fight some more. You've never given up when fighting the villains, so remember this, it was a villain who put you here, so you can't allow him the satisfaction of beating you. Anyway, you promised to marry me, so if you think you're going to use this as an excuse to get out of it, you have another think coming. You're mine, and I'm not letting you go."

Whether it was his imagination or just wishful thinking, Luke thought he saw the faintest of smiles cross her face. Whether it was real or not, he determined to use it.

"There," he said, "I'm glad you got the message and acknowledged it with a smile – I hope it was a smile of agreement though."

This time he thought he felt the slightest of squeezes to his hand.

"What did that mean? Tell you what, one squeeze for no or two squeezes for yes. After three – one, two, three." This time he felt the squeezes, "there you go, thank you, my darling, I knew you could do it."

The nurse looked at him, quizzically.

"Did you feel a response?"

Luke nodded. The nurse did another round of checks.

"Hmm, her pulse rate has increased, her blood pressure is normalising, and she's breathing more readily on her own. Good work Dani, keep fighting my lovely, this guy needs you."

There were a few peaks and troughs over the next few hours, but overall the trend was up. At seven o'clock, the surgeon visited and examined her thoroughly.

Afterwards, he took Luke out into the corridor.

"Amazingly she has turned the corner. She's not out of the woods yet, but the signs are extremely encouraging."

At eight o'clock, the nurse on the day shift announced that they had some intimate duties to perform, and they advised Luke to go home and get some rest. They promised to call him immediately if there was any change. He still hadn't moved to the area, so as Dani had given him a key, he used her flat to shower, get some breakfast and a few hours of sleep.

TESTING TIMES

WHEN LUKE ARRIVED LATER THAT morning, he was distressed to find that the crash team were with Dani again.

"What's happened?" he asked, his anxiety clear to detect, "she was doing well when I left earlier."

"As we said," replied the nurse, "she was not out of the woods. I know it's difficult for you, but the fact is Dani's heart received a massive shock, and many don't survive this long when that happens. Her lung too was compromised, so that's adding to the stress on her system. A short while ago she suffered a further cardiac arrest and the crash team are working to resuscitate her now."

About ten minutes later, the team emerged, and a doctor approached Luke.

"Mr Frazer, your fiancée has responded to our treatment, but she is fragile, so be prepared, she could relapse at any moment."

"Can I go in please?" a distressed Luke asked.

"Of course, please do so – keep talking and encouraging her."

He went in and once again took up his position beside her bed. He leaned over and gently kissed her brow, the only part of her face that was visible.

"Hey, you," he whispered, "what did you think you were doing? You had us all worried. Now come on my darling, I refuse to reschedule our wedding, you're going to get fit and well again very quickly now. I know you're tired, my darling, but you must keep fighting – do it for me. I know it's selfish, but there's no way I could live without you."

He took hold of her hand, lifted it and kissed it. "I am missing you so much – I long to hold you and kiss you, so no more messing, we've got lots to do." As he relaxed and allowed their linked hands to rest on the bed, he felt her grip tighten once again.

"Oh, my lovely, lovely girl, thank you. Today you're going to astonish the medical profession, and you're going to make progress above and beyond anything they can imagine."

As the day progressed, Dani's condition continued to improve, and she began to respond more readily than she had previously. The nurse reported that her results were steadily growing too. Having Luke there with her did help with her recovery. He determined that he was not going to leave her again but remain at her side until she was safely on the mend. The nurse arranged food for him, and although it was hospital food, he found it pleasantly appetising. When the doctor did his rounds that evening, the surprise on his face was clear to all.

"Well, young lady, keep this up – obviously this young man is good for you, I could do with his talents with a few of my patients if he has that kind of effect on people."

Dani made a grunting sound, the tube down her throat prevented any further sounds, but the gentle movement of her head from side to side and the grip on Luke's hand indicated that he was going nowhere – he was hers. Tears welled up in Luke's eyes, and so he stood and kissed her brow repeatedly.

"We get the message my darling and I agree I'm going nowhere."

"And I wouldn't be so heartless as to deprive either of you of each other – clearly you belong to each other," the doctor remarked gently with a hint of a smile, "have a happy life together."

Dani continued to get stronger by the day, and three days later they were able to remove the tubes and wires. She had to remain in ICU but was able to take liquid feeds and was able to talk a little.

Dani tired quickly, so Luke allowed her to sleep whenever she needed to, and he took the opportunity to catch up on his sleep too. Five days later, the doctors transferred to a private ward, and she was able to receive visitors for short periods.

The first to pop in was Pippa her sister and Jonathan, her brother. Unbeknown to her, they had been to the hospital a few times but had allowed Luke to remain at her side. Now though, they made up for the lost time and visited often. They were delighted to get to know Luke, and they got on extremely well together.

Both Pippa and Jonathan assured Dani and Luke that they would be there for the wedding and were overjoyed when Dani asked Pippa to be her bridesmaid, and Luke asked Jonathon to be his best man.

"Who's going to give you away?" Pippa questioned.

"Oh, I think I know, but I haven't asked him yet, so I'll tell you if and when he agrees."

Dani's recovery was, in the circumstances, very swift, and it was not long before, to her delight, the word 'discharge' entered the conversation.

"However, you will need looking after for quite some time; there can be no lifting or strenuous exercise – gentle exercise, yes, and plenty of rest."

"I'll cover all that," Pippa said, pretending to glare at Dani, "I'm changing careers, so until I know what I'm doing next, I will enjoy looking after my little sister – and I can be tough when I need to,"

"Oh no, back to childhood days – oh I remember them well, she was a tyrant to me," Dani laughed.

"Huh, some hope with you. You could hold your own with anyone."

Before discharge, work colleagues popped in too. Jenny came first, but then Paul and DCI Johnstone closely followed.

"Dani, I'm so glad to see you sitting up and looking quite well. You had us all very worried, I can tell you. Are you feeling okay?"

"Er... yes, well-ish, rather sore and not quite up to catching criminals yet, but I'm slowly getting there. Sir, I'm glad you've come in. I have a favour to ask. As you probably know, I have no parents, so would you consider giving me away at my wedding?"

The DCI was dumbfounded, and it took a while before he was able to speak. "Dani, I'd be delighted, it would be a fantastic privilege. Wow, I can't believe you'd want me of all people. Do you have a date set yet?"

"Yes, provisionally, it's exactly sixteen weeks. The invitation will include Kate and Sarah too, and I hope they'll be able to come."

"I'm sure they will, it will be an enormous pleasure for us all. Thank you, Dani, for your generosity."

"Your boss?" a surprised Pippa questioned when Dani told her later, "I couldn't imagine asking my boss. Do you know him that well?"

"Absolutely, he isn't just my senior, he had gone out of his way to help, encourage and support me and even to care for me when a criminal was threatening my life – he and his family took me into their home."

A couple of weeks later, Dani, with Pippa in tow, made a social visit to the station where she received a rapturous welcome from everyone. As she walked into CID, everyone cheered, and DI Cartwright took a pile of folders and plonked them on her desk.

"DS Taylor, get to work on those immediately, we've got way behind with our cases since you've been neglecting your duties."

He then gave her a gentle hug.

"Seriously Dani, we are missing you, but I can't tell you how good it is to see you up on your feet again. How are you progressing?"

"Very steadily," she replied with a smile, "and that's largely due to my nurse companion. Everyone, this is Pippa, my sister, she has given up her job to look after me."

Everyone went over and greeted Pippa, making her feel very welcome. Next, they went to DCI John-stone's office, only to find that he was meeting with

Superintendent Mann. She hesitated to knock, but he saw her and beckoned to her.

"Come on in Dani. We were just talking about you. It's so good to see you out and about again."

"Sirs, this is my Sister Pippa, Pippa, and this is DCI Johnstone and Superintendent Mann. Pippa's looking after me, ruling with an iron rod."

"Dani, if I may address you informally," the Superintendent said, "we are extremely proud of you and amazed at your resilience. You have suffered so much in the execution of your duties, and so we are delighted to inform you that we're recommending you for a bravery medal."

The look on Dani's face spoke volumes.

"Thank you, Sir, but I don't feel I deserve such an honour, I was only doing my duty."

"Maybe so," Superintendent Mann agreed, "but what you have faced, no officer should ever have to face that while carrying out their duty, and after that first attack you stayed at your post and stood as an example to us all. You are a credit to the force and worthy of great honour, thank you."

With that, he left the office, and DCI Johnstone invited them to sit.

"So what job were you doing Pippa?" he asked.

"I was a long-haul cabin crew. It was glamorous, a job I loved, but eventually, I realised how much I was missing family and friends back here. Also, I felt a change of career was in order, so if that was going to happen it needed to be sooner rather than later."

"You're just the right age for the force, and we need more officers," he said, looking at her quizzically.

"No, I couldn't compete with Dani. I may well pursue nursing, but I haven't convinced myself yet."

"Dani wouldn't want you to compete I'm sure, but you must pursue the course that's right for you. Anyway, talking about Dani, how are you feeling now, Dani?" he asked.

"Weak, sore and not quite ready for action. Yes, I'm progressing, though I fear it's going to take some time yet before I'm fit for work again."

"Good gracious woman, I shouldn't think you're even contemplating work yet. No, take all the time you need, we want you back, but we want you fully fit. Is there anything you need?"

"Yes Sir, I need to hear that you caught the so-and-so who shot me – I'm sure he was a Barraclough."

"You are spot on as always. We went back to basics with the Barraclough family, and eventually, we found out that Mrs Barraclough had triplets, Royston, Shelton and Ashton. While Royston and Shelton had been adopted, Ashton was simply 'given away', and that's why he didn't show up when they'd checked their family background. Mrs Barraclough's husband had left her years earlier, and she relied on immoral earnings for a living. We haven't found Ashton yet, but rest assured we will and then we'll throw the book at him."

"I'll be in touch if any thoughts come to me," Dani said.

The DCI shook his head in disbelief.

"See what we're up against Pippa? She's incorrigible. We tell her to rest, and she can't help herself, that mind works overtime. Get better quickly Dani, and you have that big date coming up, you need to be fit for that. Now be a good girl and go home and rest."

"Wow, what a boss," Pippa enthused as they left the station, "is he always like that?"

"Well, he's always fair, but he can be tough when he needs to be, he doesn't suffer fools gladly. He stands up for his team when others criticise them unfairly. I must say, Pippa, I'm feeling a bit tired now, I will be glad to rest."

Pippa was driving Dani's car, so took her straight back to the flat.

"Okay, my lovely," Pippa, said, as they arrived, "straight to bed and lay down, you look a bit wrecked."

Pippa helped her up the stairs to the flat, unlocked the door and towards the bedroom. Suddenly a voice spoke behind them.

"Well, there's a sight for sore eyes, two attractive ladies. What a pity I'm not here for a bit of fun, but I've got unfinished business with you, my little princess," he said, pointing at Dani.

"Ashton Barraclough," Dani growled, "how did you manage to get in here?"

"Oh, I am flattered, you know me. One of your kind neighbours let me in through the front door, and then I picked your lock. Not very security conscious for a lady of the law, are you?"

"Just get out," snapped Pippa, "can't you see my sister's not well."

"Now that's not very friendly when I'm here to put her out of her misery," he sneered.

"He's the one who shot me Pippa, and now he wants to finish what he started."

"Just let him try anything of the sort, and he'll have me to answer to, he doesn't scare me."

Now that was a red rag to a bull, and like a bull, he bellowed and dashed towards Pippa, brandishing a gun, "Not frightened eh? Well, maybe I'll start with you."

And that was what Pippa hoped for, his outstretched arm pointing in her direction was ideal. She grabbed it, twisted around and threw him in a somersault across the room. The gun slipped out of his grip and slid under a sideboard, but Pippa followed up by twisting his arm right up his back. He screamed when a loud click came from his shoulder as it dislocated. She then kicked him hard in the crutch and finally knelt with her knee across his neck.

The air was blue with his curses and threats, but he was incapable of doing much to fulfil them. Dani went into her bedroom and returned with handcuffs, which Pippa quickly fastened to his wrists behind his back.

"Have you got a scarf, Sis? We need to block his foul mouth."

Dani reached into a drawer in the sideboard, pulled out a scarf, and passed it to Pippa. Soon silence descended, but Pippa wasn't done with him yet, she made doubly sure by tying his legs together with her belt.

"There," she announced with satisfaction, "trussed like a Christmas turkey. Would you like to call your colleagues now, my lovely?"

Dani immediately called the station and asked to speak to DCI Johnstone.

"Hi Sir, it's Dani. We have one Ashton Barra-clough resting on the floor of my flat, would you like to collect him please?"

There were gasps of astonishment at the other end as Dani ended the call.

"Where did you learn a move like that Pippa," Dani asked her sister, "you were so quick!"

"It was part of our training in case we had threatening behaviour from a passenger. I did have to use it once on a flight to Turkey, a passenger became abusive towards another passenger, and when I intervened, he turned on me. I threw him, and he crashed against an exit door and knocked himself out. We had to restrain him for the rest of the flight."

"Well thank goodness you were here today, I don't think I could have done much with him at present."

Moments later, the door buzzer sounded, heralding the arrival of Dani's colleagues. "

How on earth did you manage to corner and overthrow that animal?" the DCI asked.

"He was in here when we arrived home," Dani answered, a little flustered, "a neighbour let him in through the bottom door, and he picked my lock. It was Pippa who overpowered him. She was just amazing."

"He may need to go to the hospital I'm afraid," Pippa explained, "I think his shoulder dislocated as I twisted his arm up to his back, though I think his temper may be a little roused too."

"Well done Pippa, you and Dani are an awesome pair. Don't be concerned about Barraclough. He deserved all he got and more besides – we'll soon cool his ardour. We'll need statements from you both, but we'll come to you tomorrow if that's okay?"

"Thanks, Sir," Dani answered, "that would be so helpful, I'm whacked and desperately need to rest and recover, so here tomorrow will be fine."

The following months flew by as there was so much happening. Pippa was invaluable in organising the wedding arrangements, without her Dani could not have coped. During this period, Luke moved to a new house, and Dani's brother Jonathan took time off to help with the move.

Spending time together was useful for preparing Jonathan for his best man role. Luke hadn't anticipated starting in his new practice immediately, but the head of practice wanted him to familiarise himself straight away so that he would be able to step straight in on his return from honeymoon.

The most significant event was, of course, the wedding day itself – it was the most spectacular day imaginable. Dani's colleagues formed a Guard of Honour, and the bride looked her most beautiful, and tears filled many eyes as she walked down the aisle on the arm of DCI Johnstone, with her cute sister in attendance. Four months earlier, this incredible spectacular seemed a most unlikely dream, as Dani lay dying in a hospital bed.

After the wedding, the couple flew off to the Bahamas for three glorious weeks and on their return moved into Luke's newly purchased ground floor, three-bedroomed maisonette together.

Dani had thought of putting her flat on the market, but Pippa offered to buy it from her as she felt that the area had now become her home and she did want to settle down. Pippa didn't yet have a job to go to, so Dani suggested she live in the flat rent-free until she got on her feet.

Almost six months to the day since the shooting, Dani received the all-clear to go back to work, but a few days before she was due to start DCI Johnstone phoned to ask her and Pippa to see him. They were somewhat nervous about going, as they wondered if something had gone wrong with the case against Ashton Barraclough for which they were responsible. When they arrived, he invited them straight in. The friendly welcome suggested that they were not in trouble, but he soon enlightened them.

"I've invited you to come in because I have a few things to share. Firstly, Pippa, I am pleased to inform you that the chief constable wants to award you with a certificate of bravery for your action in tackling an armed criminal, namely Ashton Barraclough, so an invitation to an awards ceremony will be coming in the post very soon. Secondly, Pippa, do you yet have employment?"

"Er... no Sir, I don't, though I have to admit I've not yet seriously pursued anything."

"Well, we have an admin post going in the criminal records department which we'd like you to apply for if you're interested. It's not a particularly highly paid position, but it will be a step on the ladder to bigger and better things. For instance, we feel you would make a good officer, so this post would help you along that path. What do you think?"

"Wow, I wasn't expecting any of that, thank you for even considering me. Yes, I'd be very interested in applying for the admin post. As for going on to become an officer, I'm not sure I could do it."

"Come on Pippa, if I can do it then so can you – at least give it some consideration. Sorry Sir, it's not my place to speak."

"I'm glad you did Dani because you said what I was thinking. Pippa, I'm sure you're more than capable."

"Well, if you're going to gang up on me...yes, yes, I'll do it. Thank you for your vote of confidence."

"Excellent. Now, Dani, we're looking forward to you being back in harness, we've missed your expertise greatly. However, I want to run something else by you. I've mentioned in the past that I want you to take your Inspector's exam. Well, I want to encourage you to start studying now – I have a reason for suggesting this. We want to start a new team to focus on violent crime – you must admit you've had plenty of experience recently. Anyway, we want you to build the team and to head it up. Until you pass the exam, you will be acting DI. In a few short years, I want to see you taking on my role, you have great potential, and I want to see it realised. What do you think?"

"Most certainly, Sir, I'm up for the challenge and would love to get involved in forming a new team to focus on serious crime, I reckon it's right up my street."

"Thank you both, you're inspirational, and I truly believe that this division's already excellent results are going to soar higher in the future. Will both of you be able to start on the same day?"

They both nodded.

"Great. We'll give you a couple of weeks to settle back in Dani and then we'll begin the process of change. Pippa, if you come straight to my office that first morning, I'll introduce you to the team and then show you where you'll be working."

"Sir, didn't you say I had to apply for the post, and I assumed to have an interview?" queried Pippa.

"Er... yes, I did. Hmm, tell you what, write to me and send me your CV, to keep the records straight, but I've just interviewed you, and you've got the job."

They left in happy moods, both looking forward to what the future held. The news that greeted Dani on the morning she returned was that the trials of all but Ashton Barraclough had taken place and she was delighted to hear the outcome. Ethan Roberts, as the mastermind of the whole drugs operation, received twenty years imprisonment, Lucas Evans eight years, the two gunmen fifteen years each and the other gang members eight years for carrying lethal weapons and drug-related crimes.

Goodfellow received fifteen years imprisonment for GBH, drug-related crimes and accessory to murder. Royston and Shelton Barraclough both received life sentences, the judge recommending that they both serve a minimum of twenty-five years. Both received additional five-year sentences for kidnap and imprisonment, the sentences to run concurrently.

Broadhurst, Khan, Thomas, Bright and Porter all received five-year sentences. They had pleaded guilty and protested that they'd been forced into their roles. However, the judge considered that they could have asked for protection had they so chosen. Everyone was delighted at the results, a pleasing outcome considering all their hard work over the past months. The other news was that CI Charlesworth had been encouraged to take early retirement and left without any ceremony.

Both Dani and Pippa quickly settled into their new roles. Just a few months later, Dani passed her Inspector's exam with distinction. Pippa was only in her admin post for a comparatively short time before she applied to join the force and went to Hendon for training. She was a quick learner and in due course, passed her exams with excellent grades. As was the custom, Pippa was transferred to another division in North London.

On the morning that her new team came together for the first time, it was Dani's role to brief them on how they would carry out their policing. She emphasised one thing.

"Never dismiss a member of the public when they come forward with information, no matter how unlikely that information may appear. Note it and pursue it. Sometimes the apparent time-wasters prove to be the best source of intelligence. I will never forget an elderly lady by the name of Dorothy Shackleton, who came to us saying that she 'felt' her husband had died, probably murdered. 'Feelings' – do we accept such as evidence? In a court of law, no, but some folks are susceptible and what they feel may well have substance. Your best asset is not the forensic backup, as vital as that might be, no, your best asset is your mind," she said, pointing to her head, "use it – think things through, get a feeling for the case, weigh the evidence both for and against whatever you're dealing with. Think both inside and outside the box. I can testify that some of my best leads have come from spending time thinking things through and allowing nothing to cloud my judgement. I chose you for this team because I believe that you are the best, you will give your best and together we will achieve the best possible results. Please go out and prove that I was right."

Lightning Source UK Ltd.
Milton Keynes UK
UKHW022209211119
353974UK00009B/573/P